On Track But Off Course

The Series

T.K. Richards

ISBN: 978-1-959253-10-5

First printing, 2023 LNK Publishing"

Own The Series

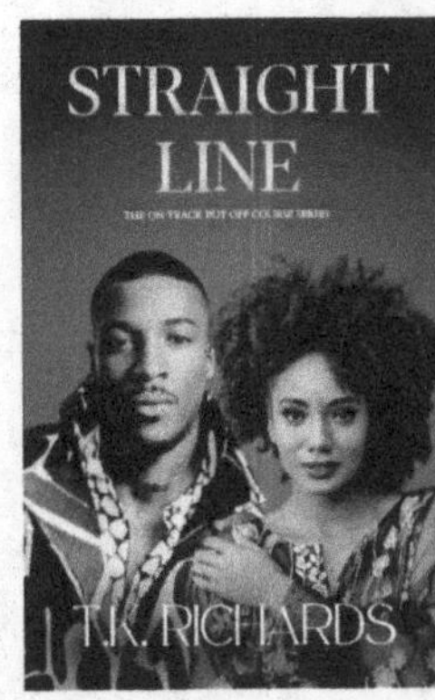

"In all the world, there is no heart for me like yours. In all the world, there is no love for you like mine."

— Maya angelou

Chapter 1

Landon

Guilty as charged. Landon's childhood friend, Millicent St. James, caught the flushed face Advertising Executive red handed.

"I saw that," Millicent teased.

"So did I," said Jen, walking into Mrs. Jeffries' office for their weekly Wednesday midweek gossip session.

Landon welcomed them into her office, glowing in her yellow flawless skin, thanks to her grandmother's recipe of slapping Vaseline on her face at night. Her thick coily hair rested down her back, and her natural no make-up, make-up look was always topped off with the perfect shade of red lipstick.

Millicent, on the other hand, never left the house without her hair in place, her face fully contoured, and a pair of high heels. Very driven and outspoken, and ambiguous to the naked eye. She loved when people guessed her ethnicity without ever giving an answer, and used her looks to straddle many fences.

Jen never shared much about her Latino heritage. Slim with smooth, brown skin and wild hair, she always wore a muted glossy lip, and looked pensive most of the time. She was the smallest of the trio, as well as the most secretive.

Landon spread the food around the table. "I ordered Chinese today. Hope that's cool," she said, closing the blinds.

"Hmm. Why are we closing the blinds today?" Jen asked.

"We have a private matter to discuss," said Landon, passing out the forks. "What I am about to say stays in the vault."

"It better not be about that tall drink of water we caught gazing at you." Millicent gave her the side eye, blinking them fast like a deck of cards being shuffled.

Landon's face turned redder. "It is. His name is Dario." She paused and glanced at Millicent up her nose. "What does it mean when you begin to fancy someone who flirts with you all the time?"

An office romance was out of character for Landon, as professionalism was her strong suit. She would never partake in mixing business with pleasure, or cheat on her husband, Todd, even if temptation of the flesh was upon her.

Sometimes Dario's voice caused her to Kegel, but no one knew that. His eyes twinkled when he winked at her playfully during meetings, but no one saw that. And when he licked his lips, she imagined him tasting her on the very table they sat, but again, no one knew what kinky thoughts crossed her mind.

"It's called being stupid," said Millicent, shaking her head. "Something you are not."

Color rushed to Landon's face. "Nothing would happen of course. He has no bearing on my life outside of work. I was simply wondering how wrong am I for feeling this way?"

The look on her friend's faces forced her to stop sharing. She dove into her lunch, wondering if they could tell how much being fetishized amused her.

Filling her mouth with food she thought, '*Is enjoying the attention of men normal in a marriage? Is this mere curiosity of the unknown, or am I bored with the routine of the repetitive cycle married couples find themselves in? Work, cook, sex and sleep.*'

Jen ended the silence in the room. "Is he what some people call a work husband?"

"I wouldn't call him that. It's nothing serious. Just a little flirting here and there. I shouldn't have said anything." Landon sighed, suddenly regretting his daily delivery of a latte and scone every morning.

"A moment ago, you said you fancied him. Is fancy your way of saying you think about him sexually?" Jen inquired.

Millicent smirked at the embarrassment on Landon's face. She stared her childhood friend of fifteen years up and down, then added, "What is this Dario person doing while you're fancying him?"

Landon blushed. "Well the other day he licked his lips in a meeting and I began imagining him using those very same lips on my... You know."

"Pussy?" Millicent asked.

"Yeah."

"Say it." Millicent poked.

"No. I'm at work."

"Even if you weren't at work, you still wouldn't say it." Millicent laughed.

"So what. I don't like saying the p word."

"The p word?" Jen laughed. "Now I'm with Mills here. Say it. Be a woman."

"Okay dammit. I imagined him slurping on my pussy. Happy now?" Landon snapped.

"Yes. Yes, we are." Her friends teased.

They shared a chuckle and Landon relaxed in her seat.

"Look at you. Able to sit back and drop your shoulders for once. Your body is thanking you for not being pretentious in a moment amongst your girlfriends. I bet you're real anal with your staff when we're not around." Jen joked.

"Maybe," Landon answered, then laughed at herself.

"And how often do you fantasize this Dario guy giving you a tongue bath?" Jen asked.

"Wait a minute, is he the scone guy?" Millicent asked.

Landon nodded. "I knew it! The first time you casually mentioned him I felt something was up. Call him in here so we can get a second look at him?" Millicent taunted her.

"I'm not calling him in here. I only told you two about him because this isn't normal for me. I have never thought of someone at work romantically."

"Romantically?" Jen scoffed. "It's not romance. It's a fantasy. He knows what he's doing."

Millicent interrupted. "I know what this is." Her hands slapped the table. "You never got to sew your oats. Your heaux phase is talking to you. It's FOMO-Fear Of Missing Out. But trust me, you're not missing out on shit."

"Mills is right. Don't let your curiosity get the best of you. Even though mine still wants to see what he looks like one more time. But I'm not married so..." Jen waved her tongue.

"Girl put that away." Landon threw a napkin at Jen's face. "But in all seriousness, he reminds me of Todd sometimes. The notes in his cologne hit my nose the same, and he's driven. I do find that intriguing. He ain't bad on the eyes either as you've seen."

"He is slick, is what he is. Men like that love to get married women in their hooks so they can pounce on them and *send'em* home. I'm not hating, but you're nothing more than a notch on his belt. Go home and be a slut to the love of your life. You know, the man who gave you his last name. 'Cause the men out here aren't doing that anymore." Millicent lectured.

"Risking it all was never an option." Landon assured.

The hour came to an end and Landon escorted her guests down to the lobby. "See you on Sunday," she said, waiting for the elevator to arrive.

"Does that include me too," a raspy voice intercepted.

Jen and Millicent turned around towards Landon, then shifted their heads to their left, where Dario stood at her side. His perfectly lined teeth were never absent in her presence, subtly forcing his infectious appeal on the unsuspecting newlywed, but her friends weren't so easily charmed by his mesmerizing smile.

"Sorry. No gentlemen allowed," Millicent responded with venom on her tongue.

"That's too bad. Maybe you ladies can bend the rules just for me." Dario grinned mercilessly.

"You wish." Jen laughed. "Call you later Landon."

Landon faced Dario. "Sorry, I don't make the rules," she said, pursing her red drawn lips, then proceeded back to her office with him on her heels.

"I imagined you were always in control," he muttered.

Landon pretended not to hear his comment. She picked up her pace and sprinted to avoid an uncomfortable conversation. But as she walked ahead, his slanted brown eyes followed her elegant curves bounce down the hall.

Her stiff suit clung to her in all the right places, and her marriage status was none of his concern. He desired her on a personal level, patiently waiting to add her to his list of victims.

CHAPTER 2

TODD

Todd Jeffries proved to be an amazing man: loyal, loving, and protective. A great provider and partner in life, he was everything on Landon's list for a perfect man: ambitious, striking good looks, thoughtful, and didn't have any priors, which represented two separate categories. The first, he didn't have a criminal history. The second, he didn't have any outside children.

Just under six feet tall, he stood out in a crowd of men. Clean shaven handsome face, chiseled jawline, dark brown hooded eyes, and a lean body.

His motto, *Mind the business that pays you,* highlighted the entrance of his print shop. He didn't talk much unless it was necessary. His moves spoke for him, while his character made him the man no one ever had a problem with.

For the past five years he courted Landon, finally marrying her roughly six months ago. From the moment he saw her, he claimed her as his, never allowing anyone to infiltrate the bond he secured. They complimented each other well from the very beginning, and he treated her the way every woman longed to be treated— Like a Queen in the streets, and a freak in the sheets.

As he rolled into the driveway, Landon hurried to throw on one of her gifts from her bachelorette party. Her phone chimed with a text from Jen.

'Delete after you read. Scone is a player. He's never handcuffing anyone. Gotta watch that one. Tread lightly. Love you.'

As instructed, Landon cleared the message, strategizing how to convey a lack of interest in Dario who was clearly gaining confidence. She spritzed her latest perfume in the air around her, and walked through the mist as the humming noise of the garage lifting, placed *what's his face* from work to the back of her mind.

Taking advice from Millicent, she greeted Todd in the kitchen completely bare, holding a beer in one hand as her shapely silhouette appeared next to the dimly lit countertop.

Todd opened the door, and a chilly breeze blew inside with him. The cold hit Landon's nipples and they perked upright. He threw his keys on the counter and yelled, "Babe we're getting the first snow tonight!"

Landon hated when he laid his dirty keys in her kitchen. "You know I hate it when you do that," she said.

Todd held his chest at the sound of her voice, then followed it, noticing her silhouette in the dark. "What the...Babe why are you standing in the dark?"

He flipped the switch, then grinned at the sight of her mocha nipples pointing at him. He turned the lights back off. "I promise I won't put my keys on the counter anymore if you promise to stand there naked every night when I come home."

"Come here," she said.

"I gotta be honest love, I can get used to this." He devilishly grinned.

"Use those lips for something more than talking," she commanded, helping him remove his jacket.

Todd towered his wife, intimidating her with his broad shoulders and cut physique. He palmed his wife's ample ass and kissed her neck, gripping her tightly in his arms. Hungry for her love, he lifted her onto the island and lofted kisses to the highpoint between her inner thighs, pleasing her desires.

Tasting her sweetness with soft licks and delicate strobing to her clit, Todd sent her into euphoria. High pitched screams of passion parted her lips, begging him not to stop, but also pleading with him to enter her domain.

She pulled him towards her. "Stop torturing me," she whispered, then latched on to his dick. With a pleasurable smile upon her face he lunged inside her fire, putting it out with strong, deep jabs, grinning at the waterworks sprouting on him.

The back of her knees rested on his shoulders, feeling his neck muscles tighten with every flex he used to pull her thighs forward. "I like how you throwing that pussy at me baby," he whirred as Landon moaned and released a sigh of relief, delighted she initiated contact.

Spontaneity was what they needed to relight the spark that got lost in the midst of bills, and work, and fatigue.

Landon's body quivered from his touch, and when they climaxed together, their eyes met, both fully committed in the moment.

In the morning, Todd woke Landon with a second round to begin their day. Lying on top of her, he rubbed his chin hair against her nose, then questioned her. "Is everything good with you? With us?" Landon grabbed the side of his face, kissed him, then nodded yes. "I'm checking to make sure what you did last night, isn't because I'm failing you in any way."

"I have no complaints where you are concerned." She brushed her knee against his thigh. "My actions last night were to spice things up. I felt we were getting in a routine."

"I expect you to come to me and tell me the next time you feel we're slipping. Okay?"

"I will. Should there be a next time." She winked, then rolled out of bed.

Todd worked at his print shop for the day, struggling to shake the feeling Landon was hiding something from him. After work he met with his partner and friend, John "Jay" Lloyd, at their sports bar on the south side of Detroit for a drink.

He sat at the edge of the bar, watching the sports reporters on the screen television discuss the latest trade for the Lions. LaTisha, the waitress he recommended when they first opened, served him his usual Guinness with a bowl of wings. "My mom bakes with this and you drink it," she said.

Todd lifted his bottle, "Forever a Guinness man."

Licking the lemon pepper from his fingertips, Todd rested his arms and slouched his shoulders on top of the bar. Jay noticed him babysitting his beer and signaled him back into the main office.

He lit two Cubans and passed one to Todd sitting on the sofa. "It's safe to sit here I hope." Todd teased.

Jay's neutral face suddenly scowled. "That was one time. You know I don't eat where I shit man. I nap on that couch."

They laughed.

Todd grinned. "You know I'm just fucking with you."

The nervous twitch in his eyes was easy to read. Jay picked up something was bothering his right-hand man. "What's going on with you T?" he asked.

"I'm cool." Todd lied.

"I know you. Speak on it."

Todd took a few sips of his beer and dropped his head. "Has Jen said anything to you about Landon?"

"Naw. I know they had lunch yesterday, but she didn't seem any different. You want me to ask her something in particular?"

"No, it's cool. Nothing like that. Just a feeling something's off."

"With you two lovebirds? Off how?" Jay released a cloud of smoke.

"I don't know. I thought she might have said something to Jen if something was bothering her." Todd inhaled, curving his lips.

"She works with all those bougie people, you know something's bound to bother her."

"Yeah. It could be work. Maybe I need to take her away for a weekend. Get her mind off of work and show her a good time or something."

"The last time I saw Landon, she seemed normal to me, but you know your wife. A getaway might be cool." Jay tipped the tray with his ashes.

The short time at the bar didn't stop the smell of smoke coating Todd's clothes. He arrived home and placed his keys on the rack. "Good boy," Landon said standing naked in the dark again. "Your wish has been granted Mr. Jeffries."

Todd carried her to the bedroom, and positioned her on all fours. "Stay like that while I shower. If you move you'll be punished," he said.

Chills traveled down Landon's spine and her opening throbbed, anticipating his return. As the steam from the shower veiled the room, her body shivered, wondering what her husband was going to do with her. To her.

The knob squeaked and the water shut off. Todd returned to the room, half dry and slick. He beamed at her liquid lips gyrating in the air, then pressed against her. The throbbing sensation excited him as if he hadn't just been in water. Fully erect, he rubbed his brim up and down her crevice, teasing her for his amusement. "I like when you jump like that for this dick." He teased. "Turn around."

Landon obeyed and faced him. "I've been thinking about you all day," he said.

Landon sneered. "So have I."

She shut him up by placing her red traced lips on his mushroom tipped pipe. A fast lick and sturdy hold of a rimshot nearly paralyzed him. Landon smiled to herself, knowing it weakened him by the shudder of his knees when she gripped him there.

"I love it when you sing on the microphone. Look at those pretty lips. Give me fifty licks," he commanded, rummaging his fingers through her hair. Landon sucked him slow, counting the times she submerged on his dick.

Struggling to hold his balance Todd stammered, "Tw-twenty more." Landon grinned, withdrawing all of her husband's power.

She mumbled, "I taste you. You want to bust in my mouth?"

Her offer made Todd tremble. Without warning, he swiftly turned his generous wife around, and deposited his spear inside his favorite place, thrusting her body into ecstasy. He jerked and pressed her shoulders against the bed, plundering her sugar walls with eager, fast thrusts. "I had to slide in you!" he yelled incoherently.

"Thank God you didn't leave me hanging. Now you give me fifty," Landon murmured face down against the sheets, squeezing her walls to hold him captive once he came.

Todd smacked her ass. "Let's go away this weekend. Anywhere you want," he said, wiping away their residue.

"I have Millicent's thing this weekend."

"Cancel it," he ordered.

"Todd you know I can't do that to her."

"Next weekend then?"

"I'm all yours."

Chapter 3

Jay

Loyalty is a fragmented ideology to John "Jay" Lloyd. A trusted businessman with the respect of the streets, a supportive friend to his team, and a reliable partner on all of his ventures. But when it comes to women, Jay is a greedy, selfish prick.

His medium built frame and disposition drew women to him. Amber brown eyes when the light hit them, the six-foot overconfident bastard exuded a hint of confidence, often mistaken for arrogance. His pecan coated complexion was clear, and the thickness of his goatee always had a fresh clean cut as if he lived in the barber shop— he owned a chain of them which solved why his appearance never lacked maintenance.

Jay was a top-notch figure in the streets, but never got his hands dirty. He was a boss amongst bosses, and when the smoke from his cigar floated from his lips, he twisted them forming o's, showing off his control.

His crooked smile could charm the panties off of a nun. His signature style— button down furlough shirts in the summer, and obscure leather jackets in the winter. Said to be the catch of the season every season, he refused to settle down until Jen came along. But even then, the ladies still loved him, the respect of his name, and more importantly his money.

Playing house suited him. He did anything to satisfy Jen's wants and needs, but avoided the topic of giving up his last name like the plague. For four years he never eluded marriage was on the table, and for four years Jen stood by him as a kept woman.

Being the sole bread winner, paying all the bills, and providing a lavish lifestyle played a major part in his disrespect to Jen. He felt entitled to do as he pleased, regardless of his living arrangement, and obligations. He was the father to Jen's son, Max, not by blood, and the home life he provided for them made it easy to overlook his indiscretions for a time.

Jen wanted Jay's rustic hands to teach Max how to be a man, given his strong work ethic. And Jay took pride into molding him into an independent, self-thinker. Molding him after himself. Making him the son he wished bled from his cloth nonetheless.

Nothing in the streets came before Jen and Max, but sometimes heauxs got in the way. The night Jen caught him red handed in the act changed everything between them. His offense was tackled by Jen's defense, and now he was losing in the game that mattered to him most. Family.

CHAPTER 4

JEN

Jen was new to the Motor City, drifting into Michigan by chance. Her son Max had been screaming for hours on and off, begging to be freed from his car seat. At the point of a nervous breakdown, she pulled over at a hotel to stretch their legs for the night. The night turned into two.

She roamed the city with her baby, feeling the vibe of the place. Tired of searching for a place to call home, she applied for a few jobs, testing her luck in the area.

A janitorial service in need of workers offered her a night shift job cleaning offices, banks, and car dealerships on the spot. Jen moved out of the hotel and into a weekly motel rental for a few weeks, taking Max with her to work at night.

Sweeping floors and pushing buckets kept her afloat and out of harm's way. The money was subpar, but the set up was perfect for her. No interaction with a lot of people, and no need for a sitter she couldn't afford or trust.

Working an assignment one night, Jen caught the attention of Jay. He sat in the parking lot of his bar, curious as to why a skinny girl would be carrying a baby carriage into the car dealership so late at night.

He circled the building, then startled her wiping the glass on a side door. "I didn't mean to scare you! I normally mind my own business!" he shouted.

Jen flapped her dust cloth at him, hoping he would leave. "Should that baby be out this time of night?!" He questioned. Jen answered, "You said you normally mind your business! It doesn't seem like it!"

Jay smiled and put his hands up. "You have a good night!" and walked away.

Her lack of interest in him, made him aroused. He hadn't been challenged for some time, and because he failed at grabbing her attention, her face was imprinted on his mind.

He waited outside the bar during the same hours as the night before, hoping to get a second chance to make an impression.

It was days before Jen returned to the dealership, but when he saw her walk in the building, he was ready to shoot his shot. He threw ice chips at the window to catch her attention and yelled, "You're too cute to be sweeping floors!" Jen shook her head yes and smiled, then went back to cleaning. "I'm going to bother you all night until you agree to have breakfast with me!" Jen shooed him away. He left, but soon returned with a plate of food from his bar and a pull-out chair. "I'm going to sit here and watch you work all night," he teased.

Jen laughed. "You are out of your mind."

"You'll soon learn I'm playing with a full deck. I know a good woman when I see one. You're in the presence of greatness." He earnestly joked.

Jen continued to play hard to get, cleaning the dealership spotless until moments before dawn barely lit the sky. After ignoring him stare at her all night, she returned to the side of the building for Max's baby bag, finding Jay still sitting in the chair outside. *'What determination,'* she thought.

Jay stood next to the glass. "Did you change your mind about breakfast? I could eat again."

Jen waved for him to meet her at the entrance. She slid a covered scalpel under her sleeve before unlocking the door, "You better not be crazy." She warned.

Jay dropped his shoulders. "I swear I'm not."

"Those cameras are activated." Jen pointed above the door. "If anything happens to me, I've told my people to check the footage."

"I own the bar next door. I promise I'm cool." Jay assured her.

Jen followed him down the street to a city classic spot, Ram's. She studied the change in his mannerisms. Behind the glass he seemed sure of himself, but sitting across from her he appeared nervous. His appearance screamed he was far from broke, and Jen had to hand it to him— he was quite attractive.

Their conversation was mostly about Jay selling himself at first. Then he began with the inquisition. "How did someone like you end up mopping floors in the middle of the night?"

Jen evaded the question. "You know. Life."

"Yeah I know. Life." He repeated.

"How did someone like you end up owning a bar?"

"I knew since I was sixteen, I was never going to punch a clock. My kind breeds different."

"Must be nice," she replied, adjusting her son's blanket.

"It is. Play your cards right and you won't have to either." He grinned.

One month later, Jay opened his home to Jen and Max, becoming a steady boyfriend and dominant figure to a fatherless child. He never knew he possessed such qualities— Reporting his whereabouts and plans to a significant other, being responsible for a little human, and sharing his private space.

As their relationship progressed, Jen grew hopeful it would lead to marriage, but Jay on the other hand, became comfortable with their current dynamic. His life changed privately, not publicly. His status as a ladies' man didn't change with a woman on his arm, but the manner in which he handled them required creativity.

Late runs in the middle of the night, senseless explanations of his whereabouts, and the overprotectiveness of his phone didn't go unnoticed. Jen knew the signs of cheating. Her bones felt it. Her mind knew it. But her heart refused to acknowledge it.

She played dumb to his philandering until it became disrespectful. The line was drawn when prank calls disturbed her sleep at night, and Jay was nowhere to be found.

For years they had a good thing going, and her catered lifestyle bought her silence. But knowing what she knew about the world, she was not going to allow designer handbags and shoes, or lavish vacations turn her into a fool.

Jen had no problem starting over. If she had to mop floors again to gain her self-respect, she was willing to do it. What she wasn't going to do, was waste her youth on a man who couldn't commit.

Resentment towards his shenanigans caused their living situation to become unbalanced, and Jen unhinged. She took note of his patterns through the week, driving past the bar where he claimed to be even though his car wasn't there, and clocking the hours he arrived home.

After several failed, unsuccessful attempts at cracking the ever-changing passcode on his phone, her imagination got the best of her. Wild imagery, and insane scenarios sent her over the edge. *I bet he's fucking some little twat, or playing taxi to some young girl, or entertaining a married woman when her husband isn't home,'* she tormented herself.

Tired of playing the fool, Jen reached out to Todd, verifying Jay wasn't with him like he said. Caught in the middle, he put Landon on the phone to deescalate the anger in her voice.

Landon invited Jen over for a drink and a chat to ease her mind of her troubles, but ended up going on one of Jen's late-night drive bys, leaving Max with Todd.

"What has Todd told you?" Jen asked.

"Nothing." Landon lied.

"You're such a horrible liar. Good thing you didn't study law." Jen joked.

"You do realize this is beneath you, right?"

Jen ignored her and silenced the music. "He hasn't brought another girl around you, has he?"

"Todd and Jay know better than to play with me like that, and I would never stab you in the back." Landon's nostrils flared.

"I'd tell you if I knew something."

"Do you?" Landon raised her brows.

"No. Todd's no fool. You got a good one."

Hearing Jen speak highly of her husband, led Landon to tell Jen what she knew. She didn't know exactly what Jay had been up to, but she could tell from Todd's actions he knew more than he led on.

Ever since Landon had known Jay, his reputation of being a manwhore superseded him. Their inner circle joked about it, but when Jen came along, the discussion of his sex addiction ceased.

In a desperate attempt to put a smile on Jen's wounded face, Landon suggested they catch a show and a bite at one of the new lounges downtown. Jen declined, determined to follow her intuition.

She parked across the street from the bar. "This won't do," said Landon, pointing to a better, secluded location with shade from the planted trees providing a dark spot two businesses down.

"This is a better view. Why do I get the feeling you've done this before?" Jen asked.

"Trust is a funny thing." Landon sighed.

"Surely you never thought Todd was stepping out?"

"A lot goes on, on college campuses, and let's just say I could have my own private detective practice if I wanted to." Landon snickered.

"Shit, sounds like I should hire you."

Landon scoffed. "You do know when you go looking, you will find."

"I know." Jen exhaled deeply.

"And if you do find something, what are you going to do?"

"Well, I have no job and no family. Everything I have is his, or is in his name. I will have to start from the bottom because I'm not touching my savings."

"I'm glad to hear you have a savings account." Landon clapped her hands.

"Yeah, whenever he gives me cash I save it."

"I love it when a woman is smart enough not to blow all of her money on materialistic bullshit. We deserve nice things, don't get me wrong, but money is freedom."

"It damn sure is."

"If you play this right, transfer the car into your name once it's paid for. We can't have you around here bumming rides."

"I can't believe I allowed myself to get in this predicament." Jen covered her face.

"We'll get through this. Once upon a time I needed help and felt like I had nowhere to go, and I hated feeling stuck. We'll figure something out." Landon squeezed her hand.

Jen was street smart, but she admired Landon's wisdom and articulation. Listening to the way Landon plotted moves, Jen knew she would be the friend to advise her when it was time. She shared a sad smile with her as Jay suddenly appeared from the corner of her eye. "Look at him thinking he's the man of the hour." Jen pointed.

"He's alone. See. You were worried about nothing."

Jay's phone was glued to his ear, oblivious he was being observed. "I hope he goes straight home," Jen said, doubtfully as he pulled out of the bar's lot. "Let's see where this joker leads us."

"I hope it's the house. Let it be the house." Landon chanted under her breath, biting her fingernails.

They shadowed him for blocks, winding up in a cheap hotel parking lot. Suddenly feeling sick, Jen held her stomach. She whispered under her breath, "Off all the places he could have gone tonight, it had to be a flea bag motel." Jen's golden-brown face turned a flushed sienna shade.

"Get out and get some air," Landon said, jumping out of the car. Jen leaned out of the car, hyperventilating and holding her chest. Landon rubbed her back. "Breathe. Try not to get too worked up."

Jen took a few deep breaths, getting lost in the fog she exhaled. "Fuck this. I'm ending this tonight. Keep the car running," she ordered Landon, and crept towards the stairwell, tailing Jay by a few feet. Careful not to blow her cover, and cautiously watching her steps, she eased up the stairs behind him, but took too long tiptoeing and lost him in one of the rooms.

She walked past a few rooms, listening for the bass in Jay's voice but came up short. Landon waved her hands getting Jen's attention, guiding her to walk further down, and telling her when to stop.

Pacing back and forth in front of the room, Jen thought of her father, recanting moments from her childhood. This was a moment she wished she could reach out to him for advice, or at least let him deal with Jay, the way he dealt with the little boys on her doorstep back in Texas.

Courage took over her body and she knocked on the room door, covering the peep hole with her finger and standing against the corridor. She heard rumbling on the opposite side of the door, and the click of a gun. "It's me. Let me see the real you." Jen breathed shakily.

The voice of a woman sounded off from behind the door. "Jay hurry up and send your wifey back home to the kitchen. I don't have all night to be fuckin' *witchu*."

Jen could hear Jay shushing the woman and cursing. In an infuriating rage she yelled, "My bad! Handle your business with your pigeon! And while you're at it, make yourself comfortable! Don't even think about bringing that bitch's fleas in my house!"

Jen began to storm off as two voices shouted at her from the other side of the door. "Oops. I touched a nerve," she said.

"Did that bitch just call us dogs?"

The door opened and Jen turned around in disbelief. Jay held it wide enough to show his disheveled face through the crack.

"You lying motherfucker! How could you do this to me?!" Jen punched his chest.

"Babe, what are you doing here?" he asked, gripping the door handle. "You following me now?"

"How long you been fuckin' around on me?" Jen pointed her fingers in his face.

"Go home." He begged. "I'm right behind you."

"Home? You mean your house? That lonely fortress is far from being a home. Fuck you Jay," Jen said with pure vitriol in her voice.

She walked away and ignored him calling her name. "Jen! Jen!" He screamed, gripping on the knob as the two fleabags beat on the door, raving to let them out.

Jen rose her hand and stuck out her middle finger, then sprinted down the stairs. Landon met her with the car near the stairwell, and sped off shouting, "Asshole!"

Jen's love for Jay was now in the transition stage of detestation and the cusp of hate. She cursed and huffed as tears fell from her face, while Landon remained silent, cruising around the city.

Todd and Jay called their phones incessantly. Both Landon and Jen turned their ringers to silent while Landon drove them on a joyride, and found themselves outside one of the new nightlife hotspots downtown. "Drinks are on me." Landon offered.

Jen opened her door and threw up the little she had on her stomach. Landon held her hair back, eighty-sixed the club, and insisted Jen and Max spend the night at her house.

When they arrived, Todd stood at the bottom of the stairs as Landon and Jen made their way inside. "Jen and Max are going to spend the night with us," said Landon.

Todd nodded. "Little man is already passed out in the guest bedroom. Is everything alright?"

"It will be," Landon answered while Jen hid her face.

"What happened tonight?" Todd asked.

"Seek and you shall find," Jen replied.

"Can we revisit this another time?" Landon asked.

"Did you know he was cheating on me?" Jen confronted Todd.

"I... Ugh...Um...I don't want to get into the middle of you and Jay's business."

"I know he told you I caught him tonight. The stench of sex on him was disgusting. He reeked of dollar store perfume and stink ass. The fuck was he thinking." Jen ranted.

Landon and Todd stood in silence. "I'm asking, what was he thinking?" Jen emphasized.

"I'll talk to him tomorrow and see what's going on." Todd lied.

"You get some rest. I'll bring you something to sleep in, in a few minutes," Landon added.

"If there's anything you need, just let us know." Todd tapped her shoulder.

Jen sat in a daze until Landon returned to the room with fresh towels, and a pajama set with the size tag still attached to the shirt. She kissed and hugged her son, contemplating her next move, rocking back and forth for most of the night.

She stewed in rage and wonder until morning. The thought of leaving what had been her home for over five years, and the man she thought she'd build a life with saddened her deeply.

Sheltering Max from the discord, Jen let him sleep as she headed to the home she wasn't ready to let go of. She hoped Jay would be there to face her, and feel the leftover rage she produced overnight. The image of his smug face kept her from crying when deep down, she could feel her chest on the verge of an explosion.

The last thing she ever wanted to be was a waif in the wind again, but she did the one thing she knew she would regret. She got comfortable.

Outraged and hurt, she prayed to her dead grandmother. "Lettie, if you're listening, I need your strength to come inside of me this very moment. Your baby girl finds herself weak and my thoughts are too unforgiving to call on the Lord."

A massive headache pounded between her brows when she thought of how the transition was going to affect Max. Jay was Max's father, the only one he would ever know. Though he had done wrong by her, he always did right by him, which complicated things.

She pressed the button to lift the doors of the garage. She parked in her space and sat inside the car for a while, resting her head against the steering wheel. Her chest fluttered from the drama, but she made it inside, grabbing all of her jewelry and designer bags to sell for cash. She stuffed them in the trunk of her car, alongside Max's video game systems and cartridges. Packing the car to capacity.

She wiped the dust off of the wad of cash she hid in the vase in the living room, then strolled the halls of the home she decorated and painted, releasing a deep sigh of despair.

Jay wasn't there, but she knew where to find him at that hour. Visions of stabbing him in the groin, and watching him bleed to death frightened her as she paced back and forth on the hardwood. "That's even gruesome for me," she said, looking in the mirror of her bathroom, chuckling as her thoughts went down such a corrupt path. *It's only infidelity. It's only infidelity. And orange is not my color,'* she convinced herself.

Shaking her head as she packed overnight bags for her and her son, Jen wondered why life constantly threw her curve balls. The life she escaped before finding herself in Detroit had not been good to her, and the love she shared with Jay erased the pain and hardships that once owned her.

The best thing she could do for everyone involved was put distance between her and Jay. After all, he might have been a boss, but he had no idea who he was really fucking with.

Chapter 5

Landon

To escape Jay and the city, Jen and Max tagged along with Landon to Millicent's house near the border of Ohio.

The plans for brunch and shopping turned into a day of children activities. And by the end of the night, Landon returned home alone, as Millicent played hostess to Jen and Max for a few days.

She threw one too many back over the weekend, and failed to reset before Monday morning. Completely off of her A game, she strutted into work forgetting to sort out Dario's intentions.

He waltzed into her office with the usual latte and scone, poised and sure of himself. Landon stopped him at the door.

"You can put that in the break room. I'm sure someone would love to have it."

Dario looked confused. "Did I miss something. Are we having a spat?"

"About that, you have to stop talking as if we have something more than a working relationship. I was going to overlook the comments you made last week in front of my friends, but I think it's best we sort this out."

"So, you did hear me?" He mumbled.

"I did. I assumed it slipped so I wasn't going to breathe life into it. It's probably best you stop bringing me coffee and treats. Okay?"

"Ooo-kay. Is everything alright at home?"

"See that's personal. I like our professional relationship. We work well together. Let's not ruin it."

"Guess I'll see you around. The office I mean." He huffed.

"We'll speak in the meeting." Landon shuffled folders, waiting for him to leave.

She fiddled with the mouse on her computer as he slowly made himself scarce. From the hallway she felt him staring at her through the blinds. "Please just go away quietly." She grumbled.

In the meeting, Landon avoided eye contact with Dario, but he gaped at her when their colleagues were focused on the projection screen. For her, it was odd how his attention was no longer warranted, once she realized the flirting on his part wasn't innocent.

To avoid conversation with him, she hurried back to her office after the meeting, surprised by an arrangement of pink tulips on her desk. *'Tulips. That's different.'* She scowled. She picked up her phone and dialed Todd to thank him.

"You have no idea how much this bouquet has turned my morning around. Tulips are a new choice, but today has been so weird I'm not complaining. It's honestly been a rough one. Thank you."

"Landon." Todd paused. "I didn't send you flowers. The fuck you got going on?"

Landon's mouth dropped wide. Todd called her name a few times as she sat speechless from putting her foot in her mouth. She looked through the blinds and saw Dario smiling at her from the hallway.

"Landon!" Todd shouted through the phone.

"I'm here," she answered.

"Talk to me."

"I am," she said, searching for the card.

Sitting between a stack of papers on her desk, was a card that read:

> *"The beauty of these tulips*
> *made me think of you.*
> *I'd like to kiss yours,*
> *Inhale your essence,*
> *And taste your nectar.*
> *I can only imagine how beautiful it is."*

~D

"Baby, I'll talk to you when I get home. I've gotta go." Landon's voice trembled. She closed her blinds, aware she had been coaxed and baited by a charming smile on a low-key manipulator, smart enough to not sign the card with his full name. She tore it in half and tossed it in the trash. Shaking her head, she muttered lowly, "I'm such an idiot. Always read the card." She tapped her forehead.

Landon hid in her office for the rest of the morning. She stared at the little hand tick slowly until lunch time, then bravely opened her door and gasped for air.

Todd stood facing her. "Grab your stuff," he demanded.

"No need. I was headed out for lunch." Her voice shook.

Landon hadn't experienced the feeling of fear during their relationship. She witnessed Todd's angry side once or twice before, but never like this. He was passed the point of being angry, and visibly livid. His chest stood out and his shoulders were straight. Blood shots of red in the corner of his eyes screamed murder, and heat expelled from his body.

They walked in silence, hand in hand and eyes straight ahead to Todd's car parked out front.

"Who the fuck is sending you flowers?" he asked.

"I will tell you if you promise to keep your cool." Landon answered.

"Why would I do that?" Todd raised his voice.

"Because I can handle it, and I don't need you to make a hothead decision and do something stupid."

"Who is it?"

"A coworker."

"Stop playing games with me Landon. I need a name."

Landon sighed as Todd drove recklessly to the restaurant, looking at the road and her simultaneously. Seeing him jealous slightly aroused her, but experiencing his fury filled her with guilt.

She resented the thought of Dario. More importantly, the fact she thought he was attractive and welcomed his easy advances. Guilt filled her for finding him charismatic, and giving him the confidence to be comfortable with his actions. Her friends were right that his intentions were that of most men, and Landon felt responsible and foolish for falling prey to his motives.

Todd refused to get out of the car once they arrived at the restaurant. "I'm not getting out until you give me the name." The silence between them grew intense, and after listening to Todd breathe hard for so long, she caved.

"His name is Dario."

"Finally. We're getting somewhere. Let's go eat."

After the waiter placed their orders Todd stated his suspicion. "I knew something was up. I could feel it. You like this cat?" he asked reading her eyes. Landon struggled to make eye contact with him.

"Nothing is up. And no, I don't like him. I don't know why he sent me those flowers."

"You sure about that?"

"What are you accusing me of?" Landon crumpled her brows.

"How do you know this jerkoff sent them?"

"I found the card after I called you."

"And if you had read the card before you called me, would you have told me he sent them?"

"Yes."

"That's what I'm struggling with. I don't think you would have."

"I called you when I saw them on my desk. That should tell you everything you need to know."

Todd paused and smiled to himself. Landon smiled and reached for his hand across the table.

"I hear you. I'm just pissed some clown got me feeling like this." Todd exhaled. "How are we going to put an end to this because you know I want to hem his ass up."

"I'll take care of it."

"Are you going to report him?"

"I'd prefer to keep it quiet. I don't want to be a part of a big mess. I want my name to remain clear."

"I get that, but if this fool is crazy...See how he's got me all wired up. I don't like this shit."

"If I can't fix this on my own, I will tell you. Okay?"

She sat with her guilt churning in her stomach. She hadn't physically betrayed her husband, but doing so with her treacherous thoughts made her think about Todd's question. *'Do I or did I like him?'* She questioned over and over in her head.

Dario was the first person to cause a rift between them since they became a couple, and Landon hadn't a clue how she could make the situation go away. It was clear Todd didn't believe she could either.

Upon their return to her office, he escorted her back inside, intensely looking at every man who walked by and asked, "Is that him?"

Landon begged him not to humiliate her, or cost her to lose her job. Todd saw the desperation in her face and obliged, hesitant to leave her side. He kissed his wife and whispered in her ear, "Call me if you need me," then walked away with the bouquet and threw it in the trash flagrantly.

'*What the fuck have I done?*'

Chapter 6

Jen

For days Max questioned his mother why they were staying in Ohio, and the whereabouts of his father. Four nights at Millicent's house, Jen began to feel they were overstaying their welcome, when she reminded her of truancy laws. The nagging of Max, and the subtle reminder from their host led her to back to Jay's doorstep. The house she no longer thought of as home.

Jay barely rested during the week. He was constantly on the go, up early in the morning, and in and out of the house during the day. To Jen's surprise, he met them at the garage door when he heard it lifting.

Max jumped out of the car before Jen turned off the engine and ran to him. She watched them laugh and play from the driver's seat, composing herself for Max's sake.

"I bought you some new clothes while you were gone little man. Go get dressed. I'll take you to school." Jay rubbed the top of his curly hair.

Jen walked past him and he pulled her arm. "I'm glad you came home," he said, with sincerity in his voice.

She looked him up and down. "You can thank Max for that."

Jay lifted the trunk of Jen's car and brought their suitcases and bags inside. Jen stood in the entrance of the kitchen eating an apple, studying the pep in his step.

'He does seem happy we're back. Typical.'

Jay returned to the living room. Max was fully dressed clinging to his side.

"I'm going to drop him off, unless you want to ride with us?" Jay asked.

Jen ignored him and replied to Max. "Have a good day pumpkin. Mommy loves you. See you when school is out."

Jay mouthed to Jen. "Be back," then rushed Max out of the door.

He returned and found Jen sitting in the living room in long sleeve pajamas, sipping a mimosa and eating a croissant. "Did you make one for me?" Jay asked.

Jen gave him a dirty look. "Why would I do that?"

"Because you love me," he said, placing her feet in his lap.

"I love---d you." Jen confirmed, jerking her feet from his hands.

"So you can stop loving me with the snap of a finger?"

"I don't owe you a response. Stop talking to me."

"I shouldn't have to say I'm sorry. You know I'm sorry. Sorry isn't going to fix what I did. Tell me what I have to do to make this up to you. New car? Fendi bag? You want to smack me?"

"You've been out here running a dick-tatorship. There isn't anything you can do. You're a nasty son of a bitch. I didn't catch you with one woman. I caught you with two. And those are the only two I have proof of. How many more have I been ignorant to?"

"Jen."

"Don't speak my name."

"Okay lady I'm in love with, I'm coming to you and telling you I have developed a fetish. If I came to you and said I want us to bring in another woman from time to time. Would you have agreed?" he asked, flexing his jawline to intimidate her.

"Am I not woman enough?"

"More than enough. I was being hypothetical."

"No. I would not agree to that."

"And I love you for being true to me. I wouldn't want to involve you into the street shit I do."

"Jay, please stop talking."

"Seriously babe. I can work on me. I can be the one woman man you want me to be. Consider the wild shit as a part of my past."

"You hurt me Jay. I've had a few days to cry and process the past five years, and we had some good times. It was beautiful actually. But once the trust is gone. I'm gone."

"You know you can trust me Jen."

"Can I? Answer this, how many times have you cheated on me?"

"I never brought nothing home. Have I?"

"Jay do me a favor. Fuck off. Please."

Jen left Jay sitting on the couch and locked the bedroom door. Breaking up with him was uglier in her head. She leaned against the door, feeling Jay's presence on the other side of it, indifferent to his collage of lies and excuses.

The magnetic appeal he once had, had worn off, and nothing about his charm could remove the disdain she felt for him. They were done.

Chapter 7

Millicent

Money was worth the long drives into the city, so Millicent could spend time with her friends. Working as a Pharmaceutical Sales Manager paid handsomely, and the plan to work from the Toledo office aligned with her ambition to rake in wealth for a few years, then move to Detroit years later.

Shaped like a Coca-Cola bottle, men of all persuasions found Millicent attractive. Her wit was sometimes overlooked, but her sharp tongue was never amiss.

On the way to meet Landon for their weekly lunch, she left her car parked at the medical office and caught a cab. "The MGM," she said to the driver, shivering from the cold and overlooking the patron seated on the other end of the backseat.

A gentleman named Mike Crumby shared the fare of the taxi, unable to take his hazel eyes off of Millicent. Mike was pale, the complete opposite of Millicent's preference in men. His lashes curled longer than hers— They didn't belong on a man, and his long face outlined a beard with specks of salt and pepper. His hands were well manicured, the second trait Millicent demands in her men, and he was brazening in his interest of the brown beauty.

Millicent never saw such lashes on a man. She couldn't stop staring at them, and Mike misconstrued her interest in them as interest in him. Her staring led him to make continuous eye contact as he capitalized on the moment.

"Please, drive this beautiful lady to her destination first. I am in no hurry."

"Thank you," said Millicent, seducing him with heavy coated mascara batting away at him.

"I'm Mike Crumby, and you are?"

"Millicent St. James," she said, shaking his hand.

"If you don't mind my asking, what's at the MGM?"

"A conference." Millicent lied.

"I interviewed a group there last week."

"What do you do?"

"I'm a freelance music journalist."

"I've never met a writer before. So, what, you get to meet a lot of celebrities or something?"

"I do, but they aren't all they're cracked up to be. After a while it gets old. I just see them as regular people now."

Millicent watched how tightly Mike held onto his briefcase, then made eyes with the driver looking at her from his rearview mirror. Mike continued to grab her attention. "The best part about what I do is travel. Sometimes I meet some interesting people like yourself along the way." Millicent blushed at his compliment. "I have to know, why is a lady of your appeal not married?"

"I refuse to settle, and I haven't met the one yet."

"Well don't count your pennies just yet."

"Excuse me."

"You met me tonight."

"So, you think you might be the one, huh."

"You never know what the universe is throwing your way."

"Mike, is it? I take what I want. I would never allow the universe to dictate my fate."

The cab driver snickered then stopped when Mike peered at him in the mirror.

"What would you say if I asked to take you to dinner next week?"

"I would say I don't know you, and I don't date people I don't know anything about."

"Google me," Mike said overconfidently.

"Google you? Did you really just say that?"

"I didn't mean to come off vain. My intent was for you to read about me, so you can change your mind, and go out to dinner with me. You'll see I'm not a bad guy."

Millicent thought about it for a couple of seconds, and responded, "Write down your information. If I call you the answer is yes. If I don't call you, then it was nice meeting you."

Mike's hand lingered against hers as he handed her his card. "I hope you use it."

He helped her out of the car and watched her until the cab became distant. Millicent went inside the hotel and waited for Landon to arrive, beaming from her encounter with the beautiful stranger.

The drama with Landon hadn't been rectified. Millicent took one look at Landon's slouched shoulders and stressed face walking towards the table.

"I planned on talking about me today, but you look troubled."

Landon exhaled and took a breath. "Trust, I would much rather hear about you. How did you enjoy your houseguests?"

"When you and Jen showed up with Max, I was upset at first. But once I learned what happened, I felt awful for reacting without knowing what she had been through."

"I was there so I witnessed firsthand how hurt she was. Is she still at your house?"

"Nope. She and Max went home this morning. Max has been asking questions and wanting to see his dad." Millicent sighed. "Jay is a real tool. You know I have never liked his heaux ass."

"Yes. We all know."

"I wish she would let me set her up with someone. I work with some nice guys."

"Since when have we ever wanted a nice guy Mills?"

Millicent shook her head and shrugged her shoulders. They both laughed and simultaneously said, "Never."

"Not to be a bitch, but how are you going to set up Jen and you're still single?"

"I actually met someone. I told you I wanted to talk about myself." Millicent sipped her water.

"Who is he and what does he do?"

Millicent bragged about her encounter in the cab, while Landon listened for key details to point out she hadn't met anyone special. The ordeal with Dario was clouding her brain and eating her alive, but she waited for the best time to interrupt and spill the tea of how she had royally fucked up.

Millicent mentioned, "I told him to give me his card so I have the power of whether or not I will call him, instead of waiting for him to call me." Landon saw her opportunity to use the word *call* as a segue.

"Speaking of making a call, I did a very stupid thing," she said.

"I knew something was wrong with you." Millicent sipped.

"Flowers were sitting on my desk after my meeting on Monday. I called Todd to thank him, and he didn't send them."

"You sat on this story for two days and didn't tell me about it. Landon…Come on now. You know you always read the card."

"I didn't see a card."

"Scones guy right?"

Landon rolled her eyes. She knew Millicent wouldn't judge her like her mother and her sister, and would help her figure out the best way to get rid of Dario. Waiting for her to respond, Landon fiddled over her food.

"I know the answer, but I have to ask. You didn't…"

"No," Landon whispered.

"Good girl." Millicent clapped her hands. "You found another man attractive. So what. You are human and not blind. Nothing happened, so no harm no foul."

"How do I get rid of him though? I tried talking to him nicely and the idiot sends me flowers. Staring at me in meetings. Then Todd showed up on my job wanting to pop off. How did I let this happen?"

Millicent giggled under her breath and tapped the back of Landon's hand. "Free breakfast and lattes, is how this happened. Being nice is how this happened. You can't smile and be nice to men. They see that as an invitation. Why do you think most men see me as a bitch? I'm not nice to them."

"I see. I thought you got off on being the dominant one in your relationships."

"I don't get off on it. I have my reasons for being the way I am. Being nice nearly cost me everything I hold dear."

Landon didn't know what Millicent was referring to. As childhood friends, she thought they knew everything about each other, but it was clear they both kept secrets.

"What kind of flowers did coffee boy send you?"

"Tulips." Landon lowered her head in shame.

Millicent burst out loud into laughter, and rocked back and forth in her seat. "Oh my God. Did he reference…?"

"Yes he did." Landon blushed.

"What I wouldn't give to read that card. I bet you aren't the only woman he is doing this to. He's probably running game throughout your entire office."

"I hadn't thought about that. I'm only interested in not being one of them, but this guy is relentless."

"File a harassment suit. That'll scare him off."

"I may have to, but I don't want this to tarnish my name."

"It's better than letting your husband put his hands on him. You don't want Todd to get in trouble. Maybe you should introduce him to me. It's been a while since I let a man tell me how pretty my tulip is." Millicent choked.

CHAPTER 8

TODD

The unfortunate events with Landon and Jen called for a men's night out. Todd and Jay both needed to let off steam with tensions running high at home. Todd reached out to McCaine and Brian, the devil's advocate and voice of reason in his circle of friends.

Since college, McCaine and Brian never participated in Todd's extracurricular activities, but they showed up wherever there was beer and a party. Years later, he kept them out of his business ventures with Jay, but like old times, they patronized the bar and showed up when necessary.

The fellas hadn't met for a round of drinks in weeks, but whenever they got together, it was mandatory they settled the score of a previous game of pool. Joking and shooting the shit with one another felt forced this particular night as Jay and Todd were neither in a laughing mood.

McCaine and Brian shared looks with one another and blew out raspberries, as Todd and Jay missed every one of their jokes.

"So, whose idea was it to invite us over here when it's obvious you two have something going on?" McCaine asked.

"Yeah man, is everything alright? Both of y'all are killing the vibe. I could have stayed home and taken abuse from the wife had I known tonight would be a bust," Brian added.

"Todd get your *mans* before I do." Jay threatened.

"Chill Jay. He's right. I'm not feeling it tonight."

"Clearly. The way you let B spank you on the table showed that." McCaine teased.

"I've got some things on my mind is all."

"Same thing as last time or something else?" Jay asked.

"Possibly related. You know anything?" Todd sipped his beer.

"Jen isn't talking to me. We might be done."

"What happened? Did she find out about all of the big booty bitches you've been creeping with?" Brian joked.

Jay crossed his arms. "You been snitching on me to your wife so she can run my business back to my woman?"

Brian's eyes widened at Jay's attack. He took a short sip from his frosted mug. "Why would I need to do that? Your name is in these streets without my help. No offense."

"He has a point." Todd concurred. "After what happened last week, can you blame her Jay?"

"Nah, I can't blame her."

"You do have a hell of a lot of karma coming your way brother," said McCaine.

"You've been living foul man," Brian added.

Todd raised his eyebrows and curled his lips, agreeing with his college buddies. "You know you're out there," he said.

"I thought you were my boy," Jay said to Todd.

"I am. But you know what you be doing."

"We're your boys too, but you can't accept the truth," said Brian.

"Can you handle the truth?" asked McCaine.

"Hell no he can't handle the truth," said Brian on cue, quoting the famous line from *A Few Good Men*.

Jay laughed with them briefly then confessed. "I don't want to lose her. And I definitely don't want to lose Max. That's my little G. I'm scared she's going to take him from me. I was miserable in the house while they were gone. I didn't like that shit one bit. But Jen talked shit to me when she got back. I don't know. This might be it."

"I hope everything works out for you man. Give her some time," said Todd.

"And what about you?" McCaine asked Todd.

Todd cleared his throat and told them a version of what happened at Landon's job, leaving out the part where she thought he sent her the bouquet.

"I trust my wife, don't get me wrong. But I feel less than a man not stepping to this cat."

"I don't know what to tell you man, I'd probably feel the same way you do, if I were in your shoes," said McCaine.

"Say the word and I'm there." Jay pounded fists with Todd.

"I feel bad for this brother, ya know. You gotta admit, you do have a fine ass wife man," said Brian. "He probably couldn't help himself."

The quad laughed at Brian's inappropriate infatuation and comment about Landon. "Chill B," McCaine lowered his hands. "You can't say what you would or wouldn't do, Todd. When you see that man, your entire plan is going to go right out of the window. You know what I'm saying."

They all agreed.

"I bet he's some punk ass, weak ass, batty boy. I'm sure I can take him. Nah mean." Silence fell amongst them. "I said *nah mean*." Todd reiterated.

"Yeah, yeah." Jay, Caine, and B chanted instantaneously to Todd's drunken speech.

He finished off his beer, "Ooooh y'all don't know how mad that mother-fucker got me."

"How about we get Trap to check this cat out." Jay suggested.

"I'm cool with that, but if my wife comes home and so much as mentions this dude, y'all better be ready to ride."

CHAPTER 9

JAY

Listening to Todd's plight, Jay couldn't handle the thought of Jen in the arms of another man. Selfishly, he glossed over how he deserved to lose her, and plotted ways of how to make her forgive him.

Drunken from the rounds of shots and beer, Jay bypassed the master bedroom and snuck into the guest room where Jen slept since her return. Giggling to himself, he stripped bare and shivered. "I've got to get that vent looked at," he whispered.

Longing for Jen's warmth, he slid under the sheets, "Jen. Jen baby. Wake up. Tell me you still love me," he whispered. Jen lied as still as hair in the 80's frozen from aerosol spray.

Jay kissed her shoulder and slipped his finger under her camisole strap. Sloppy wet kisses from her shoulder to her neck woke her. "You can't be serious right now," she mumbled. Jay's third leg stood fully erect, piercing her silk pajama shorts.

He held Jen tightly by her waist. "I'm sorry baby. I will never hurt you again. I love you baby. Tell me you love me too," he slurred, thrusting his manhood against her slim ass. "Your skin is so smooth I can't tell if I'm rubbing you or your shorts."

"Jay, get your drunk ass out of here." Jen laughed.

"You laughed. That's a good sign."

"I'm laughing because your naked ass is about to bust a nut from dry humping my pajamas." She snickered.

"I'm not letting you go. I'm going to keep you in my arms until you say you aren't mad at me anymore."

"I'm not mad anymore. Now get off of me."

Jay released her from his grip and Jen burst into laughter sprinting from the bed. "What possessed you to come in here butt naked. Look at you. And you're so drunk you can't even talk straight."

"Todd told me how some joker is pushing up on L. I'll kill a motherfucker if they try to get *witchu*. You and me are good together."

"We were good together."

"Stop all that talking like we ain't us." Jay sat up in the bed. "Let's get out this cold ass room, and go back to our bedroom, and make love like wild beasts. All night. You see what you've done to me." He gripped his firm pipe in his hand, and stroked it up and down.

"Jay, I'm not having sex with you."

"You know you want to. I miss those sweet kisses. Come here and spit on it."

Jen looked at his shiny, bronzed third leg, remembering how the girth makes her cum upon penetration. She contemplated giving into him as she watched her old love toy stand at attention. "No thanks," she said wearying inside.

"What do I have to do, Jen? You see how hard you got a brother."

"Yes. I see. And as always. Very nice. Too bad it's now tainted. Good night." She opened the room door.

"I'm sleeping wherever you're sleeping," Jay said.

"Damn Jay. It's late. I don't feel like this tonight. Just go back to your room and call it a night."

"You really not *gon'* give me none?" His voice cracked in a high pitch.

The look on his face was priceless to Jen. She held in her laughter, holding her chest as she shut the door.

"Put your clothes on before Max wakes up and sees you."

"Only if you let me lie next to you."

"Fine. But no funny business."

"I don't know why you're acting like this. You know you miss me." He growled.

Jay put on his shorts and returned to the bed. He slapped the side Jen slept in. "Come here." Jen lied down facing him. They looked at each other in silence until a smile broke between them. "I really do miss you Jen." She blushed and closed her eyes. "Are you serious about leaving me?" Jay asked.

Jen shrugged her shoulders. "I think so. I don't know. Time will tell."

"Todd was going to take L on a little vacation. Maybe we could do that."

"I could use a break. Alone. Maybe you could look after Max for a few days, and let me get some time to myself. Clear my head."

"You don't need to travel alone."

"Then pay for Landon and Millicent to come with me."

"Landon's my girl, I don't have a problem paying for her, but Millicent's pompous, *boughetto* ass can pay for her own trip."

"You don't want to pay for her because she makes bank, and doesn't take shit from you."

"I'll pay for you and Landon. That's it."

"You owe me. Three tickets, hotel accommodations, and spending money."

The alcohol began to wear on Jay. Taking Jen by the hand he whispered, "I fucked up. But that doesn't I mean I don't love you. Because I do. If you want me to pay for all of your friends, I will. Whatever you want."

Jen watched him fall asleep and studied his face. She missed their late-night talks and romps, cooling the heat between her thighs to give into him. The lie she told him that she didn't know what she was going to do bought her time to plan, as she knew their season ended as lovers, while holding out hope that a new season as friends could begin.

CHAPTER 10

LANDON

Avoiding Dario at work became impossible with the impeding rush for holiday advertisement deadlines. Landon spoke with him briefly in passing, making sure to do so when others were around, pushing him to use the heavy lineup of projects to his advantage. He signed up to co-manage two of the three ads assigned to her, clearly challenging her dismissal of him.

Sick of the game he was playing, she finally took matters into her own hands. She asked her secretary, Margie, to grab a table at The Coffee Shop in the lobby with instructions to take notes.

She dialed Dario's extension. "Coffee Shop, five minutes," then hung up before he responded.

Margie sat with her back to Landon's table, pen and paper in hand, and cell phone on standby. Dario arrived. "You bought yourself a cup already I see. Where's mine?"

Landon looked up at him with a fake smile. "I'd be happy to wait while you grab a cup on your own."

"It's cool. I've had enough joe for today."

"Great. Have a seat please." Landon's voice shook.

He unbuttoned his blazer showing off his sneaky physique, and grinned at Landon taking a glimpse of the view.

"I wanted to be clear a second time that I only have a working relationship with you. Nothing personal. I love my job and I don't want anything to jeopardize what I have worked hard to achieve. You sent me flowers that were not warranted..."

"They were beautiful. Pink." He emphasized with a smirk written on his face.

"They were inappropriate."

"Why are you afraid to admit you were flattered."

"Dario, I'm asking you one final time. Respect my boundaries and my personal life."

Landon took a few steps to where Margie was seated. "We can go now."

Together they looked at Dario sitting smug-like, then returned to Landon's office. "I hate I put you in that position, but I needed a witness in case I have to report his behavior to HR."

Margie touched Landon's shoulder. "I've been there and seen how companies protect the men and discard the women. It was my pleasure."

The audio was not as clear as Landon hoped. Background noises and nearby conversations drained out some of their conversation, but Margie's notes verified what was distorted on the tape. Landon locked the tape in her desk drawer, and instructed Margie to email a copy of the written notes to both of their personal email addresses, and file the original in her desk under the name, "Scone."

Dario returned upstairs and scoffed as he passed Margie exiting Landon's office. He stepped back a few feet and locked eyes on Landon, giving her a devilish grin. Landon leaned to one side, folded her arms, and raised one eyebrow, sending him back to his office with less pep in his step.

Margie buzzed Landon's telephone. "You have a call from Jen. Shall I connect?"

Landon closed her office door. "Send her through."

"Pack a bag, we're spending the weekend in Miami. You can't say no. The tickets are bought, and we leave tonight!" Jen screeched.

"But I can say no. I have all of these holiday ads to work on."

"You can work on the plane, and while Mills and I party. L, I need this. I'm going crazy in here. You know getting away from the cold for a few days sounds fun." Jen whined.

"It does sound nice. But..."

"But what?"

"I brushed off going away with Todd last weekend."

"I've already taken care of Todd. He's driving us to the airport."

"Let me work my magic with my boss. But look, if I have to get work done, don't hold it against me." Landon forewarned.

"I promise I won't. See you in a few."

CHAPTER 11

JEN

Excited to feel the heat, Landon worked diligently on the plane, while Jen and Millicent planned the itinerary, and googled information about the journalist Mike Crumby.

They Facebook stalked him, analyzed his Linked In account, scrolled his Instagram page and were blown away by the photos he had taken with numerous high-profile artists in the music industry. "He checks out." Jen said to Landon, stretched out in the row behind them. "Finally, a candidate for Ms. St. James." She teased.

As the plane descended from the air, the trio agreed to leave Detroit in Detroit. They settled into their separate rooms, then dolled up for a bar crawl.

"Remember to give out fake names," said Millicent.

"And get their number, don't give out yours," Landon added. Jen and Millicent shared a bewildered look at Landon. She added, "I've been out of the game for a while, but I'll never forget how to play."

The first bar was packed and impossible to get the attention of a server. They crawled down the strip to a less crowded scene, and received complimentary drinks from a group of military men looking for a good time.

Millicent flirted with the quiet one as he kept the free drinks flowing, slipping his number to her before the Detroiters skipped to the third bar.

Inside they danced on tables and took shots with a bridal party owning the bartender. Heavily intoxicated, Jen forgot about her troubles, flirted with strange men, told them fairy tales, and randomly shouted, "I'm single! Bitch wanna mingle!"

Jen's announcement drew so much attention, Landon and Millicent decided it was time to take the party back to the hotel. They walked hand in hand down the strip towards a cab station. The music from the first crowded bar caught Jen's attention. "I want to go in there. Come on people, that's my song they're playing." Jen ditched their hands and dashed through the doors.

Millicent sighed and Landon yawned, then followed her inside. They watched her dance to a different song than the one blasting into the street. "You think she knows the song has changed?" Landon laughed hysterically with Millicent, shaking their heads no.

The song ended and Jen took a seat at the bar. The bartender served her a whiskey sour and stood by, waiting to be paid. "I got it," said a male voice two seats down. Jen tended to her drink without thanking, or acknowledging the man. "I didn't catch your name. You having a good night?" he asked.

Jen kept her eyes on her drink and responded, "The name's Sam. And yeah. I'm having a fantastic night."

"You don't look like a Sam. Matter of fact. I know Sam's not your name," he said.

"Sounds like a personal problem." Jen laughed.

Landon and Millicent noticed the guy lingering around Jen and joined her at the bar. "Who's your friend?" Millicent whispered in her ear.

Jen took another gulp of her drink and continued to ignore him. "Who is who?"

"There is a guy sweating you pretty hard," said Millicent.

"Where?"

"Two seats down, light blue shirt." Millicent pointed with her head.

Jen lifted her eyes, finally acknowledging her admirer. She was too sloshed to see him clearly, so she stared past him with a goofy grin on her face.

Landon swirled her fingers. "I'm calling it. She's had enough for tonight. Let's get her back to the room."

"Noooo," Jen whined. "I'm not ready to leave."

"I'm not ready for her to leave either. She told me her name was Sam, but that's not true." The gentleman smirked.

Landon and Millicent frowned at the guy. Landon leaned forward. "What did you tell this guy?"

Jen burst out laughing. "I told him I was Samantha. And you can be Carrie."

Jen pointed to Landon. "And you're Miranda." Jen cackled at Mills. "You know. Because you're the mean one."

Millicent was stunned at Jen's drunken honesty. She didn't know she thought of her as mean, or as the dominant one per her last conversation with Landon.

"How in the hell did I get to be Miranda?!" Millicent raised her voice. "If anything, I am Carrie and Landon is Charlotte."

"Mills, this really isn't the time. We have to get her out of here. And why am I Charlotte?" Landon asked.

"You know why."

"I think McCaine's wife is a Charlotte." Jen shouted over them, then touched Millicent's face. "What's wrong with being Miranda? She was the tough one. I liked her." Jen slurred.

"Are we seriously going to debate who is who from a show that didn't represent any of us?" Landon asked.

The gentleman two seats down cleared his throat and laughed. Three whiskey sours slid behind the trio, interrupting their debate. "So, from what I could gather, your name is Mills, your name is Landon, and your name is Jen." He pointed respectfully. "Please have a drink on me." He saluted them.

Landon eyed the gentleman head to toe. "We really need to get going. But thank you." She slid her drink towards him.

"What's one for the road?" Jen snatched her drink from the bar.

Landon huffed and rolled her eyes at Jen. They had drinking binges all the time, but she had never seen her out of control before. She stood by and watched Jen and Millicent accept the drinks, and split hers in half.

"I'm Julian by the way, but my friends call me Jules," said the man in the blue shirt.

"Well Julian, nice to meet you." Millicent clanked glasses with Jen.

Jen stopped drinking and looked past Millicent at the man. His face lit up as she squinted at him. "Jennifer Mendes, don't you recognize me?"

Landon and Millicent looked at each other, then at Julian. Jen leaned closer towards him and studied his face. She was too inebriated to recognize, the friendly man with the open wallet was an old companion from San Antonio. His features had matured, but looking past them, she could see it was Jules Rossetti.

"I know this man. Girls, can you give me a second please?"

Landon scoped details to remember about Julian. His height and weight, the mole on his right ear, and the scar on his forearm. She and Millicent grabbed a table close to the bar, and watched Jen light up as Julian maneuvered closer and closer.

"What's with the name Sam?" he asked.

"Looking to escape for a night," she said.

"I can't see why you'd want to be anyone else. You look exactly the same. How long has it been?" Jules smiled.

"I honestly don't know."

"A part of me came alive when I saw you walk through that door. I thought I'd never lay eyes on you again."

"Guess you're lucky then."

"I'd have to say so. When you left, it was like your whole existence vanished into thin air. I tried to find you, but came up empty every time. And here you are, right in front of me."

"I had no control over my life back then. Sorry I left the way I did. I wanted to call you so many times, but I couldn't."

"What happened?" Jules reached for her hand.

"Let's not go down that road. That time in my life is too hard to...I just don't want to think about it, okay?" Jen's face saddened.

"You know you were my first love, right? A man never forgets his first love." Jules gushed.

"You're making me blush too much and my friends are watching," Jen whispered.

"Let them see how a man is supposed to put a smile on a pretty woman's face."

"I see you still have a way with words." Jen clasped her hand around his.

Jen met eyes with Landon and Millicent, bearing all of her teeth with a wide smile.

Jules regained her attention. "What are you doing in Miami?"

"Girls trip. What you are doing in Miami?"

"I live here. I'm a physical therapist for The Dolphins."

"That's major. So, you're doing well for yourself?"

"Not as good as the players but yeah. And you're where?"

"Detroit."

"How in the hell did you end up there?" He frowned.

"Long story."

"I have all night."

CHAPTER 12

JAY

Taking care of Max while Jen was away seemed an easy feat. Jay took him to a football game where he met up with Todd, who was overseeing their drop and money exchanged hands smoothly.

Standing near the concession counter, Max jumped over to Todd waiting in line. "What's up little man. You hungry." Max shook his head yes, then shyly asked for a corn dog and a soda. "I got you."

Jay signaled to Todd he would be back, and disappeared in the crowd. After he and Max grabbed their snacks, Todd took him up to the bleachers and sat next to the stairs near the band. He searched for Jay and found him on the side of the field, blending in with the members of the visiting team.

Todd explained what a play was in the game of football to Max, and patiently described what each position on a team meant. Jay made his way into the stands, dapping hands with the young boys who looked up to him from his old neighborhood.

The band hyped up the crowd playing a medley of classic tunes by Michael Jackson. As the drum major brought the crowd to their feet, and the commotion captured Max's attention, Jay and Todd discussed business under the noise. "I have to go to the bathroom," Max interrupted.

The band lined up to go on the field for the half time show, clearing the path for Jay and Todd to escape the bleachers before the crowd rushed below the stands. The line for the loo moved swiftly as they waited their turn to enter the lab.

Two familiar female faces from the bar approached their direction near the line. Jay shook his head side to side. One of them scowled, the other gave him a derisive smile before turning around. Todd laughed to himself and shook his head at Jay.

"What?" Jay asked.

"Nothing man," Todd answered, but Jay knew exactly why Todd gave him that look.

"Not in front of my little man," Jay said.

"Are they the two..." Todd stopped short.

"Yup."

"You did use a bag, right?"

"Most definitely. You know I don't trust these heauxs, but dammit if I didn't want to tap the thickest one raw. You see how fat that ass is," Jay said indistinctly.

Jay smiled on the side of his mouth, answering Todd without speaking. He took Max inside the restroom while Todd observed the crowd and heard the chime on his phone, seeing two missed calls from his mother.

Jay and Max returned and Todd announced, "My mom is hitting me up like crazy. I'm about to head out her way before I meet up with the ticket man and pick up the cards. You gon' be ahite with little man?"

"Yeah, he ain't never no problem."

The excitement of the band's loud music and the game tired Max. He fell asleep at the foot of Jay's bed not long after having a bath. Jay pulled him up to Jen's spot, and made himself comfortable on the sofa. Thinking about the two girls from the game, he realized he deserved the cold shoulder Jen had been giving him and called her. No answer. He dialed her again. No answer.

His buried his face in the pillow at the end of the couch, and covered with the throw, falling asleep with Jen on his mind. Hours later Max stood over Jay. He tapped him and Jay jumped. "Can I sleep out here with you Daddy?" Max whined.

Jay picked him up and carried him back to the bedroom, and laid with him until he fell back asleep. He checked his phone once more hoping to see Jen's name in a text or missed call. "Damn," he murmured at the blank screen.

CHAPTER 13

JULES

Jen stared into Jules light brown eyes, remembering how he easily talked her into doing things she never imagined when they were kids. He said he had all night, and she wanted to give it to him, but her babysitters stood in the way.

Some friends of Jules approached the bar hinting they were ready to leave. Jen and Jules were heavily engaged in conversation, and the world around them moved in a blur.

A friend of Jules tapped him on the shoulder. "Catch up with us when you're done here."

Jen snapped out of her fantasy. "I didn't know you were here with people. Introduce them to my friends." Jen waved for Landon and Millicent to join them.

"What do you say we get out of here? Go grab a bite to eat? Somewhere, where there's less noise." Jules offered.

Jen rolled her finger around in a circle. "I'd love to. But what about them?"

Jules stood up, tall and robust with his chest out. "We're going to soak up some of this liquor. Will you ladies allow us to treat you to a late dinner?"

They split two cabs and were driven to a late-night diner on a side street one mile from the strip. Jen gave the girls a brief back story on Jules, withholding the truth and details of why they lost touch.

At the diner, Jen diverted every question about their relationship to avoid further interest in her past, then dismissed them after they ate. Jules paid for

Landon and Millicent's cab fare back to the hotel, and the old friends conversed for hours, mostly reminiscing about their days of teenage love.

Jen eventually opened up about her current situation. "My life is a mess right now," she said, looking away from him.

"How so?"

"If I tell you everything, you'd be glad I walked out of your life when I did. And I don't want you to pity me. I want to remember this face," she said, squeezing his cheeks.

Jules removed her fingers from his face and kissed the back of her hand. He continued his best to coerce her into telling him what he wanted to know, but Jen refused to open up.

"Maybe you'll tell me who broke your heart one day," he said.

"I don't want to ruin this moment."

"Do you want to pay him back?" Jules traced her neck up to her chin with his finger.

"I'm afraid to ask you how."

"Because you already know how." He kissed the back of her hand again, slowly making his way up her arm.

"This might be a good time to put me in a cab." Jen sighed.

"I can respect that. But when you change your mind, call me. No matter the hour."

"When?"

"Let's be real with one another. It's going to happen. And when it does, I can't guarantee you'll leave."

"What, you gonna hold me hostage?"

"No, not hostage. You can come and go as you please, but I will make you mine again."

Jen didn't want to admit he was right. She was going to fuck him, just not tonight. As bad as her body needed a man's touch, she resisted to urge of being a fool and rush in. *'God, I love how he's so cocky,'* she thought, watching him through the cold foggy windows as he waited outside for the cab.

He escorted her safely to her room. She handed him the key card and he unlocked her door, inviting himself inside. He looked around and said, "Tomorrow night you will be sleeping in a much better bed with a much better view," then kissed her softly on the lips.

CHAPTER 14

─────────

JEN

Jen stood in the middle of the room where Jules kissed her, still as a mime. Feelings of familiarity, intrigue, and lust took over her body, and memories of his touch came rushing back to her.

She jumped in the shower, removing the stench of the bar scene from her body and hair, imagining what it would be like to sleep with her first love after ten years. *'Mmm. I bet he knows more now than he did back then.'*

Thoughts of him pleasing her forged her fingers towards her clit. She could feel it pulsating, wanting Jules melodic fingers to flick her there. The yearning for his love weakened her desire for release. Without any other options, she pleased herself thinking of the kiss they shared until the water ran cold.

The chill of the water nearly ruined her moment of haughtiness. She raced out of the shower and wrapped her robe around her *silkened* body, then wiped the steam from the mirror.

She looked in the mirror, liking the woman staring back at her for the first time in a while. The presence of Jules reminded her who she truly was, and she missed the girl smiling in the reflection.

In the morning the ladies sobered up by sun bathing on the beach. Roasting in the sun, and turning over from their fronts to their backs every thirty minutes, the heat kept them awake, but not more than the curiosity of Jen and her old flame.

"What time did you get in Jen?" Landon asked.

"Who cares? Did you sleep with him?" Millicent interjected.

"Did you use a condom?" Landon added.

Jen lifted her head and sucked her teeth. "Good morning to you too."

"Yeah yeah good morning, what was it like stepping back in time?" Landon asked.

"Why? Is there someone from your past you'd hook up with?"

"No."

"She won't answer that question honestly." Millicent looked at Landon acknowledging the truth between them. "Well if you didn't sleep with him what happened?"

"Nothing. Yet." Jen smirked.

"So, you're planning on it?" Millicent clapped her hands.

Jen nodded and placed her hands behind her head grinning from ear to ear. "I should have done it last night, but I was too drunk."

"Something was definitely brewing last night. What do you think Landon?"

"Too early to tell. Everybody's shit shows up sooner or later."

They returned inside to find Jules had sent over three fruit, chocolate, and cheese bouquets, and three bottles of wine to Jen's room for all of them. The card attached was an invitation for a small get-together at his house in a few hours, with instructions to be ready at seven o'clock for the pickup.

Jen set the trays on the table outside on the balcony, and called the girls over to her room. Millicent marveled at the array of treats and said, "I like his style. He's so much better than you know who."

A curve formed on the side of Jen's mouth.

"You know nothing about that man." Landon preached.

"But we know everything about the other one." Millicent sassed.

"Girls, this trip is about having fun. I don't want to talk about him." Jen ended the discussion. "Now. What should we wear tonight? Something beachy or something sexy?"

A private car arrived at the hotel and delivered them to a beach house in a gated community. Jules stood in his driveway filled with luxury cars around the cul-de-sac. "Nice," said Millicent. Jen blushed at her enthusiasm.

The host escorted them inside and introduced them to the other guests. A six-foot gentleman walked over and complimented their beauty. "I see why you put this shindig together at the last minute." he smiled.

"Ladies, this is Malcolm."

"Call me Mal. Can I get you ladies something to drink?"

Jules and Malcolm poured margaritas in tall glasses with salt on the tips of the rim, then led the girls to the party out by the pool. They mingled with the other guests, played games, and became engrossed in deep conversations and debates.

Jules stole Jen away and showed her the interior of the house. Jen wondered how a woman hadn't trapped him by now. "Why? Aren't you married?" she asked.

He stopped walking and looked her in the eye. "I would like to be."

"The women here are beautiful." Jen poached.

"Yes they are, but I'm not shallow. I want more than a pretty face. I want conversation. And companionship. Someone to laugh with. A mate that makes me want to rush home every day."

"Sounds like Landon's husband. He's cut from a different cloth. I thought they didn't *make'm* like that anymore."

"We are a rare breed."

They stared at each other in silence. Jen wondered if this was the room it would happen in. The room she and her old flame would reignite the passion between them.

"Do you all have plans for tonight?" Jules broke the silence.

"Clubbing. And you?"

"Kicking my friends out before they try to crash here." He joked. "Let me make a few calls. Get you on the list at the hottest club so you can skip waiting in line."

"That would be great, but you've done enough already."

"You're in my city. Allow me to show you how we do it down here." Jules wrapped his arm around her, then led them back downstairs. *'I guess tonight's not the night,'* Jen thought.

They returned to the party, catching a chill from the breeze floating in from the beach. Millicent caught the interest of a ball player from Jules's team, batting her eyes profusely.

Landon sat with her feet in the water, ignoring a bear of a man with newly growing *locs*, talking her ear off. He held himself up against the fiberglass and concrete, revealing his well-crafted arms, floating beside her.

Jen sat next to Landon and placed her feet in the water. She snickered at Landon's witty replies to her admirer, then tried to diffuse the conversation.

"Who is your new friend?" she asked.

"I have no idea. What was your name again?" Landon kidded.

"It's Murph. Your friend here has been playing hard to get." He said to Jen.

"Oh, I'm not playing." Landon flashed her ring.

"I see your little ring. I can replace that with a bigger stone."

"No he didn't." Jen chuckled.

"Yes, he did." Landon rolled her eyes.

"You must not watch the news princess; my contract is all they've been talking about. I know your husband ain't rolling in it like me."

"Nope. He isn't. But I have money." Landon corrected him.

"Now I really want to get to know you." His eyes twinkled.

Landon and Jen laughed in Murph's face. His eyes shrunk, appalled they found his flirting ridiculous. Landon calmed down and took him by the hand.

"I'm sorry we laughed at you, but women like us are educated and self-sufficient. We make our own money. And a man like you can't give me what I need."

"And what's that?"

"Loyalty. But it was nice meeting you." Jen pursed her lips.

Murph kissed the back of Landon's hand. "A man can be all of that for the right woman. Nice meeting you." He excused himself, freeing up space for the ladies to have a private moment.

"I was going to suggest skipping the club tonight. The vibe here is chill." Jen suggested.

"Fine by me." Landon agreed. "I can catch up on emails and get ahead on my work."

"Everything good on that front?" Jen asked.

"Hope so. Only time will tell."

Millicent sat on the other side of Landon. "We don't have to go out tonight, if you guys don't want to," she said. "I'm kind of feeling Mr. Head and Shoulders over there." She waved to Mal.

"I think he is feeling you too." Landon snuck a look his way. "So what's the plan?"

"Jules arranged for us to bypass the line at the hottest club tonight, but I kind of want to tell him to scratch that."

"So he can scratch that?" Millicent joked. "But in all seriousness, let's go out and if we're not feeling it, we can do our own separate thing."

"Bet," they all agreed.

A driver holding a sign with Jen's name stood in front of a limousine parked outside of the corridor. "I'll say it again. I really like this guy," said Millicent. He opened the door for them, and advised he was to be used at their disposal.

On the way to the club, Millicent probed into Jen's business. "What's the story between you and this guy?"

Jen's cheeks turned pinker than the rouge painted on them. She shrugged her shoulders and stared at the stars through the moonroof, never answering their questions.

As promised, Jules pulled strings to give them VIP status at the club. They bypassed the line and were seated at a table under fluorescent lights overlooking the dance floor.

While enjoying a complimentary bottle of champagne, Mal joined the ladies, occupying Millicent's attention. Watching them flirt shamelessly killed the vibe for Landon and Jen. Millicent snuck in a hand gesture to them, signaling she was going home with Mr. Head and Shoulders.

Landon was over the club scene and so was Jen. They left in the limousine, but once they reached the hotel, Jen closed the door after Landon got out. She rolled the window halfway down and winked at Landon. Landon sneered at her. "I don't blame you one bit," as the car drove off with Jen cheering down the pavement.

Chapter 15

Jules

Jen's body pulsed as urges rippled through her skirt. She arrived at Jules' house, impatiently waiting for him to open the door. He swung it open, arousing her in his fitted white tee and boxer briefs, exposing his assets to taunt her.

Her mouth watered as his manliness poked through his shorts. She hurdled in his arms, nearly attacking him before the door closed. In between kisses she asked, "Have you really been thinking about me all these years?"

"Yes," he answered.

"Show me," she demanded.

"You don't have to ask." He carried her into his bedroom.

Jules took full control and Jen submitted to him, allowing him to do with her as he pleased. He placed her on his dresser and recreated the scene from the night of their junior prom. He kissed her rough, then soft, then rough again on her mouth while running his fingers up and down her gardenia scented body. His fist pulled her hair back with a quick tug while he kissed her on the neck, making his way down to her aching center.

Proving he was still a selfless lover, Jules played with her chocha. Nibbling on the crease of her inner thigh, and kissing her pussy as if it had a tongue to participate. Jen let out a cat call when his finger joined the party, massaging in between both her holes. He sensed she had been neglected of love making, so he extended his pleasure into overtime.

Jen held the top of his head in utter delight, while he worked her over, rotating the use of his lips and tongue in a disorderly manner. He knew how to please her without guidance. He removed her hands from his head, so she positioned them on the back of the mirror while he osculated her hidden lips in a way Jay never had.

Once he accomplished stimulating her orally, he rose from his knees and glanced at her briefly. Jen attempted to move to return the favor, but he intercepted and lifted her quivering legs above her shoulders. He placed himself inside of her, steadily and readily kissing her on the mouth. "Do you taste the sweetness?" he asked. Jen remained silent not knowing how to respond, so he asked her again. "Can you taste the sweetness mamacita?"

Jen was brought out of her shell. She screamed, "Yes, I taste it!"

The echo of her delight aroused Jules. He thrusted her harder and nibbled on her ear whispering, "I missed that sugar," then pinned her legs against her stomach to go deep.

Long strokes, quick strokes, wide strokes, and intense strokes, Jules finished her off. Jen moaned in a pure frenzy, stuck to the dresser from the mess she made, physically incapable of moving her legs. Her thighs ached while she remained in the position he held her in. Worthy good pain below Jules calming down from his climax.

Dim light crept through the bare window, and Jules gazed at her outline, admiring her beauty. Jen was still in a euphoric state, frozen atop the dresser with her eyes were closed.

He carried her to the bed and rested beside her in silence, waiting for her to speak. He hoped she would say she missed him too after all those years, or at least compliment his efforts. With her back to him, Jen noticed the sun was rising over the water.

She smiled to herself and finally spoke. "You told me I would wake up in a better bed, with a better view, and you were right."

"I spoke it into existence." He softly kissed her shoulder.

"Not only is the view better. The company is too."

"You have no idea how it pleases me to hear you say that Jen."

"I want to feel you again." She placed his hands inside of her.

Jules did what was asked of him, giving Jen the endless pleasure she yearned. A mix between making love and an overdue fuckfest between long lost lovers tied them over as they lost track of time, and spooned each other with Jules still inside of her for the final hours of night.

The blinding sun traveled in front of the window but didn't wake her. Jules, on the other hand, slept lightly, lying awake most of the morning, bracing himself for the second time Jen would walk out of his life.

Allowing her to sleep peacefully and leave her scent on the pillowcase, he prepared her breakfast for when she woke. Sliced fresh fruit and a split toasted bagel were placed on the nightstand on her side of the bed.

While waiting for her to wake, he paced back and forth down the stairs, thinking of clever words to convince her to stay. She opened her eyes to the tray of food, and felt the bed behind her for Jules. He walked in with a notepad in his hand and blurted out. "Leave him."

Jen was stunned at his outburst. She lowered her head, hiding her flushed face. "I want to."

"Then why don't you?"

"I told you my life is a mess."

"Let me help you fix it." He offered.

"You can't."

"What aren't you telling me?"

"I have secrets, and I don't want to involve you in my mistakes." She scanned the room for her clothing.

"If you want me to beg, I'll beg."

"You wouldn't have to."

"Then why can't we be together?"

Jules dug in his drawer and threw one of his shirts to Jen. She caught it with one hand. "Because I have a son." She jumped from the bed and threw on his t-shirt.

Jules walked over to her. "I love children," he said, holding her shoulders.

"Jay is not my son's biological father, but he is the only father he has ever known. And he loves him. They love each other. I can't move him around from man to man. What kind of a mother would I be to rip them apart?"

"So, you would stay in a bad situation for the sake of your son?"

"I don't have a choice right now."

"How old is he?"

"He'll be six soon."

"Is that the only reason you're staying with him?"

"I have love for him. But I'm not in love with him."

"Do you still love me? Don't answer that. That wasn't a fair question, I know." Jules paused. "So, what are we going to do?"

"I don't have all the answers. I need to go home and sort things out."

"Don't disappear on me like before. Promise me."

"I promise."

"How much longer do I have you all to myself?"

"My flight leaves at nine o'clock tonight."

Jules held her in his arms. "Let's make the most of these last hours we have together. Anything you want to do, we'll do," he said.

Jen joked. "Well, I don't know what we *can* do with that thirst trap dress I wore over here."

Jules laughed. "We can go down to South Beach. You'll fit right in. Trust me."

CHAPTER 16

TODD

Heavy was the heart of Todd back in Detroit. The visit to his mother's house in Auburn Hills, blindsided him to his core, and came at the worst possible time. With Landon down in Miami, he had a day to sit with the news. Process it, and digest it.

Landon called to check in with him after sending Jen off into the night, but he bit his tongue and kept quiet, assured they should be together when the blow was delivered.

Jay popped up at his house with Max unannounced shortly past noon. Todd answered the door shirtless, with one hand barely tucked in his navy flannel pajama pants. "What's up Jay. Little man." He greeted them wiping his face with both hands. "Let me put on some clothes. You know where to go," he said, welcoming them inside out of the cold.

Max wasted no time turning on the television and video games in the mancave. He and Jay played GTA for a few minutes until Todd made it over to the other side of the house. "How's your mother?" Jay asked.

Todd was never sure if Jay questioned him to keep tabs on him, or genuinely cared what was going on with him. He answered him a raised eyebrow and sighed, then sat on his La-Z-Boy.

"What y'all getting into today?"

Max replied before Jay could say why they were there. "Are we picking up mom today?"

Jay looked at Todd with stretched eyes. "Tonight son. When you wake up in the morning your mom will be home." He mouthed to Todd. "Nonstop," then dropped his head and clenched the game controller. "You heard from Landon?"

"Of course. She called when they got in last night. We fell asleep on the phone."

"So they're straight?"

"Yeah. They're having a good time from what I've heard. Why?"

Jay put the controller on the arm of the chair. "Play for me son," queuing Todd to join him at the bar. "Jen hasn't called me since she left. She's ignoring my calls, and hasn't once checked in on Max. That's not like her."

"Because she trusts you with her son. She knows you won't let anything happen to him."

Jay looked away at Max. "Do me a favor man. Watch him for a few hours?"

"What? I mean yeah, but..."

"LaTisha quit this morning. I've got to get one of these birds to cover her shifts until we find a replacement."

"We've had plenty dropping in wanting to work."

"I didn't keep those applications. I never thought Tisha would pull this shit."

"Why'd she quit?"

"She's been shaking me down for money ever since...You know."

"How much?"

"Let's just say the ass wasn't worth what she's been bribing out of me. It's for the best though. This thing with Jen, I needed to clean house. I told her I wouldn't hurt her anymore. I mean it. Remember those shorties from the game last night?"

Todd nodded.

"Been blowing my phone up all morning. I hit block *on'em*."

"Damn. That's huge for you."

"I could feel my stomach knot up when I did it too."

Todd burst into laughter. Jay couldn't hold his face straight listening to Todd crack up at him. He couldn't keep his cool and laughed at himself. "If you knew anything, you'd tell me, right?" Jay asked, straightening his face.

"Anything about what?"

"Has L mentioned if Jen's really going to leave me?"

"Not to me. But I don't think she's going anywhere. She's just mad right now. She's gone to regroup with her friends and blow off some steam. She'll come back and you two will work it all out. But you got to stop fucking up man."

"She blue balling me T. And I'm a tell you something. I had to think hard about blocking my heaux's numbers. Man."

"You want me to slide that in the conversation with L?"

"Please do, 'cause I don't know how much longer I can take this trying to do right ohit."

Todd felt sorry for what Jay was going through, and considered his suffering face. "I can watch little man for you. But not all day." Todd emphasized.

"I appreciate it man."

"And for the record, Landon and I promised not to get in the middle of our friend's problems. Gotta respect the marriage code."

"What about our code?"

"Happy wife, happy life trumps that shit."

"I owe you." Jay held out his hand.

They shook. "Big."

Keeping Max for a few hours wasn't new for Todd. From time to time he sat with him at the print shop when Jay made his runs. To keep him occupied after the video games became a bore, Todd drove him into the city, sharing one of his past times with the young lad. "We're about to test your art skills," he said, pulling out two notepads and pencils.

They sat on a bench below the Penobscot Building. Todd preached to Max. "My dad used to bring me down here when I was little and say, "If you're going to draw, draw this building." We'd sit here for hours while I drew it different every time. My mom has all of them somewhere at her house. Let's see if you are better than me."

Max competed with Todd putting very little effort into it. He went through sheet after sheet, doodling the time away, not realizing how long Jay had been gone when he snuck up on him.

"I knew something was up with you," said Jay, walking up from behind.

Todd deflected. "I didn't tell you to meet us here. I would have brought him home."

"I wasn't far when you texted your location."

Todd looked at the guilt in his throat, swallowing big to engulf the reason his location was close. "Dude, we just talked about this." Todd complained.

Jay never admitted his wrongs. He avoided eye contact and changed the subject back to Todd. "You come out here to draw when something's bothering you. Why you holding out?"

"I'm not. I just need to discuss it with my wife first."

"Dad, is it time to pick up mom?" Max pulled on his jacket.

"The plane hasn't landed yet son. T, you need me to pick them up? I owe you one, remember?"

Todd laughed. "Your I-O-U won't be that easy."

At midnight, Todd stood near the ticket counters with a bouquet of purple calla lilies for Landon, and two single roses for Jen and Millicent. "Always a gentleman," said Millicent.

Todd and Landon embraced and kept the public display of affection to a minimum.

"Thank you for picking us up," said Jen, interrupting the couple.

"We can't have you lovely ladies out this time of night alone. Let me help with your bags."

He texted Jay when they turned into the neighborhood. Jay stood outside in the cold on the front steps, and met them at the curb when the car pulled up. He leaned in to kiss Jen when she rose from the car. She turned her head and gave him her cheek. "Not the welcome I was hoping for," he said, inclined towards the back window. "How was Miami? Did you ladies have a good time?" He shivered, blowing into his fists.

"We sure did," said Landon.

"How about you baby?" Jay asked Jen, grabbing her bags from the trunk.

"I had a fucking great time." She jeered.

Her intended pun went over his head. He collected her luggage. "That's good you ladies got to get away and live a little. I appreciate it T." Jay nodded. "Holla at me tomorrow." He raced behind Jen who left him in the cold.

"Will do," Todd replied.

They watched him rush to the front door, feeling the troubled vibes between them. Todd said, "I hope they sort that shit out."

Millicent chuckled in the back seat.

"What's so funny about wanting them to work it out," Todd asked.

"You men will stick together I swear," she replied.

"That's for damn sure," Landon added.

"Hold on. I didn't say he was wrong. But I talked to the man, and he wants to do right by his ole lady." Todd defended himself.

Millicent began singing, "He's a hoe, he knows he's a hoe."

Todd laughed and gripped Landon's thigh. Millicent continued to sing the tune, then stopped suddenly to talk. "Speaking of heauxs. Mr. Head and Shoulders has been texting me nonstop since we landed."

"Mr. Head and Shoulders?" Todd scowled at Landon.

"You never told us what happened." Landon turned to face her.

"Nothing happened. His phone rang non-stop. I mean of course when you're single you can do what you want, but he was a tad too busy for me." Millicent complained.

"I get the feeling all of the men down there are busy." Landon sneered and Millicent co-signed.

Todd waited until they were home to ask Landon if anyone tried to get with her down in Florida.

"This one guy," she answered, turning on the shower.

"Oh yeah." Todd moved in closer.

He covered her mouth and undressed her as the steam fogged the doorway to their bedroom. He worked his way into a quiet quickie against the wall, silencing her with kisses to spare Millicent's ears in the guest bedroom.

Todd tossed all night, holding onto Landon while she slept. At daybreak, Millicent headed back to Ohio, and Todd finally had his wife alone. He followed her into the bathroom while she primped in the mirror. "What's going on with you? I got stuck under your arm last night. You were holding me so tight. You missed me that much, huh?" Landon teased.

Todd pulled her away from the sink by her waist. "I did miss you. But I have something to tell you." His face wrinkled causing Landon to worry.

"I'm listening," she said, lightly scratching her nails against his five o'clock shadow.

"I went to visit my mother Friday night."

"Is she okay?"

"She's fine. Landon, I went over there and she showed me a picture of a boy, eight years old. He looks like me. I need you to schedule a paternity test for me."

Landon removed his hand from her waist. She backed away from him in disbelief, locking her eyes on him. "I've been torn up about this since I found out. Baby please don't look at me like that," Todd begged.

Landon stood still like a window mannequin. She took slow deep breaths, then scoffed. "You want me—to schedule you—a damn paternity test? Have you lost your mind?"

"I know you're angry, but I need my wife right now."

"Schedule your own damned test, and you better hope it comes back negative or else..."

"Or else what? What if it doesn't?" Todd huffed.

"Then we have a problem. I'm not doing the baby mama drama. I've seen first-hand how that works, and I don't want that kind of life. I have a right to live in peace."

"I would never let this ruin your peace." Todd grabbed her face.

"You have no idea how this will play out."

"So what are you saying?"

"He better not be yours is what I'm saying!" Landon screamed and slammed the bathroom door.

Todd sat on the bed and called her name repeatedly. She ignored him. "It's always gonna be you and me babe. You hear me." He reassured her.

She opened the door and fled for the closet. Todd was on her heels. He held her from behind as she struggled to dress for work. "I'm not losing you behind this," he said. Landon remained silent, until she could no longer hold back her tears. "Calm down. Let's get the results first. Okay?" Todd comforted her.

He'd never seen this side of his wife. Their relationship had been serene and ran smoothly for the most part, and now faced with conflict, an ugly side was rising to the surface, and Landon's reaction was more than he bargained for. *'Or else,'* he revisited repeatedly, wondering what she meant, and he hoped this bump in the road would be sorted out quick, and not throw them far off course.

CHAPTER 17

JEN

The homecoming Jay expected isn't the homecoming he received. He expected a relaxed, forgiving Jen would return after days away to regroup. Instead, she returned a woman further detached from the life they lived, before his philandering ways were exposed.

Jen entered the bedroom after stealing kisses from Max in a deep sleep. On the bed sat a black box with the words, **'I'm Sorry'** in bold print on the top cover, filled with a mixture of pink and gold roses. Beside it, a wrapped Tiffany box was positioned on the center of her pillow.

"That better not be a ring Jay." Jen emphasized with her eyes.

"Just open it." He dropped the luggage on the floor.

Jen untied the white bow and slowly ripped the blue paper from the box. Her hands grew clammy, afraid they were going to get into an argument on her first night back.

She opened the box, charmed by a diamond vine pendant necklace. Her eyebrows raised. "This is beautiful Jay. Thank you."

"The circle represents us." His eyes dropped like a puppy.

"Jay..." Her voice lowered and shoulders slouched.

"You don't have to say anything. I got the message outside. But I hope you wear it," he said, noticing a difference in her.

She reminded him of the girl sweeping floors. No nonsense, assertive, and head strong. Something about her demeanor aroused him as he watched her examine his peace offerings from behind. His wood tightened in his pants. "You looking good girl," he said, mannishly cuffing his set.

Jen felt guilty as she held the necklace in her hands. Staring at the circle of small diamonds she spoke. "I can't accept this. Even though I'm close to forgiving you, I will always wonder what you're doing, and who you're with. I can't live like that. I don't trust you."

"Let me show you I can be trusted," Jay begged.

"There isn't any way you can do that. We need to figure out how to be friends."

"Friends?" Jay questioned. "Fuck I look like being your friend." He raised his voice.

Jen placed the necklace on the bed. She closed the bedroom door behind Jay, and poked her fingers into his chest. "Don't you ever raise your voice at me. You don't get to do that. You don't get to tell me when I'm done being mad at you. You've been taking care of me, but that doesn't mean you own me. I was working when we met. You told me to stop so I could be home with Max. Well he's in school now, and shit is about to change. Now."

"Change in what way?" Jay leaned against the door.

"It's late. Thank you again for the lovely flowers and the beautiful necklace. I will wear it, but I'm not ready to move forward. P.S. I fucked someone in Miami. Fuck I look like being your pushover."

Jay stared at Jen wide-eyed and fuming. He assumed she threw such a dagger at him to level the score, and bit his lip as humility never suited him. "Don't I get a second chance to make things right Jen? Huh?"

Jen's mind flashed to the sensation of Jules pinning her on the dresser. Her eyes twirled and she deflected, answering his question with a question of her own.

"What if the shoe were on the other foot? Would you forgive me?"

"Yes! I would." He exclaimed softly. "People make mistakes."

Jen reached past him and opened the door, pointing for him to leave. He didn't budge.

She cleared her throat. "We can discuss this further in the morning."

Jay felt the burn from her eyes. He stepped in her face. "The morning it is," he said firmly, finally leaving her bedroom for the night.

Jen woke Max earlier than normal to spend time with him before school. She dropped him off and returned home, confused why Jay's car was still in the garage.

'Damn. He was supposed to be gone by now.'

He pressed the button near the door and jumped in the passenger seat of her car. "It's morning. Let's talk," he demanded, still dressed in his pajamas pants and white tank.

"Can I at least get dressed first?" She reached to open the door.

Jay leaned forward and removed her hand from the knob. He gripped it tight and laughed as he revealed the reason for his impromptu intrusion. "You knew that would fuck with me, didn't you?" he asked.

"What are you going on about?" Jen threw his hands off of hers, then folded her arms staring past the windshield.

Jay stared at her. "You know damn well what I'm talking about." He raised his voice.

"Fine. If you want to do this now, then let's do it."

"Did you really fuck someone in Miami?"

Jen sat quietly, rocking her legs side to side.

"Okay. I give in. If you want me to believe you gave *my* pussy away to make me feel bad. You win. I'm mad." He smiled on half of his mouth.

"You don't seem mad." Jen teased him, showing all of her teeth, then laughed in his face to piss him off further. "I swear you are some kind of stupid sometimes, you know that? Why couldn't you have been more like Todd? Not that he's my type, but he adores the ground Landon walks on. He doesn't cheat? Does he?"

"Nah. That boy is whipped like a can of cream for that girl."

"I envy her. I want to feel confident my man fancies me and me only. Don't I deserve that?"

"That and so much more." He wiped his face with both hands.

"Don't worry Jay, I'm not about to nag you into a marriage. But I still haven't decided if I'm going to keep you yet."

Jen was owning Jay with her words, but the smug look on her face aroused him. He lacked a rebuttal, but couldn't resist the urge to place his lips on hers. He threw himself on her, halfway rejected by the gear shift. His hard kiss softened once they locked eyes as Jen hesitated to pull back, giving him the green light he'd been waiting for.

His hands slid past her coat and tussled her breasts. Groping them in a hurried fashion before placing her nipples in his mouth. Jen removed her coat and pressed the button to slide her seat back, guiding Jay's head to her warmth.

He felt between her thighs, rubbing the tip of her opening with his fingers, while nibbling on her skin above it. Pacing his finger play, he moved his fingers further in to a higher mound, and rubbed until he felt her warm invitation.

He climbed back north and sucked her nipples tight in his mouth, then glanced at her leaning back with her eyes closed. "Come on this side." He sighed from discomfort.

Jen saw the eagerness in his eyes and obliged, fighting her instincts to stop the train wreck before it happened. She climbed on top of him, humored by the desperation in his eyes. He grabbed her face with one hand and kissed her hard again, deeply turned on at the spontaneity of the moment.

With a quick flick, his thermal briefs stretched down and Jen arched her back, resting her head on the dashboard. Jay lifted Jen by her ass and polished her pearl, placing it all in his mouth, shimmying his head wildly side to side.

The windows fogged on the passenger side as Jen panted heavily against the windshield. She shook from Jay's maniacal feast of her second set of lips, quavering as he brought her forward toward his rod, rubbing the tip against her fold.

Jen pivoted her body mid-air, as cruel thoughts resurfaced at the moment of truth. Flashes of Jay at the hotel, and her with Jules made her question herself.

'*Am I really about to shag two different men back to back?*'

Jay saw the doubt growing in her face while tweaking the pulse of her womanhood with his fingers. "Baby don't do me like this. What's wrong?" he asked.

The look on his face made Jen vulnerable to his desire for her. She grinned and decided to throw him a pity fuck. "Put on a condom."

The hurt of her request was visible in his eyes, but he was too aroused to plead his case. He dropped his head and strongly exhaled. "Whatever you ask of me."

He opened the door, and slipped Jen's pajama pants completely off as he helped her out of the car. She aimed for the kitchen door, but Jay held her close to him, poking his dick in her back as he reached into one of the drawers in his tool cabinet.

Palming her by a strip of her hair with one hand, he rolled the latex down his pipe with the other, and pinned her against the car facing forward.

Forcefully he broke into her womb, growling at the feeling of what he had taken for granted. Jen moaned of pleasure and pain, being manhandled with her hair in a tight grip forcing her chin to lift. "He fuck you better than me?" He barked vigorously into her ear. Jen smirked with her back to him, deliberately evading the question. "He make that ass jump like it's jumping right now? Huh?" Jay stroked harder, wanting her to feed his ego and say no.

Jen's willowy body handled the beating like a body bag. Jay mean fucked her like it was a punishment she deserved, when he in fact was the one with penalties. "Let me take it off," he begged, sucking on her neck.

"No," she refused, cuffing his hands around her shoulder to assure he didn't shred the bag.

The car rocked back and forth from the pounding jabs Jay wailed on Jen. He howled like a wolf when he climaxed, lightly digging his nails into Jen's shoulders. He released her from his cobra clutch and turned her to face him. Kissing her intently with a message. "You're mine." He grinned, proud of himself.

"Go run me a bath," Jen commanded.

Jay flipped his pants over his half brooding penis, and left Jen to collect herself in the garage. She waited to hear the pipes of the water heater kick on, and quickly counted the condoms in the drawer. Her head shook after tallying the amount of rubbers missing from the package.

She made her way inside and sat in the warm water, resting her head on her knees. Jay crept in behind her, and wrapped his arms on top of hers. Jen laid her head back on his shoulder, while he rested his cheek against hers. She was emotionally confused. Tickled at how exultant he was they finally made love, but saddened about the condoms they never used until moments ago.

A tear fell from her eye, and Jay assumed she was expressing emotions of their reunion. He wiped her face. "I cried last night. I thought I had lost you forever. Thought I would never hold you like this again. And that blow you hit me with about Miami, humph, shit brought tears to my eyes." He admitted.

Jen squinted her eyes. She neither confirmed or denied she shared the same feelings as he, laughing to herself at how he changed her truth into a lie.

She kept quiet about the matter, and asked him to massage her neck, after he sloshed water against her skin from shoulder to shoulder. The sensation of the warm water, and Jay's forceful hand kneading her stress zones, calmed her mind.

While in his hands, she thought of Jules— when and if she would see him again. And how soon. Their worlds colliding was a gift in her eyes, as he reminded her what it felt like to be adorned. He brought a new outlook with him, restoring a piece of herself that was lost. Now, she had to wait and see how it would all pan out, occupied by the images in her head of when she gave herself to him.

[illegible]

[illegible]

[illegible]

[illegible]

[illegible]

Chapter 18

Millicent

The weekly Wednesday lunch was cancelled for the week. Jen and Landon were both happy when Millicent texted she couldn't make it because Mike Crumby was back in town.

After failing to connect with Mal down in Miami, Millicent looked forward to some good company and conversation.

Mike Crumby had a respectable job and was a complete gentleman, willing to do anything Millicent suggested for a first date. Quickly, she peeped he didn't take charge and allowed her to call the shots. It wasn't a turn-on for her, but a characteristic she was willing to overlook in the meantime.

They met at Meadow Brook Hall for the annual Holiday Walk. Mike insisted he pay both their entries, starting the date off proper in Millicent's eyes.

She studied the way he talked and interacted with people, crediting his journalistic training of why he communicated so well.

After walking around on the tour, they grabbed an early dinner where their eyes met in the middle of reaching for the salt. "Is it okay to say we both know who isn't in the kitchen?" Mike joked.

Millicent laughed out loud, then collected herself as the snobbish woman at the table next to them looked down at her.

"I wasn't going to say it, but I definitely thought it," she whispered.

While giggling amongst themselves, Millicent found herself drawn to this odd man she knew nothing about, except the highlights he shared about himself, and the featured profiles she found online. She toned down her inquisition, desperate to know why the forty-year-old had never been married, or had any children.

By the end of their date, she waited for Mike to take charge and kiss her. She leaned back against her car, setting the scene, but he continued to talk, and missed her signal.

It became obvious Ms. Saint James would be waiting forever, so the dominant nature in her took control of the situation.

She pulled him in by his jacket and planted her lips on his. Mike nearly lost his balance stepping in. The kiss was clean. Soft and gentle. And perfectly timed.

Millicent pulled back and released his jacket. Mike *glamoured* her with his blonde eyes. "That was nice," he said. "Call you tomorrow?"

Millicent replied with a big smile on her face. "You better."

He opened her car door and walked backwards to the edge of the curb until she drove off. Millicent's smile lasted half way back to Ohio. She replayed the lovely moment during her drive home. Thinking about the wealth of knowledge regarding worldly affairs Mike spewed intelligibly. She was fascinated by him. '*This one's got potential,*' she thought.

Mike called to verify she made it home safe, but to also say he wished the night hadn't ended so early. Millicent was flattered, but also intrigued at his forwardness. She pegged him as passive earlier, but now she wasn't so sure.

"I like to take things slow," she answered.

"I didn't peg you to be easy. Especially since I had to wait for you to call."

"I had to google you, remember?" She kidded.

"I did say that, didn't I? I must have sounded crass."

"A little pretentious, but you said it with a smile so I figured you weren't completely in love with yourself." Millicent laughed.

They talked all night like teenagers on the phone. Millicent didn't hold back with her questions, probing him to speak candidly about his past. Quizzing him like an employer searching for a new hire.

She wanted to see if he shared the common trait of most men—selling wolf tickets and lying for the sake of lying. He came across as honest, and passed with flying colors.

When they hung up, Millicent danced as she dressed for work, energetic from the adrenaline of finally finding someone worth her time. She sang, "This might be the one! This might be the one!"

She dialed Landon on her way to work to brag about the good energy flowing within her. She got ahead of herself, expecting Landon to be in her normal, chipper mood. After reaching her voicemail twice, she swung by her office.

Landon didn't smile when she walked in during a brief with Margie.

"That's unusual," said Millicent, closing the door behind her.

"What are you doing here?" Landon frowned.

"Is this how we greet people now? What's wrong sis?"

"I'm just under a lot of pressure. I have minor problems to fix on this ad by tomorrow, and have the company holiday party on Saturday, amongst other things. I'm just not myself today. Sorry." Landon dropped a tear and slung the folder from her hands across her desk.

Millicent placed her arms around her. "Sit down. Breathe. You're just overwhelmed."

Landon's blouse revealed her heavy heartbeat, slightly flickering near the button between her breasts. "It's more than the job."

"Did scone guy do something to you?"

"God no. I wouldn't be able to handle his foolishness. It's Todd. He told me something I refuse to believe is true."

"He didn't do what his stupid ass friend did, did he?"

"No. Worse. He has to take a paternity test for an eight-year-old boy. My life with him may not end the way I dreamed. He was perfect. We were perfect. How can we survive this?"

"He hasn't taken the test yet. I'm sure this will blow over."

"I saw the picture." Landon cried.

"Oh." Millicent's mouth dropped. "Margie said you've been locked in here all morning. Let me take you to lunch."

"I can't leave. I have too much to do, and I'm not hungry."

"Then let's get some air. It's freezing I know, but it'll do you some good."

They attempted Millicent's suggestion to take a walk around the block. The cold air was so brisk, they turned back to Landon's office building, and shared a pretzel from one of the lobby vendors. Color somewhat restored to Landon's face after eating. She asked, "Why were you so lit when you walked into my office?"

Millicent dropped her head.

"There it is again. Did you finally get laid?"

"No. But I will be soon. I think."

"So, the date went well?" Landon finally smiled.

"It was perfect. Almost too perfect. I know. I know. Don't look for the negative. And I promise I'm not. I'm going to ask him to come with me to the New Year's party."

"I'm happy for you Mills. You're good on your own, but I like you having a plus one."

Millicent left Landon to her work and played crunch time with her appointments from the morning. She liked challenges, but the pressure of cramming her day went against everything she stood for.

The exhaustion from a night of no sleep caught up with her when she arrived home. She crashed the moment she plopped on the couch, and woke from her nap near midnight.

Two missed calls from Mike would have to wait until tomorrow to be returned. In that moment, she vowed not to let Mike interfere with her current schedule. She liked him enough to find a way to fit him into her equation, but not enough to disrupt her routine.

CHAPTER 19

LANDON

Very few words were spoken between the Jeffries all week. Todd asked questions, and Landon answered with one word, or said nothing at all.

She knew he hated the silent treatment, and purposefully drove him insane. When Todd asked, "What do you want me to wear on Saturday?"

Landon took her time to respond, "Whatever."

Todd left the room and balled up his fist, air punching his frustration, then returned to the closet slightly calmer. He watched her skim through dresses, waiting for her to acknowledge him. She refused, trying on shoes and organizing the already organized shelves.

When Saturday arrived, Landon dressed in all black. Todd commented, "You normally dress a bit more festive for this thing. What's with the all black?" Landon shrugged her shoulders and closed the bathroom door on him.

Every year she used this occasion to exude her beauty. Todd meant no harm with his comment, as she would be breathtaking in anything she wore. He stood outside the door and complimented her dress. "You look pretty in the black babe." Landon still didn't respond.

Todd had been on the receiving end of the silent treatment all week. His patience suddenly ran thin with Landon, and he barged into the bathroom. "I'm not going tonight. Tell your boss I came down with something. Better yet, tell him whatever the fuck you want. I'm out."

Landon's pride kept her from running after him. She finished dressing moments later, and drove to the Bagley Mansion alone. She sat in the line of traffic, waiting to pull up to the valet. Watching her co-workers arrive with their significant others, she regretted the way she shut Todd out, and contemplated leaving to go find him.

The valet approached her car, helped her out of her vehicle, and took her keys. Landon entered the old house, and checked her coat, sparkling in black sequins. She wore her hair big and blown out, allowing it to flow free for the night, and contoured her cheek bones with rose gold blush.

Strutting in solo, she wowed everyone when her red bottoms walked into the room, tightly pressing her deep cherry colored lips together.

An array of alcoholic beverages and gourmet hors d'oeuvres lined the back wall of the main room, where couples mingled and feasted along the banquet tables. Landon scoped the room. '*Where should I go and hide,*' she thought.

Nervously, she fidgeted her purse between her fingers. This was the first time she attended the party alone, and suddenly regretted her choice of dress without Todd at her side. Her body fit it flawlessly, and brought attention to her curves, nearly bringing the men to their knees. Especially Dario, who could not take his eyes off of her.

Landon made her way over to The Swendsens, getting the awkward part out of the way. "Landon! Where's Todd tonight?" Mr. Swendsen asked, swigging on champagne.

"He had an emergency. He won't make it in time I'm afraid. Hope I'm enough tonight." Landon spread her arms and raised her eyebrows.

"Of course you are. I was hoping to talk sports with your better half is all. He knows his stuff."

"Yeah, I can't help you there. I feel awkward standing here without a glass in my hand. If you'll excuse me."

Margie joined Landon at the bar with her husband closely behind. "How's it going? Saw you talking to Swendsen. He's hammered already. Where's Todd?"

"He had an emergency. I'm solo tonight." Landon threw the champagne down her throat.

"Easy there. We might have to put you in a cab you keep that up." Margie joked.

Dario walked over to the bar. He ordered two mixed drinks, staring at Landon from the corner of his eye. Sweat beads formed in the crease of his forehead as he tapped on the wood, listening to her conversation.

"How's everyone doing tonight?" he interjected.

"Good," they answered.

"Happy holidays," he added.

Margie and Landon responded half interested. Margie's husband raised his eyebrows at his wife. "Let's dance," he asked her, whisking her onto the dance floor. Landon figured Margie shared the details of the office drama with him. *'Smart man,'* she thought.

Dario cleared his throat. "I saw you come in alone. I'd happily serve as a filler tonight. Wanna join them?"

Landon took a big sip from her second glass of bubbly. "Boundaries Mr. Powers. Remember our talk on inappropriate behavior?" She lectured.

"You make it *hard*, literally, for me to behave. Don't pretend I'm the only man in here staring at you. You see it."

Landon choked on her champagne. She coughed and took a step away from Dario, making it her business not to entertain anything he had to say.

"Water please," she said to the bartender.

He nodded while passing Dario his order. "Your drinks, sir."

Dario slid a tip across the counter, and stepped closer to Landon. "What do I have to do to score some alone time with you? I know something was brewing between us before. You had my nose so open, I couldn't wait to get to work in the mornings. Hope we can get that spark back," he said, then slithered away.

The bartender handed Landon a bottled water. She sipped while embracing her chest.

"Are you alright Miss?" the bartender asked.

Landon nodded, "Yes. Just got a little choked."

A hand grazed the small of her back and she jumped. "Was that him?" Todd mumbled in her ear.

She turned towards him and smiled

"You haven't looked at me like this all week," said Todd, pressing his lips against the red paint on hers.

"I'm sorry." She grabbed a cocktail napkin and dabbed it across his lips. "Thank you for coming. You look handsome as always."

"I don't need to tell you how good you look. Always the prettiest girl in the room." He stole another kiss. "That was him, wasn't it?"

"It doesn't matter."

"What did he say?" Todd held Landon around her waist.

"Nothing important."

Landon placed her hand on Todd's shoulder. The bartender interrupted. "Sir, can I get you anything?"

"I got what I came for." He pulled Landon in closer and laughed. "Ugh, what the hell. A rum and coke. It's a party right."

"Coming right up sir."

Todd glanced over Landon's shoulder and caught Dario watching them. Mostly Landon. He furrowed his brows and squinted his eyes, slightly bearing his teeth as a warning. Mr. Swendsen broke his gaze. "Todd! I'm so happy you made it. I told your wife I enjoy our sports talks. Come, let me pick your brain about this playoff season."

As Todd was carried off into a huddle of gambling sports fanatics, Landon excused herself to the ladies' room. She relined her red lips and smiled at her reflection in the tall mirror, thrilled Todd came after all. Margie strolled in as she was leaving.

"I see Todd made it. Good thing too with Mr. Weirdo lurking about."

"I swear I say one thing, and he hears something totally different."

"If I didn't know any better, he followed you back here. The nerve. Wait on me will ya. I'll walk out with you."

Landon shook her head at the news Margie shared with her. As requested, she waited on her assistant and left the loo as a pair. Sure enough, there was Dario in the hall, pretending he was on his way to the men's room.

Margie served as a buffer, preventing him from causing a scene. They strolled past him and rejoined the party, getting soused with the other ladies who lost their husbands to the conversation of sports.

Todd laughed at Mr. Swendsen's bad jokes, being the good husband Landon asked of him. They shared a smile from across the room, and Todd excused himself from the men's corner.

"How much longer do I have to cheese with your boss?" he asked.

"You've done enough for tonight." She chuckled in his arms.

Words weren't necessary to express what they were feeling. As soon as the toast and speeches concluded, they left the party in a hurry, and raced each other home.

Todd threw his sweater to the floor as soon as he made it inside. "I've missed you these past few days Mrs. Jeffries." Todd serenaded her.

Landon walked backwards and taunted him. "Stop all that talking and fuck me Mr. Jeffries," she demanded.

He obeyed and swept her off her feet, carrying her to the bar in his man cave.

He opened a bottle of Hennessy Pure White and sipped from it, gazing at his beautiful wife. "You are irresistible babe," he said, walking his fingers up her thighs, arriving at her threshold. He forcefully tore her panty hose, barely blinking in his trance, while Landon jerked slightly at the sudden move, looking him directly in his eyes.

Todd took a final swig of his liquor and placed it on the bar. Using both hands, he shredded her under garments, freeing her throbbing flesh. Two fingers slipped inside of her, covered in slickness. An evil laugh left his mouth. "That pussy is ready for me."

Landon's dress rose above her head, and his lips met hers once she was freed. The agony of making her wait for him, increased her body heat. She spread her legs wide and pulled on his wood, trying to force it inside as her lubricated womb pulsed for him.

Todd resisted the urge for a quick bang and toyed with her, playing out the scenario he imagined while she was in Miami. Millicent robbed him of his moment, and now that he had Landon desperate and alone, he would capitalize from it.

He lifted her legs in the air and massaged them from her inner thigh, down to her perfectly pedicured feet, delivering hard kisses to the back of her calves causing her to jolt and moan. His trained hands worked their way back up to her well-rounded thighs, while he sucked the back of her legs up to her access portal.

Landon wobbled on the edge from the strong suction of his lips. Todd secured her, balancing her from the bottom of her thighs. His tension relieving tongue massage transformed into gentle kisses seconds before he surprised her with something new. He lifted her slightly from the small of her back and placed his closed mouth to her dirt road, giving it a slow, strong lick before storming her capitol.

The ride was rough and intense. Landon slipped from the edge as Todd held her mid-air, directing her walls up and down and around him, with his hands using her ass for a guide. "Don't you ever keep this good stuff away from me again," he demanded with a punishable thrust.

Landon whimpered. "Okay, just don't stop."

The liquor extended their pleasure, with Landon in a buck on the couch, riding him like a cowgirl, and finishing strong with her back arched and hair pulled by a grunting Todd exploding his seeds deep inside of her.

Their screeches and screams of passion mirrored one another. Wired to the fullest, he rose from the floor and carried his bare bodied wife to their bedroom.

He kissed her caramel coated skin from head to toe, then covered her, bonding in one another's arms.

In the middle of the night Landon woke to Todd sitting up in the bed. "What are you doing up?"

He chewed on the bottom of his lip. "Wondering what that guy was saying to you. Wondering if he's crazy. Worrying about you at work."

"I did keep my word. I handled it. I haven't had any problems out of him."

"Did you report it?"

"No. I don't want that drama attached to my name."

"Is he ranked higher than you?"

"We're equals."

"That's cute. You and I know how these places operate."

"I'm respected in my position." Landon's face tensed.

"What's his name?"

"Dario...Powers." Landon paused. "I like my job Todd. Just talk to him."

"There won't be any talking."

"This is why I wanted to handle it."

"And how is that working out for you? What did he say?"

"Nothing except all the men at the party were looking at me." Her voice rose.

"He wasn't lying, but it wasn't his place to tell you that. I'll take care of it, and I won't get into any trouble."

Landon turned her back, guilty for telling Todd half of the truth, and uneasy about Dario's reckless words. Todd promised he would defuse the situation with conversation, knowing when he approached him, he'd ask questions later, and they both went to bed liars that night.

CHAPTER 20

TODD

Christmas was tough on Landon with the results of the paternity test arriving days before. She couldn't face Todd, his family, or the new addition.

It was the first Christmas she returned home to Flint without her husband at her side, seeking the comfort of her mother Laura Lee and baby sister Launa. The kind of comfort only women you share a close bond with can give you, and even then, she still didn't feel like celebrating the holidays.

She ignored the frequent calls and texts during her hiatus back home, shutting everyone out. She needed peace and distance from the situation, and the comforting messages wouldn't let the problem escape her, so she did instead.

The tribulation was exactly what Landon never wanted to deal with in her marriage. For the longest time, she and Todd shared a bond so surreal, it was impossible for an outsider to come between them. Now things were different. She knew Todd was about to take on a role that would make him see the world differently. See them differently. And she could not compete with a child.

Having to deal with another woman contacting her husband, arranging visits, demanding his attention, and receiving money from their household was gut wrenching.

On paper she was the bread winner, and never questioned how Todd's business kept up with her earnings. Now his funds were being funneled into another woman's pockets, and Landon felt cheated— Like the world double crossed her.

Incapable of accepting the change, she sulked for a little over a week, and surprised the gang at Jen and Jay's house for their annual New Year's Eve get-together.

"Landon!" Jen screamed, when she waltzed through the door. Millicent and the wives huddled near her at the door. Jen whispered, "Don't bring it up tonight is all I ask."

"Okay," Landon mumbled.

"You look like a million bucks. Matching my decorations." Jen pointed to the silver linens, balloons, and bowls of shining lights in every corner.

"Thanks. I wasn't feeling very golden this year." Landon joked.

"Let's get you a drink."

Todd watched her walk across the room, waiting for her to give him an inch. She followed Jen to the table covered with bottles, and kept her back to him. Millicent stood next to her and refilled her glass.

"I'm so glad you're here. Todd was looking pitiful until you walked in, and I brought Mike tonight. I want you to meet him and tell me what you think."

"I'm sure I'll like him."

"It feels good to not be the stag for once." Millicent exhaled.

Landon tapped her shoulder. "There's nothing wrong with being alone." Millicent's eyes popped at her words. "True, but lately I find myself getting comfortable with it, and that scares me. I'm tired of meeting new people."

"The good old no new friends, except for boyfriends." Jen teased.

"Exactly. If this doesn't work out, I might have to recycle somebody. It's crazy out here."

"Like Mr. Head and Shoulders in Miami?" Landon asked.

"I did like him, but that would be like willingly going into a relationship and saying okay I know you're going to be unfaithful, but I'm desperate so I'll settle."

"I'll see what's up with him next time I talk to Jules," said Jen.

Millicent and Landon's faces both grimaced. They whispered to Jen, "You're openly talking about him in your house?"

"I told Jay I slept with someone else and he doesn't believe me. Go figure." She laughed, then clinked her glasses against theirs.

"I thought you two were back on one accord," Landon said.

"He seems to think so."

"Ladies, let's talk about this later. We don't want to bring in the new year with drama." Millicent suggested.

"For sure. Let's get everyone together in the living room anyway. This party is becoming separate with the men huddled over there and we're huddled over here."

Jen turned up the music and the couples got the hint. Mike walked over to the table where Millicent and Landon finished whispering about Jen's dilemma.

"Landon, this is Mike Crumby. Mike this is my best girlfriend but you may as well say sister, Landon." Millicent cozied up next to him.

"Nice to meet you, but I know who you are thanks to the fella standing over there in the cream sweater." He pointed to Todd. "He hasn't stopped bragging about the commercials you've done. I really enjoyed the one with the talking car at the drive thru window."

"Thank you." Landon blushed, then looked over to Todd.

"You wanna?" Mike held out his hand to Millicent.

Landon walked over to Todd and stood next to him in silence. They watched their friends act like fools in the middle of Jay's living room, never sharing a glance.

"I see you finally wore that sweater I bought you," Landon said.

"Yep. Thank you by the way. You look ravishing as always."

"It was a struggle tonight. I almost didn't come," she said.

"I'm glad you did. Christmas without you was hard enough." He placed his hand in line with hers.

"Same."

"So, what are you going to do?" Todd asked.

"I don't know. Can we not talk about it tonight? I just want to have a good time."

"So do I."

The couples gathered on the sofas and chairs for introspection and conversation until the ball dropped on the television. The friction between Todd and Landon was no secret, but to keep the energy light, it wasn't discussed.

The tension was mild, but still felt whenever Brian's wife discussed their children. Mike opened his mouth without thinking of the consequence.

"Why does the room tense up when someone brings up children? Am I missing something here?"

The room fell silent under the soft music. A collective gasp traveled the room. Jay said, "Of course Millicent would bring someone around who *don't* know when to shut up." Everyone in the room giggled except for Landon, Todd, and Millicent.

"I apologize. I didn't mean to intrude. Please remember I'm new here." Mike held up his hands.

"No need," said Landon. "Everyone here knows except you."

"Well since he brought it up, what is going on with you two?" Brian asked.

"B. Chill," said Jay, just before Kim slapped Brian's arm.

"It's okay. I'm positive everyone here is up to speed. Except for Mike, of course. And thank you by the way, because the tiptoeing around the subject is making everyone uncomfortable. And frankly the anger I feel inside is killing me," said Landon.

Everyone's happy faces plummeted and mouths dropped. Todd stood up. "Damn Landon, you act like I stepped out and made a baby on us. This happened before I knew you. And it's killing me too. I want my wife back. My happy wife back."

"Jesus, Mary, and Joseph I know how it happened! I'm pissed at myself because I can't get past it. I know shit happens, but this situation has turned my life upside down, and I'm expected to just roll with it. I don't want to share my husband with anyone else. How am I the bad guy for feeling this way?"

McCaine's wife Tammy interrupted them. "You two need to talk about this when drinks aren't involved, and in private."

Jen agreed with Tammy. "You two love each other. We all know it. We all see it. Give it time."

"Y'all can get past this. It's hard work though," said Tammy.

"Excuse me," McCaine asked.

"I know how she feels. Your pre-packaged family wasn't easy to deal with it."

"It wasn't that bad." McCaine argued.

"Sheeeet." Tammy exclaimed. "Maybe not for you. Humph. I wanted to pack my bags and run like hell several times. Your daughter caused friction between us, and you never wanted to hear about it. People never want to hear anything bad about their children, and you were no different."

"She's exaggerating y'all."

"That disrespectful heifer would come in my house and not even speak to me. You said nothing. And would tell her mama everything going on in our house. Landon honey, you're right to feel the way you feel. Children can ruin a relationship. Especially if the parent allows them to." Tammy stared at her husband.

McCaine looked straight ahead, refusing to make eye contact with his wife. Their interaction created humor in the room. McCaine mumbled under his breath, "My daughter didn't do those things."

"Yes she did!" Tammy's eyes widened. "Y'all! One time I picked up the phone and I heard the mama coaching the little girl on how to scheme more money out of him. Hell, the child support he was paying, paid her rent, and I heard her telling the child, "Say it like this now okay.""

"Okay that's enough hard liquor for you." McCaine reached for her glass.

Tammy chugged it down her throat and passed him the empty glass. McCaine's face turned red with embarrassment as his wife pushed the glass into his hands. All eyes turned to McCaine, watching him and his wife battle each other using their eyes.

McCaine blinked first and threw his head back into laughter, easing the tension in the room. "I can't take this woman nowhere." McCaine joked.

"Tammy, what made you stay if I may ask," asked Millicent.

"The thought of failing, and something one of my aunts told me. She said stepchildren grow up, eventually leave, and get a life of their own. Don't let anyone dictate what makes you happy. Mc makes me happy, so I made up my mind I would not be bullied out of my house and my man." Tammy winked at McCaine.

"I love you too baby." He kissed her cheek.

"Plus, I treated myself very nicely whenever they pissed me off." Tammy polished her nails against her shoulder.

"What do you mean treated yourself nicely?" McCaine asked.

"Oh you know. A bracelet here and there, a spa package, Manolos."

"Those aren't knockoffs!" He gasped.

Tammy laughed in his face and kissed his lips. Todd grabbed Landon's hand and led her into the hallway near the bedrooms.

"You won't ever have to share me," he said, and tenderly kissed her lips. "I've been wanting to do that since you walked in."

Landon relaxed her shoulders and leaned against the wall. "I miss you too. I miss us. But I can't help the way I feel. I love you no less, but it's not fair to rush me into being okay with this. I need you to respect that." She held onto his pants pockets and lured him in.

Todd charged at her, recognizing the lecherous look in her eyes. She wanted him and he knew it, happy to oblige her of the missed desire and punishment she craved. Her gloss coated his lips, and the hem of her dress rose above her thighs as Todd lost restraint trying to get to her goodies.

Jen entered the hallway. "Oh, sorry." She scurried off.

Landon squirmed and stopped the action. "As bad as I want to, let's wait until we get home."

Todd buried his head on her shoulder. "You sure, because I know Jay wouldn't mind if we borrowed one of these rooms."

Landon suffered alongside him. "It's almost midnight. Let's leave as soon as the ball drops," she said, lowering her dress.

Tuxedo hats, paper whistles, and white light sticks were passed around the room. The couples celebrated the countdown, blasting music as the ball dropped on the big screen.

The New Year was brought in with a sealed kiss around the room, lit by the glowing lights from the tables and sticks waving from everyone's hands. "Can we go home now? It's been over a week and I'm *jonesing* for you so bad, you wouldn't understand," said Todd.

Landon laughed. "I think I do." She brushed his zipper with her ass.

Minutes past midnight, the guests began to disappear. The Jeffries being the first out of the door, as for them, making up was never hard to do.

CHAPTER 21

JAY

Jay locked the door behind the last of their guests. Jen tidied the kitchen, ridding the sink of the dishes. "Leave those 'til the morning," Jay said, closing in on her from behind. "I wanted to put their asses out hours ago." He laughed.

Jen moved him out of her way, but he sprung back on her coattail. She turned halfway around and smirked at him. It was funny comments like that, and moments of him being lively with her that drew her into him.

His comedic, smart-mouthed, bad boy persona made her feel like a giddy school girl at times, exuding an unexplainable charm with the power to pull her back in.

"You wouldn't do that to them. They are the only people you like, and we both know that's a small number." Jen teased.

"I would have tonight with how good you looking in that dress."

She escaped his embrace and picked up a dish to wash. Jay put it back down. She reached high in the cabinets to store the extra flutes in the slot. Jay bent his knees, and positioned himself perfectly below where her ass would land when her feet flattened. "You feel it," he said. "I know you felt it earlier when we were dancing too."

Jen silently grinned as he took her by the waist, and pressed his eager hood tightly between her cheeks.

"Tell me you don't want it," he said. "Your nipples are on high beam, and I feel your ass twitching. You're ready for your new year blessing."

"Is that what they're calling it now?" Jen sassed.

"That's what I call it."

"You really do think you're a bad ass, don't you?" Jen laughed.

"You love that about me," he said, lifting her up on the counter. "Tell Big Papa how you want it." He groaned in her ear.

"How do you want to give it to me?"

"Unwrapped." Jay bit his lip.

"Don't ruin the moment."

"It's been weeks since you let me hit skin on skin."

Jen cooled off the heat between them and twisted her mouth to the side. She stretched her brows and squinted her eyes without blinking.

Jay panicked he was about to strike out. "I'll strap up," he said quickly, and carried her to their bedroom.

CHAPTER 22

MILLICENT

Mike's meddling and slip of the tongue curved Millicent's plans to give herself to him. Because of the hour drive back to Ohio, she allowed him to spend the night, regretfully.

Her sex life had been non-existent for over a year. She thought the drought was going to end in Miami with Mal. Now she lied next to a man whom she thought had potential, until he opened his mouth, and embarrassed her in front of her friends.

She faked snoring when he slipped his hand from around her waist, and up to her breast. He failed miserably, winding on her nipples as she pretended to be asleep. To stop him from violating her bosom, she did a sudden turn towards him and lied on her stomach.

In the morning, he tried too hard, writing M&M with whipped cream on pancakes. Dubbing it as their moniker.

"We should order towels with the M and M on it."

Millicent hummed. "Mmm hmm," scowling when he turned his back.

'Maybe he senses I wasn't pleased how he embarrassed me last night, and is trying to redeem himself,' she thought.

An hour went by after breakfast and Mike made no effort to leave. "I'm going to get a head start with some paperwork," Millicent said.

Mike put his feet up on her sofa. "Don't be long. It is New Year's Day. Thought we could go for a drive and check out some sales."

Millicent raged into her office. She worked for half an hour, ready to get this drive Mike planned over with so she could get him out of her house.

They drove to the mall to take advantage of the sales Mike made a huge deal about. He pulled out credit cards for every store they shopped in, encouraging Millicent to apply for the discount.

"That's not wise." She gave him the side eye.

He bought items he had no use for, and Millicent grew impatient with him. She figured he was a keeping up with the Jones' type of man who perpetrated more than he actually had.

On the way home, his credit card was declined and she had to pay the tab for dinner. She paid close attention to his behavior when she reached in her purse to settle the bill. Noticing he didn't make a fuss or offer to pay her back.

It only took a few weeks and one party for her to quickly grow suspicious of Mike. Now three dates later, she couldn't get rid of him.

While unlocking the door to her condo, she hinted of her plans to unwind before the work week in a bubble bath, while playing catch up with her girlfriends.

Mike followed her inside. "That sounds really nice. I'll be on the couch working on my article."

Millicent's face boiled. "Fine. You can sleep on it tonight too. I'm used to sleeping alone."

Relaxing was impossible with a man she wanted out of her house, indenting her sofa with his outline. She crept up on him in the middle of the night, and studied him while he slept.

'*Where did all the good qualities I saw him disappear to?*' she wondered.

In the morning, she dressed for work and nudged him twice to get up so they could leave together. "Babe, I worked on this story 'til late. I'm going to stay here and get it done." He rolled over into a fetal position.

"Um Mike. I have a huge client I'm meeting today and you're making me late. I need you to get moving like right now." Millicent snapped her fingers.

Mike wheezed in his sleep. Millicent stomped her heels on the floor. He didn't move. She turned on the security cameras and raced out of the door, debating to call the police to remove him.

She clenched her teeth, staining them with her blush lipstick, and rang Landon. "Please tell me you can talk?" she asked when she answered.

Landon groggily replied, "What's up?"

"What's up is I have a *wannabe* hobosexual on my couch." Millicent grunted.

"The Mike guy?" Landon perked up. "I thought you liked him."

"I did like him, but something about him is off. I'm starting to see why he was available." Millicent hit the steering wheel.

"What did he do?"

"I don't know where to begin, I just want him out of my house. Should I call the police?"

"No. Don't do him like that. Just be firm and tell him he has to go home."

"I guess. I'll be firm and see what happens. Wish me luck."

Curious about what was happening at her place, Millicent hurried home after her last meeting. The smell of curry hit her nose before the key opened the door. "I made curry for lunch. I left you some on the stove." Mike announced when she entered.

"Thank you?" Millicent questioned.

"How was your big meeting?"

"It went well," Millicent slowly responded. "Did you finish your article?"

"Oh yeah." He cheered. "Submitted it a few hours ago."

"Good for you. I'm actually about to head out to the gym, so I can come home and tend to my workload. New Year, new goals." Millicent hinted.

"Can you skip the gym tonight. I wanted you to take a ride with me to this dealership having a sale. I'd love your input since you're so good with numbers."

"Mike, I have a routine and little time to step out of it."

"I promise it won't take long."

Millicent abandoned her core class, fearing her reservations about Mike were right when they drove into a Mercedes dealership. She fumed as he drooled at the lineup on the lot, then test drove two vehicles, wasting everyone's time.

She waited for him to return in the lobby, expecting they would leave once he had his fun. As the car pulled back on the lot, she saw him follow the agent into his office. *I know this fool is not about to buy that car,'* she said to herself.

Ten minutes the door opened and he gave Millicent a thumbs up, then waved for her to join him. She sluggishly walked over to him, uninterested in whatever he had agreed to.

The agent greeted her and slid the paperwork in front of her across the desk. "Do you need me to read the terms?" Millicent asked Mike.

"Yes, but also sign and initial the spaces with the yellow highlight."

"I beg your pardon." Millicent shifted in her seat.

"He just needs your information as a co-signor," Mike said sure of himself.

Millicent looked at the paperwork, then up at Mike. She scoffed, then turned to the agent. "Sir, is there anyone here who can drive me home?"

"I'm sorry," he asked.

"I came here with this man, but I'm not leaving with this man. I need a ride home."

"I'll give you two some privacy to talk." The agent excused himself.

Mike grabbed Millicent's hand. "Baby, what are you doing?"

"Baby? Oh my God. Did you really think you could coerce me into buying you a car? Or is this a prank? This has to be a prank." She hysterically raised her voice.

"I thought we were getting serious?"

"After nearly a month? Mike, I'm sorry but this is where we part ways. Good luck to you."

"But what about my stuff?"

"Ugh. Fine. Meet me at the house."

"Meet you? Why can't I drive you?"

Millicent shook her head and walked out of the agent's office. She found him standing with his manager. "Can that ride home be arranged, or do I need to order a Lyft?" she asked. The manager and the agent paused a second too long for Millicent's taste. "I'll order that car," she said, and waited outside with Mike staring at her from the car he failed to trade in.

During the ride home, she called the police and asked them to serve as an escort, finally getting rid of Mike.

Officer Campbell reviewed her complaint, and explained the safety precautions she needed to take if Mike returned. His partner, Officer Reed, joined them inside shortly after, "He's gone ma'am. Have you checked to make sure he hasn't planted any equipment in here like cameras, or listening devices?"

"I have to check my footage from earlier today. That could take hours." Millicent sounded defeated.

"In the meantime, we're going to make sure all of your windows are properly locked, and exits secure," said Officer Reed.

The officers checked her security and left a card for her to call if she had any questions or further concerns. Millicent had plenty, but the one she couldn't shake was how she dug herself into such a hole.

Chapter 23

Jay

Happy hour at the bar on Friday eve turned into a brotherly therapy session. After taking a few shots, Jay surprisingly opened up in the conversation.

Brian aimed low and scored in the double ring of the dart board, while they waited for the pool table to open up. Feeling cocky about his shot, he grew cahones and said to Jay, "I don't know what you did for Jen to forgive your dirty ass, but you two looked happy the other night."

"Did you just call me dirty?" Jay taunted Brian. "I'm just fucking with you. Yeah, we pulling through. When she came back from Miami, I thought it was over. But she just needed a little time to simmer down."

"Tammy wanted to go with them, but my in-laws were in town," McCaine added.

"I only paid for three tickets Caine."

"Oh I know. Tammy talked shit about that, believe me." McCaine blew heavily from his mouth.

Jay took the darts from Brian's hands and threw near the bullseye. "I'm just glad the drama is over. Now I'm just waiting to get back in the free zone."

"So she is smart. I wouldn't let you raw dog me either with those scandalous heauxs you trick with," said Brian.

"Did one of y'all give B a mega man vitamin or something? He's been real slick in his mouth as of late." Jay pretended to throw a dart at him.

"No offense Jay. I'm just being real. I'm on her side."

Jay scoffed and looked at each of them to see who agreed with Brian. Todd balled up his mouth and stared at the floor. McCaine looked up to the ceiling. "So, I'm the only one who's stepped out?"

"I've never tipped on L," said Todd.

"Never?" Jay asked.

"Never. And we have never used condoms. I love that privilege."

"I don't believe you."

"You wouldn't." Todd shrugged his shoulders.

Jay and Todd shared a look of contempt. A chill disturbed the vibe between them. Jay shook it off and directed his building anger towards his normal target, Brian.

"And you play Mr. Innocent, but you're probably the main one with skeletons in his closet," said Jay.

"Me? Oh no, I learned my lesson with that." Brian shook his head.

McCaine held his head down and looked up at Brian from his nose. "Be quiet man. Don't tell them," he said.

"Hell yeah tell us. I knew you were no better than me," said Jay.

"It's not like that. I didn't cheat or anything, but man..." Brian exhaled. "The things going on in the world nowadays."

"Don't do it." Caine warned.

"Either you tell us what Caine already knows, or I'm a beat your ass in the parking lot." Jay threatened.

"Chill." Brian lowered his hands. "Remember Bell, Biv, Devoe *'Never trust a big butt and a smile'*?"

All heads nodded except for Caine, resting his palms atop the pool stick. Brian continued, "Well, now you can't."

"This ought to be good." Jay laughed and folded his arms around the cue.

"This girl had been flirting with me for months in the cafeteria. I grew curious and was like I'm going to give this girl what she's been begging for and walk away."

"Wha' she look like?" Todd asked.

"Banging body. Like a Serena ass, but she wore lots of make-up which is a turn off for me. Anyway, I set everything up making sure I didn't get caught with my dick out on cheaters. I offered her a drink and noticed her hands weren't that pretty. So of course I checked the Adam's apple..."

"Women don't have an Adam's apple." Todd cut him off.

"I—know—that. So, I told her I just wanted to be friends and took my ass home. And that's why I will never cheat on my wife."

Jay stood with his mouth open. Brian raised his eyebrows, daring him to stay silent. McCaine repeated himself. "I told you not to tell him."

"That's wild B." Todd came to his rescue. "But on the real, it's so many big asses out here now man. I was watching something with L one night and she says to me, "Do you think those fake asses look better than my real ass?" I lied to her face and said, "No." But these doctors out here are doing some amazing work."

"And putting them on men apparently, huh Brian?" Jay hollered.

To take the heat off of Brian, McCaine spoke. "I don't cheat because it seems like these women have an agenda to fuck *yo'* shit up. I swear they out here targeting married men. Ready to broadcast their success of breaking up a home. Won't catch my ass slipping."

"We all lose self-control at some point." Jay broadened his shoulders.

"No, you do," said Todd.

"Hate to bring this up, but T you must have forgot about that little filly in Atlantic City. If I recall, you slept with that girl and you and L were dating then." Jay rubbed his chin hair.

"We had just met and weren't married then. I hadn't slept with her yet when that went down. You rowing that boat by yourself partner." Todd kissed his teeth.

"Well how 'bout this. Have y'all ever been cheated on?" Jay asked.

"In college," McCaine answered. "Shit had me sick."

"I can't say that I have," Brian added. "You?"

"Not to my knowledge," Jay replied.

"I can't say that I have, but just thinking about L with some other dude gives me heartburn." Todd admitted. "She got this dude trying to get at her on the job. Shit's been keeping me up at night. And with this kid business. I ain't gonna lie, I'm worried she might run into that asshole's arms."

"L ain't like that T," said Jay.

"But she is finer than a motherfucker and that man on her job don't sound blind," said Brian.

Todd revealed his clenched teeth to Brian, growling under his breath.

"No offense, I'm just saying. Let's be real." Brian defended himself.

"Again I ask, the balls on this guy tonight," said Jay.

"I feel for you T," said McCaine. "I was trying to play it cool the other night, but having outside kids can bring a lot of problems. I knew Tammy was struggling, but I was torn between being a good dad and being a good husband. I was stressed out of my mind sometimes. I couldn't imagine dealing with that and my woman getting pushed up on."

"Well, I had Trap look into him. Turns out this dude is a bigamist in two states who doesn't pay his taxes. He's legally married in Indiana, and pretending to be married to a wife here. Trap has pictures of him playing house with multiple women."

"Sounds like you..." Brian stopped while he was ahead.

"Nah, he's worse." Todd finished.

"The good thing is, Landon isn't in any of those pics. These days women are worse than us," said McCaine.

McCaine's words cut through Todd like a knife. He couldn't fathom the thought of losing Landon, and the image of her being one of the women in the photographs raised his temper.

"You see him as competition?" Jay smirked.

"Nah, I handle mine."

"I don't know T. We all fear competition. Wonder if some lame can make our woman feel better than we do. You can't half ass in the cut man. You gotta lay down the law. Let her know this is my pussy," said Jay.

A woman sitting at the bar introduced herself into their conversation. "Your friend is right. You can't put down the lazy doodle. Ever. We don't want that shit." She tossed her hair and raised her glass in the air.

"Miss, no disrespect, but this is between me and my boys," said Todd.

"You're cute and all, but what else you got?" She batted her eyes and laughed. "I'm just messing with you for kicks."

"Say Love, what is your name?" Jay asked.

"Sasha." She lied.

"As the owner of this here establishment, let me get you a drink on the house." Jay offered.

He placed his hand on the curve above her ass and walked away from the guys. They watched him charm the woman, knowing where his flirtation was headed. "This guy never learns," said Brian. "Any who, what are you going to do about your situation?" he asked Todd.

"I'm a handle his ass. I just don't know how yet."

Jay returned with his usual smug face and weighed in. "Whatever you want to do, we got your back."

"We?" said Brian. "Landon is not my wife. I'm not getting into trouble over somebody else's woman."

"Listen to Trey getting out of the car before it cranks." Jay joked. "Well I'm down for whatever." He and Todd dapped hands.

"And on that note, I am going home," said Brian. "Make sure you do the same." He shook his head at Jay.

"You don't get to look down at me anymore." Jay patted Brian on the back.

CHAPTER 24

TODD

Todd and Jay shared a history of back alley dealings, side jobs, and secrets. Two different personalities with an interest of paper chasing, and living by their own set of rules.

Together they staked out across the street of Landon's job, in a car belonging to Charli, one of Jay's salon renters, and plutonic female friend. Charli parked one block ahead of them in a coworker's car as backup.

While waiting for Dario to exit, Jay admitted. "I didn't like Brian feeling himself last night. I might have to pimp slap him the next time I see him." Jay warned.

"You know how liquor works. Give him a pass." Todd chuckled.

"Has L said anything to you about Jen? She's hot one minute and cold the next. It's like I'm living with a stranger all of a sudden."

"My babe hasn't had a lot to say to me lately. I'm lucky to be getting lucky if you know what I mean."

"Do I ever...I'm not getting it like I used to T. I'm this close to going back to my old ways." Jay propped his thumb and index finger. "I've been keeping my word, but Jen is making it hard."

Todd gave him the side eye. "I thought y'all were getting along." Todd's voice heightened.

"We are. But it's like her mind is..." Jay paused. "Like she's somewhere else at times."

"I wish I knew what L was thinking. Once I get rid of this numb nut, I hope we can get back to how we used to be."

"At least she's still taking care of you man."

Todd hissed through his teeth. "Not to brag, but it's too good between us for her not to. Just saying. My key was made for that lock."

Jay fanned him off and raised his chin. "Aw whatever man. I hear you. I hear you. Hopefully this surprise birthday party I'm planning for Jen will turn things around. Hold up, hold up— that's his car leaving out."

The energy shifted as the car pulled from the metered parking. Jay texted Charli and tailed them, keeping two car spaces between them. He drove calmly as Todd's face tensed with anticipation.

Mindful of the CCTV cameras around, Todd sat low in his seat, and Jay drove with his brim tilted down on the left side to block the upper half of his face. They followed Dario into bumper to bumper traffic. "Damn." Todd wiped his hands on his black sweats, nervous they would lose him in the process of changing lanes.

"Don't worry T. We have his address. We know where he's headed." Jay assured him.

Charli crossed in front of their path, taking the lead of the tail, and putting Jay and Todd two car spaces behind her. The address Trap provided was three miles ahead, yet Dario turned into an apartment complex.

Charli continued to drive past the entrance, as Jay followed him in the compound. They kept the engine running and watched him retrieve a key from his coat pocket and enter a unit on the second floor.

"You catch that?" Jay asked, parking the car in an open space at the next unit.

"Sure did." Todd smirked.

Charli circled back and called Jay on the burner phone. "This isn't the spot. What's going on?" she asked.

"Small detour. We'll give him ten minutes, then it's up to T on what he wants to do. How we looking on cameras?"

"One at the entrance, and one at the front office." She reported.

"Stay close. I'll hit you in a short." Jay hung up the phone, and turned to Todd. "What do you want to do?"

Todd seethed at the change of plans. He pulled his ski cap low on his brows, rolled on his fleece gloves, and covered his head with his hoodie. "I promised my wife I was gonna talk to him, so I'm gonna go talk to him. Where did Charli say the cameras were?"

"Front gate and on the office." Jay pointed.

"It's probably some in those lights too. Go 'head and pull out. You or Charli catch me on that side of the bushes." Todd pointed to his left.

"Your burner on?" Jay asked.

"I'm good."

He climbed from the car with his gun at his waist side. Jay left the complex and drove slowly towards the wooded area Todd would exit, while Charli waited on the other side, still as backup.

Todd held his head down from the lights and knocked on the door. Dario boisterously announced. "Wrong apartment," looking at the back of Todd's hoodie.

"I just came to tell you some kids scratched your car and ran off man."

"They did what!" Dario opened the door.

Todd pulled his cap over his face and stunned Dario with a punch to his gut, then pushed him to the ground by his head. He mushed the side of his face into the cement. "I have friends all over this city. It was easy to find you Dario."

"How do you know my name?"

"How is it that you don't know mine? Hear me good. You will stop harassing my wife. If I have to make a second visit, it won't be this civil."

"You've got me mixed up with someone else." Dario pled.

"I don't like repeating myself. Understood?" Todd pressed his head harder.

"Understood." Dario cried.

"Now you lay there until you think it's safe to move. And you better be smart about it. If you move too fast, the person in that blue Chevy will shoot you in the leg. And he never misses. If you run for the door, he'll shoot you in the neck. I wouldn't try and get cute. And one last thing. If you call the police, your neighbors will tell me, and I'll give them the okay to break in your house, and finish what you started. By the way, your wife in Michigan will be happy to know about your double life."

Todd eased up the hold on his head, and kicked him on his side and in the chest. He dropped copies of the detail photos next to him, and took his time walking with his head down toward the bushes, then jumped the fence to make it to the road. He walked on the side of the street and hopped in the car with Charli passing by.

"Got him." She reported to Jay.

"You know where to go," he said.

Jay drove back to his side of town and stopped at his usual burger joint. The server passed his order to him through the window, and he gave her the bag back with the burner phone inside. "Wrong order!" the server shouted and discarded the bag in the garbage. He passed Jay a second order.

"Your sister will have your money," Jay said, then drove to Charli's salon.

He parked Charli's car in her designated space, leaving the keys above the visor, and met Todd in the office of the bar.

Todd sat with his head leaning back against the wall holding a nearly empty bottle in his hand. Jay smacked on French fries and rustled the paper bag digging for more. "She get rid of those?" he asked.

"Yeah. Paid too," Todd replied.

"You straight?"

Todd threw Jay the deuces sign. "I'm trying to decompress. My adrenaline is still running heavy. I need to hit something."

"Is the problem solved?" Jay cleaned his teeth with his tongue.

"Think so. I'm gonna head home. Face the wife. As always..." Todd dragged and stretched his hand to Jay.

"Don't mention it. It's what we do." Jay pounded his fist.

A throbbing pain shot through Todd's right hand. He entered the kitchen and rumbled through the cabinets in search of a Ziploc bag.

Landon came downstairs. "Why are you making all of this racket?"

"Do we have any plastic bags?"

"In the pantry." She grabbed what he needed and passed him the box. "What do you need this for?"

Todd flashed his hands before her.

"Do I dare ask?" Landon questioned.

"It's nothing." He filled the bag with ice. "How was your day?"

"Fine until now." She eyed him closely. "Why are you dressed like you're auditioning for Creed?"

"Jokes and beauty. Ain't I a lucky fella." He moved in closer. "Have you showered?"

"No. I was about to work out."

"I have just the work out for you." He stepped in her face and gazed intensely in her eyes.

Landon placed her arms over his shoulders. "Why are you so riled up?" She blushed.

Todd pressed his swollen manhood against her, filled with adrenaline, aggression, and lust. He slipped off her bra and ran his palm against her nipples.

Landon twitched. "I'm not complaining, but damn, what's gotten into you?" She asked, placing her hands down his sweatpants.

Aroused by the look in his eye and the brick texture of his shaft resting in her palm, she dropped to her knees and placed the tip in her mouth, kissing him softly and slowly. Her eyes to his thighs, she listened to him sigh and moan when she swallowed him, touching the back of her throat. His weapon strengthened and he gasped. "You trying to make me shoot my gun too soon," he said, softly gripping the bun on top of her head.

Landon hummed and grinned, captivating him with her eyes. Todd grunted at the speed Landon maneuvered her lips while tickling his tip. Up, down, and circling his rim sending chills through his body.

The joy of her service and changing speeds from fast to slow was just what he needed to relieve the angst built up inside him. "You know I love it when you suck me and fuck me," he said, easing her mouth from around him.

He lifted her abruptly and tasted her nectar before carrying her to the stairs. "I can't hold out any longer," he said, stopping midway up and placing himself inside.

He exhaled a squeal at the touch of her heat, and Landon arched her back, sending her supple breasts north near his mouth. He sucked them hard and stroked her pussy the same, caressing her upper back with every stab. "You feel so good girl," he said, profoundly stroking her depth.

Singing a blended tune of ah's and grunts in Landon's ear, Todd spread her legs into the shape of a V. One foot rested against the wall, while the toes on the other gripped the bars on the banister. Todd gurgled from the push and the pull, using Landon's bum as a handle, bringing her closer and tighter.

He felt Landon's increased heartbeat through his chest. He snogged her mouth, lost in the moment of pleasure. Her juice dripped on his fingers, stirring him wild. He slipped a finger between her cheeks and circled her backdoor. Landon's eyes opened as she pined, "We've never."

He played with her flesh and studied her reaction to the sensation, exciting him further. "I don't want to go Greek, but it seems you do." He tested his chances.

She shook her head no. "But what you're doing feels good," she respired, as Todd's scrotum tightened and his tip ballooned.

He pressed her button as he burst inside her, growling to her siren. Paralyzed on top of her carpet burned back he moaned, "I fucking love you Landon. I hope you know that."

She clung to him from below with a step piercing her back. "I do know it. And I love you too."

Neither husband or wife shared the happenings of their day. Both withholding information to savor the moment of harmony between them. Their adulation and sexual chemistry of one another would always be ubiquitous, yet their perfect marriage was deteriorating, and neither knew how to stop it before it was too late.

CHAPTER 25

MILLICENT

Landon removed Todd's arm when the alarm sounded. She turned and faced him, ready to talk about the papers he received in the mail. He felt her gaze upon him and opened his eyes. He smiled at her being within arm's reach, and took a deep breath to inhale her scent from her side of the bed.

"Get back over here?" He pulled her closer.

"Papers came for you yesterday," she said, playing with his clavicle. "I opened them."

The look in her eyes told Todd what papers she spoke of. He kissed her forehead and stroked her face with his finger. "Don't let that worry you. Don't let that come between us." Landon pouted and turned to leave the bed. Todd pulled her back and they locked lips fervently, then she left him lying there in a pensive state.

She strolled into the office distracted, primarily focusing on the midweek gossip session that could not be missed. The beginning of the year shifted south in its first week, and marriage woes and breakups needed to be discussed.

Dario walked past her in the blink of an eye. He didn't speak or engage. "Such a strange fellow," Landon said under her breath.

The moods of Millicent and Jen were identical to that of Landon when they arrived to her office. "What's up," Jen asked, plopping down in her usual seat by the window. "Why don't people put curtains up in their office? It would help with the draft this time of year."

Landon went to her cabinet and passed her a throw. "This should help. The food will be here shortly."

Millicent exhaled and tapped her fingers on the table. Silence swept the room until Jen broke it. "Okay I'll go first. I'm definitely leaving Jay."

"What? After the way you two were entangled on New Year's." Landon stated.

"I can't stop thinking about Jules. I don't know if it's the excitement of sneaking around and having conversations with him, or the fact that he doesn't want to waste my time I find appealing, but I want to see where it goes."

"You've made this decision from one magical weekend?" Millicent sarcastically sassed.

"We do have a history."

"If you love it I like it, or is it the other way... however the saying goes," Millicent added.

"Okay, what's up with the energy in the room?" Landon asked.

"I'm just being pissy. After being alone for nearly a year, I found myself involved with a weirdo." Millicent shook her head. "I think I'm allowed."

"Jesus, I haven't spoken to either of you in days and missed out on this tea. What happened?" Jen inquired.

"Where to begin. He tried to get me to cosign a car loan for him, and I had to call the police to escort him out of my house. I haven't slept a full night since."

"You could have stayed with me." Landon offered.

"I would have asked if you didn't have enough on your plate. How is that working out by the way?"

Landon's eyes couldn't lie. She stared off into space for a few seconds before answering. "I wish I knew. I love my husband and our life together, but this child makes me feel like a big secret has come between us. I feel like he's not all mine. I'm not explaining it properly because it's such a confusing issue. It's so much I want to say but..."

"Better to release it than to hold it in," said Jen.

"Well to be completely honest, it's like this. If a woman calls my husband's phone or texts him, I have every right to question why this woman has access to him. But how do you justify feeling that way when a woman is calling your husband when a child is involved?"

"You set boundaries," Jen said firmly.

"Is that realistic though? This woman has already sent papers to our house. I know how this goes. I've never felt the need to go through Todd's phone, and now I'm wanting to check it to see what they are discussing. I don't like this feeling. Call it insecurity, jealousy, whatever. I don't like the territory we're in."

"Landon, after finding out Jay was two-timing me, I understand how confused you feel. It's not easy to trust your mate when another woman has access to them."

"And I trust Todd, but I'll never trust another woman when it comes to my man. That's my truth." Landon confirmed.

Dario walked past the office and Millicent perked up in her seat. She assumed he would look inside to get a glimpse of Landon. When he didn't she asked, "Did he lose interest or something?"

Landon scoffed. "He said something to me at the Christmas party, but I think after he saw Todd and I together he realized he was wasting his time."

Millicent smirked at Landon. "Humph."

Landon and Jen looked at each other and scowled. Landon responded, "I can't stop you, but if you want to give it a go be careful. And be mindful he doesn't respect other people's relationships, so why would he respect yours."

"At this point I'm preparing to be a spinster or a cougar." Millicent joked.

Millicent's joke of testing the waters of younger men, or turning into an old bitty in her prime livened up the room as the food arrived. The mood of the room finally achieved its normal warm sense of sisterhood, opening the floor to speak freely. They shared the ala carte Landon ordered and spilled more secrets.

"I make Jay wear condoms when we're together. I'm also counting them and one has been missing from the stack. I found it in his wallet, so what does that tell you?"

Jen looked to both Millicent and Landon. Landon replied first, "That he's being safe?"

"That he plans on being safe when he inevitably steps out?" Millicent guessed.

"Bingo. Now do you still think I'm wrong for breaking up with him?"

"You know I have no qualms about it." Millicent laughed.

"Besides, I'm not mad at Jay anymore. He cheated, and will continue to cheat. And I evened the score with Jules. Right?"

"I'm not sure the one time equates to however many times he's done it?" Landon twisted her face.

"Call me desperate, but I called Mal's whore ass. He wants to fly me down to see him."

"My birthday is in two weeks. Schedule your trip so I can go with you." Jen hopped in her chair.

Landon and Millicent deviously glinted at one another.

"What was that look?" Jen asked.

"Jay is planning a party for you."

"I suppose he thinks that'll make me want to love on him again." Jen rolled her eyes.

"You really are over him. How does he not know?" Landon asked.

"I throw him a fuck to shut him up."

"And now it's all about Jules?" Landon followed.

"Now it's all about me." Jen tapped between her breast.

"Jen, since we're being honest here, I've been wanting to ask why Jules called you Jennifer Mendes and not Jennifer Carson?"

Jen stopped eating. Her face turned a flush burgundy and her demeanor stiffened before them. She cleared her throat and stared Landon down. "Never ask me that again. Are we cool?" she said firmly, bringing a chill into the room.

Landon adjusted her hips in her chair. "Yeah. We're cool."

Feeling intimidated with Jen's response and delivery, Landon ended lunch and rose from the table. "You guys can wrap this up and take it with you. I have a proposal to prepare."

Millicent called Landon from the parking lot. "What was that about?"

"I don't know and I'm not sure I want to find out. That was unsettling."

"I've never seen her switch up so fast," Millicent whispered.

"Why are you whispering?"

"I think I'm a little scared." She laughed.

A beat didn't skip when Landon arrived home. She went straight to Todd's liquor cabinet and squirmed at the sip of Crown burning her chest, then replaced it with a bottle of flavored vodka and orange juice.

Todd arrived home shortly after and grabbed a beer from the fridge. "I'm in here," she yelled.

He followed the sound of her voice into his mancave. Twisting the cap off the bottle he asked, "Bad day?" Landon nodded, curled up in the lazyboy. Casually Todd continued. "Has that guy been bothering you at work?"

"Nope. All clear on the work side." She sipped from the glass.

"That's good to know." He grinned behind his beer. "So what gives?"

"I had a spat with Jen, and overall, just a shitty day." Landon twirled the straw in her concoction.

"I hope what I'm about to say doesn't make it worse?" Todd leaned against the wall. "Ephram's mother came by the shop to discuss the support case and visitation. She wants me to get him this weekend."

"I see. So, I assume you'll be spending the weekend at your mother's house?"

"No, that's not what I was planning at all. I want to bring him here and introduce him to you."

"Todd." Landon's voice cracked holding in her cry.

"Think about it."

"I don't want to think about it. All I do is think about it!" She raised her voice.

"Okay. Okay. It was just a suggestion. I'll make other arrangements."

Landon wallowed into her bathroom and turned the shower to boiling. She sat on the edge of the tub, sweating from the steam. Her dewy face dripped as the steam moistened her skin, blending with her tears. The pain in her chest felt different with this cry, for this was a silent one, as before it was heavy and thunderous and crazed. The calmness of her weeping alone in the shower forced her to recognize she could no longer lie to herself. She could foresee where they were headed, and it wasn't pretty.

LANDON

The vibe of the party wasn't what Jay imagined. Jen didn't appear surprised or thrilled, Todd arrived without Landon, Millicent was overly nice to him, and if it weren't for McCaine and Tammy's lively interactions, the party would have been a bust.

Landon arrived an hour late and placed her gift on the table. Her aura matched that of the room, *banterless* and withdrawn. Jay looked around the room and grew upset at the lack of interaction and conversation. "Does somebody wanna explain what's going on?" he asked.

"Thank God somebody said it," Brian mumbled.

"I invited you all to a party to celebrate my ole lady. But you all are acting like a stick is up your asses. What's going on?"

"Jen and Landon need to air out a small disagreement, I'm once again the third wheel at the party, and everybody knows everybody's business, so it doesn't feel much like a party. Sorry." Millicent expressed.

Jay turned to Todd and shrugged his shoulders. He looked to Jen. "What'd you two fall out about?" Jen rotated in her chair and noticed how uncomfortable Landon looked hugging the edge of her seat.

She stood. "Landon, can I talk to you for a minute?"

Jen led the way to her bedroom. She closed the door behind them and wrapped her arms around Landon. Landon briefly lost her balance with a look of wonder on her face, and patted her on the back.

"I'm sorry for the way I spoke to you. You're the sister I wish I had and I hate we haven't spoken in weeks." Jen's voice softened.

"I don't like us not talking either. To be honest, I'm still confused how I offended you."

"It wasn't you. It's me and my crazy past. We all have secrets and my past is one I have to protect. Even though I love you guys, I still have to be careful of who I can trust."

"You know you can trust me, but I won't pressure you about your secrets. I just want us to be like we were before."

"Let me make it up to you. Brunch and massages tomorrow."

"Is this a secret we're keeping from Mills?" Landon teased.

"I guess she can come along too."

They returned to the party hand in hand and Jay announced. "Looks like they made up, now can we have some fun." He placed the game box of Conversation on the coffee table, and lowered the music with the remote on his phone.

McCaine topped off the glasses with the rum punch from the snack table as Tammy dealt Millicent the first card.

Opening the game, Millicent read her question aloud. "Should an ex be invited to your wedding? Of course, I would get this question. What wedding will I ever have." She joked, throwing her hands up midair. "Um, I'm going to say no. Why have your past taint your future."

"I agree," said Kim.

The consensus of the room mumbled in agreement as Tammy dealt the next card to Kim. She flipped the card over and read aloud. "What turns you on?" Brian's eyes popped open. "Yeah baby let's hear how I turn you on."

Jay cackled, creating a chain reaction of chuckles in the room. Kim cleared her throat. "This is all healthy and honest fun, right?" she asked.

"Yeah," they said in unison.

"Well, I watched a movie once that got me wondering what it would be like to go to one of those key parties."

"Swinging!" Brian's voice raised. "Hell no. We're not doing that!" He crossed his arms.

"It's not about you. It's about her." Millicent reminded him.

"Who in here besides my wife wants to swing?"

All eyes looked to the floor and the ceiling

"Exactly." Brian emphasized. "Ask me the next question," he demanded.

Tammy placed his card in front of him and he read. "Which do you think is worse, physical or emotional cheating?"

"Both." He answered.

"No, no. You have to pick one," said Tammy.

"Then I'm going with emotional being the worst one."

"Why?" Kim asked.

"Because a man can sleep with a woman and not give a damn about her. He just wants to get in and get out. But a woman cares and daydreams and fantasizes about a man which is worse because it lingers on."

"Why can't a woman get in and get out?" Tammy asked.

"Y'all aren't built like that." Brian rolled his shoulders.

"Says who?" Jen asked.

Jay looked at Jen with a side eye. "Well educate us. Are you ladies in this room telling us men—that women—not heauxs, but nice respectable women like yourselves, can sleep with a man and not catch feelings?"

"Yes!" they answered in unison.

The men stood up and looked at their women.

Millicent continued the conversation. "You men don't realize the climate you've created. The roles are slowly changing. Women are no longer the docile beings you want them to be."

"Mills, we get you are in a league of your own." Jay snided.

"Jay, why do you always single me out?"

"Because I think you're a secret man hater spitting poison in my ole lady's ear."

"Your ole lady doesn't need my help. You do that on your own." Millicent waved her hand.

"Okay, you two go to your corners." Jen stood between them. "It's my birthday and I was enjoying this game. Especially seeing Brian lose his cool because Kim has a freaky side no one knew about."

Jen's joke served as the perfect deflection of her side dealings. Tammy then posed the question. "Who's next?"

Brian answered, "Todd."

Tammy shuffled the deck and handed Todd his card.

He sighed deeply. "Should your partner be allowed to go through your phone?"

Millicent shouted, "100 percent!"

Todd hesitated with all eyes on him, and the room growing silent. "Yes. Sure. Why not. I have nothing to hide from my wife." He squeezed Landon's thigh.

"Landon, I don't mean any disrespect, but what kind of voodoo do you have on my boy?" Jay erupted. "100 percent hell no your partner shouldn't go through your phone."

"Why not?" Millicent asked.

"You stay out of this." Jay pointed to Millicent.

"If you don't have trust, what do you have?" McCaine commented.

"Caine please. You change your password every week," said Tammy.

"How do you know that?" McCaine's voice shrieked.

Tammy puckered her lips and shook her head at her husband. McCaine waited for her to answer. They locked eyes, bringing heat into the room. Tammy opened her mouth. "Here's your card honey." She passed McCaine the next one on the top of the deck.

His gaze turned comical. "Are you looking for a new boyfriend or girlfriend? Hmm. Not today," he answered.

Tammy slapped him on the arm as everyone laughed, but admired their chemistry.

"How about you? You looking for a new boyfriend or girlfriend honey?" McCaine asked.

"No, but sometimes I fantasize you, me, and another man having a kiki." Tammy sipped her drink.

"A whata?" McCaine's face scoured.

"I'm just curious to see how I would perform."

"I'm not!" McCaine scooted away from her. "Jay, what the hell with this game man?"

"I like it. It sparks great conversation." Tammy leaned towards him. "It's actually Jay's turn."

Jay's hand met Tammy's halfway. He looked at his card and asked for another.

"It doesn't work that way," the guests all said.

"Well can I trade with someone? What are the rules to this game?" Jay questioned.

"The rules are you answer the question you are dealt." Tammy emphasized.

"Humph. This is a set up." He shook his head.

"You picked this game." Brian reminded him.

Jay grinned at everyone in the room. "How long is too long to date without commitment? My answer is there is no answer."

"Objection!" Millicent shouted. "That is not an answer."

"It's my answer." Jay covered his chest.

"He's right." Jen silenced the uproar and agreed. "It's been five years, and I'm not ready to commit. It's not for everyone."

"Wow. Look at them tag team for the win," said Brian. "Y'all are starting to act like these two." He pointed to Landon and Todd.

Landon looked straight ahead while Todd stared at her. The spotlight broke Landon down. "Happy birthday Jen. Call me in the morning. If you all will excuse me." She threw her coat around her shoulders and walked towards the front door.

"Todd, what the hell man?" Millicent asked.

"Trust me Mills, I'm fighting a losing battle." Todd sat back on the sofa.

Landon turned around and cut Todd with teary eyes. "Yeah, I'm the bad guy."

"No one said that." He explained.

Landon frowned and stormed out of the party.

Tammy followed her outside. "Landon! Don't leave!"

"Don't mind me! Go back inside and enjoy yourself!"

Tammy caught up with her. "I hate to see you like this. You've always been poised and composed and calm. Don't let this baby mama situation change who you are."

"Tammy, it's freezing out here. I can't have this discussion right now." She shivered.

"It gets better. Trust me it does."

Landon exhaled a cloud from her mouth. "How are you and his daughter now?" She struggled placing her fingers inside her gloves.

"Believe it or not, we are in a good place." Tammy danced to warm up. "We have been for a few years now. Time healed that wound. She grew up and stopped looking at me as the enemy. She even admitted her mom put her up to most of that mess."

"But that's just it. I don't want to go through that." Landon's teeth shuddered. "Go back inside. We'll talk some more. I promise."

Tammy returned to the party that had become Todd's therapy session.

"Listen to me. I don't want this woman. I didn't want her whenever she became pregnant. She was the campus jumpoff. All I want to do is take care of what's mine, and Landon wants no part of it. Do you know how hard it is to keep your wife in the loop who doesn't want to talk to you, or hear what you have planned, or how hard a change like this has on me?"

"Todd, you brought the boy to your house when she told you not to," said Millicent.

"And she acted like it was going to kill her to speak to the boy. Then she up and left. Stayed gone all night."

"You know she was at my house," Millicent added.

"Still. The boy knows she doesn't like him. Then I had to hear his mother's mouth."

"Because outside children spread your business, and create problems. Sometimes." Tammy chimed in.

"She's being childish if you ask me," said Brian.

"You come home with a baby mama and you'll see childish. No offense Todd," said Kim.

Todd stood up to leave.

Jen grabbed his hand. "Your situation is unfortunate, but I get how it's all a bit much for Landon to smile and bear it. Men are built different from women and she's embarrassed and hurt. Why can't you men understand that?"

Millicent chimed in. "You answered your own question. They're men."

CHAPTER 27

———

TODD

The long route home wasn't long enough for Todd. He circled the block ten extra minutes, putting off what awaited him. To his surprise, Landon appeared calm, packing an overnight bag. He cornered her next to the bed, and turned her bag upside down.

"That's not funny." Landon huffed.

"You didn't yell. Good. Maybe we have a chance to actually talk and fix this problem tonight. Notice I said *WE*. As in you and me."

"And how do you propose we fix this?" She challenged him with her eyes.

"I hear you. You want nothing to do with this. But do you want anything to do with me?" he asked sincerely.

Landon placed her hands against his chest. She felt his heart racing in her palms, and choked up on emotions. "The last thing I want to do is lose you, but I can't find a way around this. I hope you can understand." She buried her face in his chest.

"Landon, the boy is here. I can't undo what's been done. I need you. I want you. I want you to help me with all of this. It hasn't been easy for me."

"It seems easy."

"It's not. I've got a strange kid looking to me for answers. A woman wanting child support and texting me so much I have to mute my phone, and my wife who I love more than anything in this world wants to leave me. How is that easy?"

"I'm sorry. I really am. I haven't thought about how you felt in all of this.

Everything you mentioned is what bothers me. The money going out of the house, welcoming a stranger into mine. But most of all, it's the access another woman now has to you. I am now sharing my husband with another woman."

"You're not sharing me. I'm co-parenting. And those pennies aren't hurting us. We are good. I've seen to that. But are you with me?"

Landon took a deep breath. "I'm with you."

Todd flashed his pearly whites and held her tight in his arms. "He's a good kid. You'll see, but I won't bring him over until you're ready. Now give me those luscious lips I've been craving. Eight weeks and two days is too long for me to be without you girl. You knew you were punishing me," he said, forever falling under her spell.

Chapter 28

Jen

Incessant knocking at The Jeffries door woke Todd, lying naked and wrapped fully around Landon. Her cell phone vibrated off of the nightstand. Todd listened to it buzz with his eyes focused on the window, listening for the footsteps of the person interrupting his morning wood.

"Landon!" Millicent shouted outside their bedroom window.

Todd shook Landon. "Baby, why is Millicent outside?"

She jolted in his arms. "I forgot we were having brunch with Jen this morning. I owe you one." She sucked on his cheeks and squirmed in his arms.

"You owe me five. Maybe six." He teased, holding onto her as she wiggled out of bed. He threw on his shorts and stood shirtless in the window, holding up his index finger to Millicent.

Looking up she shouted, "Good! Y'all made up!"

Landon opened the door and let her inside. "I totally forgot."

"Judging from the happy man in the window you had a good reason." Millicent grinned.

Landon snickered. "Wait for me in the kitchen. I won't be long."

Jen held a table for the duo at Nero's inside Caesar's. They did a quick recap of the highs and lows of the party, with emphasis on Landon's abrupt departure.

"I thought about you all night," said Jen.

"No need. They looked like they worked things out to me this morning." Millicent reported.

"Oh, good. That makes me happy. We can't both transition at the same time. We'll drive Millicent crazy with our drama," said Jen.

Millicent raised her glass and eyebrows before taking a sip of her mimosa. "I was thinking you would change your mind about Miami after your party. Guess I was wrong."

Jen huffed and flared her nostrils. She sat back in her seat, sipping from her glass with a smirk written across her lips. "The condom in Jay's wallet isn't there anymore. And two more are missing from the box he keeps in the garage. I'm over him. I'm over us."

"You know what they say about fools. The mistakes of the fool are known to the world, but not to the fool himself." Landon quoted.

"Listen to Niche over here." Millicent chortled.

Jen asked, "Are you still going down to Miami?"

"No need. They're coming here for the playoffs."

"I know, but I don't want to wait that long to see Jules." Jen bounced in her seat.

Millicent observed the sparkle in Jen's eyes when she talked about Jules. She hailed the waiter for another pitcher of mimosas as Landon spoke. "You really are throwing them back today."

Millicent placed her hand across her chest to catch her breath."Because I feel bad for something I'm about to do." She reached in her purse and pulled out a small, lilac square box with a purple ribbon tied around it. She set it in the center of the table. "The last time we were together things got a little heated. I was lonely and thought you two needed some space, so I returned Mal's call. I entertained him. You know, late-night phone sex. That sort of thing. Anyway, because of the playoffs he couldn't come here, so he flew me down for dinner one night."

"You finally got laid," said Landon.

"I did. And it was lovely, but nothing to make me wanna move down there. But it got the job done." She blushed. "While I was there, Jules told me to give this to you on your birthday. "She pointed to Jen. "But I couldn't do Jay like that. As much as I would have loved to see his face on the floor, I do have a heart. So, here's your present a day late. He says read the note first."

Jen reached for the box and Millicent swatted her hand. "I can't believe he did this. And you've been sitting over there with it in your purse this whole time." Jen crinkled her nose at Mills, producing an envelope with her name written on the seal.

She unfolded the note and read to the girls:

> *I promised myself I would find you.*
> *That promise came true.*
> *Now I promise I will do whatever I need*
> *to keep my promises to you.*
> *With this ring I promise love*
> *will always be your friend.*
> *This promise ring promises you*
> *that my love for you won't end.*
> *Promise me we'll be together.*
> *I don't like being apart.*
> *This ring is just a start.*
> *A bigger one is tied to my heart.*
> *Love, Jules*

Jen threw the ribbon on the table and tore the paper from the box, blinded by a flawless, clear-cut diamond. She placed the ring on her finger and stared at its beauty.

"Didn't I say he was a keeper." Millicent bragged.

"He most certainly is." Jen agreed.

"You're practically glowing." Landon smiled. "It's beautiful."

"I said from the beginning I liked this guy. He has a nice aura about him." Millicent added.

"What are you thinking right now, Jen?" Landon asked.

"How to execute my exit strategy," she muttered, studying the ring.

"Does Max know you and Jay aren't getting along?"

"Not a clue. He's going to be crushed. Jay is the only father he has ever known and is good to him. But mama ain't happy."

"Speaking of fathers, I've always wondered who is Max's biological dad, and why isn't he in his life?" Millicent asked.

"His father is dead."

"Oh. Sorry to hear that. Is it okay to ask how he died?"

"I killed him."

Millicent and Landon backed away from the table, stared at each other, then turned back to Jen. They belted with laughter, then stopped abruptly as Jen sat stone faced.

After her behavior in the office weeks ago, Landon believed her words to be true, but didn't want a repeat of that eruption. She sat quietly and let Millicent take the fall. "Why would you say something like that?" Millicent whispered across the table.

"Because it's true." Jen admitted.

"You actually murdered your son's father, and sit there as if it isn't a big deal," said Landon.

"It is a big deal, it just isn't a big deal to me anymore," Jen replied.

"Are you in some kind of trouble or something?"

"Not at the moment."

"Do we need to lookout for red dots on our faces when we're with you or something? Like really, what's going on here?" Landon asked.

Jen tucked the ring back in the box and placed it in her bag. "Before I fill you in, I need to tell you if anything happens to me, you and Todd are to have full custody of Max, with full visitation from Jay okay?"

"Jesus Christ." Landon nodded.

"My birth name is Jennifer Mendes. When Jules spoke of my family suddenly disappearing one day, he was telling the truth. The reason he couldn't find me was because I was placed with a foster family under witness protection. The agent in charge of dropping me off at the foster home knew their department had a mole inside, and hid me at a safe house until she could help me run away. That very night, the foster home was shot up and set on fire. She knew people were coming for me and risked her life saving mine."

"You could be dead right now." Millicent gasped.

Landon placed her hand across her neck taken aback. She looked on in horror, nervously twitching her legs against the table.

Jen continued. "My papa was involved with money laundering from a fortune five hundred, and embezzling money from whoever he was working for. Those powers that be found out he had been stealing from them, and so they threatened to kill all of us if he didn't return what he stole. Him, my mother, and me. My father knew once he gave them the cash, they were going to kill us anyway. So, he blew the whistle on the operation to save me and my mother, and offered to testify against the company, in exchange for our protection."

"So…child protection services took you away from both of your parents?" Millicent asked.

"They had no choice. Keeping us together as a unit would have made it easy to find us. My agent promised to look after me as a side deal with my dad, so when she removed me from the safe house, she took me to a nursing home, and gave me a new identity under the name Manuela Reyes. I had a new name, new life working as an aid, legal driver's license, and one on one tutor to finish high school."

"How long did you have to pose as Manuela?"

"Three years. Remember when I did Tammy's hair on that trip to Vegas, and you guys went on and on about how professional it looked?"

Millicent and Landon nodded. "Yeah."

"I have a beauty license under the Manuela name."

"I feel like I don't know who I'm looking at right now," said Landon.

"I'm still the same person. My name changed. Not me." Jen tapped her chest.

"If I hadn't heard Jules call you Mendes, would we be having this conversation?"

Jen shrugged her shoulders as the table remained silent from the shock and awe of her revelation. "Probably not."

"It's true what they say, you never know what dark secrets people hide behind their eyes," said Millicent. "Did you know your dad was involved with cleaning dirty money?"

"Nada. We lived a normal life like everyone else on my block. Paycheck to paycheck as far as I knew."

"So how did you become Jen Carson?" Landon asked.

"I'll give you the quick version. After I got my cosmetology license, I continued to live at the nursing home. When the owner died, his children took over the business. They knew nothing about my arrangement, so before they questioned who I was, and why I was living there rent free, I left. I searched for my agent, but when I failed to find her, I moved to Brooklyn and worked at a salon as Manuela. I was scared to look for my parents, I trusted no one, and all I did was work, worry, and look over my shoulder."

"That had to be lonely." Landon placed her hand over Jen's.

"Very. But I woke up every day thankful I was alive. Then the loneliness crept in and that's how I got Max. A courier named Alex started coming by the shop, and flirted his way into my bed. He was the only man that ever touched me after Jules, and as far as I knew, I was in love."

"What was Alex like?" Millicent nestled in her chair.

"He was kind. And had a funny brownish olive tone. Curly hair like Max. About my height. Cute in the face, again like Max. He did this weird thing where he stared at me, like he had so much on his mind, but when we were together it always felt nice."

"So what happened to him?" Millicent questioned.

"Well, I got pregnant and he suggested we get married. I put it off as long as I could, but being alone in the world with a new baby— I eventually said yes, and we eloped at city hall."

Jen dug in her handbag and opened her wallet. She pulled out a photograph of Alex, who looked like a bigger version of Max. Briefly her eyes watered. She wiped away the one tear that escaped her ducts, then placed the picture behind another picture in her billfold.

Millicent sat quietly biting her nails staring off in the distance. Landon swatted her hands. "Nasty habit."

"I'm over here trying to make sense of all this. One of my dearest friends is also a complete stranger. I still love you the same, but it's hard to imagine you on the run, working in a salon, and in witness protection." Fully loaded with questions and curiosities, Millicent continued her forward inquisition. She leaned over the table and whispered, "So why did you kill him?"

Landon choked at the question and creased her face at Millicent.

Jen lowered her head, spoke indistinctly to herself, then sat straight in her seat. "Because he forced my hand." She paused, collected herself then continued. "After we married, everything seemed normal. I went back to work to save up for our delayed honeymoon, then one day I came home to my mother holding my baby in our living room. I was no longer alone and soooo happy to see her, but I didn't know how to explain who she was to Alex. I can still feel how I felt in that moment. I just stood there as if I had seen a ghost."

"You kind of did," said Landon.

"Alex came out of the room and smiled at me differently. Like he pitied me, but at the same time saw me in a new light. Kind of like the way you two have been looking at me the past five minutes."

"We don't mean..."

"It's cool. I'm a big girl. I can handle it."

"Apparently." Millicent shaded her.

Jen overlooked Millicent's remark. "So Alex came out of the room and said to me, "You could have told me the truth, but your mom explained everything, and it explains why you get cold with me sometimes. I'm here. I'm not going anywhere." I was relieved, but still wary, ya know?"

"Of course. You survived a traumatic experience. I would have issues with trust too." Landon agreed.

Jen took a deep breath. "I was also insecure. I hadn't quite got my figure back after the baby, and was taking this mommy and me exercise class. So, I asked my mom to come with me, so we could talk in private, and she could tell me where she'd been, what story she told my husband, and find out what our plan was going forward. She claimed she was too exhausted, and stayed behind at my apartment. As I was headed down the second flight of stairs, my neighbor stopped me to hand me my mail that was thrown in with hers. A bank envelope addressed: 'Mr. Manuel Reyes C/O Miss Manuela Reyes' was in the pile. Inside was an I.D. card with a note taped in the crease of the cardboard. It read:

"I pray this finds you in time. I'm sorry to notify you like this, but your father has been murdered, and I fear your cover could be blown. Get out of town and use this new name from now on. Your new identity is Jennifer Carson. This is the name your father used to hide the money at this bank in Sweden. He figured the moles wouldn't search for you under your real first name since you've been exposed under Manuela. Be careful going after the money. If I could help you more I would, but I am now in hiding myself. Take care until we meet again."

Signed, A Friend

"What are the odds," said Landon.

"Exactly. I received that letter and didn't want to accept my dad was gone forever, but also feared I had already been compromised. But what instantly stuck out at me, was the presence of my mother. The odds of her showing up when I had a child, was newly married, and news of my father's death sent chills down my spine. But I played it cool."

"What did you do?"

"I handed Max to my neighbor and asked her watch him while I grabbed his toy from upstairs. I snuck inside and crept to the kitchen to retrieve my revolver from behind the microwave. Noises from my bedroom sounded like a woman in distress, and I feared whoever found me was attacking my mother. I tiptoed towards the echoes and slowly opened the door. And there was my mother with her legs high in the air, beneath Alex."

Jen's face became flushed. She shook her head while tracing the rim of the plate in front of her, recanting the scene in her head.

"So you shot him in the back as a crime of passion?" Millicent edged her on.

"No. I watched them." She confessed, tapping her temples incessantly. "I sat on the floor and let them finish, thinking of something clever to say when I confronted them. And that was what I was supposed to do, because everything became clear. My mom didn't bring trouble to my door. She was the trouble at my door. She hired Alex to get next to me, thinking I would tell him about the money."

"Jen, I thought you were about to say you overheard them practicing what lie they were going to tell you about sleeping together," said Landon.

"Nope. They were in cahoots the entire time, and my mother was going to use him, to get the money from me, so she could have it. She never planned on me having Max. As I sat there, it hit me. I couldn't trust either of them. So I opened the door pointing my pistol at them both and asked, "Which one of you bitches wanna die first?""

Jen dropped her head against a formed fist under her chin. "You don't have to tell us anymore if it's upsetting you like this," said Landon consoling her, rubbing her shoulder. Millicent slid her chair closer and did the same.

Jen's hands shook as she confessed. "My mother downplayed the situation, accusing me of being jealous because she fucked my husband. I played along, acting like I didn't hear their conversation. Alex thought I didn't see him easing his hand under the pillow, so I shot him, then shot over my mother's head to shut up her screaming."

"Jesus," said Millicent.

"Alex wouldn't let up, making me out to be a fool. "Baby this was an accident. Your mother threw herself at me," he said over and over making his way to me. I warned him, "Stay back," but he kept coming closer, so I shot him in the chest and he fell to the ground. I pointed back to my mother and asked her, "How much did he cost?" Her eyes grew big when she told a lie. And she lied to my papa all the time when I was a child, so I recognized the look," Jen said fading into her memories.

Landon and Millicent watched her travel in her thoughts, drifting into another time and place. "Jen," Landon called her name, snapping her back into the present.

"I wanted to kill her, but I couldn't. I was still her little girl, waiting for her to find me in that nursing home, and tell me we were going to be a family again. Seeing her face complete with shame and guilt pacified my vengeance in that moment as she pleaded, "Jen don't shoot. Please don't kill me." And I didn't. She proved I was weak and had some serious growing up to do. In order for me to survive I would have to eliminate anyone that came after me, and I failed myself by letting her go."

"She's your mother," said Landon.

"Yeah, the mother that was screwing her husband. The mother that was planning to double cross her," said Millicent.

Jen interrupted their debate. "She is the woman who gave birth to me. Not a mother. She only cares about herself."

"Where is she now?" Landon asked.

"Yeah, what happened to her?"

"She insisted the money belonged to her. Claiming she helped my father do his dirty work, but I was wondering how she even knew my dad left the money to me. Then it dawned on me that someone else was in on this thing. I lied and told her I would let her live if she cooperated. I made her dress Alex, and rip the seams in her underwear before ordering her to put them back on. I undressed and told her to cover up in my clothing, while I threw on dirty clothes from the hamper, and wiped off my prints on the gun. I hit Alex in the head with the lamp, then emptied the clip of the bullets in Max's diaper bag. I put the gun in my mother's hands, and placed mine on top of hers, and told the police that I came home and saw Alex forcing himself on my mom, so I hit him in the head with the lamp to get him off of her, but he came after me, so she shot him."

"Did they believe you, or did you have to prove it?"

"The police believed what we told them after my mother was examined, and cleared her in self-defense. And when it was all over, I told her I never wanted to see her again."

"How are you sure she won't try to contact you?" Millicent asked.

"After that night, my mother was still watching me. But I was also watching her. I needed to smoke the third party out in her little scheme before I could move on, so I deliberately had luggage delivered to my apartment, giving her the idea that I was about to take a trip. I thoroughly cleaned my apartment of my DNA, and sublet it to new tenants to erase any trace of me. Max and I slept at my neighbors for a few days, and when I was ready to make my move I took him to his sitter, and left my apartment with my suitcase filled with wigs and jackets. I saw my tail on the way to the airport, so I did some twisting and turning until I lost them in one of the restaurants. I went to the restroom and put on a wig and changed my jacket, then looked out for the person tailing me. Turns out, she was working with the agent who took me to the nursing home. My mother knew where I was the entire time, and the whole time I thought the agent was protecting me, she was really working with my mother, and waiting to be led to the money. She was double crossing my papa, my mother, and me. And I feel deep in my bones, she and my mother had something to do with my father's death."

"So what did you do?"

"Exactly what they did. I paid some guys to take them out, and left town as Jennifer Carson. I drove west and was offered a job cleaning at night. Then I met Jay, and here we are."

The waiter interrupted, reaching over the ladies with fresh water refills and the check. Landon reached for the bill and placed her credit card in the slot at the top of the folder. "If it wasn't your birthday I would let you take care of the bill Richie Rich," she joked. "That is if it's really your birthday."

"Is it really your birthday?" Millicent scrunched her face with a curious smile.

"Yes, it's really my birthday. It may not say so on my license but this is the day I entered this crazy world."

Landon placed the paid receipt in her tote, and the trio finished the afternoon enjoying a spa package. Upon leaving the hotel, Jen caught Landon looking over her shoulder, and scouring the parking lot before they exited the building.

"I wouldn't put you in danger L." Jen exhaled, walking ahead of her. "I never got the money, so no one's looking for me. You're safe."

CHAPTER 29

JULES

Jay found it strange Jen and Millicent went to a football game together. Landon served as Max's babysitter until Todd and Jay arrived at her house, raising questions about the outing.

Todd peered over at Landon, preparing her for the interrogation Jay was bound to initiate. She raised her eyebrows at Todd, and stood her ground with the barrage of questions thrown at her.

"Why didn't you go? Jay asked.

"Because Millicent only had two tickets, and I don't care for sports."

"How did she get the tickets?" He paced the floor.

"Her job."

Jay scoffed. "Jen's been acting off lately. You know something?"

"I don't."

"If you did, would you tell me L. Remember we knew each other first and I always have your back."

"Jay, we are close and if I knew something, I doubt I would tell you, because I don't like getting into people's business. But I do love you, and have been rooting for you since...um...you remember that night."

"I've changed since then." Jay pled.

"Have you?" Landon gave him the side eye.

"You do know something."

"I know you haven't changed is all I'm going to say."

"Is that what Jen told you?"

"Jay, talk to her when she gets home."

"I think your little friend has her ear. I don't like that shit. Jen came home 5:30 this morning from clubbing with her. And now they're at a game. I know she is trying to introduce her to one of those players."

"I seriously doubt that Jay." Landon struggled to hold a straight face. "Why do you hate Mills so much?"

"Because man hating Mills is a bad influence for Jen. I like when she hangs out with you. You're loyal. Got your head on straight. You take care of my boy and got his nose wide open. You're good people. But that Mills. She's poisoning Jen against me. I can feel it."

Landon looked to Todd for help. "Alright man, that's enough with the third degree." Todd interrupted.

"Baby, fix him a drink while I gather Max's things." Landon patted Jay on his head then left the room.

The crowd was loud at the game, but Jen and Millicent kept warm in the box with the wives of the players. One of them enjoyed the high status more than the other.

When they were alone, Millicent revisited the story Jen shared with them. "You are lucky to be alive. And filthy rich." Her eyes narrowed, studying her reaction.

"I will never see that money. I don't know who is waiting on me to show up and cash out. That day could very well be the day— I cash out."

"So you are just going to let it stay there and what, go fund their government or something?"

"What do you mean?" Jen frowned.

"I am sure there is some sort of stipulation after a certain amount of time, if the money isn't claimed, then it becomes the property of their bank or government." Millicent stirred.

"Can one of you nerds help me research that?"

"I'll see what I can do. Give me some time to check with one of the techies on how to hide an ip address before we search anything," Millicent paused. She leaned in closer to Jen. "These women up here love to stare."

"I noticed that too. But don't worry. I can turn into Manuela if need be."

The two stared back at the women eyeing them and laughed. Jen gave one of them a daring look, putting an end to their gawking, then back towards the field. "I guess we can give them a pass. They're probably worried we're here for their man." Jen chuckled.

After the game, they sat in Jen's car outside the hotel. While waiting for the team to arrive, they people watched and heaux watched, then turned to each other bursting with laughter.

"How dare we judge them when we're out here lurking in the lot like them!" Millicent cackled.

"Speak for yourself. I got a promise ring."

When the giggles settled, Millicent revisited the elephant in the room. "Do you have any reservations about leaving Detroit? Or us?"

"Of course, but I follow my instinct. And it says I need to go and live my life. My main concern is how Max is going to handle all of this."

"If you find yourself overwhelmed with everything, just call me. Leave Max with me for a while."

"In Ohio? Away from his dad? Jay will never let that fly."

"I'm serious though. He livens up my house. It can get quiet in there sometimes."

"It's too soon for your clock to be ticking Mills." Jen scowled.

"I never told you this, but when you two stayed with me those couple of days I loved it. I mean I like quiet, but the noise was comforting. It felt good not to be alone."

"If anyone understands that, it's me."

The bus pulled into the lot and the groupies swarmed inside the lobby. Mal texted Millicent:

Mal: U here?

Flashing lights: Mills

Mal: I see you.

He walked over and opened the car door for Millicent to get out. "How you doing?" he spoke to Jen. Hanging on the door, Millicent propped her foot on the floorboard. "You spending the night with me, right?" he asked.

"I don't know. It's late and I have work in the morning."

"We have a couple of hours. Our flight leaves at five."

Millicent leaned down and looked at Jen. "Are you staying the night, or do I need to go and get my car?"

"I'll be here, but I can't say how long after last night. Of course, I won't leave you stranded though."

"Mills knows good and well I'm a take care of her. And I know for a fact Jules wants you to stay. Come on. Let's go in." Mal guided Millicent and Jen out of the car.

With sweaty palms and a racing heart, Jen trailed behind Millicent and Mal. In gentleman form, Jules sat at the bar waiting for her to arrive. He swept beside her as she walked past the piano and grabbed her hand. She recognized the feel of his touch, and continued walking without looking up at him, confident that the hand belonged to her beloved.

They stepped inside the elevator and locked lips before the doors closed. The smell of his cologne ravished Jen feverishly, while the feel of her moist lips made him come alive.

The elevator stopped on the floor below them, and they briefly stopped Frenching. "I'll hit you up," said Millicent, exiting with Mal. A patron entered and smiled ear to ear, staring at Jen's lavender lipstick smothered on Jules's mouth.

The elevator doors opened on their floor, and they lip locked without any regret, stumbling to the room. Jules placed the do not disturb sign on the knob outside, and twisted the double bolted lock.

When he turned around, Jen was standing in his view, completely naked wearing nothing but the ring he gave her, and her coat at her feet. "I have missed you." She tempted.

"I missed you more."

"The birthday girl has a gift for you," said Jen, holding her hand near her cheek flashing her ring.

"It fits you," he said, gripping her fingers softly, and admiring the stone. "It's your birthday, so why would you have a gift for me?"

Jen lowered her position and dropped to an open stance. She unzipped his khakis, releasing the bulge from his pants that was toying with her since the elevator. She kissed his manliness with her lips closed, then embraced him with a strong pull using her tongue. "You don't have to do that." Jules weakened voice trembled as Jen returned the favor and pleased him the way she remembered he pleased her.

She was never great at pleasuring a man orally, but the sounds coming from Jules made her feel as if she had improved.

"I hope I did that correctly," she said. "I don't have much experience, and ever since Miami I have been dreaming what it would be like to do that to you."

"I don't think there's much more for you to learn, but I don't mind instructing you along the way." He caressed her chin.

"Shall I continue?"

"No. Allow me," he said, springing her body in the air, placing her wet cup on his mouth.

He balanced her body with his closed lips pressed on her spot, kissing it slowly and humming at her scent. Relying on sound, he could tell she was pleased. He continued to deliver wet kisses, strong licks, and his twirling tongue a few times more until she uttered, "You're driving me crazy."

When he was done teasing her, he opened wide and hollowed her sweetness with his full mouth gently. His top lip on her clitoris, and his bottom lip on the edge of her fold, holding it firmly.

Jen let out a shy scream as he commenced to taste her and tickle her, holding her high above his head. The raunchiness of it all thrilled Jen, enjoying the performance of Jules's balancing act.

There was no doubt in her mind, Jules wouldn't let her fall. She compared her ride in heaven to her ride with him in life. Wanting every part of him.

He brought her back down to earth, and she whispered, "You take such good care of me." He silenced her with his finger placed over her mouth, and turned her towards the wall.

"Are you ready for me?" he asked.

"Yes."

Jules rubbed himself up and down her track teasing and teasing her, making her beg for him to put it inside. He kissed her on the nape of her neck, and waited for her to stop expecting it, then entered her base without any regrets of holding his fire.

Jen squirmed in delight and gasped for air, as Jules fucked her fast then slow, fast and then slow again, prodding her pussy 'til it wept. She panted and she moaned, losing herself in his grunts and compliments.

Jules slammed his hand against the wall, holding Jen next to him by the waist. "Huugh." He relieved himself, clutching onto her shoulders, constricting her closer to him.

He caught his breath, sniffing her hair in between powerful jolts of unfolding heat between them. Clinging to her body like he was trying to win a game of tug of war, he rubbed his forehead against her back, weak and motionless from the rush.

Defeated from the exploit of her body, Jules picked her up from behind and placed her over his shoulder as a cave man would. He unveiled the covers, laid her down in the bed and climbed in with her.

Jen placed her head on his chest. "Thank you," she whispered.

He placed his arm around her back, cuffing her close to him. "For what?" he asked.

"For being in Miami at the right place, at the right time. For being patient while I figured out my messy situation."

"Have you?" He sighed.

"I have. I'm all yours." Jen smiled.

"You mean it?" He stroked her shoulder.

Jen sat up, biting her bottom lip and smiled at him. "I'm coming to Miami."

"And Max?"

"Not just yet. I'm still working out the details, but he definitely has to meet you before I commit to this wholeheartedly."

"So what, if he doesn't like me, you're not gonna stay?"

"I have to make sure he is okay with whatever decision Jay and I agree upon."

Jules grabbed her face and fervidly kissed her, stealing her air, and breathing his into her mouth. "It's going to work out," he said. "You're finally free. Finally, mine."

CHAPTER 30

JAY

Jen arrived home just before the sky turned light blue. Jay and Max sat at the breakfast table quietly when she walked in. "Mommy!" Max shrieked, fully dressed for school.

Jen lowered and kissed his cheeks. "Don't you look handsome. Do you want me to take you to school?"

Jay cleared his throat. "Why don't we both take him," he grumbled, putting a spoonful of cereal in his mouth.

He was pissed, but he hid it well. Jen admired him for keeping their drama and their issues a mystery to her son. "Sure thing. It's about that time so let's get going baby," Jen said, ignoring the devilish gaze coming from Jay.

The ride to the school was a mix of emotions for Jen. She felt anxious to blurt out she was in love with another man, sad at how happy Max was in the backseat because both of his parents were dropping him off to school, and exhausted from the dynamic of their situation as a whole.

She held herself together and kissed Max once more on the cheek, waving as he ran inside the double doors of the entrance. Several deep breaths later, she sat back in the passenger seat of Jay's car. He locked the doors and smirked at her, then lit into her calmly.

"I've never raised my voice at you, but you're making it hard for me Jen." Jay fussed.

"You've been good to me, minus the infidelity." She snarled.

"See right there. That was a dig to get me wound up, but I'm not going to lose my cool because you want an argument. You've made your point. Okay?"

"What point is that exactly?" Jen scrunched her face.

"You're still punishing me for what I did."

"You mean for what you still do."

Jay's eyes bulged out slightly. His voice cracked and lips opened before he formed his words. "I don't know what you're talking about, but this acting like a lady of the night shit gotta stop."

"Lady of the night?" Jen held her chest and laughed.

Jay pulled into the lot of a closed general store. He swiped his hand across her thigh, then squeezed. "I'm trying not to disrespect you and call it what it truly is."

Anger blossomed Jen's repressed emotions. Irritated by his words and the touch of his hand, she gained the courage to speak her truth. "I'm in love with someone else."

Jay removed his hand from her leg. Their eyes met, and for the first time he saw he had lost.

"With who?"

"You'll meet him soon enough." Jen held her hands up.

"What? Why am I meeting this motherfucker?" Jay pointed his finger at Jen.

"Because I'm leaving Detroit."

"Yeah. Okay. And going where?"

"That's not important at the moment. We need to discuss Max..."

"Let me stop you right there." Jay cut her off. "Blood or not that's my boy. Whoever this cunt you running around with all hours in the night will die before he gets a hand on him. Heard me."

"Now you hear me. I would never want another man to be Max's father. I know you love him. But..."

"There is no but!" Jay slapped the steering wheel.

"We wouldn't be here if you didn't fuck this up. And I can't help it that I found someone who doesn't make me wonder if I'm good enough to be the one. You don't do that for me."

"You wanna get married? Huh?"

Jen shook her head no.

"What do I need to do to make you come up off of this bullshit?" Jay lowered his voice.

"You could have stopped fucking random bitches."

"You gotta let that go. That's old news."

"I've been counting your condoms Jay, so come up off that." Jen smacked him.

Jay laid back in his seat. He wiped his lip and stared at the hydrant to the left of him. He had been cornered, with no way of getting through the web he spun for himself.

"We need to decide how we're going to tell Max we're no longer together." Jen preached.

He refused to listen to Jen and demanded he be given the opportunity to redeem himself.

"I don't trust you." Jen reminded him. "Here's my proposal. I leave Max with you temporarily until I'm all settled. I'll introduce him to…"

"No one." Jay shut her up. "Let me help you out, Jen. Go do whatever it is you need to do. Get it all out of your system. Me and Max will be here waiting for you when you come back."

It was exhausting for Jen talk to Jay at times, with this being the most difficult.

"I need to get some sleep. Take me home." Jen rested her arm on the car door and leaned her head on her fist.

Jay left for work and she fell asleep with ease once the house was clear. Halfway towards town, he recognized the change taking place and refused to accept Jen walking out on him. He circled back and returned to the house to fix the future he didn't want to face— losing his family.

Struggling with a way to make Jen want him again, he sat at the foot of the bed and watched her sleep, remembering how it felt the first time she left him. He didn't like the emptiness of the house, and found the quiet unsettling. Not hearing Max's voice run about drove him insane.

Angry with himself for taking Jen for granted, he knew deep down he'd lost her. He tapped her foot and woke her. She sat up with squinted eyes, delirious from two days of no sleep.

"I thought you left," she said.

"How can I change your mind?" His head faced the floor.

"Just accept it Jay. Please."

"I can't have another man raising my boy. I wasn't good at considering your feelings, but I hope you understand how that makes me feel."

Jen examined Jay's face. He was serious about Max, and even though she was tired of dealing with him, she couldn't deny how great of a father he was to her son.

"A boy needs a father to help him become a man. You can't do that. I failed you, but I won't fail him."

"What are you suggesting?" She leaned her head back on the pillow.

"I'm hoping you change your mind, but if not, give me custody."

"I'm not giving up my son."

"Our son. I'm the only father he will ever know."

"I'm leaving you. Not abandoning my child."

"I fucked up. I don't expect you to give me another chance, but I'm hoping you will. In the meantime, leave Max with me, like you said. Take a break from me. Go live a little. Experience some new things, and then let's decide what's best for him. I can take care of him. Things are too heated right now for us to make a permanent decision."

Jen agreed knowing Max would be in good hands. When he came home from school, she explained she was going away for a few days. Landon and Millicent were on board to help out with him in any way he needed, and helped her legally document the terms of her and Jay's agreement.

That night she slept in Max's room, assuring him of her return. While he was in school, Jen packed a few bags and parted for Miami, leaving a note taped to the television.

Tears fell from her eyes as she closed the door to the house she wanted to make a home, and hopped into the back of a cab to begin a new life with Jules.

Her departure was felt in Jay's bones. He circled home during one of his runs, happy to see Jen's car in the garage. "Jen!" he repeatedly called out, hearing nothing but the silence he feared.

He searched their bedroom and found the note taped to the television. He paused before opening it, conjuring up the nerve to read the words he didn't want to accept. Jen's dried tears softened and stiffened the lines of the paper. Jay traced them with his fingers, shocking himself as salty tears of his own skated down his cheek and dropped onto the page.

He hadn't cried since he was a child, and to be broken by a woman changed him immensely. He folded Jen's note and placed it in her dresser drawer on her side of the bed, then smiled it hadn't been emptied completely, giving him hope she would soon return to them.

BOOK TWO

DERAILED

CHAPTER 31

FLAG ON THE PLAY

MILLICENT

"I know those eyes," Millicent muttered before she screamed, alarming the neighbor's dogs. The masked face stood at her bedroom window, eerily piercing into her soul and grinning at her fright before he took off into the night.

Millicent stood frozen atop the shattered glass sporadically spread on the floor, paralyzed as her life flashed before her—The mistakes, the secrets, the betrayals, and most of all the failure of finding love. She was a catch after all: beautiful, educated, and well-off, but single and alone inside a townhouse of *pictureless* walls.

"Ms. St. James! Ms. St. James!" Her neighbor pounded at her door. "Are you alright in there? Please say something! I've called the police!"

Hopping around the broken glass, she made her way to the door and peeped through the keyhole. Back and forth her neighbor paced with the telephone pressed to her ear. Millicent flung the door open.

"Did you see anyone?! Did anyone run past you? Did you see a car at least?" she asked.

"She's opened the door. I'll wait here with her until the police arrive," her neighbor answered with the phone now pressed to her chest. "Thank God you're okay. I told the lady who answered my 911 call everything I know. I heard you scream, and my dogs went crazy. I didn't see anyone."

"Argh!" Millicent tugged at her hair.

"Why did you scream like that? If you don't mind my asking?"

"A man wearing a mask was staring at me in my window, and he threw something at me." Millicent's voice cracked.

"My Lawd. Which way did he go?"

"He took off that way," Millicent pointed towards the entrance.

Faint blue lights flashed in the distance, growing brighter once the police cars turned the corner on Millicent's street. Her neighbor placed her hand around Millicent's.

"You are more than welcome to spend the night at my house. My husband can fix your window in the morning. A woman staying alone, I am sure he will be happy to help."

"I don't feel comfortable staying anywhere close to here tonight." Tears formed in the corners of her eyes.

"But where will you go this time of night? It's times like this when being neighborly is required of the Lord."

As Millicent's neighbor repeatedly called on the Lord and squeezed her hand, Millicent wished she'd stop talking. She suffered listening to her prayers with passive commentary of her being a single woman living alone until two officers approached them. "Not such a great night it appears. Which one of you live here?"

Millicent raised her hand. "I do. Millicent St. James."

"I'm Detective Scott. This is my partner, Officer Reed. Sorry you had to call us out here tonight."

"I called," the neighbor interrupted.

"You want to tell us what made you call 911?"

While the neighbor gave her account of events, Officer Reed escorted Millicent inside. He picked up the object centered between the broken glass.

"Does this look familiar to you, Miss...?"

"St. James, and no, officer."

"Notice anyone lurking around?"

"I can't say that I have."

"Any enemies out to harm you? Kids you may have stopped playing in the street?"

"No enemies. Pretty good with kids."

"And you saw the perp. Yes?"

"I didn't see much. A man dressed in black with a ski mask over his face staring at me. When I saw him, he threw whatever that is through the window."

She pointed to the mess on the floor. "I screamed, and he ran away in that direction."

"Can you estimate the height and weight of the perp?"

Millicent sighed. She had a clear idea who was terrorizing her. She stalled, contemplating if she didn't make a huge deal of the broken window, she could avoid facing her dreaded ex in court, and move on with her life. "I'd say pretty tall. Maybe five-foot-eleven, six feet tall, slender build."

Detective Scott entered Millicent's bedroom. He briefed Officer Reed on his conversation with the neighbor then suggested to Millicent, "Your neighbor mentioned she offered for you to stay with her tonight. I would advise you to take her up on her offer until you get this window fixed. Hopefully, whoever did this will slip up, and we'll have him in custody soon. Make the streets a little safer. And this is a nice neighborhood. We don't get many calls in this area."

Millicent shook her head. "I have friends in Detroit. I'm sure they wouldn't mind me staying a few nights. Can one of you stay in here with me while I pack a bag, please?"

"Certainly," said Detective Scott. "I'll be outside checking the perimeter. By chance do you have a trash bag and some tape for this window?"

"Top shelf in the pantry."

While packing, Millicent became overwhelmed and dropped a few tears. The hatred in the intruder's eyes spooked her. Her gut told her it was Miles, and her mind raced back to their breakup months ago. She thought she had seen the last of him, and buried the image of him and the embarrassment she felt from being duped by a psycho. But now his eyes found a way to haunt her forever.

Officer Reed carried her bags to the front of her house while she turned off the lights. A man-shaped silhouette appeared behind the blinds in the living room. "Ahhh!" Millicent screamed.

"My apologies! Ms. St. James, it's me, Detective Scott. I was checking your windows," he shouted through the glass before making his way inside. "Forgive me for scaring you. I was making sure your windows were locked so you'd be safe whenever you return."

Millicent placed her hands on her chest. "This is too much."

"Again, I apologize, but I also have some bad news. A witness that lives in your division said they saw someone running from your house and into the woods. I've called for backup to comb the area and see if we can find anything. And your neighbors have pointed out that your vehicle has four flat tires."

Her arms dropped to her side. Her shoulders slouched and she fell to the floor. "How the fuck am I supposed to get to Detroit now!"

The officers looked at each other.

"I apologize. I didn't mean to curse, but fuck! What the hell is happening?!"

"I already have an officer checking your car for fingerprints. Here's hoping we find something to help catch this menace."

"Sir, excuse me for saying, but is it safe to say this wasn't random?"

Detective Scott sighed. "I agree with Reed here. It appears you were personally targeted. Any enemies that may want to..."

"We've already been there, done that." Officer Reed shook his head.

"Can one of you stay while I make some calls? It's late, but hopefully one of my friends will drive out tonight and pick me up because I can't stay here. I just can't."

Examining Millicent with a close eye, Officer Reed offered to take her to Detroit if his supervisor granted him the clearance.

"How long will that take?" Millicent asked.

"Someone's gunning for a promotion with community service." Detective Scott nudged his head to the door. "The captain's outside."

Officer Reed stepped out to speak to the captain with Millicent's bags in tow.

"Nice place you have here." Detective Scott aimed for small talk.

"Thank you. It was."

"Was?"

"It's tainted now. If it were daylight, I'd put a for sale sign out front right now."

"It must be hard dealing with this all on your own."

"I'll manage."

"Well, you know you could..."

"Detective Scott, right?"

"Hmm."

"Thanks for all your help tonight. I'm going to go make some calls. If you'll excuse me." Millicent stepped away into the kitchen.

Officer Reed popped back inside. "Ms. St. James, if you're ready," he said, carrying her bags to his squad car.

CHAPTER 32

CHARIOT

WALT

The officer made small talk with Millicent to get her mind off of her troubles. She barely cracked a smile at his jokes, or listened to a word he'd said until she felt the car exit off of the highway.

"Where are we going?" she asked.

"So you were ignoring me. To the station to switch cars. It was the only way the captain agreed I could offer my services. And besides, you don't want to ride to Detroit in a police car. Am I right?"

Millicent shrugged her shoulders. "Thank you for not making me sit in the back."

"That space is for criminals. You don't look like much of a criminal to me." He raised his brow.

"Normally I'd laugh at that, but due to the circumstances..."

" I understand."

"If I haven't said it before, thank you for doing this. I can pay you, or at least give you gas money for your trouble."

"That won't be necessary. I'm happy to do it. Besides, you seemed pretty shaken up back there, and I don't like seeing women in distress, or sad, or hurt, or abused. Are you positive the place I'm taking you is safe?"

"Yeah. It's my best friend's house. She's like a sister to me, and her husband is pretty cool. They always make me feel welcome. I practically have a room at their house."

"That must be nice."

The car turned into the station lot and Officer Reed opened her car door. "This will be quick. Follow me." He took her by the hand and helped her to her feet. The word about his charity spread throughout the office before they arrived. "Sit right here, Ms. St. James. I'll be right back, and we'll be on our way."

Millicent pretended not to notice the many eyes shifting in her direction, or the whispers coming from the desks surrounding her. The staff at the precinct sized her up like a piece of meat at the deli counter. Second guessing the arrangement, she repositioned herself in her seat, waiting for her officer to return from the corner where she spotted him signing paperwork.

"Reed here offered to be this pretty lady's chariot!" A loud voice shouted from behind a cubicle wall.

"She's out of your league, Reed!" said another voice from the opposite corner.

"Oh, what a knight in shining armor!" Another teased in a high pitched voice.

Reed apologized to Millicent from afar and signaled he needed one more minute. He fanned off his unit and shouted, "Pipe down! Pipe down!"

A husky officer approached Millicent. "What brings you in?" He snorted.

"I beg your pardon?"

"What's a babe like you doing in here?"

"A 'babe?'" Millicent rolled her eyes.

Officer Reed returned and picked up her bag. "Leave her alone, Jamison. She's waiting for a lift."

"Oh yeah, where to? I can take her wherever she needs to go."

"I already offered." Officer Reed placed his hand on his belt.

"I bet you did." Jamison smiled and walked off.

"Ignore them. They don't get out much."

"Obviously."

"Let's get you to your friend's house."

They left the station nothing short of catcalls, whistles, and cheers. She lowered her head and smiled so the officer couldn't see she was amused, and erased it when he opened her door and helped her inside his classic, renovated Chevrolet Impala. "If you will, can you plug in your friend's address?" Millicent called out Landon's address into the system. "And off we go."

The hour drive felt like an interrogation. Walt hadn't realized the dry answers Millicent gave him, extended from his lack of conversational skills outside of his job.

"I feel like I'm annoying you," he said.

"You're not." Millicent's tone was less than convincing.

"That was a lie."

"Excuse me?"

"No offense. I could tell by your tone, you lied just now. I'm training to be a detective."

"Okay. Good for you, but how dare you insinuate I was lying?"

"But were you? I won't be offended by the truth."

"Okay, yes, you were annoying me with the third degree. I felt like I was still back at the precinct."

He exhaled deeply. "I'm working on that. It's my job, so I kind of can't help it at times."

"No worries."

"Now that I have you talking, and you've told me I basically suck at having a normal conversation, may I ask you something personal?"

"That depends."

" I can't place your ethnicity. What are you, if you don't mind my asking?"

"I get this question a lot."

"I'm sure. What I'm about to say isn't going to come out right, so forgive me if I do offend you, but sometimes when I am on the phone with a person I can tell if they are black or white or Spanish and so forth. Have you ever found yourself mentally visualizing what the person on the other end of a call looks like?"

Millicent chuckled. "Um, I think everyone does that."

"Well, for me and I can only speak for myself, I can even tell when I am talking to a black person that is talking white."

"What is talking white?"

He paused. "Let me try to dig myself out of this hole."

"Yeah, let's see you do that." Millicent grinned.

"I noticed you laughed a second ago."

"I did. Now dig, Officer Reed."

"Please call me Walt. Short for Walter."

"You can't dig yourself out, can you?"

"Tough crowd." He smiled. "I think the term I'm looking for is code switching. I can tell when my people are code switching—you know, talking in a tone and manner that is not their normal voice or projection."

"Nice save." Millicent smiled. "I knew what you meant. I just wanted to see you squirm."

"That's cold, Ms. St. James. You have a sense a humor. I like that."

"Are you flirting with me, Officer Reed– I mean Walt?"

"I am, Ms. St. James, who still hasn't answered my question."

Millicent stared at the officer other than an officer for the first time that night. She noticed the smoothness in his dark skin, and the fullness of his lips and felt him worthy of an answer she normally evaded.

"My family tree consists of many different backgrounds. My grandmother was raised in the Bahamas. My grandfather was from England. He and his real family took a trip to the islands where he met my grandmother and conceived my dad in a vacant hotel room she was cleaning. My grammy never heard from my grandfather again, and the only thing she knew of him was his last name, St. James. She gave that last name to my dad, and he earned a free ride to a university here in the states. There he met and married my mother, who is mixed with everything associated with slavery and fraternizing with the Indians. And no, I don't know which tribe."

"And all of that created a world class beauty."

Millicent's cheeks flushed pink and red.

"I didn't mean to say that aloud."

Silence sat between them as the navigation system announced they were about to arrive at their destination. "I wish that drive was just a little longer," he said, parking in front of The Jeffries' house. He carried Millicent's bags to the door. "This house looks dark. Are you sure the people that live here are home?"

"It is pretty dark, but I'm sure someone's home. Landon would have told me if she were leaving town." She rang the bell.

"Who's that?" Walt pointed to a car pulling behind his in the driveway.

Millicent turned around and sucked her teeth. "Nobody."

"Whatchu doing here, Mills? And with the police no less."

Millicent turned back to Walt. "You know how you told me to ignore those people at the precinct? Do the same for him."

"Officer." Jay snickered. "You with the police? Of course you would be. What kind of trouble you got yourself into, Boughetto? I thought you were all white collar and shit. How you doing tonight overseer, I mean officer?"

"Your friend has jokes, I see." Walt muttered.

"Is this your new man, Mills?"

Walt extended his hand to Jay. "Officer Reed. And you are?"

"Talking to the lady." Jay shook his hand. "All jokes aside, Mills, you in some kind of trouble?"

"Not anymore. Where are Todd and Landon?"

"The hospital."

"Why? What happened?"

"Todd damn near burned his eyebrows off trying to outdo me on the grill. He burned his elbow pretty good, but he'll be alright. They're going to be there for a while, and you know how you and L bougie asses are. She's cold and wants a blanket, but God forbid she lays on one from the hospital."

"Well, let me in since you have the key."

Jay walked between Walt and Millicent, gave Walt a onceover, then grinned at Millicent. "Is this yours?" he asked, pointing to Millicent's bag. She nodded. "I'll take that, officer."

Walt handed the duffle to Jay as he stared at him with a curve on the side of his right lip. "You have some pretty interesting friends, Ms. St. James."

"You ain't bringing another Kevin 'round here are ya, Mills?"

"Who is Kevin?"

"No one." Millicent sighed and buried her head below her hand.

"Some clown she had taggin' along wit' her a while back."

"Kevin and I work together. Nothing more. Stop playing around, Jay."

"It was none of my business. I shouldn't have asked." Walt chuckled.

Jay grinned at Millicent. "You still haven't said why the police is dropping you off this time of night."

Millicent looked away.

"She had an intruder in her home. I offered to bring her somewhere safe."

"Get the fuck outta here. Did y'all find the person?"

"Not yet."

"I hope you do before...Thanks for looking out for my people. Millicent ,you could have called one of us to come out there."

"I didn't mind. At all." Walt stared at Jay with his chest out. "Again, pretty interesting friends, Ms. St. James."

"I'll leave you two kids out here to say good night. I would invite you in, but I'm pretty sure my friends wouldn't like Mills entertaining some strange man in their house. Nice meeting you Officer...Reed?"

"Call me Walt."

"Ahite then, Walt."

Free from Jay's quips and intrusion, they stood on the steps clueless of what to do next. Like a teenager sneaking around behind her parents' backs, Millicent kept watch on the door, waiting for Jay to interrupt them. Walt conjured up the nerve to speak first.

"What happened to you tonight was horrible, but something good came out of it. Meeting you."

"I can't thank you enough for bringing me all the way out here. As I said before, I can pay you."

"I would never take money from a woman." He scowled. "Ms. St. James, are you seeing anyone?"

"Not at the moment. I take it you're single?"

"As a one dollar bill. Ugh, that has to be the corniest thing I have said all night."

"Yes, it is." She laughed.

"Well I'm going to get my corny ass back on the road. It was good to see that frown turn upside down."

Millicent lost the resistance to blush.

"Can I try to make you smile again— at a later date— when you feel up to it?"

"I'd like that."

Millicent watched him walk away with one foot inside of the house. She yelled, "Don't you need my number?!"

"What do you think took me so long at the precinct! I was hoping this night ended like this!"

Jay crossed Millicent's path. "Let this be the last time you bring the police to folk's house."

"Scared?"

"Never dat. You gon' be good staying here by yourself?"

"No."

"Come on and ride with me to the hospital so I can talk shit about ole copper ass."

"I'd rather you shut the hell up and just drive."

Jay opened the passenger door for Millicent. "For you, milady."

Millicent rolled her eyes and hopped in. Jay plopped in the driver's seat and revved the engine.

"What you know about cars, Mills?"

She sighed. "How to buy them and trade them in."

"Where is yours by the way?"

"Four flats in front of my house."

"Who did you piss off, girl?"

"Jay, just drive."

"How about I take L her blanket, and you come home with me? She doesn't have to know you're here. I can keep you safe tonight."

"No thank you." She scoffed.

"You'll change your mind. And when you do, holla at me."

"That won't happen."

Jay grinned. "That pig was square. Don't get too close to him."

"Why not?"

"Cuz he's gonna hate my guts when he finds out I'm the motherfucker that stole his woman from under him."

CHAPTER 33

NEW MAN WHO DIS

JEN

In a new bed, in a new house off the southern coast of Florida, Jen woke up to clear blue skies, and waves crashing on white sands outside her bedroom window.

"What do you call that?" Jen asked Jules, kissing her shoulder.

"That's what you call a good morning fuck that will have you thinking about me all day." He squeezed her ass until she squealed. "Good morning."

"Good morning." Jen sighed between a smile and her hair covering half her face. "What was that move you did in the end?"

"You like that, huh?"

"I did." She giggled. "You haven't done that before."

"That was just a little something something. You want me to do it again?"

"Duh." Jen laughed playfully as she and Jules wrestled on the soiled, mangled sheets beneath them. "But it will have to wait until I get home tonight."

"Listen to you. You've only been here a few months and already making me second in your life."

"Don't be like that. You know I hate being late."

"I know. It's good you like working at that spa."

"I'm doing more than working there. I'm planning to open my own spot as soon as I finish tying up loose ends with Max."

"I thought Jay was going to have full custody of him?"

"He wants to, but I can't agree to that. I'm his mother."

"And a boy needs a father."

"Are you saying you don't want Max here with us?"

"Don't put words in my mouth. What I'm saying is that as a man myself, I can honestly say I would rather my real dad be in my life instead of a substitute."

Jen sat on the edge of the bed. "I'll take that into consideration. Jay and I will do what's best for our son in the end. You had me scared for a second."

"Why?"

Looking back at Jules over her shoulder, she said, "I thought you were going to say my son wasn't wanted here. I was afraid I was going to have to leave your ass and crawl back to Detroit with egg on my face."

Jules inched closer to her and wrapped his arms around her waist. "I would never. He is a part of you. And I love every part of you. Besides, don't you think it's time you let him meet me?"

"Soon. Jay is not on board with that idea yet." She tapped the back of his hand.

"It's not like you to let him call the shots. Like you said, you are the mother after all."

Jen turned around and smirked. "Have I made a mistake?"

"What do you mean?"

"Letting you believe because you fuck me every which way even sideways you can talk shit to me."

"Whoa. Let's start this morning over." He pulled her closer. "Good morning, my long lost love."

"I need to get my day started."

Jules followed Jen into the closet slinging clothes on the rack. He stood at the entrance and blocked her from exiting.

"I'm not letting you leave if we're on bad terms."

"We're not. But we will be if I'm late."

He moved out of her way. "Do you want my lawyer to look at your business plan?"

"No. I've got it all under control."

"I don't like when you're mad at me."

"I'm not mad."

"Then look at me."

Jen threw her clothes on the bed and faced him with her brows slightly raised higher on one side.

"Point made. I'll wait for you to cool off to ask about your plan.

"I'll tell you now. I'm opening a makeup bar. A salon dedicated to giving women makeovers, and teaching classes on how to properly apply their make-up. Not this caked-up shit all over the internet. I'll make house calls, tend to celebrities when they roll into town. That sort of thing."

"Sounds like you've done your research."

"I'm confident it can work. I envision three makeup artists and two stylists at the bar. Girls can come in and get serviced before having their pictures taken or going to prom. We'll provide self-care to women who need a day to spruce up."

Jules kissed her forehead. "You haven't opened the doors yet, and I'm already proud of you. When you finish your certification, expect a big donation from an anonymous donor."

Jen looked as if she had seen a ghost when Jules asked about her certification. He was in the dark of her flawed past and would never know her secrets, though they weighed her down. Despite her maternal attachment and hidden cries at night, she sacrificed her selfish longing to be with Max, knowing with Jay he would be heavily protected and kept safe in case anyone from her past came looking to settle the score.

Once out of the house, Jen breathed out without Jules picking her brain. She thought about her first husband, Alex, and how he ruined her ability to trust anyone, something she wished she could fully experience with Jules. He knew Jen the girl, not Jen the woman, and she had a life she could never share with him.

Jen knew he was the man for her by the way he gazed upon her when he thought she wasn't looking. His desire for her was what she longed for as he loved her in the purest form, but when she listened to her gut, the man she felt the most trustworthy with her secret was Jay. Philandering, two-timing John Jay Lloyd of all people.

Jen further questioned if being loved, and adorned, and craved would be worth it in the end, and wondered if she had been wise, or a fool for the sake of love. *Should I have found a way to make it work with Jay? Was I weak for falling in love and thinking I could run into the arms of another man with ease? I could have followed Jay's lead and had an affair with Jules. No. Jay would have found a way to screw it up for me.*

Thinking of Jay led her to call him. His greetings were cold in the beginning. Dry conversation. Quick hang-ups. This time he surprised her.

"Missing me yet?" He chuckled.

Jen scoffed. "How is my baby? How are you?"

"You don't have to ask that every time you call. I'm handling my business as usual."

"Of course you are, but how is my son?"

"Watch your words. 'How is *our* son?' And he is doing just fine."

"I'm coming to see him."

"The two times you have aren't enough?"

"Jay, I don't need your shit today. Okay?"

"What's wrong? Lover boy ain't living up to the hype?"

"Lover boy is perfectly fine and wants to meet Max. Are you good with that yet?"

"Nah. My boy got one daddy and one daddy only. And his mama is always welcome to come home when she's done bullshitting in the streets."

"You told me to take all the time I needed. Now you're throwing it in my face."

"Maybe I should have been clearer. I thought you would take off for a few weeks, maybe even a month. I didn't know your fling was going to result in you moving outta state."

Jen sighed. "I didn't call for a lecture."

"I might have fucked up, but did we deserve to be abandoned? You took it too far."

"What we're not going to do is blame me for our breakup."

"Our son asks me every day if you've called."

"And I do. You choose not to answer."

"I know, but I lie to him. I tell him you called while he was at soccer practice, or asleep in the car. But why do you call every day? Tell pretty boy to fuck off and come home."

"Jules is not a pretty boy."

"Whoa whoa whoa. Don't call his name to me."

"Why? Because you have never called out your coleslaw's name to me. Like Sasha."

"Who is Sasha?"

"It's been that many? You can't remember their names?" Jen sucked her teeth. "You haven't changed one bit."

"Whether you believe it or not, some things have changed."

"Like what?"

"Things," Jay muttered.

Jen took a play from Jay's book and abruptly ended their call. He dialed her back. She swiped her phone and sent him to voicemail faster than a person scrolling past the pictures they weren't given permission to see.

She called Landon. "Who is the new bimbo?"

Landon coughed. "Good morning to you too. How is the sunshine state?"

"Hot. Now fill me in. Have you met her yet?"

"I have not. And Todd hasn't mentioned anything to me. I've been around pretty heavy, filling in your shoes until you come back. When will that be?"

"I don't think I could come back if I wanted to."

"Why do you say that?"

"Because I could tell in Jay's voice that he is about done with me as I am him."

"Men don't pine away for a woman that long. My uncle got himself a new wife in less than a month when my aunt died."

"They really are pieces of shit, aren't they?"

"Facts. And this is Jay we're talking about. What did you expect?"

Jen hit the steering wheel and pulled over to the side of the road. "Hold please." She screamed with the phone pressed to her chest.

"I heard that. Do this. Close your eyes and tell me who do you see yourself with?"

"Jules."

"Do you feel anything other than hate for Jay?"

"I don't hate Jay. I'm disappointed in us. He hurt me and humiliated me, but I do like how he used to beg for me to come home. He didn't do that today."

"Jen, if you come back Jay will continue to be who you know him to be, and you will regret losing the man who obviously truly loves you."

"I guess I just needed to hear that from the wisest person I know."

"You should come home this weekend. Stay with me. It'll be fun. Millicent is already here, so we can make it a girls' margarita weekend or something."

"Why is Millicent there?"

"She's been living here for a few weeks now. Someone vandalized her place, and she's too scared to live alone at the moment."

"That person really did a number on her. Now I understand why she hasn't given me an update on how long I have to collect that money in Sweden. Give her my best, will ya? Better yet, I'll do it myself this weekend. I'm coming to see my boy. But the girls' night will have to wait. I'm not coming alone."

CHAPTER 34

THE OUTSIDER

LANDON

Landon's party for Jen turned out to be a disaster before it got started, thanks to Todd inviting Jay, and his son Ephram, without clearing it with her first. His apology for doing so was not received on her behalf, therefore setting the tone for the party.

Jay showed up in rare form. Flamboyant and cockier than ever. He pulled a page from The Book of Nas in his attire. Casual black chinos and matching blazer above a black label tee and medium gold link chain shining from his neck, with fresh white sneakers with fat laces. Landon gave him the side eye when he arrived.

"Now you know Jen is coming home to see her baby. Why would you agree to come tonight instead of being at home so Max could enjoy seeing both of you getting along?"

"He likes going to Mrs. Latham's house. I told her Jen was coming to pick him up."

"Did you tell Jen that?"

"I'll tell her when she gets here."

"Jay, I want you to know I'm biting my tongue. Okay?"

"Ey, I ain't the one who left. Don't be mad you got stuck with the realest in the breakup. Let me kiss the host." He puckered his lips. "Where is T?"

"Boy, come in and go out back."

"If you need me to make sure he doesn't burn those thick ass eyebrows, just say that."

Landon took a deep breath, then hurried into the kitchen to lay out the food while eavesdropping on the conversation between the men. Millicent popped in.

"You need some help?"

"Yeah. Grab that pan and meet me outside. I'm trying to listen in on what the boys are talking about. Jen thinks Jay is seeing someone. I'm trying to find out before she gets here."

"Did her and Jules break up or something?"

"No. But she said she can tell he's into someone. Come on and help me listen in."

Millicent pretended not to notice the look Jay gave her when she walked outside. She recognized he was undressing her with his eyes, and it puzzled her that she liked it.

"What time did you tell Mr. Officer to drop by?" Landon asked her.

"Eight o'clock."

Jay blew from his nose loud enough for Millicent to hear him.

"I can't wait to meet him." Landon squealed and rolled her shoulders.

"Todd, did you know these two invited the po-po to your house?"

Landon cut him off. "Jay, I need you to simmer down. The party hasn't started yet, and you are already starting shit. Todd, check him please."

Jay clicked his teeth, glancing at Millicent with a seductive eye. She followed Landon back inside, blushing with her head hung low, guilty of playing phone tag with both Jay and Walt. The doorbell rang. "I'll get it." Millicent sprang for the door. "Oh, it's you guys," she said to McCaine, Tammy, Brian and Kim.

"Well, hey to you too." Tammy narrowed her eyes and passed her a bottle of wine. "You're looking well, given what you've been through."

"I didn't mean to offend you guys. I just thought you were my plus one. Everybody's out back."

"Is Jen here yet?"

"We're waiting on her too."

Landon greeted her guests and followed everyone to the deck. Todd swiped a kiss from her as she brought out the final dish. "Everyone can eat," she announced over the music, shaking on the top step. Todd returned and lowered the sound of 90's hip hop playing over the radio and gained everyone's attention.

"Everybody, Landon and I have two special guests tonight. I want you all to meet my son, Ephram."

The shocked faces of their guests had a hard time settling on who to look at, the boy or Landon. He stood next to Todd, looking at the adults with big dough eyes, twisting from side to side. Landon created a space between her and Todd, red faced with a fake smile on her lips and a stiff forehead.

"He's a cutie," said Tammy, coaching Landon to relax with muttered lip movement.

Millicent whispered, "We may have to drag her off of that step. She looks like a mannequin up there."

"I've never seen someone blink so much," Kim added.

"Come over here, baby. You hungry? You want me to fix you a plate?"

"No. I wanna go back in the house and play my video game," he said, looking up at Todd.

Todd smiled down at him. "That's cool. I just wanted you to meet your family. These people are always going to be around, so get to know them. Okay?"

He nodded his head, then repeated himself. "Can I go play my game now?"

"Yeah. Go 'head." Todd rubbed the top of his head.

He ran off, and Todd inched closer to Landon. "See, that wasn't so bad. Was it?"

"I think Jen may be at the door. I'll be right back."

She went inside and leaned back against the door, holding her hands to her chest and exhaling in short breaths. Todd turned the music back on as Jen's silhouette formed at the door. Landon opened it before she rang the bell. "It's so good to have you home." She and Jen hugged.

"I missed you," Jen whispered in her ear. "You know Jules."

"Nice seeing you again. How did she manage to sneak you away?"

"I'm actually flying out on the redeye."

"Yeah, he can't be away from the team right now. I just wanted him to meet Max. Even if it was for a hot minute."

"How did that go?" Landon asked under her breath.

"It went. Jay wasn't happy about it, but he held his composure in front of our boy so...cool points to him, I guess."

Landon bit her bottom lip. "Ha. That explains it."

"What?"

"He's in rare form tonight."

"Shit. Well, Jules and I are only staying for like an hour. I have to drop him off at the airport, and I promised Max I would pick him up and let him sleep at the hotel tonight so he can get in the pool tomorrow. I hope you won't be mad?"

"Jen, with the way the night is going, I might kick everyone out after you leave."

"What happened?"

"We'll talk later. Jules, let's go make you feel awkward and introduce you to the boys. Mine won't bite, but Jay…"

"I expect nothing less from him after meeting him earlier today." He laughed.

A record might as well have scratched when Landon walked through her patio doors with Jen and Jules on her heels. Jay turned up his lip and snickered with Todd. Landon narrowed her eyes at her husband, and summoned him to her side. "The chain is pulling her ball. You better go before you get sent to bed with no dinner." Jay chuckled and gave him dap. Todd placed his hand in the small of Landon's back as she formally introduced him to Jules.

"You taking care of my people?" Todd and Jules pounded fists.

"It's been my pleasure."

Millicent walked over. "Good to see you, Julian."

"I told you, my friends call me Jules. And it's good to see you too. Mal's been asking about you."

"Tell him I'm cool."

"Landon told me what happened. Did they ever find the guy?"

"Nope. Not one lead, but I don't want to talk about that tonight. I've put it behind me, put my house up for sale, traded in my car, and am moving on. But we'll catch up on all of that tomorrow at brunch, right?"

"Fah sho."

"I'll be right back. I think my date finally arrived. Look at me. I'm no longer the fifth wheel. Excuse me."

Landon tapped her arm. "I'll join you. I need to check on Todd's son."

"Wait. He's here?" Jen asked.

"Yeah. I'll bring him out so you can meet him."

Millicent looked through the blinds from the front room. Landon comforted her. "I'm sure he'll be here. Go hang out. I'll keep watch." She raced off to Todd's man cave. The television had animated army men on the screen, turned up loud as the music outside. "Ephram!" she called. No answer. She checked the kitchen, sure he decided to finally eat. It was empty. She sped down the hall and gasped.

"Get down from there before you fall and break your neck," she warned him, sitting on the edge of the banister.

"What would you do if I fall?"

"What? I'd call 911. Now get down!"

"I would tell the police you pushed me."

"What did you say?"

"You heard me."

"Get your little ass down from there right now!"

Landon watched him climb back over the banister and sent him to his room. The room Todd was thrilled to paint blue and decorate with sports decals, shelves of balls from golf to basketball, and pictures of the local legends. She pulled Todd away from Jay, sending heat signals to Jules's back.

"Didn't take you long to escape Jules, I see."

"You mean Julian? His friends call him Jules." Todd and Jay chuckled.

"You two are so childish."

"He hit it off with Brian and McCaine pretty good. You know. Talking that college shit."

"I need you inside. We have a problem," she exclaimed in a whisper and repeated what Ephram said to her.

"You must have heard him wrong," Todd replied.

"Todd, I know what I heard, and he has to go home."

"Landon calm down. The boy just got here."

"And he threatened to lie about me to the police. The cops and the media will take a child's word over an adult's word at the drop of a dime! And they wouldn't care that he's lying. I have too much to lose over this ridiculousness!" Landon exclaimed.

"Where is he?"

"In your cave. I'll go pack his belongings."

Todd found Ephram playing his game. He sat next to him and picked up the extra remote. "I used to be pretty good at these things. Let's see if I still have it," he said, working his way in. "Are you hungry yet?"

"I ate some of those chips Ms. Landon put on the counter."

"We have more than chips out back. How about I fix you a plate after I beat you one round?"

"No thanks."

"Say, did you say something to Landon to upset her?"

"No."

"You sure? She says she asked you to not sit on the railing upstairs. She was scared you would hurt yourself. Did you say you would tell the police she pushed you if you fell."

"I didn't say that."

"Okay. Do you remember what you said?"

"I haven't said anything to her."

Todd paused the game with his remote. "Stop playing for a second. Ephram, look at me and tell me the truth. What did you say? Landon wouldn't make something up like that, Son."

"I thought you would be on my side."

"On your side for what? You said nothing happened."

Ephram sighed.

"Come on. I'm going to take you home. We'll try this another time." Todd's voice cracked.

Landon walked in with Ephram's bags. Her chest was tight and her back stiff from the stress she predicted when news of Ephram ruined her happiness. She watched Todd from behind, feeling the hurt he released in the room. "I'm going to leave these here. It was nice to have you spend the day with us, Ephram." Landon dropped the bags and rejoined her guests outside, intruding on a conversation between McCaine, Tammy, and Jay, entertaining the comedic couple of the group with all of the nicknames he created for Jules.

"I guess the police ain't showing up tonight, L. It's probably for the best. This party went down the moment Rick Fox dropped in. Where my boy T at?"

Landon stumbled on her words with a lie on the tip of her tongue, and a tear forming in the corner of her eye. Tammy read her body language and noticed the water bubbling above her lower lash. "Something's wrong." She scowled, nudging Landon to a private corner.

Landon nervously shook her head. "It's happening. Just like I said it would." She sniffed and wiped the tear. "Don't mind me. I'm just a little upset. Todd has to leave and take his son home."

"Now?"

Landon nodded. "You won't believe what happened in the house."

"Remember I've been here before. Try me," said Tammy.

The friends noticed Landon wiping tears and gathered around. With shaky breaks she retold what transpired in the house.

Tammy's mouth dropped. "I was hoping you were wrong. Secretly I wished this would be an experience you'd actually enjoy."

"I tried. I don't know what more I can do. And in every outcome, I am the bad guy, but how can I trust being around a kid who would say something like that?"

"Todd has himself in deep shit with this one." McCaine blew from his mouth.

"That boy wouldn't set foot back in my house," Kim added.

"I was thinking the same thing. The law will make an example out of innocent people when it comes to children." Brian sighed.

Millicent interrupted. "If he would say something like that, do you think he would steal? Never mind. Excuse me, I need to check my room."

CHAPTER 35

———

WHO YOU WIT'

JAY

Jay's eyes followed Millicent running into the house, tuning out the group sympathizing with Landon. He chimed in, "L, that's messed up what the little boy said, but it doesn't change the fact Todd is his daddy. Give little man time to adjust. He's been over here how many times. Two? Three?"

"Jay, you hate the police more than anyone I know. How would you honestly feel if a kid threatened to have you arrested for absolutely nothing."

"He was just talking. He wasn't gonna do that, L. He was just being a kid."

"Well, let him be a kid over at your house."

"Um. No." Jen interrupted. "I don't need him influencing my sweet boy."

"So just like that, the kid has been alienated," said Jay, looking around at everyone. "If y'all will excuse me."

Landon pointed at Jay walking up the stairs. "See. I'm the bad guy no matter what. I knew this shit would happen."

Jay went inside and sought out Millicent. He posed in the entrance of her room door with a grin on the side of his lips. Millicent, busy fumbling through her bags counting credit cards and jewelry, didn't feel his presence as he gawked at her curves.

"Is anything missing?" He propped himself against the door.

Millicent gasped and held her chest. "You scared me. And no, it looks like everything is still here."

"Good. That kid has everyone outside in a tizzy. I would hate for them to add thief to his name."

"What are you doing up here?"

"Checking up on what's soon to be mine. Especially since the overseer is a no show. But that's good for me."

"The night's not over."

"It is for him. Stop frontin, Mills. You probably read my texts over and over at night, wishing I was here keeping you company."

"You're really doing this with Jen downstairs?"

"Jen has moved on, and so have I."

Millicent studied Jay with a close eye. She did enjoy reading his texts, and thought of how one in particular made her believe he truly was into her.

"In one of your messages, you said you knew this would happen."

"Like you didn't."

"Jay, what do you want with me?"

"You already know." He moved closer.

"Nothing about you and me makes sense."

"That doesn't mean it wouldn't be right. And I bet it feels right too." Jay touched her skin for the first time, tracing the curve below her cheek.

Millicent shivered. "I am smarter than this."

"That might be your problem. You think too much. That's why you don't have a man. Take a chance for once. I swear you won't regret it."

"I don't want to hurt my best friend."

"How can you when she doesn't feel anything for me anymore. She's made her choice and she's happy. Don't you deserve to be happy too?" He stunned her with a kiss to her lips. "Tell me you didn't feel that."

Millicent looked into his eyes and didn't answer. Jay stole a second kiss, this time with his eyes open. "How have I not noticed you before now?" he said, and took her in his arms, taming his dominant beast within. Millicent brought out a sensual side in him. He wasn't what she was used to, and he acted according to her needs, hypnotized by the softness of her skin blessing his fingertips. Passion he didn't know existed flowed through him, causing him to see Millicent more than the dollar store fucks, or corner girl quick jobs he was used to. She wasn't to be played with or fucked in that moment. She needed to be made love to.

The way Jay held her close, gently kissing her lips and giving her body the attention it craved surprised her. This wasn't the Jay she had come to know over the years. The Jay who bigoted his way through neighborhoods of women. The

Jay who taunted her for calling him on his bullshit. This was a man who seduced her with charm and wit, successfully convincing her to go against what she knew was wrong, and made it feel right.

Millicent surrendered her body to her longtime adversary, giving him control of it to do as he pleased. She weakened from his strong hands and allowed him to lift her legs into the crease of his elbows, and place her pussy on the hard knot tightened against his zipper

"That's all you," he said. "You ready to let me taste?"

She nodded.

Jay laid her on the bed, pressing his trapped dick against her with pressure until she squirmed. He smiled. "I know it's wet." He pecked her lips, creating a trail towards her neck. Her gasps for air excited him more than when she played hard to get, and he rose above her for another look of his latest dream turning into reality.

Over the past few weeks, he imagined how this moment would be— him pounding on her from the rear and pulling her long wavy hair towards him while arching her back like the letter C. But he couldn't handle her that way once the moment arrived.

"What is it?" she asked.

He puckered his lips. "Show me you want me."

Millicent's legs spread eagle. She removed her panties and threw them at his face. Jay caught them and placed them in his mouth.

"This better not be some sort of game, Jay," she said.

Jay freed his mouth and dropped to his knees. "Let me clean up your mess."

His breath against her throbbing flesh and admired its beauty with his fingers. Tracing her entrance like a delicate flower before licking her center. His tongue tasted the nectar dripping from her folds and he moaned. "This pretty pussy hasn't been tended to."

He kissed it with a long steady motion from the bottom to the top. Millicent mangled the covers in her hands. Jay thrashed his tongue against her shaking body hard, counting how many times her ass jiggled in his face. "Yes, Jay. Just like that. Keep doing it just like that," she groaned. He shocked her with fast soft licks and a full mouthed kiss to her quivering pussy. The aggressive tongue stabs and repetitive, soft pecks to her slit made her stomach cave as she erupted in his mouth.

Her hands cradled his head tight to her hole, restricting him from breathing, and the intensity of her orgasm shook the bed and his soul. He was ready to plow.

Jay rose to his feet, reached in his wallet, and covered himself while Millicent squirmed and held herself on the bed. Seeing him protect them made her think of the stories Jen shared of finding condoms they never used. She respected him for it, but also questioned herself. *'This is a mistake. What the fuck am I doing with him?'*

Jay wiped his mouth with her panties, slid between her legs where they once covered her, and positioned himself to enter her world. Millicent contemplated telling him she'd changed her mind, but feeling his very grown manliness against her aching womb clouded her judgment. She wanted it. Needed it.

Slowly he danced his way inside of her, holding back the fast paced assault he imagined he'd do to her in his dreams. He *grinded* his cock hard and slow into her corners, listening to her breathe sighs of relief. Millicent's nails sunk into his back.

"Scratch me, baby, I don't care," he whispered, digging harder and deeper in her zone. "You like that?"

"Yes, Jay, yes."

"Say my name again."

"Yes, Jay." Millicent panted in his ear.

He cuffed both of her thighs from the back and brought them forward. The faster their hearts beat, the weaker Jay's elated mind could no longer tame his beast. "Can I go deeper, baby?" he asked, doing so without her permission.

"Mmm hmm," she answered, clenching her walls around him so tight he nearly burst early.

"What is mmm hmm? I wanna hear yes Jay. I like how you sound when you say my name."

"Yes Jay. Go deeper." Millicent thrust her hips forward.

Jay lowered his torso and kissed her. "You want everybody to hear you outside?"

"I don't care," she whispered.

Jay grinned and kissed her to silence the pleasure escaping her lips.

CHAPTER 36

A WOMAN & HER INTUITION

JEN

The dilemma between Landon and Todd killed the mood of the party. Jen shifted the attention to herself and lied, "Jules and I decided Max would love to see the planes take off at night. We're going to get him and call it night. Are we still on for brunch tomorrow?" Landon hugged her. Jen turned to Jules. "I'm going to go tell Millicent bye and visit the ladies' room. Meet you in the car."

Jen freshened up in the downstairs guest bathroom. Faint whispers and moans traveled through the vent. As she continued to primp in the mirror, the sounds grew louder and familiar. She stepped out and turned towards the stairwell, doubting herself as she climbed. The sound of Jay's voice grew stronger behind the door in Millicent's room.

Her eyes widened after cracking a thin opening. Jay stood behind Millicent, his body draped around hers, kissing her neck as she giggled and swayed in his arms.

She closed the door shut, dashed down the stairs, and went back into the bathroom. She stared at herself forming tears in the mirror, questioning her feelings and reaction to what she saw. After tiring of looking at herself, she rested her back against the door. One tear fell. She wiped it from her cheek, took another glimpse of herself in the mirror, and consoled her reflection. "That's all they get."

Frozen from the betrayal, thoughts of the times they all spent together flashed in her mind. She wondered if she had missed something over the years. Had she missed a flirtation between them, or signs they shared a connection? She came up empty.

A knock at the door broke her trance.

"Jen, are you alright?" Jules asked.

She opened the door. "Yeah. You ready to go?"

"Been ready. There's a guy outside asking where he should park."

Jen scoffed as he rang the doorbell.

"You sure you okay? You seem upset. Did Jay say something to you?"

"I'm fine. Really. Let's get out of here."

Walt stood at the door with flowers and a bottle of wine. Nervously he smiled. "You must be Todd and Landon."

"No," Jen replied sharply.

Jules scowled at her tone. "They are in the back. Julian." His hand reached forward.

"Walter," he replied, shaking Jules's hand.

"And this is Jen."

"You must be Millicent's date. She's been waiting on you to arrive. Nice to finally meet you. We were actually on our way out, but please come in. Everyone is on the deck. Just go right through those doors." Jen pointed past the kitchen.

"Nice meeting you."

As Jen and Jules finagled their way between the cars parked in the yard, Jay stepped onto the porch with his phone to his ear. Jen's face turned red. "Do you need me to drive?"

Jules huffed. "Something definitely happened. You're acting strange out of the blue."

"Now is not the time. Just get me out of here. Please," she begged as Todd pulled up behind them.

He waved to them leaving, receiving a cold stare and cut eyes as the car drove away. Jay met him in the driveway, smoking a joint.

"What's with them?" Todd asked Jay.

"With who?"

"Jen and Miami Beat."

Jay laughed. "That was probably my best name for him, ain't it? Shit, I don't know. I haven't said a word to either of them. You got problems of your own from what I hear. Your ole lady's out back crying. You got your hands full, T." Jay passed the joint to Todd.

"Don't I know it." He inhaled a long toke.

"You think he said it?"

"Yup."

"Whatchu gon' do?"

"Shit if I know." He exhaled. "Let me go check on my wife. This is gonna be a long ass night."

"If you need some privacy, send Mills over to my house. I got a special place for her." Jay smirked.

"Shut up man." Todd laughed.

Their joking ceased immediately as they walked out to the deck. Todd's eyes rested on Landon's red face, and Jay's eyes widened at the sight of Millicent sitting next to Walt holding a bouquet of flowers in her hand. He whispered to Todd, "That's the po-po."

Todd looked over to Millicent. "Is this your friend who can't tell time?"

Walt stood up. "Sorry for being late. In my line of work, you never know when someone decides to do something stupid and force you to put in overtime."

"I'm just fucking with you. Todd. Glad you could make it." He offered a shake of hands..

"Walter Reed. And this is…" Walt's eyes shifted to Jay as his inquiry lingered.

"Jay. We met the other night." He grinned. "I see you found your way back."

"That I did."

"Well, enjoy what's left of the party. As for me it's over. Be easy, man."

Todd made his way over to Landon. He held her at the waist, waiting for a moment to interrupt Brian telling one of his long-winded stories. "I'm going to steal my wife away for a minute." He pulled her aside, surveying every eye upon them. "So everyone knows what happened, and you've been crying. You know I don't like seeing you sad." He kissed her cheek.

"How did it go?"

"He finally admitted that he said it."

"Did he say why?"

"No, but let's talk about it later. Right now I want to dance with my wife, get drunk, and send these people home."

"We could send them home now. Both guests of honor have left so…"

Todd laughed. "And so has Jay."

"Don't get me started on him."

"What did the homie do now to piss you off."

Landon pulled back from Todd. "Read this text from Jen."

Todd guffawed with a smile fighting for a place on the sides of his mouth. "Yo! That motherfucker!" he exclaimed in a whisper.

Landon took the joke further. "More like friend fucker."

Todd laughed hysterically and glanced at Millicent sitting with Walt on the back porch. She looked like a deer trapped in headlights, bored out of her mind as the cop yapped his gums endlessly. Todd pulled Landon close, chuckling in her ear. "Yeah, it's time to send everyone home."

CHAPTER 37

IT'S A NO FOR ME

MILLICENT

One by one, they rid the house of their guests, with Walt and Millicent as the exception. For at least an hour, Todd and Landon sat with them listening to music, and listening to Walt tell them about the high speed car chase that nearly killed him before he made it to the party.

Todd took more of an interest in him than he did Jules. Landon loved when he engaged with others besides Jay, showing an interest in new avenues and personalities.

"We should get together and go out on a double date one night." Landon suggested.

Todd caught Millicent sneaking a dirty look her way and laughed to himself.

"Sounds good to me. I'll wait on Millicent here to tell me when's a good time, and hope to make it happen. And on that note, I better get going. It's been a hell of a day, but I wouldn't dare keep this young lady hanging on a string. I had a good time tonight. Lovely meeting you two."

"Let me show you out." Millicent hopped to her feet.

The sky was black above them, and so was Millicent's heart, dragging her feet to come clean with Walt waiting for a kiss good night.

"I need to tell you something," she said.

"I can tell there is someone else."

"Huh? No. Um. I put my house up for sale. I'm not coming back to Toledo.

I've been offered a job and will move out of my friend's house once my place is out of escrow."

"Sounds like you're saying we should quit while we're ahead."

Millicent took a deep breath and bit her fingernails.

"I respect you letting me down easy. But what was with the texts you've been sending me?"

"I do like you. It's just not the right time. I hope you understand?"

Walt sighed. "I would understand if you allowed me to take you out on a proper date. One where I'm not late. And if you want to write me off after that, I'll bow out of the running."

Millicent blushed. "And when do you propose we go on this date?"

"How's tomorrow? I'll settle for a late lunch date to not put any pressure on you."

"You would drive all the way home tonight, and back here again tomorrow just to take me out?"

"Pick you up at three." Walt kissed the back of her hand and left.

Millicent followed the sound of dishes clanking in the kitchen. Landon stopped wrapping food with foil and loading the dishwasher, and stared at her, hoping she'd crack.

"He's good for you." Landon led to kill the silence between them. "You won't find another good one like him is all I'm saying. He's a good catch. He's handsome, well-mannered, polite, attentive, a conversationalist with an actual job this time. When was the last time a man brought you flowers?"

"I don't know."

"And excuse me for saying, but I can tell he has a nice body. Those broad shoulders on that smooth chocolate skin, and bald head." Landon sucked her teeth. "You are crazy to let him slip through your fingers. I'm trying to understand why you aren't in the car going home with him tonight. He was practically begging you to like him with those slanted smoldering eyes."

"We have brunch tomorrow."

"Girl, fuck brunch. A fine ass man drove out of his way to see you to safety, came to meet your friends, brought you flowers and the host a bottle of wine. What do you want?"

"Chemistry. I want chemistry. Hell, you felt more for him than I did. Do you want his number?"

"I'll take it if Todd doesn't get his shit together."

"Girl, please. Todd is crazy about you, and you ain't going nowhere. You two are just going through a rough patch."

Landon sighed. "Nice try. We're talking about you."

Millicent laughed off Landon's attempt to steer the conversation. The buzzing of her cell phone silenced the both of them and they stared at each with guilt ridden eyes.

Jay: You still over there entertaining five-0?

No: Millicent

Jay: Are you sliding through or am I gonna have to kidnap you?

Let me think on it: Millicent

Jay: Quit playing. Your mind is already made up.

Cocky much?: Millicent

Jay: I'm trying to☺

After watching Millicent with a close eye, Landon pried. "You've got that look. What did he say?" Millicent continued to text and ignored her question. Landon stopped talking. She looked on as Millicent typed a mile a minute, blushing and smiling every time she pressed send..

"You were saying?" Millicent asked Landon.

"Who is that?"

"I'm sorry, why is this conversation so weird?" Millicent frowned.

"I'm trying to see where your head is."

The phone buzzed again.

Jay: I'm ready to see you now. #unfinishedbusiness

Millicent blurted, "Landon, I think you and Todd could use some privacy tonight after what happened today. I'll be back in time for brunch tomorrow."

"Where are you staying?" Landon giggled.

"I don't follow."

"Toledo or Jay's house?"

The look of a stuck deer returned to her face. Landon packed the foil covered dishes into the fridge, laughing like a movie villain. "So Jay fucks that good huh?" Her laugh grew louder and insulting.

"How do you know?" Millicent whispered.

"Why are you whispering? Todd knows what y'all did in the upstairs of his house."

"But how?"

"Jen saw you."

"Oh fuck. I'm not coming to brunch tomorrow."

"Yeah, if I were you I probably wouldn't."

"How the hell did this happen? You two have hated each other for so long."

"Landon, it was so intense. I have no idea how we got here. I agreed to go over his house and talk about it."

"You must think I'm slow. Ain't no talking happening over there tonight." Landon snickered.

"Jen hates me, doesn't she?"

Landon shrugged. "I don't know. If she does, you can't blame her."

"I have been pushing Jay away for weeks. I told him I didn't want to hurt Jen, but he refused to let up."

"Because he's Jay. He's used to getting what he wants."

"So what should I do?"

"The safest choice is Walt, but you're grown. Do what you want. Technically, you already have. So…"

Millicent stared at the latest message on her phone. She exhaled deeply and typed her reply as Landon shamed her with whimsical eyes.

"Don't wait up."

CHAPTER 38

THE STRAW

LANDON

The sink was clear, the counters wiped, and the final light switched off for the night. The hours she spent avoiding her husband were hours he spent waiting for her to come to bed, and a looming conversation of the mishap they dreaded, but needed to have.

Landon climbed in bed, sighed, and turned her back to her husband. He sat up against the headrest, shirtless and bright-eyed.

"This is the first time in weeks we've had the house to ourselves, and this is how we're going to spend it?"

"I thought you were sleep."

"I waited up for you." Todd stared at her back, waiting for her to face him.

She didn't budge. "You know I can't go to bed with dishes in the sink. And after Millicent left, Jen canceled brunch. I figured I should tackle everything tonight so I can sleep in and relax tomorrow. Good night."

"Landon, you know damn well we can't go to bed like this."

"I know we shouldn't, but I was hoping after we came together to get everyone out of here tonight, we could just go with that and call it a night. I'm tired."

"Landon, the boy is my son. I can't send him home every time he does something you don't like."

She rolled her body and faced him. "Is that what his mother said to you?"

"No, that's me telling you that I'm not doing that again. I only did it tonight because we had a house full of people. But don't ask me to do that again."

Landon sat up in the bed and looked straight ahead. She replayed Todd's words, mouthing them to herself over and over until she worked herself into a tizzy.

She stared at him as if he had stolen money from her purse. "Don't ask– you– to make me feel comfortable in my own house? Don't ask –you– to have my back, like you've been asking me to have yours? And don't bring light to what threatens me– if your son is involved? Did I hear that correctly?"

"I didn't say..."

"Not in those words, but it's the same thing. You know, against my wishes and better judgment, I went along with this because you promised everything was going to be fine. For you, I stayed. I put in effort. And what do I get? A pre-meditated threat from a child that could ruin me, and his daddy telling me how shit is going to be no matter what."

"I didn't say..."

"But you did. Just not in those words. How can you not see what he said is no laughing matter? This shit is serious, and you're instructing me to take it lightly."

"I had a talk with him. He doesn't know why he said it, but I'm going to work with him so he doesn't do anything to make you not want to be around him."

"Work with him where? Here?" Landon raised her voice.

"So you're back on that?"

"I am." Landon took a breath. "I don't hate the boy, but I don't trust him after tonight. I need to tread carefully around him. I can't make where I stand any clearer. I hope you get that. And again, good night. Love you."

Landon turned her back to Todd a second time and drifted off to sleep with ease. He sat on the edge of the bed, cradling his head between his legs as his feet tapped the top of his leather slippers below the foot board.

In the morning, Landon reached over to Todd's side of the bed. She opened her eyes when cold sheets stunned her fingertips and groaned. "And so it begins." She threw on lounge wear to put on a pot of coffee, fixing Todd's the way he liked, one cream, one sugar, and added a hack his family swore by– a pinch of salt. She strolled into his man cave. The television was off, the bar light was blacked, and the blanket resting on the corner of the sofa was still folded with the creases and tucked triangles on the edges. She checked the backyard. No Todd. She peeped through the shutters, assuming she would catch a glimpse of him finally cutting the branches that were scratching against the living room windows. Still no sign of Todd. Her face turned to stone when she made her way to the garage and saw his car was gone, and the reality of their new chapter crept in their house without a grace period, or manual on how to navigate through the troubled waters drowning them.

CHAPTER 39

HOUSE OF WHORES

JEN

Jen's hidden rage didn't fool Jules. He missed his flight, concerned he was on the verge of losing her a second time. With Max spending the night, he checked into the room next door. "Let's eat breakfast downstairs. You, me, and little man," he suggested, standing outside what was his room the night before.

"I canceled brunch with the girls, so that works." She looked over her shoulder before giving Jules a kiss good night.

"And you're sure you're alright?" he hounded her.

The light in her eyes dimmed. "I'll tell you about it tomorrow. I need to sleep on it before speaking on how I feel at the moment."

"Just tell me. Is it me?"

"It's not you. You've been great."

Jules exhaled and snuck a quick peck to her lips.

In the morning, he surprised Jen and Max wearing his swim shorts to break-fast. "Somebody wanted to go swimming today, right?" Max jumped up and down pulling off his pajamas.

"Thank you," Millicent mouthed.

"I couldn't sleep much, so I ordered room service last night. It was nothing to brag about. After the pool, I'm taking you two to lunch. Wherever you want to go."

"It'll be just you and me. Max has been invited to a birthday party at one o'clock."

"I better impress him in the water then."

To Jules, Jen seemed more like herself sitting by the pool watching him lose swim races to Max. As the love of Jen's life warmed up to him, he saw a life with them both in Miami.

On the way back to their rooms, he whispered in her ear as Max ran ahead of them down the hall. "You can't be without him. Bring him to live with us."

"I will have a battle on my hands to do so. It would have to be shared custody."

"Have you asked?"

"I will, but I know who and what I'm up against."

On the way to the birthday party, Jen asked Max if he would like to leave Detroit and move with her to Miami.

"Is Daddy coming too?"

"No, baby. You and I will live with Julian."

"I want Daddy to come too."

"He will visit you whenever you want."

Max frowned. "When are you moving back in our house?"

Jen felt a sharp pain in her chest. Knots formed around her heart, and she teared up behind her sunglasses. "Look, Mrs. Latham is already here to watch you at the party. Mommy has to go see Mrs. Landon for a second. But I promise I'll be right back to pick you up. Go have fun."

Jules saw Jen wipe the second tear dripping below her lens. "I'll take him over to her," he offered.

She looked away from them and stared at herself in the side view mirror. Caught in a daze, she missed Mrs. Latham and Max waving goodbye to her as Jules raced back to the car.

"Jen, I can't stay in the dark much longer. What has you so upset?"

"Plug in this address," she said.

"That's not an answer."

"I'm about to show you what's bothering me."

She entered her old home and exhaled a deep breath at the scent of loud vanilla musk diffusing from the plug at the entrance. "This place hasn't been dusted in weeks," she mumbled, tapping her heels across the hardwood floor in the living room. Jay burst from the back of the house— dick slinging with his gun cocked pointing at Jen. She sat on the couch. "Put that away." She fanned him off.

"What the fuck are you doing in here? Where's my boy?" He placed the safety on the gun and hid it behind his back.

"Birthday party. Whose car is out front?"

"You don't live here no more, Jen."

"Did she tell you I know?"

Jay covered his penis with his free hand. "Yeah. She told me."

"Tell her to come out."

"Jen. Why are you here?"

"I'm testing myself."

"I think it's best if you come back later on so we can talk about this. I'on want no drama at my house, Jen. You know what's up."

"I do." She shook her head. "How long?"

Jay sighed and locked eyes with her. "A day."

"You expect me to believe that?"

"I don't have a reason to lie."

"Never behind my back?" Jen raised her brow.

"Now I've down some stupid shit, but I wouldn't do you like that. Neither would she."

"How did it happen?"

"Damn, Jen! Come on!" Jay shuddered.

"You know I know where the guns are hidden." Jen pointed a gun made with her thumb and index finger at Jay. "Bloooow! Right in the pinga. The thing you've tricked to death."

"The fuck, Jen." Jay softened his tone. "I'm to blame. I went after her when she moved in with L. She gave me the cold shoulder until yesterday. It just happened."

"You love her?"

Jay stuttered. "Th-th-this just started last night Jen!"

Jen shook her head and scoffed. Her scoff morphed into an inaudible whispering monologue, followed by an uncontrollable snicker. Jay looked over his shoulder and eyed Millicent peeping through a crack from his bedroom door.

Jen's chuckles stopped. "I could tell the last time we talked you were falling for someone, but damn, I didn't expect this." She rose from the couch. "What is with you? Do you get off by doing fucked up shit to me? Were my feelings a game to you?"

"I can never make up all the wrong I've done to you. I took care of you, but I know that wasn't enough."

"Loyalty is all I wanted."

"I know that. But don't act like you didn't leave me for that pretty mother-fucker when I was trying to make things right between us."

"You are full of jokes. Making things right by fucking my friend." Jen sucked her teeth. "I have the answer I was looking for. I don't care. I'm not losing anything here. You were never going to be what I needed." Jen smiled. "And lawyer up. I'm coming back for my boy. If you still want to be in his life, we can set up visitation, but he's coming with me."

"I'll see you in court."

Jen grinned. "He's all I have, and I will not lose. And I'd kill you if I did."

"She means it, Jay. Don't push her." Millicent's voice echoed down the hall.

"You might want to listen to your new fuck buddy."

CHAPTER 40

EVERY GIRL HAS A SECRET

MILLICENT

Jen strolled out of the house that used to be hers and left the door open. Jay secured the house and told Millicent it was safe to come out. She cut the corner draped in a sheet, and threw Jay his shorts.

"What did she mean I need to listen to you?" he asked.

"Give her some time to cool off. I'm not at liberty to say more than that."

"Sounds like you know something I don't."

Millicent looked at the clock on the wall. "Oh shit. I forgot to cancel my date with…"

"You better not say that cop."

"He's nice. He doesn't deserve to get stood up."

"Fuck him. I got you."

"But for how long? The way you stuttered when Jen asked if you loved me says I need to tread carefully with you."

"I don't throw that word around, Mills. But I do feel something for you. And I don't want you to leave. I want you to move out of those married folk's house, and move in with me and my boy. They need privacy right now, and I don't want you to be alone. Everything is out in the open now. Let me make you feel safe. Let me take care of you."

"I can take care of myself."

"But you don't have to. Don't act like you don't know me. You know how I roll."

"That's just it. I don't know you. What's your favorite food?"

"Steak. What's yours?"

"Anything Italian. Who is your favorite rapper?"

"Snoop and Jeezy." Jay nodded his head.

"Jeezy? Really?"

"What's wrong with Jeezy?"

"Nothing's wrong with him...I mean, I like to turn on trap music in my cute clothes riding to work sometimes, but he hasn't been out long enough to be someone's favorite rapper."

"Who is yours?"

"I love J. Cole, Andre 3000, and Kendrick Lamar."

"What could your boughetto ass possibly know about Kendrick Lamar?"

"I know *'We Gon' Be Alright.'*" Millicent sang in tune.

"Look at you." Jay curved the side of his lips. "Mills has a cool side."

"Don't seem so shocked."

"I took you for a Swiftee."

Millicent choked on a laugh. "The fact you know what that is, is unbelievable."

"Why? Because I look like I don't listen to Taylor Swift?"

"Name one song by her."

"This one seems appropriate after what just happened." Jay paused, staring into her eyes. "'*W-e–e-Are-Never-Ever-Ever.*'"

"Okay stop. I believe you." Millicent held up her hands, and the sheet covering her naked body fell to the floor.

"See we have more in common than you thought." Jay snatched the sheet. "And right now I want to get back to our unfinished business."

"What about my date?"

"Like I said earlier. Fuck the police."

Chapter 41

Which One of Us Is The Fool

Landon

Ten minutes early this time, Walt arrived at The Jeffries' home. A sudden shower formed above him, and he frowned at the sky before taking cover under the porch. He rang the doorbell, shaking off beads of water before they absorbed into his shirt.

Landon opened the door dressed in a tracksuit and sunglasses. She gasped at the flash of lightning striking behind him. A thunderous roar shook the house, and rattled the light fixture above Walt's head.

"Please come in. I can't let you stand outside in this mess." She waved him inside. "I had no idea it was supposed to rain today."

"Neither did I. Did I catch you on your way out?" He alluded to her sunglasses.

"The rain has changed those plans. I was going to go for a run and clear my head."

"Bad day?"

"I'm afraid to say I'm not alone in that department. Millicent isn't here."

"I am a little early."

"What time were your plans?"

Walt raised a brow. "You said were— as if— you don't plan on her showing up?"

Landon scowled.

Walt raised both brows. "Did something happen?"

"A lot happened."

Landon's body language and the shakiness in her voice forced Walt to switch into work mode. "I'm not in uniform, but I'm still an officer of the law. May I ask, is everything okay?" He asked, quickly getting over the news he was being stood up.

"Everything's fine. Why do you ask?"

"Your husband hasn't come to say hello. I thought we got along pretty okay last night. Millicent isn't here for our date, yet here you are telling me I've been stood up behind a pair of sunglasses on a rainy day, inside your house no less."

"I guess it's safe to say you don't know how to clock out, do you?"

"I'd feel a lot better if I could make sure you aren't hiding something behind those shades. Please?"

Landon huffed. "I'm not hiding anything. I just had a little crying spell, and my eyes are puffy."

"Still, if you don't mind." Walt insisted.

Landon lowered her lenses. "See. Puffy. I told you I'm fine." She chuckled.

"You're laughing. That's a good sign."

"I can't believe you thought I was a battered woman. Todd would never."

"He didn't give me that impression, but you never know what goes on behind closed doors. Sorry for prying. The job seems to never leave me, and I had to be sure," he said, opening the door.

"I appreciate it. It's still coming down pretty hard out there."

"Yeah, I don't think you're going to get that run in today." He gazed at Landon staring at the rain pouring onto the porch. "I'm going to make my way back to my side before the roads get flooded. Here's my card. Use it if you need anything."

"Thank you, but I don't need it. Trust me. These bags won't be under my eyes for much longer."

Walt's face twitched from her choice of words. He stepped on the porch and turned around. "Landon, if you don't mind my asking, am I wrong to think there might be something going on between Millicent and that Jay character?"

Landon snickered. "Jay character. You summed him up in one word," she replied, and turned silent.

Walt waited for her to confirm. "Well, it was nice seeing you again. You take care of yourself."

Landon closed the door and called Millicent one more time. She watched Walt strut his broad shoulders and muscular chest down the pavement through the blinds. The prompt beeped to leave a message on Millicent's voicemail, and she said, "I'm watching your shot at happiness walk away while you lay it low and wide for Juy of all people. I hope you know what you're doing."

CHAPTER 42

INSULT TO INJURY

LANDON

The Jeffries had become strangers in their house. The once model of what a husband should be was now cold to his better half, and she, disengaging and curt. With no resolve of the matter with the child, and Landon insistent he was not welcome in the home, the brick wall they hit stacked layers between them a bulldozer couldn't knock down.

Todd's first attempt to reconcile came weeks later, reminding her of his mother's birthday party. Landon knew it was his way of trying to find a way back into her world. She agreed to tag along, disheartened by the continued struggling conversation between them in the car. Her heart ached at every beat of silence. Her body shivered of fear. They were in uncharted waters, with no sign of rescue.

The pain in her chest grew stronger when she noticed Ephram playing outside with the other children. She sighed at Todd's lack of communication. "I should have known and should have stayed home," she said to herself.

"What's that?"

"Nothing." She mumbled below her breath. "God be with me today."

Mother Jeffries was aware of Landon's decision to postpone having a child. She pushed for her to change her mind when Todd shared the news of a spontaneous miscarriage Landon suffered while they were engaged, so it was no shock of her passive aggressive digs, and gloating about Ephram in front of the entire family.

The insurmountable sneaky looks, smirks, and pity taps on Landon's shoulder from the family were endured with grace, and a poker face, while she screamed on the inside.

"Isn't he the cutest little thing?" said Mother Jeffries.

Her sister chimed in."He looks just like Todd and PJ when they were boys." She turned to Landon. "Wonder what y'alls baby would look like?"

Mother Jeffries turned up her nose. "We'll never know. She has a career."

"We sure won't," Landon snapped back, and made her exit.

She found herself a spot on the front porch as she waited for a cab. The smell of wood burning in the backyard comforted her as her emotions ran high, thinking of the baby she lost. She wondered if it were a boy would it have looked like him, and the pain in her chest churned, reflecting on the wound that never healed.

The more she held back her tears, the wider the pain spread. Reality sunk in she was no longer a part of Todd's family. Their marriage was over, and love wasn't enough to save them. A smile crept on her face when she least expected it. She'd arrived at the inevitable moment she feared for months. To begin a new chapter of her life and walk away gracefully, giving Todd what he desperately wanted. To be a father.

PJ appeared out of nowhere, standing in front of Landon, reeking of beer, weed, and smoke from the fire out back. She gasped and jumped when he called her name.

"Landon, whatchu doing out here by yourself?"

"Getting some fresh air. Where did you come from?"

PJ pointed to the side of the house. "You were gone just now. What's on my favorite sister-in-law's mind?"

"You got another one I don't know about?" Landon smiled.

PJ laughed. "Yeah, I do. You know Nardo, my sister's husband. That's the biggest bitch I know."

They both cackled.

"I know you're out here 'cause them hens is clucking inside, ain't they?"

Landon rolled her eyes.

"Todd told me what's going on. I hate y'all having problems. My brother has always been crazy about you. To see you two fizzle out over something like this. Be tough, Sis. Don't let nobody come in and fuck up what the two of y'all got."

"I can't compete with a man and his seed."

"I told my brother he should have put his foot up that boy's ass and handled it. That was some fucked up shit to say. I don't know, Sis. I'm witchu on this one.

I've been to jail more times than I care to think of, and it ain't no place for the likes of you. I wouldn't want to be around the little joker either if he said some shit like that to me either."

"PJ, you are the only person who agrees with me. Thank you for helping me realize I am not crazy."

"You ain't crazy. These kids on some next shit these days. It's a little bad ass down the street that talks so much shit to me when I walk to the corner store. I ride Little Man's bike past his house to make the insults go by faster."

Landon held her side laughing. "What does he say to you?"

"One time he followed me and called me a mama's boy. Said I was still teetin,' and my teeth was gonna rotten from suckin' old ass sour milk. Last week, I thought I was in the clear. His little ass shoulda been in school, but he was home playing hooky. That little fucker lifted up the window and shouted, "Fuck you, punk ass PJ, with your dirty bitch ass!"

"No he didn't." Landon cackled.

"I ain't lying. I threw a rock at his window. I'm a bust his little ass one day."

Landon held her chest as the pain subsided but grew tight from the heavy laughter PJ blessed her with.

"I needed that laugh. But don't go back to jail beating up somebody's child."

"That's where you're wrong. That ain't a child. That's a demon hiding inside a kid's body. Fuck them kids."

The taxi drove up, and Landon bounced from the porch. "Do me a favor and tell your brother I'm gone."

"No, Sis. Don't just up and leave. You know how family is."

"I do. But I don't think I'm a part of this one anymore." Landon blew PJ a kiss. "See you 'round, maybe."

In the back of the cab, Landon's tears dropped like water from a faucet. The faces of all of her friends flashed in her head to call for comfort, but the only one she wanted to hear from was Jen.

With murmured speech and endless sniffles, she managed to greet Jen coherently. "Can you talk?"

"Always for you. What's going on? Millicent sleeping with your man too?" Jen joked.

Landon screamed out a laugh, and her cry paused. "How did you say that calm and carefree?"

"Chile, I'm over it. I hope your friend is happy with her community peen. Now were you crying, or was I hearing things?"

"I was, but thanks to you I'm crying and laughing. I'm glad I called you."

"Talk to me."

"Todd and I are over."

"Don't say that."

"We are."

"You wouldn't be crying if you didn't still love him."

"I will always love him, but I can't live like this. Neither of us are happy, and the only person who agrees with me is PJ."

"Now Landon, I'm on your side too. But I wouldn't go around bragging that PJ is your support system with his crazy ass." Jen chuckled.

"PJ is cool. But you wanna know something eerie?"

"Besides the fact you are listening to PJ, please."

"The little boy looks more like him than he does Todd."

Jen scoffed. "That happens in families though."

"But remember when this first came to light the guys said the mother got around?"

"I see where you're going, but Landon, he took a test. It's his son. I don't think you're ever going to make peace with that."

"You're right. I don't know why I'm backtracking. I've already made up my mind. I am going to file. I feel like Todd wants to, but he's doing that man thing where they push the woman to take action so the blame doesn't reside with him."

"I know exactly what you mean. Men do stupid shit like that all the time. Fucking cowards." Jen clicked her teeth. "You should come down here before making any moves. Come help me with my makeup bar and step away for a while."

"If I won't be imposing I'd love to get away for a few days."

"Call me with your flight details. Can't wait to see you."

The invitation to visit Jen didn't rust. Landon arrived home and booked the next flight down to Miami in the morning. Todd stumbled in the house as she packed for her trip.

"So that's it? You just leave and don't say shit to me?" Todd griped.

"I'm sure I wasn't missed."

Todd's speech slurred. "Why are you packing bags at this hour? You ain't going nowhere, Landon. You my wife. You carry my last name."

"I know I do. I'm going to spend a few days with Jen."

"You didn't discuss that with me." He snatched a blouse from her suitcase.

"We haven't discussed anything in weeks. Todd, you are out of your mind right now. The first conversation between us should not be when you're like this."

He threw her blouse on the floor. "You got something to say to me, then say it."

"Did you drive home like this?"

"Why you care? You left and didn't say shit to me. Don't you never pass messages to me through my brother again. You hear me?"

Landon sighed, holding in her laugh at how ridiculous he sounded. She picked up her blouse and placed it back in her luggage. Todd threw it back to the floor.

"Stop packing this fucking bag. You not going to see no Jen and get hooked up with one of Pretty Ricky's boy toys."

Landon laughed in his face.

"Don't laugh at me. I ain't say shit funny." He grabbed her and held her close. "I miss you, baby. Why you wanna leave me?"

"I'm not leaving you. I'm just going to see my friend for a few days."

"No." Todd sniffed her neck. "You always smell so good. Look what you did." He placed her hand on his manhood.

"I'm not fucking you like this. Get over yourself."

"You know you want to." Todd snickered.

Landon huffed. "I have something to ask you."

"Go ahead. Ask me anything baby."

"Is there a chance Ephram is PJ's son, and not yours?"

Todd pushed Landon away and looked at her in a way she'd never seen before. His red eyes, filled with hatred and disdain for her narrowed, and his voice raised so loudly, she was sure the neighbors heard their quarrel.

"I took a fucking test, Landon! It's just a child. They lie, They tell stories. They do bullshit. Give it a rest!"

Landon shuddered. "You know what, you're right. I am giving it a rest."

"What does that mean?"

Landon threw more clothing in her suitcase and stuffed her duffel bag until it overflowed and wouldn't zip.

"You've made a big deal about nothing. All you had to do was let it go. Why'd you do this to us baby? Huh?"

"Todd, I have wrestled with this for far too long. I can't anymore. You have been mad at me for how I reacted, and that isn't fair. We'll never agree on this, and I've made my peace with it. My flight leaves in the morning. I'll be back in a few days. We can talk about a separation when I get back, and when you're sober."

"I'm not leaving. You are the one talking about walking away."

Landon faced Todd and gazed into his eyes for the first time in weeks, searching for the version of him she once knew. The version she fell in love with. The husband that made her feel nothing came before her. He wasn't there.

"Todd, if Ephram had fallen, and I was the one to find him, I wonder would I somehow be blamed for that too."

"Landon, just let it go."

"And there's my answer!" Tears poured from her eyes. "No matter how that day played out, it's clear we are no longer what we once were. You are attached to another woman, and there isn't anything to change that. When I get back I'm filing for divorce, and I want to get through this as amicably as possible."

Landon stormed out of their bedroom and Todd ran after her. Down the stairs he stumbled, holding onto the railing and yelling in a drunken stupor. "We're not getting a divorce! What's gotten into you?! How you gon' leave me, girl? You know you love me. I'll unpack all those fuckin' bags! You hear me!"

"Don't follow me. Go sleep that shit off at Jay's house or something."

"I'm not leaving this house! You gonna have to burn this motherfucker down with me in it. I ain't leaving my house and you ain't leaving it either!"

Todd pressed on Landon's heels from room to room, cornering her in the kitchen. "Come here girl," he said in the low, slick tone that used to entice her. "You don't want me no more, baby?" He kissed her lips. Landon squirmed in his arms and blew a raspberry from her mouth. "Remember what we did on the counter a while back?"

"Todd, go to sleep! Please."

"I don't want to go to sleep. I wanna make love to my wife. You see what you do to me." He pressed his dick against her folds. "You don't wanna leave me. Do you? Tell me you were just bullshittin'."

Buzzing from his phone vibrated between them. Todd grinned on the side of his mouth and kissed Landon again. "I saw that look in your eye. That got you excited. You been handling business without me these past weeks." He cracked himself up and nibbled on her ear. "Where you keep your toys? Show me what you've been doing."

Landon maneuvered from his clutch. "Just answer your phone."

Todd's face turned squeamish when he answered, "Yeah."

"Thank you for letting E come today. He said he had a good time," Ephram's mother said faintly through the phone.

Landon shook her head and slapped her thigh.

Todd studied the aggravation in her face and stuttered. "Okay."

"He also mentioned your mother said you and your wife are having problems. If that's true, we can go on and give this a shot of being a family. E would love that."

"Nah, that's not true. And that's not happening. Is there a reason you're calling?"

"I just told you. People get together for the sake of their children all the time. You think about that."

He ended the call and held his head down. "I'll talk to my mother."

"No need. This isn't the marriage I signed up for."

CHAPTER 43

I'VE BEEN DRINKING & I'VE BEEN THINKING

JEN

Buried below Todd's arm, Landon slid to the side of the bed and escaped the hungover madness before it began. She arrived in Miami an emotional wreck, crying at the sight of Jen waiting for her at baggage claim.

"Stop crying. You're going to make me cry, and I'm trying to advertise my business." Jen teased.

"Take me to see it."

Tears rolled down Landon's cheek as she admired the light in Jen's face walking her through the make-up bar.

"You did it. You left behind all that toxic shit, and look at you. You're thriving. It's like you have a whole new life. You've given me hope."

"So your decision is final?" Jen squeezed her shoulder.

"I told him last night."

"So it's a heavy drinking kind of night, huh?"

"Let's start now."

Jules kept the drinks flowing while Landon and Jen hung outside at the pool.

"Are you sure you don't want me to call some friends over? Have a little party to get your mind off things?" he asked.

"I'm positive. This view and my friend is all I need."

"Let me know if you change your mind. Babe, I'm going to go make that run. Call me if you need anything."

"I'll be back, Landon. Let me walk him out."

Before the sun set, Landon was drawn into the waves roaring under the near dusk sky. She closed her eyes, placed her feet in the azure water and held her arms out wide. The breeze calmed the raging, confused spirit she brought with her to Miami, and the water cleansed her clouded mind. When she opened her eyes, she witnessed the sun slide below the blue horizon, and dropped a tear into the Atlantic.

"You alright?" Jen stood at her side.

"I think so." Landon pointed towards the sunset. " That was us. Falling off into the unknown."

"And like tomorrow morning, we'll rise again." Jen held her hand.

"I haven't listened to his messages. I feel free not hearing his voice. That's a good thing, right?"

"None of this is good, but it's a start to moving on. Don't let your thoughts beat you up. Hear me?"

"I'll try not to."

"Mine did for weeks. Most of all Milli Vanilli's fake ass. I think she hurt me more than Jay. I can't make sense of it." Jen kicked the water.

"Because you expected something like that from him."

"Right. Jay sticking and moving doesn't surprise me. But with her? Who would have ever thought?"

"Millicent's date. That's who." Landon laughed. "Poor guy drove all the way back to the city in the pouring rain the next day, and Millicent left him hanging. His instincts are sharp, that one. He asked if something was going on between them, and I had to cover for her when I was at my absolute worst."

"That guy was hot as fuck."

"Smoking!" Landon and Jen tossed water on each other.

"I'm glad Millicent fumbled that. As much as I am mad about what she's done, I still win."

"What do you mean?"

"I have Jules, and she has Jay." Jen spun around in the water dancing and screaming. "But now I have to rethink Jay having custody of Max. I don't want my baby calling Millicent 'Mommy.' I'd...You know."

Landon was familiar with that tone. Chills ran down her spine while her imagination ran wild on how Jen would have finished that sentence. She ended the silence with a confession.

"I'm going to be honest. Our friendship hasn't been the same lately either. I find myself questioning if she would have done the same thing to me."

"And you're wise to ask that question. I found myself thinking about some of the questionable things she's done and said over the years. Do you remember on our girls' trip when she said you were living vicariously through me in regards to an old flame?"

"Yes! I was pissed she brought that up! She was talking about my old crush, Reynaldo, back in Flint. The star of the baseball team who broke up with me and had everybody calling me DT."

"What is that?"

"A dick teaser." Landon blushed. "I deserved that nickname. I was too afraid of the dick back then, and I led on a lot of guys but never put out. I was a good girl." Landon laughed. "Until one night, I came real close to doing it with ole Rey Rey. We kissed and kissed and kissed until there was nothing left to kiss, so naturally he did what any horny teenage boy would do. He whipped his shit out and blinded my ass. I hadn't seen a lot of penises in real time, but I know the one I had in my hands would have destroyed my virgin ass. It was priceless."

Jen fell to her knees in the water laughing. "Priceless? Was it gold or something?"

"It should have been. It looked like one of those mushrooms you see growing out in a country field standing tall above the other shrooms that weren't so blessed. Wide, long, and pretty. Like I said, priceless."

"I may have to call Jules back for a quickie hearing you talk like this."

"I'm getting flustered myself just thinking about it. Anyway, Millicent knows that I will carry that moment with me forever. Before I met Todd, I confessed to her that I wanted to go back home and find him, have my way with him to kill the curiosity of what it felt like to be with such a man."

"Well, you might become a free woman soon. There's time to fulfill that dream, and if it's anything like me and Jules finding each other again, it's going to be so explosive I might feel it down here." Jen and Landon chuckled. "All this talk about pretty pipes has me riled up. Wear your earplugs tonight."

As Landon listened to her hosts moan, and the bed knock against the wall, her legs squeezed tightly around her hand. Her fingers rotated above her panties as eroticized thoughts owned her body. She was weeks without pleasure, thinking of the hard dick she left begging to please her at home. Her mind wandered, imagining Todd's lips against her nipples as Jules groaned in the other room loud enough to make her want to offer herself to whichever friend he said he could invite over.

Their echoes of pleasure invaded her mind, remembering the make-up fuck sessions she and Todd had over the years. How he made her scream with passion and climb the walls with spontaneous bouts of love making at any given time of the day. The more Jen shrieked of ecstasy, the raunchier her thoughts traveled, back to the high school lover she regretted passing over.

She replayed the night she nearly lost her virginity in her head. Her white shorts pulled to the side, her cotton bikinis shredded in the seat of her folds, and Reynaldo sucking all the juice from her cup. She grinded his face from the top of the slide on the playground where the shade from the trees blocked out the street light. His nose stimulated her clit, his hungry eyes looked up at her, begging her to agree to let him put in the tip.

"I'll let you do the finger," she said.

Reynaldo grinned at her permission, spread her soaked lips apart with his fingers, and hunched her with his dick about to rip through his briefs.

"I can tell you want to," he whispered.

"I do, but I'm scared."

"Don't be. I know what I'm doing."

"I don't want to get pregnant my first time."

"You won't."

"And I don't want to get called a heaux."

"Nobody's going to know."

He relieved his cock from the pressure overflowing in his shorts and rubbed it against her thigh. Landon jumped, "What's that?" she asked.

"That's how excited I am to be with you right now." Reynaldo lied.

Landon stroked his penis, disgusted by the fluid leaking out, and terrified at the girth between her palm.

"I'm still not ready. What if I give you a hand job?"

"Landon, I can't keep doing this with you." Reynaldo's soft tone turned harsh.

"I'm sorry. I'm just not ready."

"I was damn near in. Come on. Don't leave me like this." Reynaldo's foot slipped from the bottom step.

Landon covered her exposed nature and giggled. "See that's a sign. I can't let my first time be on a dirty park slide. Walk me home."

"Nah. You walk yourself."

Landon woke from the dream and opened her eyes. The grunts stopped next door, so did her recollection of the past. She reached for the light, unsatisfied and beaten as her phone lit with a text from Todd. *'Come home.'*

Jen found Landon sitting out on the deck at day break, stretched out beneath a blanket with a bottle of wine resting on the end table.

"Morning," said Landon, tipping her glass to Jen's empty hand.

"Are we skipping the mimosas and diving straight in today?"

"If I can stomach it. This is my second bottle. I'll pay you for them."

"Don't be silly." Jen placed the empty bottles in the blue bin. "Something set you off?"

"Todd. He messaged me last night. Two words. *'Come home'.*"

"So you saw the flowers?"

"What flowers?"

"Jules left them on the table. I thought they were for me, but the card said those exact same words. *'Come home.'*"

Landon scoffed. "I would prefer we didn't spend my last night here talking about him."

"Done. What do you want to do?"

"Honestly. Sleep."

"That's depression talking."

"And I welcome it. If you and Jules don't mind, I'd like to lie around all day and do absolutely nothing."

Jen wiped the tear strolling down her cheek. "You got it. Give me a holler if you need me."

"Thanks. I knew I came to the right place."

The sun circled the house while Landon drank and napped. Jen snuck in her room and left cheese, crackers, and mini sandwiches by her bed for when she woke, switching out her tray with fresh fruit and toasted bagels when she emerged the next morning. Landon hauled her luggage down the steps.

"Jen, you are a lifesaver. I don't know where I would be without you. Thank you for taking care of me."

"I love you like a sister."

"You are my sister. Remember that."

CHAPTER 44

HOME NOT SO SWEET HOME

TODD

Landon returned and dropped the bomb Todd feared. He sat on the edge of the bed with the world shut off, processing the words *trial separation* in his head.

His eyes were glued to the floor as Landon pranced in and out of the bedroom, glancing at him from the corner of her eyes, waiting for him to make a move or a sound. His lack of response made her break a sweat, and the confidence she lied to herself about, slowly crumbled.

"That's the second time you've said you don't want to be in this marriage," Todd mumbled. "What's going on? You hate me now or something?"

"I don't hate you. But you know as well as I do this isn't working."

"But you think living separate lives will work? Splitting up is not how you fix problems."

"Some problems can't be fixed. This is that problem."

"You are overreacting about this like a motherfucker." The muscles in Todd's arms flexed.

"Staying together when joy has been stripped from a union is not an option for me."

"So fuck my options is what you're saying?"

"Todd, answer this. The next time I have a problem with your son, what are you going to do? Be mad at me again, punish me for having my own feelings, force me to be present when I'm uncomfortable?"

"It's a major change that's going to take some time getting used to."

"I don't want to get used to it. I'm done."

"Done? Are we separating, or going straight for a divorce?"

Landon refused to look at Todd, or give him an answer.

Todd exhaled. "If it's a divorce you want, I'll give it to you. I'm done pleading my case."

He sped off into the night, drowning his sorrows at the bar, and venting to anyone who would listen. The bartender sent word to Jay he was needed. He arrived and shared a few shots with Todd, listening to his drunken stupor and make believe scenarios. When his speech slurred, Jay cut him off and delivered him home to the woman he spent all night ranting about.

"You did a number on my boy," he said.

"You did a number on my girl." Landon sassed.

"Yeah, yeah. Take it easy on him. And cut out all that separation talk, L. You know damn well ain't nobody gonna love you like my people. I never pegged you for the selfish type. Work this shit out. You hear me?"

"Thanks for watching out for him tonight." Landon shut her door.

She covered her better half with a blanket in the guest room downstairs. Todd grabbed her hand. "Look at my pretty wife." Landon ignored him, slid her hand away, and eased to the door. She shut off the light as her husband continued to mumble. "Don't leave me baby. I love you girl. Don't leave me baby."

His stupefied speech troubled Landon throughout the hours of the night. Guilt and fear of ending her marriage shot pains to her heart. She worried how he would take care of himself when he was on his own, and how she would manage the cold winter nights without him. With a clouded mind she tortured herself with what ifs and regret until she found herself laid next to him.

Todd inched behind her, kissed the back of her shoulder, and placed his arm around her waist. "I love you too. Don't give up on us," he said, mid-snore in his sleep.

Landon lied with him until the sun crept through the thin sheers on the window. Todd reached for her with one hand, and grabbed his morning wood with the other, expecting to grind his way back into his wife's good graces.

"Landon!" He sat up on the bed.

She popped her head inside the room. "Coffee is on the stove. It should help with that hangover."

"I'd prefer some of your coffee." Todd patted the sheets.

Landon blushed.

"Did I imagine you in my arms last night?" he asked, rubbing the crust from his eyes.

"No. I kept you company."

"You know next to me is where you'll always belong."

"Then keep it warm for me in ten years. I'm running late. Let's put a pin in this until tonight."

Work didn't distract Landon's mind from wrestling with her heart for a win. She enjoyed sleeping next to Todd, being in that familiar space of protection and love. In a haste, she prepared to escape the confines of being reeled in by her husband's charm and devilish good looks. He arrived home with flowers, candy, and passes for a matinee to the first movie they saw, blindsided with a note waiting for him under a magnet on the fridge.

I'll be working remotely for the rest of the week. Headed to my parents for a few days. We'll talk when I get back.

CHAPTER 45

SHE WENT TO FLINT

LANDON

Mother Davis knew the surprise visit from her eldest daughter came with the need of wisdom and approval. She welcomed the younger version of herself with loving arms and suspicion, happy to know she was still needed in her headstrong daughter's life.

Landon crossed over the Davis Family doormat, rushed by memories of her childhood. The fights between her and her younger sister Launa, standing on the stool to help her mother cook dinner, and the day she left for college, oblivious she would never live there anymore. The scent of blackberry cobbler and coffee stained in the walls brought the taste to the tip of her tongue. The pictures of her and Launa at prom hanging in the living room brought a smile to her face as she passed the hallway where the many talent show awards dressed the shelves near the piano.

Landon stopped and stared at the life size painting of her grandmother gracing the top of the staircase. It held her attention for so long, everything faded into the background.

"What brings you home?"

Landon gasped. "I didn't hear you walk up. Nice to see you too."

"That's no way to welcome your sister, is it, Launa?" Mother Davis chastised.

"I didn't mean anything by it, but seriously, when does Landon ever come home and it's not a holiday? Must be trouble in paradise."

"Why are you like this?" asked Landon. "Don't answer that. I know it's because you've been stuck here your entire life."

"And look who came back." Launa smirked.

"Girls."

"Sorry, Mama. I won't be staying long. This one has me already cutting my visit shorter than I planned."

"I hear fussing," Mr. Davis interrupted.

"Daddy!" Landon pushed Launa out of the way.

"Look at you. It's like looking at your mother all those years ago." Papa Davis wrapped his frail arms around Landon.

"Yay. Daddy's favorite daughter remembered where he lives," Launa mumbled.

"Chile, be happy we're all together again, and hush up with all that griping and carrying on. I thought you had to go to work?" Mother Davis added.

"On my way like a good soldier." Launa laughed at her sarcasm alone. "Tough crowd. Don't forget Tim's bus will be here at 3:15."

"I don't need reminding." Mother Davis fanned her off.

Landon shook her head at her sister talking under her breath, stomping down the stairs. Mother Davis sighed and rubbed the sides of her face with her palms.

"Just once I wish my prayer came true and you girls got along."

"We do get along. Once she gets all of that hostility out, we'll be fine."

"I hope so. I don't want you to cut your stay short. But to what do we owe the pleasure?" Mother Davis asked. "Is she right about trouble in paradise? I don't see your better half with you."

"I did come home to share some news in person, and get your advice on a certain matter."

"Well, let's go into the kitchen. This sounds like it calls for comfort food."

Mother Davis pulled out pots, pans, leftover dinner, and filled a bowl with butter and flour. As she rolled fresh biscuits, Landon and her dad sat at the breakfast table where her nephew, Tim, drew pencil and crayon markings into the wood.

"It's like looking into a time machine, baby girl."

"I wish to age as beautifully as Mama."

Landon's natural coiled hair was exactly like her mother's. She shared her light brown eyes, symmetrical face, and full lips, but took after father with a light brown complexion. The only feature she and Launa shared. Launa, on the other hand, was her father's child. A spitting image of him with coarser and fuller hair, with nothing of Laura Lee except for her petite shape and small feet.

As the chicken boiled and the biscuits entered the oven, Mother Davis probed Landon to find out what was going on.

"How is my son-in-law?"

"Pretty upset with me. I came home because I wanted to tell you in person that I've decided to file for a divorce. I know this is not what marriage is about, and I wish I could have stuck it out like you two, but we have a situation that is not going to go away anytime soon, and I am unhappy."

"Well, I was hoping for the good news of a possible grandchild." Father Davis sighed.

"But Todd is a good boy." Mother Davis dropped her hand from her hip. "I don't understand. Did he put hands on you? Cheat on you?"

"No, and not that I know of."

"Well, if he didn't cheat on you or beat on you, it must be you."

"I guess I am to blame. I said for better or for worse, but the worse involves a child he fathered before we met, and the little boy has been causing us to have problems."

"How old is the boy?"

"Eight."

"I'm not happy about hearing the word divorce. What kind of problems is the boy causing?"

"He threatened to put me in jail for pushing him down the stairs."

Mother Davis held her chest. "What kind of child is this? And what did Todd say?"

Landon's voice choked. "In a nutshell, I need to get over it."

Father Davis scoffed, "Baby girl, I love Todd. And I trusted him with your hand. But if he isn't making you feel like the diamond you are, I'll support you leaving. I know you love him, so it must be pretty bad in your house if you want to end your marriage with him."

Her mother smacked her father's arm. "Don't be so hasty. Aren't you afraid of being alone, Landon? Your sister says there aren't any good men out there, and judging from what she's brought home, she is telling the truth. They don't make'em like they used to. And Todd is a good one. Careful you haven't already driven him into the arms of another woman while yours end up empty."

"I can survive on my own, Mama."

"I'm not talking about survival. I'm talking about loneliness." Mother Davis kissed her teeth. "It's okay to weather some storms."

Father Davis interrupted, "But Laura Lee, some storms come around and wipe shit out, leaving people to start from scratch. If you need a new start, your Daddy has your back."

Mother Davis threw her hands up. "I guess my advice ain't worth a damn."

Landon kissed her mother. "Of course it is. Just have my back when Launa throws this in my face."

"Don't pay your sister no mind. She has no room to talk."

"What you know, Mama?"

Mother Davis tightened her lips and removed the biscuits from the oven humming a church hymn to stop from spreading family gossip Landon knew the sound of her mother's hymn meant to move on. She admired the handmade crafts her nephew created that lined the kitchen walls while her dad updated her on his plans for retirement, and schooling her about putting her money into separate bank accounts before the legal proceedings.

"You know who else is divorced? The Felix boy from down the street. Wife took him to the cleaners. He had to move home."

"I'm not worried about that, Daddy."

"You know who ain't never got married? Reynaldo. Saw him at the football game last Friday night."

Landon's interest grew in her father's stories after hearing Reynaldo's name. His admiration for the former baseball star increased her curiosity of how he turned out after so many years. She chuckled internally, recalling her recent conversation about him with Jen.

"How is Reynaldo? I haven't heard that name in years."

Mother Davis raised a brow.

Papa Davis smiled. "He's doing good. Took an assistant coaching job at your alma mater."

"Really? Good for him."

"You know, I always thought you would end up with him. Thought I was going to be flying off to games, sitting in a sky box somewhere watching him play."

"I don't know why you thought that, Daddy. We were kids. Nothing serious."

"You were stuck on those old rich boys from across the bridge. Only my daughter would give the baseball star the pink slip to chase pretty boys."

"It was all for the best. You dodged a bullet." Mother Davis winked at her.

Landon gave her mother the side eye before excusing herself to unpack her car. She settled in her old room and napped before her nephew made it home from school, demanding the attention of everyone in the house. His footsteps stomped up and down the hallway, waking Landon. She listened to him make noise throughout the house, putting a stop to it with a kiss to his forehead. "You've gotten so big." She stole sugar from his cheek. Tim blushed and sat down, studying the aunt he hadn't seen in months.

Landon recognized the way she interacted with her nephew was how she wished she interacted with Ephram. Quickly she recognized the difference, and her decision became clearer than it had before. She knew she was making the right choice to set Todd free to be a father, and begin her journey to finding the happiness she'd lost.

Launa strolled in after dinner. Landon sat on the screened porch in the dark, snickering at her loose walk coming down the sidewalk.

"You party through the week, I see." Landon dug at her.

"I thought you would have been halfway back to your bougie world by now. Tell me, how has the world come crashing down on your head?" Launa laughed.

"Silly of me to wait out here for you with hopes we could talk like sisters for once. What was I thinking? I must be crazy for trying."

"You called me a heaux the last time you wanted to have a sisterly chat. You remember that?"

"Yeah, I remember." Landon snickered. "I wouldn't have called you that if you weren't so nasty to me."

"Doesn't sound like an apology."

"You know what, never mind." Landon opened the door to go inside.

"That's right." Launa clapped her hands. "Run off like always. Run back to your degree and your big house and your stuck up husband thinking y'all are better than everybody else."

"I don't walk around thinking I'm better than anyone, and Todd is far from stuck up. You're just mad I left you behind."

"Don't act like you are my savior, L boogie. What you gonna do? You gon' rescue me? You gon' take me under your wing and make me dress like you and act like you? No thanks."

"Just tell me what I did that caused you to hate me so much."

"Ain't nobody got time to be hatin' you. You don't make my world go round."

Landon stormed into the house. Launa stayed behind on the porch and sat where her sister had. "It's good to have you home, Sis." She raised her glass punch bottle and took a swig.

The next morning, Tim asked his aunt to drive him to school. "My friends said you have the coolest car," he said. Launa gritted her teeth at his request. Landon happily did what her nephew asked of her, getting a brief taste of what life would be like as a mom. For two days she got up early every morning, rushed to get two people out of the house, helped her mom take care of the home, prepared meals, and caught up with her work. And after those two days, she understood why her sister was so bitter and angry.

Neither sister apologized with words. They carried on as if jabs hadn't been exchanged, and softened up to each other during the rest of Landon's visit, finally making progress on improving their bond. Hearing her girls laugh and carry on a conversation without discord was music to Laura Lee's ears.

"Maybe now your daddy will take you three to the game with him. He's been wanting to ask you, but with the way you two have been acting, he's been dancing around it."

Landon and Launa looked at each other and laughed.

"You want to tell him?" Launa asked.

"You do it. I'll go get changed." Landon dashed to her old room.

The field was packed with old classmates and their children, local college scouts, and former frenemies of The Davis Girls, the one thing that would always unite them. They put on airs and gossiped like the best of friends, whispering in each other's ear about the people they came across in the stands.

Landon had forgotten how good the hot dogs were at the ball field stand, and after devouring the one her dad bought, she offered to pay for the second round of dogs, peanuts, and Coke. She stood in the long line cheering on the home team as they scored, looking back at her sister laughing at how ridiculous she looked making all that noise by herself.

The line cleared ahead in front of her, and she stepped ahead to order. "I thought I would never lay eyes on you again." Reynaldo Williams' low voice rumbled in her ear.

Landon turned around to big white teeth and wet lips. "Hey, you. I thought the same thing."

"I'm glad I was wrong." He licked his lips.

"Un-huh."

"Did your old man tell you I ran into him the other day?"

"I can't say that he has." Landon lied with a sly smile on her lips. "How are you?"

"Doing good. Working as a coach at the school. I can see for myself how you're doing. Still fine as hell after all these years."

Landon blushed until her face turned red, thinking about what she and Jen discussed. She examined his handsome face, and athletic build, noticing the only change about him was he had grown a mustache on his baby face, and gotten his ear pierced. The smell of his woodsy cologne was still the same, and when the wind blew it danced across her nose, bringing back the memory of the night they shared in the park.

"You don't look too bad yourself," she replied.

"How long has it been?"

"Six, seven years maybe." Landon shrugged.

"I mean how long has it been since that night?"

A man interrupted. "Ma'am, are you going to order?"

"Uh, yeah sure. Four hot dogs, three cokes and one bag of peanuts."

"That'll be fifteen dollars," said the clerk.

"Don't worry about it. It's on me," Reynaldo offered.

"You don't have to do that."

"I insist."

The old lovers stepped to the side as the order was being prepared. Reynaldo talked nonstop about his injury that ended his college career, and how thankful he was to be able to coach the sport he loved. The people in the line and behind the counter stared at them playing catch up, and when the food was ready, Reynaldo helped Landon take her order to the stands, making Papa Davis all smiles in the bleachers.

[illegible]

[illegible paragraph]

"[illegible]," [illegible].

"[illegible]."

"[illegible]," [illegible].

"[illegible]."

"[illegible]," [illegible].

"[illegible]."

[illegible paragraph]

CHAPTER 46

THAT OLD THING

LANDON

While Launa and Tim cheered on the plays, Reynaldo sat next to Papa Davis and talked his way into a dinner invitation. Landon and Launa shared a disapproving look.

"What is happening right now?" Launa asked.

"I wish I knew. Make him stop," Landon whispered.

When the conversation between Reynaldo and their father finally offered a segue, the old flame asked Landon, "Care to take a walk?"

Landon whispered to Launa. "I'll try to undo the damage daddy's done. I'm not divorced yet."

"Say what?" Launa stopped sipping from her cup.

"Yeah. You and I have a lot to catch up on. Be right back."

Reynaldo didn't beat around the bush. He asked Landon to meet him at the park where they created the memory stuck in her head. Hesitant to answer, she fumbled over words to disinvite him to dinner.

"If I say yes, will you find a reason to cancel having dinner at my parents house?"

"If you say I'll get some alone time to catch up with you properly, I'll let your pops down easy."

Landon chuckled. "Right. Then, yes, I'll see you at the playground."

Upon her return to the bleachers, she assured her sister the crisis had been averted.

"Good." Launa sighed.

"By chance, do you know why Ma said I dodged a bullet with that one?"

Launa scowled. "Why? What did he say to you down there?"

"I got him to promise not to come to dinner if I hung out with him tonight. Should I cancel? I'm curious what Ma knows about him."

"You know how old ladies gossip in church. You'd be amazed how much you think you know about a person, then the saints and sanctified blabs out your business, and you're stuck clutching your pearls in the pew. What's going on with you and Todd?"

"He has a son who has ruined our marriage. I'm filing for a divorce. End of story. You were right. Trouble in paradise."

"I didn't want to be right. Sorry about that."

"It's not your fault."

Launa held her sister's hand. "Be careful tonight. Don't think for one second you need to back pedal because you and Todd are uncertain right now. Okay?"

Whatever Laura Lee and Launa knew ate away at Landon, bugging her to pieces. It was all she could wonder about as she looked at the night sky in Reynaldo's eyes. The park was dimly lit below the moonlight, but illuminated just enough she didn't worry her old flame would try anything out in the open.

Slightly bigger than when they were teens, his five-foot-eleven frame made his chest stand robust in his t-shirt. His amber brown eyes stared into hers as his moist, kissable lips puckered at her with ill intent. Landon maneuvered her way over to the swings set. They laughed like children as Reynaldo pushed her back and forth, reciting his smooth lines from back in the day as if he were trapped in the past. The swing stopped in the air, and Reynaldo closed in on Landon from the rear. His hands wrapped around her waist, gently gliding to her thighs. She shivered from his touch, freaked out by the pounding in her chest and set of hands fondling her that didn't belong to her husband. "We weren't so lucky on the ladder last time. Maybe the swings will allow fate to finally take place." He whispered in her ear, spreading her legs apart.

Landon removed his hands and hopped off of the swing. "What's your big secret?"

"I don't know what you mean."

"I think you do."

"If you have something to ask me, just ask me."

"That's just it. I've been given a sprinkle here and there, but no one will come right out and say whatever it is you're hiding."

"Is this why you don't want me to come to dinner?"

"Sort of."

"I don't know why she didn't just tell you." He exhaled deeply. "Did your sister tell you to uninvite me?"

"She did."

Reynaldo grinned. "Your sister is jealous of you."

"I beg your pardon." Landon rolled her hips to the side.

"We kind of hooked up when you left for college."

Landon picked up a rock and threw it at his chest. The rock gently pierced his skin below his shirt.

"Ow, girl. Shit. Let me explain."

"Why the fuck did you ask to hang out with me when you've already fucked my sister?" She threw a second rock at his dick.

"Stop, girl. It wasn't like that. The day you left for school, I came by to see you. You had already left, and your sister threw herself at me."

"So it's her fault?"

"She put the moves on me."

"And that makes you innocent?"

"Look, what happened was wrong in a sense."

"In a sense? Please. Stop talking."

"I came looking for you, and things got out of hand."

Landon laughed. "God, I feel like a fool being here with you." She sucked her teeth. "Please don't show up at our house tomorrow. It's seen enough of you, don't you think?"

Landon fled the scene in a rage and made the short walk home in record time. She stormed inside and overlooked Launa watching television in the living room.

"So?" Launa asked, startling her on her way upstairs.

Landon stepped back down and glared at her sister. "You could have just told me you fucked my boyfriend. I'm sure it made you feel absolutely superior to have that one over me all of these years."

"Sounds like he's painted me as the bad guy."

"Aren't you? You came on to him knowing how I felt about him."

"That son of a bitch lied."

Laura Lee popped in from upstairs. "What is going on down here?"

"Reynaldo is what." Launa folded her arms.

"You are my sister. I would never want your sloppy seconds. And you should never want mine."

"I knew it would come to this one day." Laura Lee sighed.

Reynaldo knocked on the door, and the ladies grew quiet. The floorboards creaked above, and Papa Davis limped down the stairs.

"Why hasn't anyone gotten the door? And why did it sound like you girls were arguing? You were getting along so well earlier."

Launa gritted through her teeth. "Daddy, don't answer that."

"What? Child, pipe down. What's gotten into you?"

Papa Davis smiled at the sight of Reynaldo standing at the door. He welcomed inside, and all of the ladies shouted. "No!" Reynaldo paused with one foot inside and the other midstep.

"What the devil is going on?" Papa Davis asked.

"Reynaldo, don't you think it's time you came clean, Son?" Laura Lee advised.

"Come clean about what?" Papa Davis frowned at Reynaldo.

"Mr. and Mrs. Davis, I would like to apologize for any confusion I may have caused."

"We don't need the apology." Laura Lee shook her head. "You owe that to our girls."

"Mama, you knew about them all this time?" Landon held her chest.

"A mother knows everything."

"Boy, I ought to knock your ass out." Papa Davis charged at Reynaldo. Laura Lee held him back. "Why am I just finding out about this?" he asked Laura Lee.

"Because you always favored Landon, and I didn't want you to hold a mistake this big against Launa, who is desperate for you to see her the way you see her sister. She's grown so much over the years. Neither of you should hold this against her." Laura Lee looked between Landon and her husband.

"Why is this coming out now?"

"Because this weasel is using your fondness of him to work his way back into the picture knowing good and well what he has done. That takes a special kind of lowdown selfishness, don't you think, Son?" Laura Lee scolded Reynaldo with her eyes.

"Ma'am, I truly am sorry. I came by tonight to apologize."

"To which one of my girls?"

Reynaldo stuttered. "Um...I um..."

"I have a question. Did it end between you two because Mama found out, or did he throw you away after he got what he wanted?"

"I ended it." Launa confessed. She turned to Reynaldo. "You want to tell her why, or will you lie about that too?"

Reynaldo huffed. "Can I see him?"

"See who?" Papa Davis fumed.

"My son."

Landon's shoulders wilted as she looked at Launa. Laura Lee exhaled as the secret she had been carrying for years finally released her from its shackles, and Papa Davis dropped his head to the floor.

"This boy is Tim's father?" Papa Davis asked.

"He most certainly is, and Launa has been too ashamed to tell anyone. I can do math, sweetheart." Laura Lee pressed her lips tight.

"I would like to clear the air and say I offered to take care of the situation, but Launa chose to go through with it. Just like she knew I was in love with Landon, and she proposed that she and I get together."

"That's a lie!" Launa yelled.

"No, it isn't." Laura Lee intervened. "I was sitting in the living room listening that day. You were flirting with this boy, and he was so horned up he didn't care where he got it from."

Landon threw her head back at Launa.

"I'm not the only one you need to be pissed with," Launa pleaded to Landon. "There's more you don't know."

"How is that even possible?"

"I'll show myself out." Reynaldo edged for the door.

Papa Davis shut it closed. "You can leave after we discuss your responsibilities, Son."

"Landon, as bad as this looks, I do love you. I'm sorry for what happened years ago, but when you met Todd and found the happiness you deserve, I hated myself for what I'd done. And I think you should know everything has worked in your favor by not taking up with the likes of him." Launa pointed to Reynaldo. "The day I found out I was pregnant, I went to tell him, but when I got to his house, he was kissing another girl in his driveway."

"Is that why you chose to keep the baby? To spite me?"

"No, I kept my baby because I wanted him."

"None of that matters now." Papa Davis shut them up. "The boy is here now. Son, you gon' ahead and get out of here. I need to think if having the likes of you around is a good idea."

Reynaldo looked at the family ignoring his existence without a glance in his direction. He left the Davis home, and with the air cleared, Landon and Launa shared their realest conversation in years.

"What you did hurts, but not to the point I would ever disown you as my sister," Landon confessed.

"Even when I act like I hate you, I love you still." Launa reached for a hug.

"I'll always choose my sister over a mister." Landon squeezed her tightly.

"I can't breathe." Launa gasped.

"Good. That's for being stupid." She squeezed tighter. "And that's for being bitchy all of these years. Well, maybe you weren't bitchy. You were acting out of shame."

Launa fought her way out of Landon's grip. "You win. And again, I'm sorry. But there's something else you should know."

"Un uh. I don't want to know anything else that's going to gut me. Be a loving sister and bury it with you."

Chapter 47

Stronger Than Pride
Todd

The Jeffries began playing the game of who could outdo the other with the separation in tow. Todd didn't receive Landon's note well, and being the first time she went home without him spoke volumes she was serious about calling it quits on their life together. As the days went on without a phone call from her, he decided to move out of the house, and into the back room of his print shop.

The transition of living out of his beautiful home and into the mediocre living quarters of one room with a mini fridge and microwave, old television, and leather sofa were humbling and depressing. Jay's constant intrusive thoughts didn't help Todd's mental or emotional state.

"You put yourself here, man. You haven't known that kid for eight years. I wouldn't have let him come into my life, and take away everything I love. Look at you, man. No house. No good woman. And back in the streets with gold diggers and bitches playing more games than me."

"I'm not worried about bitches. This is temporary. I'll let Landon see she and I can't be apart for too long, then we'll find our way back to each other. Everything will work itself out."

"If you say so. But if I were you, I wouldn't stay here long. I'd move my ass back in my house and live like *The War of the Roses*. I wouldn't let no muthafucka get next to L if I were you."

"I'll win her back at McCaine's anniversary party next weekend."

"And what if she doesn't miss you?"

"She will."

The night of the party, Todd surprised Landon on their doorstep with a corsage attached to a gift wrapped box with a diamond tennis bracelet inside. He complimented her as he always did. "Forever the prettiest woman at the party. If you don't mind, I would love to be your date." His puppy eyes looked up at her standing in the entrance like he was lost. And he was without her.

Landon lowered her head and smiled. "Sure. Let me grab my bag. Come in."

Confidence filled him as he stepped inside, pacing the floor and smiling to himself as the first part of his plan worked. Landon made her way back down the stairs, capturing Todd's full attention. He couldn't resist how stunning she appeared, floating in the fluorescent light like an angel without wings. Marveling at her beauty, he fought to hold his tongue in his mouth when she stepped in front of him. Todd extended his arm. "Allow me." He placed the corsage on her wrist and fastened the bracelet on the other. "Shall we?" He leaned in and stole a kiss from her cheek.

The date was a mind fuck on both of their parts. Slipping into old habits of familiarity and love as Landon had no intention of changing her mind, and Todd had no resolution regarding the scale that weighed against him– His wife on one side, his son on the other.

Their friends cheered when the two of them walked into the party together. Landon flashed a brief smile. The men pulled Todd into a huddle, congratulating him on a prize he hadn't won. She wiped the smile from her lips after hearing them slap hands and championing man. "That man went home and got his woman back," said Jay.

A shooting pain pierced through her heart and down her back. She shook it off and joined the ladies gathered around the love nest Tammy and McCaine created for the party.

Rose gold and off white decorum covered the closed in patio from the ceiling to the floor. Champagne bottles matching the candles and centerpieces on the tables illuminated the room, surrounded by all of the guests dressed in different shades of ivory and white. T&M trinkets added a personal touch of the couple of the hour, and Tammy was more than thrilled to tell the women all about the planning process.

"I saw a party like this online and knew this was how I wanted our place to look for this anniversary."

"You may have missed your calling," said Kim. "I'd hire you to be the visionary for my next party."

"Speaking of visionaries, Landon, you and Todd looked gorgeous as always walking in together. Does that mean you've called off the separation?" Tammy inclined.

"Jesus, men gossip more than women." Landon sighed.

"What separation?" Millicent looked at Landon.

"Tonight is not about me." Landon excused herself from the line of fire.

"Right." Tammy changed the subject. "Let me show you ladies tonight's party favors."

Tammy pulled out engraved copper mugs with metal straws. Kim inquired about the price, and McCaine's face wrinkled with strain.

"We don't talk about price, dear. McCaine would have an aneurysm if he knew."

Kim giggled at his reaction behind Tammy's back. She turned around and Kim changed the subject. "Has anyone heard from Jen?"

"I invited her, but never received a response."

Landon returned to the circle of women. "I went to see her recently. She's doing well down there. Jules couldn't attend tonight, so she sat this one out. She sends her love."

"So you've been communicating with people, just not with me," Millicent snided her. "I bet she knew of the separation."

Tammy cleared her throat. "Whatever's brewing between you two, don't hash it out at my party, but fix it before we go to Castillo Mas next week."

"Are we still doing that?" Landon frowned.

"Don't be a prude." Kim tapped her shoulder. "Everyone I know who's been to a voyeur club says it made their sex life even better."

Landon smirked. "And if you aren't having any trouble in that department, what good is it?"

"I don't know. Maybe spark new ideas."

"It's as if I don't know the women I have been friends with all these years." Landon rolled her eyes at Millicent. "Anyone else want a glass of champagne?" She left the ladies at the table.

"To be continued," Kim muttered.

Millicent pulled Jay away from the guys and wrapped his arms around her shoulders. They kissed and danced in the corner with every eye in the house studying their chemistry. Landon recognized she was in love, but couldn't see past their conflict to be happy for her. She wondered if jealousy played a part of her sudden detestation for the friend she's known her whole life. For their roles were reversing, and she would soon be alone.

As she watched the new couple put on a show of affection from across the room, Todd was watching her. It inspired him to confess he was ready to come home. He walked over to her. "May I have this dance?" Landon gave him her hand. He held her close and whispered in her ear, "I see how you're looking at Mills. I once made you feel that way. I'd like to see you smile like that again. But for real, not for a show like those two spotlight whores." He and Landon chuckled cheek to cheek. Todd gazed into her eyes and squeezed her lower back. Landon felt the connection still between them. She resisted the tears bubbling in her eyes, spiraling on the inside of what she was about to lose. "I cried while you were gone. Waiting with my phone in my hand, hoping you would call. But you never did. It's why I moved out. It gave me time to realize the situation I put you in. And I'm sorry."

Landon hugged him tighter. "Let's not do this here."

"Tell me how to fix it. Us being at odds while those two of all people find love with each other. It's just not right. I'll never understand how that is working out and we're not."

"I'm against it, but I'm happy for them."

"I am too, but...."

"Honestly, it doesn't matter if we understand it."

"You're right again."

"Wanna know what bothers me the most about it?"

"Please. Tell me."

"That it could have been you over there with her."

Todd stopped dancing. "Not if she paid me."

Landon and Todd were so engrossed in their conversation, they didn't notice Millicent standing next to them.

She tapped Landon on the shoulder. "Can I borrow the Mrs. for a second?"

Todd waited for Landon's approval to let her go, leaned in, and whispered in her ear, "Not if she paid me."

They shared a quiet laugh.

"It would kill me." Landon pinched his cheek, then followed Millicent to the kitchen.

"You two don't look like you're separating to me. I see two people madly in love."

"We'll always love each other. Surely this isn't why you pulled me away?"

Millicent huffed. "What's going on between us?"

"I wish I knew. Things feel off since…you know."

"So I'm being punished for falling in love? I have to go at this alone. Not share how I feel with my best friend in the world? Because honestly, I need you right now."

"Why is that?"

"Because I'm terrified. Jay looks horrible on paper, but it frightens me how good it feels to be with him. I haven't felt this way in a long time."

"I'm happy for you. I truly am. I just can't help but wonder if you would do to me, what you've done to Jen. I'm finding it really hard to trust you all of a sudden. I'm sorry."

Tears formed in Millicent's eyes. She confessed, "I think about Jen every day. I'd love more than anything to repair our friendship. I regret hurting her. That was never my intention. But if I have to lose her to feel the way I feel with Jay, I'll do it. I wouldn't trade the happiness I feel for anything. Love has finally found me, and I'm not letting it go."

"And I hope it works out for you both."

"You do know I wouldn't do anything to hurt you. Not talking to you feels like I have lost a sister."

Landon looked at her, expressionless.

"So what have you been up to? Besides going to Miami?" Millicent continued to reach for a moment to bond.

Landon sensed her desperation. "I went home for a few days. Spent some time with my folks."

"How is everyone?"

"Everyone is well. I ran into Reynaldo while I was there."

"Did you?" Millicent's eyes grew wide.

"I dodged a bullet with that one. Tell you about that later."

"So you didn't?"

"God no. And I'm glad I didn't back then either."

Tammy intruded. "There you two are. Come. We're about to watch a video,"

After hours of dancing, eating, drinking, and viewing a slideshow of Tammy and McCaine over the years, Todd drove Landon home. The drive was quiet as old love songs played on the radio. So far he was two for two on his plan to show Landon she was the love of his life, and he would not go away easily. Now that the tone had been set, he hoped his final act to win her over was granted for the evening– Especially since Landon could be frisky when intoxicated.

Todd stroked the back of her hand as he walked her to the door. He held it up to his mouth, kissed the back of it, and got lost in Landon's eyes. He kissed her lips as they stood on the steps, praying for an invitation inside. Landon returned his advance, succumbing to desire by the minute. Todd's cock blossomed between them and she pulled back.

"I'm going to invite you in. But listen. No matter what happens, I want us to always be friends."

"I'll say what you want me to say if it gets me on the other side of that door, but I'd be lying if I said I could be your friend. I want to be your husband. Friends don't sound too good to me, baby."

"We love each other." Landon leaned in and placed her forehead against his.

Todd pulled her close and kissed her neck. "Baby, you are the only woman for me. The only woman I have eyes for. The only woman to get me excited like this."

"I want you just as bad, but promise me in the morning you'll go back to your place."

"I promise. I don't want to, but I will if that'll make you happy. Now, can I please have you?"

Landon led him to the top step. Todd pushed through the door, unwrapped his tie and threw his jacket to the floor. He lifted Landon's dress above her thighs. "You miss me laying pipe, don't you, baby?" He sighed in her mouth, then coiled his tongue with hers. With full desire bursting between them, he ripped her stockings to shreds, grinding against her on the wall below the staircase.

"Fix my plumbing, baby." Landon begged, stripping away his belt and unzipping his fly.

"Consider it done." Todd plunged inside her dripping walls. "Ahh," he groaned, biting his lower lip. "I'll leave my bill on the nightstand in the morning." He thrusted deep inside her pussy.

Landon wailed by his force, panting uncontrollably as the zipper on the back of her dress scratched her back. "Take this off," she whispered, lifting it above her head. Todd freed her and she elicited relief. He dipped between the line of her cleavage mounted like twin dome towers, unhooking her bra with the flick of a finger. His lips sucked her brown nipples until a rolling moan resounded from her throat. Lost in the sensation of his talented lips, she wound her aching pussy around his wand to the rhythm of his orchestrated tender jabs.

Every inch of Landon's cave vibrated. Todd reminded her how he knew to please her cravings, lifting her body up and down on his dick while his tongue traced her tanned skin from her bosom to her full lips. Familiar with her outline and corners, he stabbed her flesh side to side, making her slit sputter the warm cream he missed raining on him the past few weeks. "Daddy's home, baby." Todd pounded harder and stronger, drunk punching her walls until her come covered his dick completely and trickled down his legs. Wailing of ecstasy, Landon clutched her legs around him, enjoying the punishment of depriving him of her love for weeks. "That's my good girl. Show me you missed this dick. Cream for me, love. Ahh. You feel so fucking good," Todd groaned, lifting her legs above his shoulders. "I'm not finished with this good pussy yet."

He fucked Landon going up the stairs. Carrying her as she rode his stiff dick until they crash landed on the bed. Landon squealed at the painful pleasure of him ramming into her hole and grinding her fast, then slowing his strokes when he dug into his favorite corner at the top of her canal. He drilled until her legs weakened above him, trembling for more gluttonous punishment. He lifted his body and flipped Landon over on her stomach, kissing the center of her back down to her ass channel. "You've trickled all the way back here. Let me clean you up," he whispered, tonguing her dripped juices with tender strokes.

Landon gasped, "Oh! You nasty motherfucker."

"Mmm hmm," Todd moaned, prodding the center of her forbidden with circular motions.

Landon was destroyed, quavering uncontrollably. Todd failed to hold her still as she wiggled and wriggled at his mercy. He slowed down the pace, delicately kissing her back door, then smacked her ass and squeezed it like putty as he plowed his way back inside her warmth.

Strong, stiff and sturdy, he held his wood to the end of her fountain, pressing her clit with his thumb. Landon moaned. "I love it when you do that."

"I know you do," he said, rubbing her nub until she came again.

Todd joined her in exertion, holding her tight in his arms so she couldn't escape the perfect position her ass rested around his dick. He jolted in place, biting the back of her shoulder until his clip was empty.

They laid in their mess, still and contempt, listening to the insects trill outside the window, and the nightingale sing from the bush below their bedroom. Todd circled Landon's hair around his fingers.

"I was thinking we should go away. A change of scenery might do us some good."

"I just had a change of scenery, and it did do some good. Going away together will only further complicate things between us."

"After what just happened, you still want to separate?"

"Todd, remember the night of your mother's birthday party?"

"What does that have to do with us getting back together?"

"That phone call you received, how do you suppose that woman knew we were having problems?"

"I haven't given it much thought."

"I can think of two people. Either your mother has taken a liking to her, or your son ran back and told her about what he's heard. That's not the family I want to be a part of. I'm not fighting for your mother's attention or respect, and I don't want my business being shared with people in the street."

"Baby, I can't control what the boy tells his mother, or my mother's gossiping."

"That's my point. You and I aren't in control of us anymore. You and I have different paths now. It's why we have to end this. It's not going to work between us."

Todd kissed her good night, and fell asleep with her in his arms. He woke first as the rays of the sun graced him another morning next to the woman of his dreams. He watched her sleep for a short while, kissing her forehead while her hair found a way to tickle his nose each time he brushed it back. He lifted his sticky body from next to Landon's, and opened the drawer on his side of the bed. The notepad with The Jeffries printed across the top made him smile as he wrote Landon a note before keeping his word that he would leave in the morning.

Here is the bill for my service:
Call me when you change your mind.
I'll wait forever if I have to.
T

CHAPTER 48

THE EMPTY SEA
LANDON

It was weeks before Landon convinced herself to file the papers, but she persevered and hated herself for it. She couldn't bring herself to face Todd, ignoring his calls and late night visits sitting outside in the driveway. And when the files arrived with the date to finalize their decree, she read *Jeffries vs. Jeffries*, and grew physically ill.

Admitting to her mother she couldn't go through the process alone, Mother Davis and Launa surprised Landon the morning she was due in court.

"You don't have to go through with this, baby. Call it off. Todd has been praying you'll change your mind."

"Listen to Mama. Todd has been calling us night and day, begging us to convince you to change your mind," said Launa. "You are not going to find anyone better. I'm telling you, the sea is dryer than the desert."

"You both will hate me for saying this. Hell, I hate me for saying this. I can't be around that boy. And from what I've seen, he needs his father. This is best for everyone involved. Myself, Todd, and that boy. I have to walk away."

Todd refused to make eye contact with Landon when she entered the room. She stared at him, waiting for one final moment to look into his eyes and ask him to forgive her.

The lawyers mediated the terms of the agreement prior to their meeting, but Todd's lawyer stopped the proceedings to make an announcement. "My client has changed the terms of our previous agreement."

Landon tensed in her chair, still staring at Todd studying his phone below the table. Mr. Jeffries has agreed to give Mrs. Jeffries everything with the exclusion of his vehicles, his business, and partnership ventures with other parties. He is offering to relinquish any ownership of joint bank accounts, as well as his rights to the home on Mongrain Avenue, and continue to pay the mortgage while Mrs. Jeffries resides in the home, and gives full sale of profits to Mrs. Jeffries if, and, or when she decides to sell the property."

Landon's lawyer whispered with her, asking if she agreed to the changes. She wondered if his generosity was a final attempt to make her change her mind, and she called his name.

"Todd?"

He finally met eyes with her.

"Why are you doing this?"

Todd's lawyer interrupted. "Mr. Jeffries has also offered to pay off Mrs. Jeffries's vehicle if she agrees to abide by one request, submitted by Mr. Jeffries this morning."

"What is it?"

Landon's attorney intercepted. "Mrs. Jeffries, You hired me for a reason. I'll take it from here."

"My client requests that Mrs. Jeffries keep the last name Jeffries."

"Landon, do you agree to these terms?"

"Yes, unless I marry again." Landon added to the amendment.

Her attorney silenced her. "My client agrees to this request, and would like to add, pending upon a new marriage, she holds the right to remove the surname Jeffries at that time."

Landon signed the papers and stormed out of the hearing. She raced to the lobby and commanded Launa to get her out of there. Laura Lee stayed put, and waited for Todd to arrive at the exit.

"I'm sorry. You'll always be my son, and are still welcome in our house." She squeezed his hand. "You take care of that boy now."

"I will, but I'm not giving up on your daughter. If we have to do the whole wedding thing again, then so be it. These papers mean nothing to me. She's still my wife." Todd kissed Laura Lee on the cheek. "Love you, Ma."

CHAPTER 49

SEX EVERYWHERE

LANDON

Landon survived the first night as the former Mrs. Jeffries with the help of her mother and sister. Their company in the house kept her sane, but when they left the next morning, the shock set in. She struggled getting out of bed, her spirit was low, and her appearance staggered. The once sharp dresser switched to ill-fitting work attire with big jackets and flats, replacing her fitted dresses, skirts, and four inch heels.

As time went on, the house grew lonely, but Landon slowly worked her way out of the fog. Her circle kept her entertained, and for the one year anniversary of their visit to the sex club Castillo Mas, the ladies reassembled once again for a filthy night of voyeurism and fun.

They assembled at Kim's house. For an hour they lushed on homemade margaritas and wine before the limousine arrived to chauffeur them for the night.

"How the hell did we allow this one to drag us back to this place without the guys?" Tammy asked.

"Stop faking like you aren't happy the balls aren't dragging behind us this time." Kim slapped Tammy's leg. "This way we get to experience it freely. It's a girl's night!"

"Let's set some rules," Tammy suggested over the music. "No one get on that nasty ass bed in the middle of the floor, keep your feet on the floor, and come out of there with your panties on."

"What if we have a hall pass?" Kim teased.

All eyes shifted towards Kim.

"Did Brian give you the clearance tonight?" Tammy asked.

Kim blushed and looked at us up her nose. "Nah!" she shrieked. "I'm bullshitting y'all!"

Beyond the city limits they arrived at the house turned club, flashing red neon lights outside the heavily guarded gate. The chauffeur gave the security guards the password, and the gate opened.

"Y'all ready for a wild night?!" Kim fired up the squad.

"No turning back now." Landon sighed.

Kim passed a condom to Landon. "As the single lady in our group, you have clearance to do as you please. Just make sure you are protected."

Landon passed it back to her. "I'm good in that department."

"Somebody's got a maintenance man and been holding out." Kim raised her brows.

"Thank God." Millicent clapped her hands. "When do we meet this mystery man?"

Landon cleared her throat. "Shall we go inside?"

"And on that note, ladies, if you get uncomfortable or just not feeling the club, our driver has movies cued up, drinks, and snacks. Just come chill out in the car if need be until everyone is ready to leave. Hopefully that won't happen. Now let's go have a good time. Castillo Mas awaits!"

The club had been renovated since their first visit. Red lights flashed at the entrance as fog veiled the air. The laughter of the friends echoed between the slowed beats as they entered the first room, witnessing a naked woman in black spiked leather getting spanked on her exposed cheeks by two men licking wooden paddles.

Millicent whispered in Kim's ear. "How did you find this place?"

"We all have our little secrets, dear. You getting turned on already?"

"I don't need assistance in that department." Millicent turned up her nose.

As the lights switched from red to blue, and the fog cleared the passageway to the next exhibit, the ladies entered a foreplay room. Participants on a stage, some fully naked, others half dressed, pleasured their lovers for voyeurs circling the room, holding up rating cards. They watched a woman deepthroat a seven inch dick, receiving a perfect score of ten by the judges, and a man eat the pussy of a woman until her torso fell off of the table as she balanced and spread wide with his face planted up her ass.

"Give him a ten too!" Kim shouted.

"Give her the ten for balance." Millicent chuckled.

"We have been in this room for twenty minutes," Landon pointed out.

"Seriously?" Tammy's eyes twirled.

Landon showed the girls the time on her phone.

"Damn. Then give all of them a ten for holding people's attention," Tammy joked. "Y'all ready to move on?"

"Yeah," they mumbled.

As they trekked down the hall, the lights went out, and the music stopped. Neon arrows blinked on the wall, guiding them ahead into a gold room with a woman chained in a stirrup machine with cables connected to her breast.

"This is so much better than the last time we came," Landon said. "These exhibits make it more of an experience than horny people fucking in a room."

"I agree. I was prepared to be bored." Tammy laughed.

Buzz, electrical shocks stimulated the model's breasts. She shook and hollered, then smiled of delight. A man walked onto the stage with a purple dildo in his hand and placed it inside the front of her panties. It vibrated against her as she begged him to turn it up higher. He zapped her breasts again with the push of a button on the machine, then gripped her face. "I give the orders," he said, then licked the side of her face.

"Okay, I'm gonna head to the next room. This one is a bit much for me." Tammy squeezed through the group.

"Wait," said Kim.

"Ah!" the woman screamed and shivered on stage uncontrollably.

"I'm a little intrigued," Millicent confessed.

"Then you stay and watch this shit." Tammy led the way out.

The fog grew thicker as the gold room faded behind them. Down the murky hallway, they grew silent until the arrows pointed them inside a dark room where the lights flashed from wall to wall every two seconds. The ladies held hands, ensuring they stayed together in this room. With every flicker of light a couple appeared to surround them, engaged in a random sex act. Their heads turned like they were watching a tennis match. Left to right they were stunned by men on women, women on women, two men on one woman, and countless other arrangements shown only when the light flashed on each wall.

"Which way out of this room?" Landon whispered.

"I don't know. I'm scared to move and end up in the mix." Tammy giggled.

"This way." Kim led them.

Slow music played ahead with a purple haze clouded above. A hostess holding wrist bands stood at the entrance next to a security guard with a nightstick.

"Read the rules for entering this room." She pointed to a sign on the wall behind her.

- *All are allowed to enter.*
- *You may look.*
- *You may touch.*
- *To participate, you must wear this band as your form of consent.*
- *Do not take off the band while in this room.*
- *Doing so will result in removal from the property.*

All of their heads peeked into the room of moans and groans from sex crazed party goers going at it like beasts in the wild. A man fingered for them to come inside while he fucked a woman from behind.

"I'll pass," said Landon. "I don't want to be touched by none of these people"

"We all will," said Millicent. "How do we get to the bar?"

"Speak for yourself." Kim held out her wrist. "I'll see y'all in a few."

The hostess pointed to the door on the left. "Follow the stairs. Bar is down below."

Bass pounded louder than the music from the other rooms as they entered a neon blue room with a pool sitting in the corner opposite of the bar.

"Welcome to the pool party of your dreams," said a hostess welcoming them inside.

"I'm in the wrong business," said Tammy.

"I want to dance." Millicent shook her hips to the music.

"I'll join you two later. I need a drink. That was a lot to take in." Landon headed to the bar.

The bar area was filled with regulars that immediately noticed the newbie. Thirsty hounds surrounded her as she searched for an opening to place her order, while Tammy and Millicent were crowded by dirty dancing rejects. A man offered Landon his seat at the bar.

"What's your poison?"

"Strawberry daiquiri."

"That's Kool-Aid."

"That's what I want."

"Get the lady a strawberry daiquiri," he ordered. "It's on me, pretty lady."

"Thanks, but I can manage to buy myself a drink. I appreciate the offer though."

"I'm sure you can. What brings you to a place like this?"

"Bachelorette party," Landon lied.

"Oh. Someone is getting taken off the market. I hope it isn't you."

Landon looked at her naked ring finger and rubbed it.

"Not yet."

"So, what's your name?"

"Lashika."

"Nice to meet you, Lashika." He leaned in her ear. "I know that's not your real name, but I love role playing."

Landon moved her head away from his and paid for her drink. The man placed a twenty dollar bill in front of her and told the bartender to keep them coming. He leaned in towards her again and whispered," There's more where that came from. How much to leave your friends behind for the night and come home with me."

"Sir, I am not a hooker. Have a good night."

"Tell me your price, and I'll raise it."

Landon rolled her eyes and took her drink to the dance floor. She grooved with Millicent and Tammy, giving them a laugh at her weak offer at the bar.

"At least you know you still got it," said Tammy.

"Please. That man would go home with the first woman who says yes." Landon laughed.

"Guys, I have a question. Who told the guys we were coming here?"

Landon and Tammy followed Millicent's eyes to a table above the pool area.

"Them being here has Brian written all over it." Tammy shook her head.

CHAPTER 50

WHAT'S MINE IS MINE

TODD

On an upper level deck above the pool, the smell of marijuana perfumed the air. One by one the men at the table took a toke from fat rolled cigars, ending in the hands of McCaine.

"You can't hit this. Your job has random testing." Jay snatched it from his hands.

"I don't need you to babysit me. I'm grown," McCaine argued.

"Go ahead and be grown and unemployed then. Don't ask me to pay your bills either, bruh," Jay snapped.

"Okay, okay. I'll pass. I'm going to get another drink. This round is on the babysitter." McCaine held out his hands.

Jay passed McCaine a Franklin. "Keep the change for the next round too, errand boy."

McCaine ogled a couple of half naked women making out on the stairs on his way to the bar. He worked his way through the horde and placed an order for four beers, noticing his wife, Landon, and Millicent near a crowd of men chanting, "Shots!" at the end of the bar. He moseyed back to the table and reported to the men, "Brian was right. They're here."

"Ain't this 'bout a bitch. Coming to a place like this without us. What the fuck was Kim thinking?" Brian stuck out his chest.

"What are they doing?" Jay searched the crowd.

"Shots with a bunch of jerkoffs."

"Do they look drunk?" Brian asked.

"I didn't see Kim down there. Tammy is nearly blitzed. Millicent might not be too far behind."

"And Landon?" Todd asked.

"She's lit." McCaine shook his head.

"I don't care what dummy buys Tammy's drink. I'm still recovering from that damn party."

"Alright, fellas. It's been a fun night. Time to go shut this shit down." Jay led them to the bar area.

They wormed through the crowd, separating to find the party girls. Brian stood by as Kim whipped her hair around, dancing risque in a sandwich between two men on the dance floor below a shadow from the balcony. Jay crept up behind Millicent.

"You don't belong in a place like this."

Millicent faced him and laughed. "Who blabbed?"

"It don't matter."

"You mad?"

"Nah."

"Then shut up and dance with me."

"I only do that at the house."

Todd tapped Millicent. "Where's Landon?"

"She was right next to me."

Todd searched through the crowd with a glint of desperation in his eyes. He spotted Brian and Kim laughing on the dance floor, Tammy and McCaine raising hell on one end of the bar, and Jay and Millicent on the steps wrapped in each other's arms. He forced his way through the crowded bar and scowled at the faces of men glaring at him until he landed eyes on Landon having a conversation with Dario Powers.

He walked up on them and stared at Landon talking to Dario more than he could handle. She felt his eyes burning her back, turned her head full of hair around, and locked eyes with him. She would never get the look on his face out of her mind. It was endearing and passionate and angry. It made her feel like a villain for pulling the plug on their love, and selfish for placing her happiness before their bond. It also made her feel guilty for the way she mishandled herself with Dario at work, even though they were no longer man and wife, and she never crossed the line with him.

Todd smiled at her and she felt at ease. Glossy-eyed and grinning, she smiled back at him and lowered her head with rosy cheeks glowing like a blood moon. In her drunkenness she revealed to Dario she was now divorced, and he used that information to rile up Todd.

He placed his hand around her waist and stared Todd up and down, grinning at the anger raging in his face. Todd pushed Dario's shoulder. "Don't fucking play with me, man. You ain't 'bout that life. You ain't learn your lesson last time?" Todd barked, then knocked his hand from Landon's waist.

"She ain't yours no more," Dario taunted him.

"She'll always be mine." Todd stood in his face, clenching his fist so tight the muscles in his biceps amplified.

Dario smirked. "I knew the moment your hood ass showed up to my house it was only a matter of time before you lost her. A woman like this has no business with ghetto trash like you."

Landon stood at Todd's side. "What's he talking about?"

"Landon, go over by the stairs with Jay and Mills."

"No baby. You stay over here with a real man." Dario reached for Landon's hand.

Todd smacked it away. The people standing near them at the bar grabbed their drinks and left. He stepped to his left, shielding Landon behind him. "Landon, get from over here," Todd ordered. She listened this time. "If you think for one minute I'm going to let you put Landon in the middle of your bigamist shit, you got another thing coming."

"It must suck to have a woman like that leave you. Baby girl is good and liquored up, and was all smiles over here until you showed up. But that's cool. I have forty hours with her through the week. We'll send you a wedding invitation."

The clenched fist at Todd's side rose to the air. The anguish, humiliation, regret, sorrow, and frustration he kept hidden inside flowed through the blood rushing to his head, and veered to his fist as he knocked Dario with a sweet punch to the jaw.

Dario held his lip and smiled. "I have witnesses this time."

"Fuck your witnesses." Todd sucker punched him in the nose.

Blood dripped from Dario's nostrils, splattering on his shirt and to the floor. Rumbling of the crowd rushing towards the exit, and creaks of chairs sliding across the floor muffled Dario shouting at Todd when he sneak attacked him with a glass full of beer to the head. Todd remained composed and checked for blood where the glass broke above his ear. Splotches of beer drenched the sleeve of his shirt. He glared at Dario with the eye of a tiger, and grabbed him by the back of his shirt as he attempted to flee from the bar. Todd slammed his head on the back of a wooden stool. "I told you to stay away from my fuckin' wife!" He repeated as he pounced on top of Dario, beating him to the floor until security bum rushed him.

Dario rose to his feet with the help of a few bystanders and security. He wiped the blood from his lip, closely watching the other security officers rough house Todd. When the grip of one of the security team holding him up loosened, he broke free and snuck a blow to Todd's stomach while he was heavily constrained with both of his arms above his head.

"She's fair game now! It's over for you!" He laughed, spitting out blood.

Jay caught Dario from behind and jabbed him in his ribs. Security lost control of the situation and hemmed up Jay while Todd freed himself from their restraint. He snaked between the chaos and clobbered Dario with a one-two combination. Dario leaned forward. He held his stomach, stumbling like a drunk, then patted his eye. Todd caught him again and stunned his other eye.

The crowd dispersed into chaos. Dario swung punches in every direction, landing an accidental blow to Todd's eye, but in turn was hit with a wind up uppercut to his chin, weakening his knees, and laying him flat on his back. Todd kicked Dario until he curled up into a ball between two stools.

Security grabbed Todd and threw him and Jay out the back door of the club. They fled to the side of the building, blending in with the staff gathered by the employee entrance smoking cigarettes. They eased their way to Jay's car, slid inside and called the girls.

Jay: I'm parked by the gate. Bring Landon with you.

We've left the lot. Stuck in this traffic. :Mills

Jay: Pull over at the first exit and wait for me.

Okay. :Mills

. . .

The gang met at the gas station at the first exit off the highway. Todd walked over to the limousine, led Landon out by the hand, and sat with her in the back of Jay's car.

"I'm not apologizing. Do you see what I would do for you?"

Landon shook her head yes.

"Promise me you won't ever have anything to do with the likes of that guy."

"You don't have to worry about that. I don't fancy him."

"And I believe you. Because I love you. I'll always love you."

"I know."

"How you been?" He grabbed her hand.

"Okay. I have my days." She smiled at her hand inside of his.

"Still the prettiest girl in the room."

Landon looked up and gazed into his eyes. Todd licked his lips and leaned in to taste hers as Tammy knocked on the car window.

"Todd what the hell was that? You need to work on that temper, boy. Landon, can we get out of here?"

She waved her hand. "You guys go ahead. Tell Kim I'll pick up my car tomorrow."

Tammy grinned at the look in Landon's eyes. "Talk some sense into slugger here."

Jay returned to the car with Millicent, cranked it, and merged into traffic. Millicent turned around with her arm posed against the headrest, smiling at Todd and Landon having a moment.

"What got into you, Todd?" She grinned.

"Millicent, not now." Landon sternly glared at her.

"You didn't need to beat that poor man like that. Landon has never liked him."

Jay tapped Millicent's leg. "Baby, it's been handled. Let's just stay out of it."

"What was all that stuff you were saying in the club about learning his lesson the last time?" Landon asked.

Todd stuttered. "A while back I had him investigated when he was harassing you. I found out some devious things he's involved in, and warned him not to get you caught up in the middle of his mess. But don't worry about any of that. Just promise you'll stay away from him."

"I promise."

"Yeah, Landon. Stop dangling that string on my boy's head and getting him into shit. You know you still love him. Quit fuckin' around." Jay fussed.

"I know you ain't talking after you broke up a friendship. Somebody needs to put a foot up your ass."

Jay stared at Landon and Todd in the rearview mirror. "T. Since when your girl talk like that?"

Todd chuckled and shrugged his shoulders. "I'on know, but I like it." He grinned, kissing the back of Landon's hand.

Jay grinned at Landon. "I hear you, Sis. Message received. I won't fuck up this time. I give you my word. I'm in love with Mills." He called Millicent over and kissed her on the side of his mouth as he drove. " I love you, girl."

Millicent smiled. "Love?"

"You heard me."

Jay swerved on the road as he attempted to maul Millicent's face with one hand on the wheel, and the other caressing her chin. Todd and Landon chastised him to cut it out. "Pull over," said Millicent, pulling on his shirt collar, kissing his cheek. The car slowed down and veered off at the next exit, stopping in the safety lane in front of the stop sign. Jay turned off the engine and tackled Millicent.

"That place got you turned on, I see," he mumbled.

"And you just said you love me." Millicent sighed.

Todd and Landon watched them go at it, squirming in the back seat.

"I don't think they're coming up for air." Landon joked.

"I remember the last time we were like that."

Landon's eyes grew big.

"What's it been? Two, almost three months?" Todd stared at her with his teeth sinking into his bottom lip.

Millicent gasped and pushed Jay back. She sat up and turned towards Landon. "Todd is the maintenance man!"

"You ain't know that?" Jay scowled.

"You knew and didn't tell me?" Millicent complained.

Landon whispered to Todd, "You told him?"

"He figured it out on his own." Todd smiled on the side of his mouth.

Todd grabbed Landon by her thighs and pulled her body closer to his. His eyes tempted her as they gazed deep into hers, coaxing her to stop fighting the urge he sensed growing inside of her. Their lips finally locked in a tender, sensual kiss as Jay and Millicent cheered them on.

Todd lowered his back against the door, sliding down to the seat. He pulled Landon with him, then waved for Jay to turn around and give them privacy.

Jay and Millicent returned to their own desires, giving into the heat firing between them. They opened their eyes and snickered at the sound of Todd's zipper coming undone, and held their laughs when Landon's lips smacked around Todd's pipe.

Todd, unable to grunt silently and control the passionate sighs of Landon's lip service, held up his hand and waved for Jay to get out of the car. The door slammed and Todd moaned, "Baby, can I come home!" softly massaging Landon's scalp as she filled her mouth with his dick, holding her gag as his hips pressed forward. "Hop on top before I bust," Todd ordered.

Landon's quivering legs climbed on top of him, and the car rocked side to side. Millicent hopped on the trunk, her breasts jiggling from the motion. Jay kissed the cushion of her pillows bouncing under the moonlight, and pulled out his penis. He rubbed it on Millicent's leg. "You trust me?" he asked, sliding her thong to the side. Jay's arrogance and imperiousness overpowered Millicent's detestation for him, and brought out a wild desire she hadn't felt for some time. She nodded and spread her legs wider, then held on to his shoulders as he stroked his dick with his hands and coached his tip between her southern lips.

The car squeaked and shook from the throttling of Landon working Todd over on the inside and Jay pressing Millicent's ass up and down the edge of the car on the outside. Landon contained her squeals, huffing as Todd long-dicked her from below, rolling her supple ass around his cock. With a glimmer in his eyes, he traced the lines of her mouth, worshiping her while she took command of his vigorous thrashing.

Outside, Jay would not be outdone. Roughly, he fucked Millicent in the dewy night air, making her scream into his shoulders. The excitement of being seen by passersby made her feel like the models in the exhibits at the club. She grinned as Jay put on his own display with beating hearts between them, racing to the finish line.

The car settled, and the couples headed back to the city with the music blasting and not a word spoken between them. Jay dropped Todd off at Landon's house, and the former lovers carried on for days, unable to break the soul tie that bound them. "Baby, what are we doing?" Todd begged for the answer he desperately wanted to hear. Landon never gave it to him. She kept quiet, accepting they couldn't go on like this for much longer.

"I'm confused. I have to let you go, but I can't."

"This is fuckin' with my head, baby. We always had great sex, but since we've been sneaking around, I want you more than ever. I want to come home."

"This is all my fault. I should have never reached out to you."

"I'm glad you did." He held her hand.

"I should have let you move on with your life. Can you forgive me?"

"There's nothing to forgive. But we gotta fix, whatever this is. I can't keep going on like this. I want my wife back."

Chapter 51

Seasons change

Jen

Summer came to an end, and it was time for Max to leave fun in the sun and return to Detroit. Jen stayed with Landon for the week, caught in the adventures of Todd's midnight visits, and intense conversations between him and Landon when it was time for him to say goodbye.

She interrupted them one night, and asked for a moment alone with Todd. Landon was relieved the departure wasn't going to be torturous for once.

"I need a favor from you, Todd."

"What you need?"

"Has Jay mentioned anything about full custody?"

"I don't know if I need to get in the middle of that, Jen."

"Look, I want to have a sit down with him, but he's vague whenever I ask him, and I just need an idea of how he'll react if I file for full custody."

"All I know is he was excited Max was coming home this week, and he talked about him the whole time he was away."

"I just want my son to be happy. And I don't know if he's happier here, or with me. It's hard to tell. Being that you are going through your own father/son thing right now, I thought I'd ask your opinion."

"I feel that. All I can tell you is, have the conversation. It's been a minute, and you both seem happy, so let all that past shit go, and work it out. You see I'm still trying."

Jen squeezed Todd's hand. "And don't give up. I think you're wearing her down."

Jen took Todd's advice and arranged for Jay to meet with her for lunch on The Jeffries' back lawn. Jay arrived ready for a battle with his smug face in tow.

"You can put that away today," Jen said, opening the door.

"What you talking about, girl?"

"That look. I didn't invite you over to argue. Leave the hostility outside." Jen welcomed him into the house.

Jay stepped inside and they stared at each other. "It's good to see you too, stranger."

"Todd and Landon are out back. Shall we?"

He followed her to the deck. "Looking good, Jen." He clicked his teeth.

Jen shook her head. "Thank you. I see some things haven't changed."

"You'd be surprised."

They sat with the divorced couple like old times, staring at one another around the table.

"I'm just going to say it. This has to be the most bizarre luncheon I've ever attended." Jay joked. "It's like we traveled back in time or something. You got L & T sitting over there divorced, but carrying on like they're not, and us." Jay pointed to himself and Jen. "What is this about?"

"About mending our friendship and keeping the circle tight. It's been a strange, difficult year. Wouldn't you agree?" Jen asked.

"I do."

"And we need to fix that. I asked you over today because I don't want to hate you anymore."

"What about Millicent?"

"Let me deal with that in my own time. My main concern is you. Our issues are starting to affect Max. We both want custody. Neither of us is going to budge, so we need to work something out better than we have right now."

"What do you propose?"

"Split custody six months of the year."

"Sorry, Jen, but no. I think you should move back to Detroit. You do that, and I'll agree he can live with you, while I'm still active in his life. I don't trust another man raising him full time. No disrespect to your boy toy."

"His name is Julian."

"Yeah, him. I'm the one responsible for helping Max become a man. I don't know that cat like that."

Jen sighed.

"You know what I can do for him and will do for him. It was hard enough letting him come down for the summer without seeing him."

"The travel is starting to wear thin, Jay. On me and him."

"So move back."

"And a part of me felt like he was distant with me. I could tell he missed you and that hurts me. He's sad, and I'm starting to feel like I'm not enough anymore."

"A mother can never be replaced, Jen." Jay assured her.

"So if I stopped coming up as often as I have this past year, you won't poison him against me?"

"Never dat."

"And…stop him from calling someone else Mama."

"Is that what this is really about?" Jay frowned at Jen. "Max would never call another woman your name. I won't allow it. You gotta trust me."

"It would kill me, Jay. And make sure you tell him I called and I love him every day. Even if I don't. Tell him."

"I give you my word." Jay squeezed her hand.

"Then that's settled. You and I no longer need to argue over custody, and we can work on becoming friends again."

"Jen, don't get me wrong, I'm happy we finally settled on this, but I gotta know. What changed your mind?"

Jen looked at Landon. "There are some things I will share with you at a later date. As of right now, you're the stable one and what's best for him."

"I don't buy it." Jay huffed.

"Everything is fine. Jules offered to transfer to the league here, so I could be closer to Max, but I just opened my makeup bar and need to see a profit before opening a second here."

"I have the cash if you want it." Jay looked at Todd. "If that will get you back here to be with our son, T and I will both invest."

"I need to discuss that with Jules."

"For what? He hasn't married you yet."

"He has a point," Landon added.

"Men don't think with their heart like women. We think with our head," said Jay.

"Which one?" Jen snickered.

Jay buried his head beneath his hands and laughed. "I know that low blow was directed at me, and good one. I'll give you that." He clapped his hands, flicking a toothpick from side to side in his mouth. "I had that coming."

Jen raised her brows. "Accountability. That's new."

"Do you want this money to start this business or not, 'cause you talking rather slick."

"I should be allowed as many as I want. Don't you think?"

Jay was humbled. He looked at Jen down his nose and showed all of his teeth before holding up his hands and nodding.

"I'm the bad guy. That'll never change, but I have to admit. I missed this. I miss you. Aside from what I did and am doing, we had a good time together until my shit caught up to me. But I like being able to talk to you like this."

"Then let's build on that."

"Agreed." Jay reached for her hand.

Jen shook it, then smacked it away. "One more thing. You, Max, and I need to go out for dinner before I leave so he can see we are getting along."

"And what about...?"

Jen silenced Jay before he uttered the words. "You, me, and our son. Capiche?"

"Got it."

"Now, go pick up my son and bring him to see his mama."

"Yes, ma'am. Think hard about that business proposal. Me and Todd are always down to make a little money."

CHAPTER 52

FALL LEAVES

TODD

Autumn turned the green leaves to orange, yellow, and red and plummeted them to the ground in time for the annual Dine & Drink Festival. Todd hadn't heard from Landon in a month. When she didn't call to confirm they would be attending the event together, he arrived solo, surprised to see Landon already sitting amongst the group.

Her energy was off. Her greeting was cold, and he couldn't help but notice how it seemed intentional she was seated at the end of the table when two chairs were available at the opposite end. He sat across from Jay, leaving the seat open between him and Tammy.

"That finally stopped..." Jay eluded in code.

"Seems so." Todd poured the wine in front of him into the empty glass. "Jen send that proposal?"

"Got it this morning. I'll bring it by your place tomorrow."

"Cool."

Todd glanced at Landon, searching for the right moment to say hello. All night they stared at each other, turned away, and stole looks when the other wasn't watching. By the end of the night, they found their moment, and took a walk away from everyone. A light breeze blew Landon's hair wild with the wind. The night air drew them close. Todd stood with his hands in his pockets. His elbows brushed against her sweater, tempted by her icy rose scent the swirling draft perfumed in the air.

"How you getting home?"

"I drove." Landon sipped her last drip of wine.

"How many glasses have you had?"

"Shit, I can't remember. But I'm good."

"How about I follow you to make sure?"

"As much as I want to say yes, I'm going to have to pass tonight."

"What, scared your boyfriend is going to see you with the likes of me?" Todd teased.

A curve formed on the side of her mouth. "No boyfriend. Just being smarter."

"Is that even possible?"

"Todd..."

"Have we actually arrived at the end of the road?"

"I think so. Sneaking around has been nice. Really nice. But I found myself becoming attached to you. Craving you more and more, and that has to stop. It's time we both move on."

"I knew this was coming. The one time I wish I was wrong."

"I wish I was too."

Todd exhaled sharply. "So the last time was the last time?"

"I'm afraid so. I better get going. You take care of yourself."

"Shit, I'll try."

Against Landon's wishes, Todd followed her home. He watched her pull into the garage and waited for the bedroom light to turn on, then made his way home in disbelief they were officially Mr. and Mrs. No More.

CHAPTER 53

SOME GETTING USED TO

LANDON

The snow fell early in October, dusting the city with a warning of one of the coldest winters to come. By November, one inch turned into three, then four inches as the brutal cold settled into the Midwest, forcing travel plans to delay, and loved ones to be missed for the holiday.

Tammy always held a huge Thanksgiving feast at her house, but with the rumor mill circling Todd was back out on the dating scene, Landon chose to host her family at her home. They piled in from Flint, helping her decorate for the holidays, and change her home's appearance. The old was out, and the new arrived for days with delivery men in and out with furniture and appliances.

The pictures on the wall were updated, the frames new in color, and accented corners with deep hues of auburn and caramel toned the house, making it warm and inviting for the season. The changes made her feel better about her single life, and the presence of her family livened up her spirits, serving as the perfect distraction for the loneliness looming above her at night.

With Jules traveling with the team, Jen arrived on Thanksgiving Eve with Max at her hip.

"I couldn't let you spend the first holiday of this season alone," she said.

"You are a sight for sore eyes. Come in. I want you to meet my family."

"I should have called. I feel like I'm intruding."

"Not at all. You being here is perfect. I was afraid my nephew was going to be bored out of his mind, but he and Max can keep each other entertained in Todd's old mancave. He already has a video game set up in there."

"Can I go, Mama?"

Jen tapped his shoulders. "Yes and be nice."

"Yes ma'am."

The lonely house was suddenly the lively house, full for the long weekend with good company and loving vibes. And though Laura Lee's words were eating her alive, "You're going to run him into another's woman's arms," she accepted her fate and dodged any further conversation about Todd. But Laura Lee wasn't easily fooled. When everyone spoke what they were thankful for during Thanksgiving dinner, she knew Landon was hurting.

"You girls should get out of the house. I'll keep watch of the boys with the help of your father. Go out. Be young."

"The clubs in the city are pretty fun during the holidays." Jen suggested.

"You don't have to ask me twice. I'm game." Launa kissed her mother's cheeks. "I'll be ready in twenty."

Plowed snow lined the salted, cleared streets, and the downtown night sky lit the mood. The ladies popped into the latest rave, stuck in a long line of partygoers. The wind blew so strong, the temperature felt ten below.

"I can't feel my toes anymore." Landon shivered.

"Fuck this. I'm going to wait in the car." Jen ran off.

Launa and Landon followed.

"I have an idea. Let's skip the club, and go warm up at one of those Spanish Coffee Houses that sells those nose warmer drinks with live acts.

"I know just the place," said Jen, driving them to a late night café near the dealership where she once worked.

They piled inside a booth and found more than music and warm drinks. A group of friends were seated next to them and struck a decent conversation. Against the owner's wishes, they slid their table closer to the booth, keeping the girls laughing and entertained while the night's act sang slower, softer renditions of the most popular songs. "I know this one!" Launa shouted, singing the tune loudly from the audience.

"You girls want to do something fun?" the husky one asked.

"We don't know your names." Launa pointed out.

"I'm Caleb, this is Seth, and this is Coran."

They saluted the ladies.

"I was going to suggest we get out of here and go ice skating in Martius Park."

"Isn't it closed at this hour?" Landon asked.

"So, we'll have it all to ourselves."

They followed the gentlemen, stoned and glossy-eyed. Bundled up like snowmen, they snuck into the park, and slid around on the ice like kids without skates until the wind gusts became too heavy. The guys escorted them to their car. Landon and Jen sat inside, warming the engine and defrosting their hands against the vents, watching Launa put the moves on Caleb.

"It's hard to believe you two came from the same woman," said Jen.

Launa hopped in the car..

"You get that, Little Sis?" Landon teased.

"Was there any doubt I would?" Launa laughed.

Early in the morning, the aroma of a famous Laura Lee breakfast woke the house. She put on a pot of coffee, fried sausages and eggs, baked biscuits and griddled pancakes for the boys.

"Girls!" Laura Lee woke them, passed out in their rooms. "Get up and go eat. I want you to take me to catch the sales."

"Ma, you could have mentioned that before you told us to go out and get shitfaced," Launa complained.

"I know you didn't catch a suitor with that mouth. Get up. Let's not waste the day."

Jen tiptoed into Landon's room after Laura Lee woke her. She keeled over laughing in Landon's bed.

"Your mother just woke me up and told me what I was going to do today. I have never had a mother do that. I love her so much."

"She set us up."

"That's what Launa said." Jen cackled. "I love the shadiness of it all."

Papa Davis gave his word to keep an eye on the boys while the women shopped, grabbed lunch, shopped some more, and ran into Millicent in the food court of the mall.

"Fancy seeing you girls here. Hello, Mother Davis." Millicent kissed her cheeks and hugged her. "How are you?"

"Doing good. Having a blast with my girls. And you, dear?"

"I'm doing well. How is Pops?"

"He's at Landon's with the boys." Laura Lee noticed Jen and her girls rolling their eyes at Millicent. "Well, it was good seeing you. Hope it's not so long next time."

"You too."

"Girls, I'll be sitting over here while one of you grabs that fancy latte drink for me." Laura Lee tightened her lips at her girls as she excused herself.

Millicent glanced over Jen and questioned Landon. "Why didn't you tell me your family was in town?"

"Time got the best of me. You wouldn't believe how exhausted I am."

"The holidays, right. Well maybe we'll catch up at Kim's game night, or are you not coming to that as well?"

"We're definitely coming to game night." Launa smirked.

"Good. Well, see you all there."

Millicent walked off, confused why Launa rolled her eyes at her. She waved at Laura Lee, then looked back at the ladies whispering amongst themselves.

"We're not going to game night. It's always couples, and I don't want to see Todd's new fling." Landon crossed her hands.

"Yes, we are, and it's going to be epic." Launa snapped her fingers.

"I'm with Landon. I'd feel better if Jules was with me."

"You two need to learn how to chill. Like me. I've got this under control." Launa grinned.

"What aren't you telling us?" Landon narrowed her eyes at her sister.

"Caleb and his friends want to hang tonight. He'll bring his friends, and we'll show up, ruffle a few feathers, start some ruckus, win some money, and be out. Besides, don't you both want to watch everybody get uncomfortable when we walk through the door?"

Jen laughed out loud. "Why hasn't your sister hung out with us before?"

"This is exactly why."

CHAPTER 54

GAME, SET, MATCH

LAUNA

'*Funky fresh dressed to impress ready to party*', Launa riled up Jen and Landon with her blend of throw-your-phone hip hop hits. With *Ante Up* blasting through her speakers, she and Jen bonded, shaking their hair and nodding their heads while Landon remained prim and proper in the backseat, nervous about seeing Todd with another woman on his arm.

They swung by the grocery store closest to Kim and Brian's neighborhood to meet the trio from the café. Smoke seeped through the cracked window of Caleb's car, signaling he would follow them to the party.

He and Launa hugged when they got out of their cars. Jen and Landon watched them bond, huddled together on the sidewalk.

"Your friends getting out or what?" Launa asked.

"Yeah, we just weren't expecting to be led to a neighborhood like this. We didn't take y'all for bougie people last night."

Launa laughed. "My sister is the bougie one. This is her friend's house, and I assure you they are a little bougie, but mostly cool people. I promise we'll have a good time."

"I am not bougie." Landon mugged Launa on her way inside the house.

"Shee-it." Launa swiped at her, snickering with Jen behind Landon's back. "She knows she is. She just doesn't like to hear it," Launa whispered to Caleb and Jen walking on each side of her. "Caleb, tell Seth and Coran to get out of the car."

Caleb waved to the guys. "It's cool."

Fashionably late, the odd mix entered Kim and Brian's house. The chatter silenced and all eyes shifted to Landon, Jen, and Launa walking in with three strange men behind them.

"The fuck is this?" Brian mumbled.

"It's about time you got here. And you brought dates." Kim's voice went south. "Great. The more the merrier."

"Yeah. More suckas to lose their money!" McCaine shouted.

"Ignore him. I'm Kim, this is my husband Brian, and welcome to our home."

Landon spoke. "Kim and Brian, you've met my sister Launa before I'm sure, and these are our new friends, Caleb, Seth, and Coran."

"Nice to meet you all. Come on in, put your coats over there, and let the games begin." Kim smiled nervously, then pulled Landon to the side. "You vouch for these people?"

"Right now, yes. But if something pops off, blame my sister." Landon raised her brows and made her way into the living room.

"What's up, everybody? Who was in here screaming about losing money? I'm ready to get in that ass! Sup, Bruh-law?" Launa leaned down so Todd could kiss her cheek.

"Winning so far."

"Not for long." McCaine slammed his cards on the table.

"You must be the shit talker," said Launa. "I have my eye on you."

As the night started with a serious game of poker, Launa sat on the sidelines, peeping at who was the real competition. Todd and Landon glimpsed at each other for the first hour, smirking with one another about Launa increasing the awkward vibe in the room.

"We are not playing poker all night. Save that for when you all meet up at Jay's house or something." Kim stared at Brian.

"Let this be the last hand, so we can play whatever Kim has on her list." Brian folded his hand. "But make no mistake, we will end the night at the card table."

"Time for Trivia, everyone!" Kim announced.

"We already know who the smartest person is in the room. Do we really need to play this?" McCaine pointed to himself.

As the game proceeded, tension began to build thanks to Launa's shenanigans. Whenever Todd answered a question correctly, she shouted, "Alright Bruh-law!" Landon tapped her a few times when she thought no one was looking, but Jen saw it every time and couldn't contain her laughter.

Todd's date allowed the dig to roll off of her back the first few times, but the more Launa ignored her presence, the more she lost her patience and decided to speak up. "Hi. I'm Shanice. I don't think we've been introduced."

"We haven't, but I'm sure you know my name by now. Everyone in here has it on their tongue. Ain't that right loser...I mean, McCaine." Launa snickered.

"Landon, get your sister please." McCaine held up praying hands.

"Todd told me about the others, but I'm afraid he didn't mention anything about you, Launa."

"I ain't the one you need to be worried about." Launa chuckled. "Caleb, baby, can you bring me a beer and keep me warm? It's a bit chilly where I'm sitting."

Jen looked at Landon, and they smirked. Jay saw Landon and Jen communicating across the room. He leaned over to Landon and said, "Your little sister is feisty."

"You like that don't you, Jay?" Launa winked at him.

Millicent cleared her throat.

Launa turned to Jay and smiled. "My bad. I didn't mean to get you in trouble. I thought I was about to be your flavor for the week."

Todd giggled. "Yooo Launa. Chill, Sis."

"I'm just playing around. Speaking of playing, where is Kim? Ah, there you are. What's next on this list? I came to bet and take you rich people's money."

"How are you two even sisters?" McCaine asked. "She needs to come on the guys' trip to the casino next time."

Tammy pinched his leg. "Take a chill pill, old man."

Landon looked at Kim and mouthed, "Cut her off for the night."

Kim held up *OK* with her fingers.

Caleb twisted off the top of the beer with his bare hands and passed it to Launa. She patted the seat next to her and slid closer to Jay to make room for him.

"I think it's time we partner up and bring down the house. Whatdya say, Caleb?" Launa ran her fingers across his head.

He blushed. "Ey. I'm here with you."

"What are your friend's names again?" Todd asked Caleb.

"That right there is Coran. And that's Seth." Caleb adjusted his shirt from beneath his stocky arms.

"Seth, you look familiar to me. T, he look familiar to you?" Jay asked.

"Yeah, that's why I asked. But I can't put my finger on where."

"We'll figure it out before the night is over. I'm sure," Jay added.

Landon and Jen rolled their eyes at Jay and Todd's banter.

Kim put an end to Launa's display of being a bad guest and slid a drawing easel into the living room.

"Time to test those art skills. Pictionary is up, but with a twist. We are going to draw names and pair up that way."

The guests sulked as Brian walked around the room with a hat filled with the male guest names on a folded piece of paper. The women pulled from the hat and revealed their new partner's name. The room was already full of jokes and laughter as they switched seats, and the odd pairs teamed up ready to play.

Landon partnered with Jay, Todd with Launa, Brian with Millicent, Seth with Tammy, Caleb with Shanice, Kim with Coran, and McCaine with Jen.

"We'll go first." Brian picked a card from the deck. He drew his best artwork of a man kneeling down on top of a fist, and an arm with muscles.

Millicent struggled to make sense of it and guessed incorrectly, "Neil Armstrong."

"No. It's Mike Tyson. It's a fist and muscles."

"But why is the man kneeling down instead of lying down?"

"Because I couldn't draw a man lying down."

"Next!" McCaine hit the wrong answer buzzer.

Todd went second and with ease drew a bird and a worm. Launa stood and calmly answered, "The Early Bird Gets The Worm." She and Todd high fived, then Launa belted out, "That's right, Bruh-law. Show 'em how it's done."

Shanice let out a loud sigh.

Coran took to the board and drew a circle, vigorously pressing the marker in the middle of it. The dot grew bigger each time he hit the easel. Kim shouted, "Center of the Universe!" Coran's eyes grew big when he nodded. Kim guessed, "On Point! Um, period in a circle! Point, blank, period!"

The timer dinged and Coran dropped his head. "It was center stage," he muttered.

"But where is the stage?" Kim asked.

"The circle is the stage. I was nodding yes when you said, "Center," but you moved on from that word.

"Well, good try." Kim frowned when his back turned.

Seth took to the board and showed off his art skills. Standing at six foot three, his skinny frame kneeled down to the board and drew a fast caricature of the rap artist Drake. Tammy guessed it correctly and everyone clapped at how great the drawing turned out.

Kim sprung from her chair and patted Seth on the back. "You are definitely invited back, and will be my partner next time. Can I keep this drawing?"

"If Landon doesn't want it. Sure." He blushed.

The room grew silent and all eyes shifted to Todd, looking at Landon's rosy cheeks with wounded eyes.

The offer and the silence tickled her. She said to Kim. "I'll let you have it since it's your party." Kim rolled up the drawing and tied a string around it with one of the ribbons from the gift bag. Landon turned to Seth. "But I would love to see your art collection and hang something on my wall."

"You got it." Seth winked at her.

"Who's next?" Todd huffed.

"That would be the best dressed motherfucker in the room." Jay stood up.

"Jay, I got this." Landon tapped his shoulder. "Just get it right."

She stepped to the podium and drew a devil, a pair of high heels, and a square with dollar signs inside.

Launa shouted, "Is it someone we know?"

Landon looked at Launa and begged for her to behave.

Jay silenced Launa and started yelling answers, "Money is the root of all evil! If it don't make money, it don't make sense! The devil don't fuck with broke bitches!"

Landon added the movie cut clapboard to her drawing, and a box of popcorn.

Jay jumped up and down and screamed, "*The Devil Wears Prada*!"

"Ah, hell nah. How would you know that?" Tammy fussed.

"I love me some Meryl Streep. That white lady can act."

The room went into chaos of laughter, and all the men stood and patted Jay on the back. Shanice stood, and the room fell silent. Too silent as everyone turned to Launa snickering in Todd's ear. She rolled her eyes at Launa as she drew a calendar, and a rain cloud. Caleb correctly guessed, "April Showers," and earned them a point.

McCaine jumped up from the floor and attempted to top Seth's drawing with his rendition of big hair, a television that looked like a robot, and a microphone that resembled an ice cream cone.

"I have no idea what a robot would be doing with an ice cream cone and wearing a wig, I'm guessing," said Jen.

"No. It's The Oprah Winfrey Show. Look at the hair. And this isn't a robot. It's a TV," McCaine explained.

"Okay one more round of this, then back to the card table," Brian told his guests.

The group played one more round of Pictionary with their dates and spouses, followed by a quick break to eat at the food table. Todd snuck looks at Seth making Landon laugh, waiting for her to lock eyes with him like they always did. He worked his way closer towards them, eavesdropping on their conversation.

"Is it possible I can see you again?" Seth asked Landon.

Todd interrupted. "Can I talk to you for a second? In private."

Seth answered, "The lady is still eating right now."

"I asked the lady. Not you." Todd flared his nostrils.

"I'm done eating. I'll be right back," Landon pinned her lips together towards Seth.

She followed Todd to the edge of the living room near the front door.

"Are you for real with this clown?" Todd pointed to Seth.

"It's not what it looks like."

"It looks like he is sizing you up. And he ain't good enough for you to be doing that."

"I'm only here with him because I heard you were bringing a date, and I didn't want to show up by myself. Shanice seems nice."

Todd stared in her eyes and exhaled a long breath. "You and I both know Launa has made sure I never see her again."

They both laughed.

"And she's not so nice. She's after money. And beginning to bore me."

"So why'd you bring her?"

"Same as you. Didn't want to show up by myself. You been good?"

"So so. And you? Well, don't answer that. I've heard how you've been doing. It's good seeing you. Friend."

"You too. Now don't make me beat that clown's ass tonight."

"Tell that to my sister." Landon pointed to Launa.

Launa saluted them with a drink and shimmied her way over towards Caleb. Todd and Landon cackled at her dance, then rejoined everyone back at the food table. Jay was overheard asking Jen about Jules.

"Where's Pretty Boy?"

"Turn on the television and see. You know the league plays on the holidays."

"That's right. I wasn't thinking about the games. I was really wondering where I've seen that Seth cat before, and what are you doing showing up with some random men?"

"Why do you care who she's with?" Millicent asked.

"A man's gotta know who is being brought around his kid."

"Jay, I didn't take you as the kind to be questioned about your business," Launa butt in.

"Launa, this conversation has nothing to do with you." Millicent sucked her teeth.

"You're right. It was between him and her." Launa pointed to Jen and Jay. "So why are you in it? Snobby sneaky ass bitch."

"Whoa. Whoa. Did I miss something?" Jay asked.

"Now hold up. We won't have any of that tonight," said Brian.

"Yo, Landon's little sister, chill out." Jay slid her a drink.

"I'm cool." Launa smirked.

"I beg to differ. You've been taunting me all night." Shanice joined the debate.

"Shalice, is it?" said Launa.

"It's Shanice."

"Sorry, babes, you aren't even relevant." Launa laughed.

"That is my cue to leave before I beat a bitch's ass. Todd! Take me home."

"What is your problem, Launa?" Millicent frowned.

"Trust me. You don't want me to go there."

"Damn, is it time to call it a night already?" Tammy asked.

"But, baby, we haven't whipped their asses in Spades yet," McCaine complained. "I don't care if they knock each other out. I came to eat, drink, and play some cards. And afterwards go home and have butt naked sex on top of all of the money I won."

The tension died and everyone laughed. Launa apologized for her unkind words and made a promise. "From here on out, I'll be on my best behavior, and beat all of your asses in Spades. Let's do this!"

Todd walked over to Launa and whispered in her ear. "You made me laugh tonight, Little Sis. Look after my baby. And don't let that clown put a finger on her. I gotta take Shanice home. Love ya."

"Be safe out there on that road, Bruh-law. And Todd, do me a favor. Do better. Please?" Launa grinned.

Shanice yelled from the porch. "I can still hear her talking about me!"

"I better get going guys. I'll see y'all later." He tipped his head. "Landon."

Todd smirked at Seth on his way out and shared a smile with Landon as he opened the door for Shanice. He nudged her outside as she yelled, "She doesn't know me like that! And trust me she doesn't want to! I'll fuck up these nice people's house with her narrow ass!"

"Ooohhh she's mad now." Jay rubbed elbows with Launa. "Why did you pick at that girl like that?"

"I meant what I said. He could do better." Launa shuffled the deck. "Caleb dear, do you need me to get you anything before I deal?"

"I'm good, babe."

"Now that that's settled, I have something I want you to do for me."

"What's that?"

"Steal all of his books." Launa pointed to McCaine.

"Landon, come get your trouble making sister. She does not want none of this!" McCaine slapped the table.

"I'll follow your lead, mama." Caleb blew Launa a kiss.

Launa moaned. "Twenty bucks a game starts now."

As the card game commenced, Tammy tried to learn more about Seth and Coran. They gave Coran the third degree until Seth mentioned he was shy, and didn't talk much around people he didn't know.

"You weren't this quiet last night," said Jen.

"Y'all hung out last night?" Tammy asked.

"Yeah, we had coffee downtown and took the girls ice skating. We had a good time," Seth replied.

"Wonder what Jules would say about that?" Jay chuckled.

"I haven't been ice skating in decades." Tammy spoke loud so McCaine could hear her at the table. "Why don't you take me ice skating anymore?"

"Because I need my hands to work and pay these bills! Now leave me alone. I'm concentrating."

Tammy fanned him off. "Excuses, excuses. Next time y'all go, invite us along."

"'Cause we sure weren't invited last night." Millicent sighed under her breath.

"I'm trying to get Landon here to tell me when she wants to go back out there and show me what she's got." Seth grinned in her face.

Jay cleared his throat and shouted, "I'll take that!"

The party gathered around the card table serving as the entertainment for the rest of the night. Landon was impressed at the card shark her sister had become. Launa's game matched her mouth, and Caleb had fallen in love with her fun girl persona, while Jay failed at hiding he was turned on by her hustling abilities.

The time passed one a.m. as the final hand of the night was dealt. "Take your sister back to the country," said McCaine, sweating from his armpits and shaking the table with his knees. Lauma snatched another book from the table and smiled at McCaine, who was eyeing her like she was the devil.

"You don't know about them country girls." She laughed.

"I know bout'em." Caleb snarked.

Lauma stared in Jay's eyes, and Millicent grew uneasy. With a poker face, she winked at Caleb to follow her lead, and played her final card. Caleb snatched the book and smacked the table. "Eight it up! Get up from the table!" Lauma and Caleb eliminated McCaine and Jay— the first time in the history of their tag teaming efforts.

"That'll be $500," Lauma said to Jay, winning a side bet from bypassing the points total.

Jay pulled out a wad of cash. "You have got one hell of a little sister, L. Y'all are like night and day."

"I'll teach you how to play one day, Jay." Lauma held out her hand for her winnings.

"Well, this has been fun. Brian and I want to thank you all for coming. This one is in the books."

"Thank God this night is over. I don't know how much more I can take," Millicent mumbled.

"What are you griping about?" Landon asked her.

Millicent nodded at Lauma. "Your sister has been on one. Taunting Todd's date. Coming in here with one guy, and flirting with Jay in my face. So disrespectful and unnecessary."

Jen laughed out loud.

"My sister was not flirting with Jay."

Lauma put on her coat. "Lighten up, Millie. I'm here with someone. Whatchu so nervous about? Oh yeah. I forgot." Lauma snickered.

"Like that! She's been saying slick shit like that all night!" Millicent argued.

Jay chimed in. "Lauma, you are cool as fuck, but on the real you have been coming for folks pretty hard all night. My girl being one of them. What's up?"

"What's up is your girl is grimey and a fraud."

"Please enlighten me." Millicent clung to Jay.

"Landon, that issue we recently resolved back home, where I told you who my son's father was?"

"Yeah."

"Remember when I said I found out he was seeing multiple girls, and the day I went to tell him I was pregnant I saw him kissing someone?"

"Yeah."

"It was your best friend." Launa pointed to Millicent. "She was fucking him too."

"So there's a pattern," Jen chimed in.

Landon's face turned bright red. "Why would you keep that from me after all of these years? Like you've had so many opportunities to tell me you did that."

Millicent sent daggers with her eyes across the room at Launa. "I didn't want it to come in between our friendship. You can't possibly hold that against me now. That was eons ago. Neither of us give a shit about that guy now. Landon, this is stupid."

"Fuck Reynaldo, this is about you being my friend. And Jen's friend. You did the same thing to both of us. I don't even know who you are anymore."

"Yes, you do. I'm your best friend. One mistake can't change that."

"I'm not so sure anymore. Kim and Brian, thanks for having us." Landon grabbed her coat and led everyone out.

Millicent stepped out into the cold calling Landon's name. Landon kept walking and hopped in the car with Jen in the driver's seat.

"Ain't no way in hell I'm letting Launa drive us home. How you feeling?"

"Confused. Like I can't trust anyone."

"Hmm. You can trust me, 'cause I damn sure trust you."

Launa and Caleb slammed into the side of the car, making out with condensation clouding around them.

Seth knocked on Landon's window. "I don't know what tonight was about, but if you ever wanna get together or talk, here's my number. Hope to hear from you."

"I'll give you a call," Landon lied and rolled up the window. "I have no intention of ever seeing him again."

Jen chuckled. "Your sister promised us tonight would be epic. She could have told us she was holding onto a hand grenade."

"Makes me wonder, what I would do if...Never mind. I'm not going down that road."

"So let me get this straight. The guy we talked about when you came to visit me turned out to be your sister's son's father, and fucked your best friend?"

"Yup."

"Ain't you glad you held your pussy hostage?"

Jen and Landon burst into a roaring laughter.

Launa hopped in the back seat. "Well, didn't I say we would have a good time tonight?" She waited for the two of them to pipe down. "Now you know she has the tendency to stab you in the back."

"You could have told me this months ago, ya know."

"Yeah, but I wanted to see her face when I exposed her secret. She has never liked me, and I have never liked her. She had too much influence on you growing up. You and I were thick as thieves, and then one day you and her became friends, and you pushed me to the side."

"That's not true. Well, maybe just a little."

"I forgive you." Launa squeezed her sister's shoulder.

"And I you."

"You two make me wish I had a sister." Jen's lips curved.

"You do. You have me." Landon pounded her fist.

"And me," Launa added. "You are the realest person Landon has hung out with. Welcome to the family!"

CHAPTER 55

LOOK AT US

JEN

Jules surprised Jen before her week ended in Detroit, proposing they fly to Vegas and elope. Jen's mind went blank for a second as flashes of Alex smiling at her from the grave formed tears in her eyes.

"I didn't mean to make you cry." Jules wiped her cheeks.

"I wasn't expecting you to ask so soon."

"Is that a yes?"

"Yes." Jen hesitated. "But Vegas?"

"At Christmas. That gives us a few weeks to get a plan sorted out. Whatdya say?"

"Something small and intimate."

"However you want it."

Before she shared the news, she questioned Max about his feelings for Jules and Millicent. His response would determine if she would go through with the wedding. To her surprise, Millicent was the victor of the two.

"I love Ms. Millicent. She reads to me a lot, and is nice to me, and tells me she loves me and my mommy every night."

Jen was shocked by Max's response. She reflected on the memorable moments they shared, and figured with the care Millicent was providing for her son in her absence, she could forgive Millicent for being a backstabbing bitch, but would never forget it, and no longer harbored any hatred towards her. She thought, *'Was them falling in love a fluke?'*

Still undecided on what to do, Jen kept the proposal from everyone. She returned to Miami with a racing mind, and spent days tallying the pros and cons of saying "I do," once again.

Jay called her to settle Max's schedule for the holidays. Jen had no choice but to come clean with her decision, and kept her word that she would explain to him why she said what she said the day they put their differences aside.

"Can you come down here, so we can talk?"

"In person? Is that necessary?"

"It is. You should come see where we live."

"I'll call you when I get in town."

The urgency in Jen's voice was recognizable from the years they spent together. Millicent wasn't pleased he was leaving on short notice, or where he was headed, and acted out.

"Are you done playing with me, and now chasing what you've lost?" she asked.

"Stop your worrying. I'll be back soon. And I'm coming home to you."

"Is Jen in some sort of trouble? Can I help?"

"Why would you think that?"

"Just be careful. And tell her I miss her and I still love her. Even if she hates me."

Knowing Jen's secret, Millicent did have something to worry about. If Jen was getting Jay involved with her hellish past, she feared the worst for everyone involved, and Jay could see in her eyes she knew something he didn't. He touched down in Miami and followed Jen's directions, meeting at a hotel on South Beach.

They walked a long way from the hotel to a secluded location past the strip, where the waves could distort the sound. Jen looked over her shoulder repeatedly making Jay nervous.

"Why did I have to leave my phone at the hotel? Should I have brought my gat or something?"

"Sorry. What I have to say can't be said near a phone, and I'm always on alert. I'm surprised you never noticed."

"What's going on, Jen? You got a brother on edge coming down here by himself."

"I wanted to run a few things by you."

"I do as well." Jay looked over his shoulder.

"Jules asked me to marry him, and I said yes.

"You're gonna marry the pretty boy? I didn't think it would last this long. When?"

"Christmas in Vegas. Max will be out of school for the holidays, so it all works out."

"Are you sure this is the guy for you?"

"It feels right." She smiled. "I feel loved."

"I'm coming at you with nothing but truth, girl. I don't like him. I've tried, but I follow my gut, and I just can't put my finger on it. You call me shady all the time. Well maybe shady knows shady like real knows real. I feel like he is a pretender. And I don't want to see you get hurt. If dude hurts you, I'm going to hurt him. That's my word."

"Unfortunately, I'm the pretender."

Jay stopped walking and looked in Jen's eyes. She confessed her true identity and told him what she'd endured before he came into her life. As he listened, he saw a version of himself staring back at him. In that moment he realized why they were compatible more as friends than lovers, as they both kept secrets, and both couldn't be trusted in their relationship.

As Jen wrapped up her story involving the money, the murder, and her menacing mother, she revealed she knew he and Todd's hands were dirty.

Jay laughed. "You don't know nothin' girl."

"I know more than you think. That's why I'm having this conversation with you. I followed you a few times before I caught you cheating. I know about the gambling ring where y'all fight cocks, the number houses, the sporting bets, and the you-know-what.

Jay rubbed his goatee. "Is that right?"

Jen lifted her blouse. "I'm not wearing a wire. I don't need you to deny or confirm. I'm bonding with you. I may need you to come through for me one day."

"Why do you say?"

"I'm going to go after the money." Her face turned grave.

"Are you nuts? You don't know anything about that country. The laws are different. The streets are foreign. We know nothing about that place, or how they operate."

"I didn't say I was going now, but one day I will, and I might call on you. Will you answer?"

"I'm not going over there." Jay spoke with his chest.

"What are you afraid of?"

"Why aren't you afraid is a better question?"

Jen turned around and led the way back to the hotel. Jay repeated his question.

Jen huffed. "Because it's mine. And my daddy lost his life behind it."

"Doesn't mean you need to lose yours. You have more than enough, I'll see to it you never go without. Leave that shit where it is." Jay grabbed her hand. "Look, a part of me will always love you, but I'm thinking we didn't work out because I didn't know the real you, and I thought you didn't know the real me. And maybe that's what broke us. But you and Max are always gonna be my responsibility. I'm here for you if you need me. But leave that shit over there with them people."

"I'll give it some more thought."

"In the meantime, send a pic of your boy to my phone just in case he ain't who you think he is."

"I will when we get back to the hotel. Now what did you want to run by me?"

"Where do you stand these days on Millicent?"

"We're all human and allowed to make mistakes I suppose."

"Did somebody body snatch the Jen I know? Who are you and what have you done with my son's mother?" Jay joked. "But on the real, she loves you and Landon. Talks about y'all all the time. I'll be glad when you three make up, and shit can go back to the way it used to be."

"One day. Maybe?"

"Women have the hardest time letting shit go. Look at me down here on pretty boy island. Be like me. Let it go."

Jen laughed. "I don't hate her. You might get your wish soon enough. So how do you like it down here?"

"It's alright. But I'm catching the red eye back out tonight."

"Why?"

"This is ain't my stomping grounds, and these ain't my streets."

Jen nodded her head. "Some things about you will never change, but I noticed a few things are different about you."

"Like what?"

"You seem happier. A little more free and settled."

"It took for you to leave me to look at myself."

"And maybe Millicent had something to do with it. She's good for you. You and Max."

Jay narrowed his eyes on Jen. "Again, where is the Jen I know?"

"I'm happy now."

"Seems so. Are you gonna tell your soon to be husband about the business venture before or after y'all are married?"

"After."

Jay shook his head. "Have it your way. It will be a few months, but once all the leg work is complete, I'll fly you out to see it. Then you can take it from there."

"Can't wait."

"Look at us, working as a team." Jay grinned.

"Max would be proud."

CHAPTER 56

PEACE OF MIND

JAY

Hours before the red eye delivered Jay back to Michigan, he made the most of his short trip with a business dinner in the city and caught the game at the arena where Jules worked. His associates treated him to the hottest strip club in the Miami nightlife. And after being entertained by drinks and slutty women, he flew home with a lot to think about from a night to remember.

The sky was still dark when Millicent welcomed him in their bed. Wide awake, wearing nothing but a smile, she pulled the covers back. "I prayed you'd make it back in one piece. How did it go?"

"It went well. I have some things to process, and work on with Todd, but overall things are looking up," he replied.

"Did she tell you anything new?"

"Let's just say we got everything out in the open."

"Did y'all talk about us?"

"We did."

"And?"

"Like I said, things are on the up and up."

"What does that mean?"

"Give it time, Mills. It will work itself out."

"If you say so. What is that smell on you?"

"The beach, booze, and bitches from the strip club."

"Strip club? You can't be serious coming in here with heaux juice all over you. Get out of my bed."

"Your bed?"

"It became my bed when I moved in here and had it delivered. So yes, my bed."

"Come here, girl. I like that feistiness." Jay slid her to the bottom of the bed by her feet.

"Don't touch me with those nasty ass hands either." Millicent pushed him away. "Is this where it begins to end for me?"

"What are you talking about?"

"Am I going to have to count condoms and worry you are out there cheating on me with ratchet bitches and heauxs in the club too?"

"Slow down with that. I caught a game, dinner, drinks and went to the club with some business associates. I have never cheated on you. I got what I want, and I'm wiser now. You gotta leave my past in the past if you want to be my future. You hear me?"

"I hear you, but I am not listening."

"This dick belongs to Millicent St. James. You listening to that?"

Millicent kicked back to the top of the bed.

"I'm going to take a shower, and when I get back I'm going to write my name all over your ass. You'll hear me, feel me, and listen to me then."

He rushed back to Millicent dripping wet with his gear in shift. They tumbled and tussled for a few rounds, while Jay pled his case for trustworthiness. "You think your man has been tipping out? You need your man to prove his love for you?" Millicent resisted his kisses and didn't answer. Jay groped and tickled and fondled her until she folded with low screeches.

"Okay, okay I believe you."

"Good. I don't want you to ever think I'm being disloyal to you, Mills. You are the woman for me."

Jay placed his vodka infused lips on hers and kissed her sloppy, rough, and long. The thought of her walls had been on his mind during his flight home, and he played out what he imagined now that she was in his grasp.

Clutching her ass tightly from below, he *grinded* on top of her, fighting his penis to stop the quick entry it aimed for. It bounced and shifted side to side, ready to feel her slick lips gyrate around him. The plans to taste her walls were forced to wait as his mind lost the battle to his dick. It forged inside of her pussy, pushing and pulling as she quietly "Aaahed" in his ear.

Rough from the start, she held onto his shoulders, her nails scraping his back while her body welcomed the lashing. Jay was lost in a euphoric state listening to her pant and gasp for air, digging deeper and deeper in her world. He grinned at the extra warmth drizzling on his pipe. The vodka in his system added to his stamina, giving him the power to fuck her long and hard, fast then slow, slipping and sliding inside her walls, weakening her with broad strokes until she quietly released sounds of ecstasy into the pillows.

The sun was now high above the trees, but the pound fest was far from over. Millicent laid wrecked on top of the bed she bragged about. Jay removed the pillow from her face and placed his hands over her mouth, continuing a high performance of rigorous strokes to the back of her wall, while fingering her clit. Millicent moaned and bit his hand, shivering below him like a razor in a barber's hand. Jay fucked his liquored soul to his peak. He grabbed her withered body and grunted, pressing his face against hers. "I love you," he whispered in her ear.

"I want more of that when I wake up," she said.

Jay laughed, looking at the clock. "Then that's in ten minutes."

CHAPTER 57

MOVING FORWARD

JEN

As requested, Landon escorted Max to Las Vegas for Jen and Jules' big day with Launa and Laura Lee as a surprise.

"I couldn't let you go on lockdown forever without showing you the best night of your life," said Launa.

"Maybe." Landon frowned. "It's Christmas, and we can't let her walk down the aisle looking tired and beat."

"And we still need to check the venue. How about a post-marital night on the town next time we're together?"

Jen hugged the girls. "I like the sound of that."

The trio visited the hotel's wedding chapel in the heart of the building. An intimate, beautifully decorated gazebo filled with colorful bouquets of lilies surrounded by candles couldn't have been more pleasing. "So much better than the first time," Jen mumbled.

Ms. Rosetti, Jules's mother, arrived to survey the chapel. She looked at Jen as if it were the first time they'd met. "We should have met you a long time ago. Who can get to know a person the day before a wedding?" she grumbled. Jen got the sense she pretended not to know her because she disapproved of her family's history. She gave Launa and Landon a look of concern and laughed nervously. Launa stepped in as the family Jen needed to support her against her future mother-in-law, throwing subtle jabs back at her so Jen didn't have to.

"A wedding in Vegas. The place of sin," Ms. Rosetti complained.

"The place of love. Where your son chose to get married. Not Jen," Launa answered.

"When do we meet the boy?"

"'The boy' has a name, Max. And you'll meet him tomorrow, at your son's wedding, and it will be beautiful." Launa cringed with a smile.

The tone of Jules's mother heightened. "And who are you?"

"I'm Launa, Jen's baby sister. Nice meeting you."

After the hostile meet and greet, the Davis sisters met in Jen's bridal suite. They decorated a miniature Christmas tree and exchanged gifts early. Jen clung on to Max, taking in every moment with him to make up for the time she missed.

"Max is going to have three Christmases this year. Tonight, when we get back to my house, and at his dad's house." Landon tousled his hair. "Did I tell you an elf dropped off some presents for you at my house this morning before we left?"

Max's eyes grew big.

"Speaking of gifts..." Launa went to the closet. "An elf dropped this off for you."

Launa handed Landon a gift bag from one of the boutiques downstairs in the hotel. She frustrated everyone, carefully untying the red ribbon, feeling for the tape on the edge so she didn't tear the paper.

"We'll be here all day." Laura Lee sighed.

Landon opened the card taped to the box and read it aloud:

"Making sure you have something under your tree.
Merry Christmas
~Love Todd"

She opened the box and held the latest Louboutin bag to her chest. A tear formed in her eyes, and Laura Lee passed her a tissue from her purse.

"I can't keep this."

"How long are you going to make that man suffer?" her mother asked.

"That's not my intention, Mama. I thought we were finally making progress as friends."

"He doesn't want to be your friend, chile. He wants to be your husband."

Landon felt guilty. She had broken her vows and broken his heart, but reached a comfortable place with having him in her life without having to deal with his baggage.

"When did Todd put you up to this?"

"A few days ago when he found out you weren't going to be home for Christmas. What are you going to do?" Launa asked.

"Definitely send him a Christmas gift, but I think I might have to cut off all communication for a while, or I'll never move on."

"And neither will he." Launa squeezed her sister's shoulder.

Like sisters would do, Landon and Launa showed up at Jen's door in the morning with coffee in hand, ready to tend to their maid duties. They ordered a light breakfast for the bride, prepped for her dressing with hair and makeup, and made sure Max looked sharp to carry the rings.

Time stood still in the room when an unexpected knock sounded at the door. "We're coming down in five minutes!" Launa yelled. The knock startled them again. She counted everyone in the room. "We're all here. Who the hell is being an asshole at the door?"

She opened it and gasped. "Of course." Launa chuckled. "What are you doing here, Millicent?"

"I come bearing gifts and apologies. If you all will have me."

"Come in," said Jen, surprising Landon and Launa.

Millicent hugged her and passed out cards and gifts.

"I'm glad you came. I've been meaning to call you, but things moved so fast I never got the time. I forgive you, and would like it very much if you would come to my wedding."

Max entered the room and hugged Millicent. When Jen saw the happiness on her son's face, she knew she had done the right thing, and took it as a sign of good faith that the day was going to be beautiful.

"How about you?" Millicent asked Landon.

Jen tapped Millicent on the shoulder. "It takes time, Millicent. Quit while you're ahead."

Landon withdrew and smiled to herself in the corner. It felt good to know Jen had her back and silenced Millicent so she didn't have to. Launa exhaled and took control of the room. "Ready?" she asked Jen. She nodded, and followed her team downstairs to her ceremony.

Jules lifted his bride in the air after the minister declared, "I now pronounce you man and wife." He kissed her as their witnesses celebrated them, stopping the lip lock when Max pulled at the back of his tuxedo.

The guests laughed at Max's protection of his mom. Jules took his hand and placed it inside his mother's, covered theirs with his, and kissed them both. It was the first time Max looked him in the eye and smiled, bringing the room to tears.

In a separate suite, the happy couple held a small reception for their guests. The Rosettis disappeared to Jen's bridal suite for a quickie in her wedding gown. The tulle on her dress was flipped above her waist for twenty hard pumps and back at her feet before the guests could worry about their whereabouts. When they returned to their party, they danced in the middle of the room.

"That is the only time I'll forgive you for that driveby." Jen kissed her husband's ear.

"That is the only time I plan to rush tearing that wet ass up."

They laughed forehead to forehead.

"I wonder if this is how most couples talk to each at their wedding?" Jen whispered.

"I don't know. But I bet most husbands are thinking what I'm thinking."

"Which is?"

"I wish these people weren't around so I can fuck the shit out of my wife again."

The couple laughed hysterically in the middle of the dance floor. As the chuckles settled, Jen noticed Launa tossing her braids in front of Jules's brother, Juan, while Millicent babysat Max, and Landon kept Laura Lee company. She took one final look around the room and laid her head on her husband's chest.

"Today couldn't have been more perfect."

"It's not over yet. You ready to get out of here?"

"I am."

Their party threw rice and rose petals when they exited the front entrance of the hotel. Jen tossed her bouquet directly to Landon, blew her a kiss, and cried as she waved goodbye with her new husband on her arm. Landon caught the kiss in the air and smelled the lilies in the bouquet. She looked up at Jen. "Thank you," she said under her breath, hoping the happiness she saw in her friend would extend her way.

CHAPTER 58

PRESS YOUR LUCK

MILLICENT

Launa decided to come up for air from Jules's brother and try her hand in the casino before they left Vegas. She ran into Millicent trying out her luck on the slots.

"I thought you left town?" Launa plopped down in the seat next to her nemesis.

"Nope. Enjoying some me time."

"Trouble in paradise?"

"You would love that, wouldn't you?" Millicent rolled her eyes. "Unfortunately for you, everything is just fine at home. I saw you had that cute guy all over you earlier."

"Yeah I did. Didn't I?" Launa polished her nails with her shirt.

"Jules's brother, right?"

"Yup."

"What happened with you and that guy you brought to game night?"

"He's still around. I don't have a ring on this finger." Launa flipped her hand front to back.

"Very smart. Until there is a ring on it, you can't put a claim on it."

A waitress approached carrying a tray of complimentary champagne. Each took a flute from the tray and sipped.

"Tangy," Launa exhaled.

"Cheap," said Millicent. "I believe this is the first real conversation you and I have ever had, Launa."

"I think you're right. It was because I didn't like you."

"And what, you like me now?" Millicent sneered at Launa.

"I didn't say that, but you coming out here to show Jen some love and apologize to my sister makes me see you a little different."

"I miss them both. They were like sisters to me."

"I know how that feels. You took my sister from me, but I'm over it now since we put all of that behind us."

"Launa, whatever I did to make you hate me so much, I apologize for it. Truce?"

"Thank you. That's all you had to say. And stop there before you kill my buzz."

"So are we good?"

"We're good."

"Will you help me get back in good with your sister?"

"I'm not getting in the middle of that. Let her hold her grudge for a while. Time will have to heal that wound," Launa advised. "I'm curious, though. Why didn't you tell her about you and Reynaldo?"

Millicent lowered her head and took a deep breath. "Have you ever regretted doing something stupid?"

"Ugh, hello. I love my kid, but if I could pick another daddy for him I would jump inside a time machine."

"Well, I was mad at myself after it happened. I felt like the biggest dummy alive. He saw me at the store, and we got to talking, and all I could think about was how Landon described what it looked like. I wanted to see if it really was as pretty as she said it was, so when he put the moves on me I went to his house. He whipped it out, and I was mesmerized. Next thing I knew, I was added to the hit list, and never heard from him again."

"It truly is a work of art attached to the most vile human being," Launa added. "And he talks a good game, doesn't he?"

Millicent shivered. "If you find that time machine, swing by and pick my ass up."

"Will do."

They clinked glasses.

"Alright, enough of that. Let's make a toast," Launa suggested. "Here's to good sex."

Millicent laughed and raised her glass. "To good sex I wish I could give back."

"And may I get some tonight."

"Launa, you are crazy as hell."

"People tell me that all the time. See you 'round."

CHAPTER 59

CURVES

LANDON

Landon handled her first New Year's Eve as a divorced, single woman with a bottle of melatonin gummies, silk pajamas, and a bedtime before the clock struck midnight. The winter storm blowing in from the west was too brutal for anyone to get in or out of the city, and everyone was buried behind white ice castles and mounds of frozen snow.

A neighbor's kid made a few bucks off of Landon shoveling her snow and tending to her yard, clearing a path for her to get in and get out. Landon paid him handsomely as the months went on, but also treated him to the baked cakes, cookies, and pies she began baking on the regular to soothe her loneliness.

She became a fan of comfort food, and a Food Network enthusiast. If it looked good, she cooked it, and baked it, and fried it, and ate it. And if she couldn't make it, she ordered it to be delivered to her doorstep.

Her workout room turned into a dust haven, and her waistline nonexistent. It wasn't until winter was over that she noticed she was on the pudgy side. She'd put on so much weight, her clothes size went up by four, and her ass was so plump, men stopped whatever they were doing to stare. Todd couldn't believe his eyes when he ran into her.

"And I thought you couldn't get any prettier," he said, admiring her curves.

"You're being kind. How are you?"

"I would ask the same, but I see you're doing fine. I heard you put on some weight, but damn Landon, I like the extra roundness on that ass. You got some baby making hips on you now."

Landon twisted and moved her hands nervously. "Life treating you good?"

"It is today." Todd licked his lips.

Landon chuckled. "Well it was nice running into you. I might see you at the next party."

"You sure about that? You haven't come around since Thanksgiving."

"I just needed to take some time for myself. I'll be back around in time."

"I hope so. I heard you and Mills aren't on speaking terms. Do yourself a favor, and stop pushing away everyone who loves you." Todd winked.

"I'll keep that in mind."

Landon knew she went up a few sizes in her clothes, but it wasn't until Todd pointed out how much weight she gained that she decided to throw away her sweet tooth, and find the woman she used to be.

The calendar said spring, but the weather said not yet. Snow continued to fall, so Landon got a head start on her weight loss by dusting off her equipment in Todd's old man cave. When the treadmill became boring, she danced in a Zumba class, working off the pounds twice a week, and once on the weekend.

Spring arrived past its due date. Landon jumped to the opportunity of neighborhood runs once the snow melted, and participated in weekend charity races. By summer she had run the twenty pounds she gained off of her, and had come to love the way running made her feel physically and mentally.

She continued to run regularly to maintain her figure, or whenever she felt anxious to turn on the oven and whip up something sweet.

Expanding her range of charities to donate to and stay in shape, she signed up for a race near the Eastern Market where the neighborhood had been gentrified, and the vendors sold fresh produce. The competition was fierce in that district, pushing her far from the front of the pack, but motivated her to return to compete with the best.

She placed closer to the front on her second race at the market, meeting some new friends to broaden her horizons. She tagged along with them to the market afterwards, flipping through the hues of green and yellow vegetables, and ripe fruit. Sweaty from the race, she hurried to make a decision on what to buy for the week before someone got a whiff of her workout.

Landon didn't know what possessed her to follow those people to the market without showering first. She hid below her hat, thumbing through the carrots, and stepped on someone's foot. "Sorry," she said without looking up, and nudged past the person.

"No need to apologize," a man's voice replied.

She reached for a batch of broccoli, and brushed against the fingers of another shopper. She lifted the brim of her hat, and the voice from before spoke.

"Oh, hey you."

"Hi." Landon smiled, showing all of her teeth.

"Landon, right?"

"You remembered my name."

"Of course I remembered your name. A man never forgets the name of a pretty woman. Especially one who was kind enough to bring him out of the rain. How are you?"

Landon blushed below her hat. "I'm doing good. What brings you this way?"

"My unit sponsored a race here this morning."

"Small world. I ran that race. You didn't mention you run before."

"Since I was in the marines, I run every day if I can. I don't know how I missed you out there." Walt sneakily checked out her physique. "Pardon me for asking, but do you always run without your wedding band?"

Landon fidgeted with her ring finger. "I'm actually divorced now."

"Sorry to hear that."

"It's okay. We are still good friends. Just no longer a ball and chain."

"I hate to hear you and your husband split up, but I can't say that doesn't make me smile. I'm sorry if that's weird." He gazed at her eyes peeking at him below her brim.

"Not weird at all." Landon's top teeth sank into her bottom lip.

"I know I don't live around here, but is it okay if I call you sometime. Maybe take you out to dinner?"

"I would love that."

"Here is my card. If you'll accept it this time." Walt laughed.

Landon read it and placed it in her pocket.

"I hope to hear from you." He slowly strolled away.

"You will."

Landon beamed from ear to ear. Running brought her back to life and helped her find herself again. It reintroduced her to the feeling of self-worth, and snapped her out of her obsession with food that masked her depression. It freed her mind and her waistline, and now it had introduced her to someone she could share all of that with— Detective Walter Reed, the man she rooted for her estranged best friend to give a chance. But as it turned out, the odds were in her favor, and when he came knocking this time, he'd be knocking for her, and her boots if he played his cards right.

BOOK THREEE

THE CROSSING

CHAPTER 60

TEA

LANDON

Turning heads as always, Landon arrived for a mandatory lunch date with Tammy, who wouldn't take no for an answer.

"We haven't seen you, Ms. Jeffries." Tammy stood, kissing the air next to her cheeks. "Looking good as always. You're glowing so bright I can see a halo above your head."

"I missed you, too." Landon hugged her.

"I tried to get you on the phone yesterday. I'm surprised you showed up today. Everyone thinks you've written us off."

Landon stuttered, "I—I have a good excuse. Tell everyone I've been super busy."

"When you stutter like that you are telling a quick one. I see being a horrible liar hasn't changed. What's really going on?"

Landon peered at Tammy with a side eye.

Tammy danced in her chair and slid her hands together. "Ooh. This ought to be good."

"It's not *what's* been keeping me busy. More like *who*?"

"Well, I know it isn't your former maintenance man, who still talks about you every-damn-time I walk in on the guys having a moment. His face lights up at the mention of your name."

A blended grin and resting bitch face curved on Landon's lips. "That was a mouthful."

"Yes, it was." Tammy sipped from the glass of water in front of her.

"And no, it's not him. I couldn't continue to see Todd and function properly. I had to cut off all ties with him in order to move on. Believe it or not, he made it easy for me to cut him loose the last time I saw him."

"How?"

"Can you believe he said he heard I had put on weight, and was loving how the thickness looked on me? Who the hell says that to a woman?"

"But he said you looked good?"

"What if the extra pounds *didn't* look good on me?"

"Ah. I see your point. Now enough of this deflection. Who is the mystery man you're keeping a secret? I promise I will keep it in the vault."

"Please, and do not use this as pillow talk tonight."

Tammy coiled her pinky around Landon's. "I give you my word."

"The man I'm seeing is kind, attentive, generous, sexy, athletic, good-looking, well-mannered."

"I'm waiting for you to stutter because all of that sounds like a lie. If it's too good to be true, it probably is." Tammy gasped. "It better not be a married man, Landon."

"He's not married, and you've met him already."

"The slim guy who could draw that you brought to the party last year?" Tammy guessed.

"No, not him."

Tammy sat back and huffed, struggling with the mystery. The long pause and smile on Landon's face tickled her, so she gave up as her mind went blank.

"I'm stumped. I don't recall seeing you with anyone besides the artist, and I'm bored with this guessing game."

Landon stained the glass of water sitting in front of her with the red paint on her lips and whispered, "His name is Walter."

Tammy frowned. "When did I meet anyone named Walter?"

Landon raised her eyebrows and took another sip.

"Wait a minute." Tammy leaned forward. "The cop Millicent ghosted was named...Get the hell out of here!"

"See my dilemma?"

"How in the hell did that happen?"

"We ran into each other at a charity race—Literally bumped into one another. He remembered my name, asked why I wasn't wearing my wedding band, and if he could take me out. I've been under him for weeks now." Landon stared at the floor in a daze, smiling to herself while drawing circles in the middle of her chest.

Tammy watched her get lost in her thoughts, chuckling at the goofy grin on her face that resulted in her cheeks turning rosy. A moment of silence crept between them with Tammy observing the early signs of love blooming. She remembered that look. The feeling of butterflies fluttering in the stomach, and recognized the entranced look in Landon's eyes.

"Do I dare ask where you went just now?" Tammy snapped her fingers.

Landon's grin blossomed into a smile.

"You're falling." Tammy lowered her voice. "Refresh my memory. Millicent never hooked up with him, right?"

"Nope. She hooked up with Jay instead."

"How long do you think you can keep this a secret?"

"Why does anyone have to know?"

"Because we're your friends, and you know you can't bring him around us."

"Eh." Landon shrugged her shoulders.

"It's only been a few weeks, but surely you remember Jay. He will clown that poor man. You know how he is."

"I couldn't care less to be honest."

"This guy must really be something."

"He is. I wasn't expecting to meet anyone like him, when you know, I already had one great love. How the hell did I get two?"

"Love?"

"I'm speaking too soon, I know. But when I say I've been under him since the day we met—I'm being literal. He called me an hour after we ran into each other, and brought me some chocolate covered strawberries a few hours later. I left him standing at the front door while I put them in the fridge. When I came back so we could leave, he softly kissed me on my lips and said, 'I didn't want to wait until the end of the night to do that. I couldn't help myself.'"

"Well okay then."

"Right!" Landon tapped Tammy's hand. "Then, he opened my car door, and kissed me again before taking my hand and seating me. I was wet before we pulled out of my driveway. He had me flustered sitting across from him at dinner thinking about those kisses."

"Damn, Landon. It's getting hot at this table." Tammy fanned herself. "Please go on."

"At dinner I learned he doesn't have any children, major points for me, and he has never been married."

"Did you discuss Millicent at all?"

"Not once. Anyway, while we were waiting on the valet to bring his car around he said, 'I wish the night didn't have to end so soon.' Then I said, 'It would be a shame for you to drive back home tonight. You could stay at my place.'"

"And he did," Tammy muttered.

Landon chuckled. "Then he said, 'It would be impossible for me to stay at your place in another room and get any rest knowing you are close by.' Then I said, 'Who says you have to stay in another room?'"

Tammy covered her mouth. "This is so unlike you."

"It is, isn't it? I don't know what got into me, but I'm glad he did. We stopped by the store to get some eggs, juice, snacks like cupcakes and chips, and protection." Landon muttered the latter.

"Good girl."

"You should have seen how the lady at the checkout was grinning at me, and looking at him and the condoms. After he paid her, she winked at me and whispered, 'Go get'em, girl.' And boy did I ever. We made it back to my house, and he followed me into the kitchen. He put the groceries away and snuck behind me in the pantry. His lips hovered over mine as he gazed into my eyes, breathing in all of my air. We kissed—hard this time, and he didn't let go of my lips so easily like before. He drew my tongue from my mouth and held it hostage, picked me up, and came up for air to ask me which way to the bedroom. I pointed upstairs, and everything after was fucking magical."

"Are you sure? Because you haven't had sex in months. Close to a year if I remember correctly. Could it have been that your body was appreciative of being touched by strong hands?"

"Tammy, the man laid me across my new bed and stared into my eyes, slowly pacing himself as he undressed me. The anticipation of what was to come was sexy. It was like I was being seduced while he read my mind, planning what he was going to do to me. The man was in tune with my mind and my body."

Tammy smirked at Landon.

"Why are you looking at me like that?"

"I'm waiting for you to stutter."

"You'll be waiting forever." Landon exhaled. "This man traced my lips with his finger, and told me to relax while he ran downstairs. He came back with one of the cupcakes and spread the icing across my breasts. His lips felt like magic going across my nipples like a slow midnight train taking its time with my body, careful when speeding across all major bumps with intricate soft kisses and finger play—locking his eyes with mine to study my reaction."

Tammy interrupted. "I'm going to need a drink listening to this." She hailed the waiter. "One peach margarita, please."

The waiter scurried off and Tammy begged for Landon to continue.

"After the slow burn of teasing, and fingering, and tracing my body from head to toe, he rolled the condom on. I'm thinking he's about to put it in, but he lifted my ass up in the air, grated my cheeks with his teeth, and tongued me everywhere. Blew my fucking mind! I was done. But he wasn't. Out of nowhere he slipped inside of me and touched every corner that needed dusting." Landon clutched her hands around her glass of water, stroking the sweat lubing the outside.

"I'm speechless," said Tammy.

"So was I. After he came the first time I was thinking we are going to roll over and go to sleep. I was wrong. He went downstairs and brought up the strawberries, and fed them to me. Had me licking chocolate off of his fingers which led to a second round. I straddled on to him and rode him like my life depended on it, and when I was done, he got back on top and finished himself off without my help. I was too weak to assist. Now here's the freaky part." Landon's cheeks rosed. "He went back down on me after we both came, and tongued my pussy like it was my mouth until I came again. But what has me so fucked up is after I was shaking like an earthquake, he rubbed my body with deep thrusts of his wrist. I have never been so relaxed in my life. He then took me by the chin and turned my face towards him. He stared into my eyes as he gently swept his hands across my face, caressing me in one arm while the hand on the other massaged my scalp until I passed out. Have you ever had that done?"

"I can't say that I have. Is it possible to put it in a bottle so women can open it as needed?"

Landon laughed. "The next thing I knew it was morning and he was cooking me an omelet."

"Well I'll be damned. A unicorn that fucks your brains out and cooks? I might need to trade Caine's ass in. Does he have a brother?"

"Nope. One sister."

"After hearing all of this, I assume you were being catered to yesterday, which is why you ignored my call?"

"Sort of. We were active yesterday, but he was also helping me fix a few cracks he found around the house."

"Is that why you mentioned the love word?"

Landon sighed as she smiled. "This isn't a fling or a one night stand as you can see. The man woke me this morning with a foot rub. He said he loves me. I believe him."

"But do you love him?"

CHAPTER 61

COSMIC

WALT

Walt was pressed hard on Landon's mind when she returned to the office. The day turned into a waste, so she called it quits early and went home, wrestling with Tammy's question, unsure how to process her feelings.

As the evening hours turned into night, she picked up her phone several times to call him, then shied away from the idea that she should make the first line of contact. She liked him. She missed being in his company. More importantly, she missed having a man around.

Finally, his number appeared on her screen. She let it ring a few times, pretending she wasn't waiting by the phone to hear his voice.

"So how was your day?" he asked.

"Great actually. How about yours?" Her voice cracked at her failed attempt to hide how big she was smiling.

"It started off great since I woke up next to you." He threw in a laugh to hide he was smiling, too.

"And how did it end?"

"I can't answer that."

"Why not?"

"Because it hasn't ended yet." Walt sighed. "I don't want to freak you out, Landon, and if I do, be honest with me. Please."

The smile on Landon's face dropped as she thought to herself, *'Oh boy. Here goes the reason he's still available.'*

Walt coughed. "I feel like there is something special between you and I. Am I alone?"

She held in her breath for a second, then stammered. "I know what you mean. I feel it, too. I was scared to tell you I thought about you all day." She thumped her forehead for speaking too freely.

"You have?" His voice heightened. "I mean. You're not the only one. I made so many mistakes on paperwork today because I couldn't stop thinking of you. I know I'm being too forward, too quick even, but I was wondering when I could see you again?"

"That depends. Will I have to drive there, or will you drive here?"

"You are always welcome to come to my home. It's not as lavish as yours, but it's cozy and clean."

"So you want me to come there?"

"I tell you what. I'll come down this weekend, and drive you back to my house. That way I won't worry about you getting lost."

"I'd love that, but I have to warn you."

"What's that?"

"I have some peculiar ways, and if your house is not clean like you say it is, I'm going to want to come home."

"That just hurt my feelings."

"No, no. I didn't mean to hurt your feelings, I just don't want you to be mad with me, or feel offended if I change my mind about staying."

"Well I hope I can make you feel right at home."

Landon hoped her obsessive compulsive disorder didn't ruin a potential serious boyfriend. She attempted to correct her delivery and statement with hope she hadn't turned him off.

"I'm sure I'll love your house just fine if it's anything like the person I've spent the past few days with. Never mind me and my ridiculous funny ways. I hope I didn't put you off."

Walt beamed in his response. "I think you're perfect. There's no way you could put me off," he said.

Landon blushed, placed the phone to her chest and silently squealed. She placed the phone back to her ear and took a deep breath.

"Have you had dinner?"

"I was just about to ask you the same thing."

"I was about to reheat my leftovers from lunch when you called," she confessed as the doorbell rang. "Excuse me one second."

Scowling on her way to peek through the foyer window, her heart raced, wondering who was at her door at that hour.

She tapped on the window. "You're at the wrong house," she said to a man standing on the porch dressed in a red hat and shirt.

"Delivery for Landon Jeffries."

"I didn't order anything."

"I believe that guy did." He pointed behind him to the bottom of the stairs.

Walt stood up and waved to her with his phone in his hand. Landon covered her mouth as she opened the door, and took the paper bags from the delivery guy. Walt tipped him and met her at the door grinning from ear to ear.

"Get in here," she said.

"I had to see you." His lips planted a soft kiss on hers.

"I'm glad you're here. I didn't want to seem needy or clingy, but all I could think about today was how I wish you were here when I got home. That's crazy, right?"

His hands stroked her back. "It doesn't sound crazy to me."

Staring into his glowing brown eyes, she added, "I want you here, and you obviously want to be here, but we just started seeing each other. Not that I need a label or anything, but what's happening between us?"

"Are you sure you don't want to put a label on this?"

"If I were to say yes, would that make you want to run away?"

"I'm not going anywhere until you tell me you're tired of me." Walt closed the door behind him and locked it.

"Mr. Officer, something tells me I won't ever get tired of you."

"Officer? Oh, it's like that tonight."

"I hope so."

Walt raised Landon's leg and gripped her below the knee.

He gazed in her begging eyes. "What say we work up an appetite?"

Landon placed the bags on the picture shelf. Walt kissed her with so much conviction, she knew he came back to heal her aching body.

He moaned in her mouth, fondling the curves below her robe with strong tugs on her buttocks pushing her up against him. Wet from the moment she smelled his rosemary and cedar wood scent, she sighed in between kisses, jittery in the knees. Drenched from the friction of their bodies colliding, Landon gave into her urges and led him to the bottom of the staircase.

Tackling him to the floor, she spread her legs wide for the taking. "Look how bad I want you inside of me." She slid her panties to the side.

Walt licked his lips. He stared at her with love in his eyes and lust below his waist with an engorged dick erupting behind his zipper. Swiftly he revealed the bulge Landon yearned to bear witness. "I've got to satisfy my sweet tooth first." He dropped to his knees with a thirsty tongue.

Softly and gently he licked every nook of her hidden flesh.

Landon's fingers clung to the railings. "Ah," she whined.

Walt nibbled and sampled, humming into her hole. "I ain't stopping until you rain."

The slow, gentle tongue fucking forced Landon's hips to jolt and sway. Walt palmed her ass and cupped her pussy to his mouth, tonguing her center until her body vibrated.

Landon cried out. "You were right. The night was far from over."

Walt squeezed her ass as she came.

Shaking with relentless moans, she shrieked. "I'm ready." She crowned his head in place. "No, don't stop." She respired, changing her mind quickly from the swelling sensation bursting inside of her. "Mmm. Okay–I'm ready."

Walt's lips released Landon's pussy. She pushed him on his back, climbed on top of him, and yanked his belt from his pants. He wiggled them off, and her mouth slightly parted from the bulge in his underwear telling her hello. She drove his boxer briefs down to his knees with one finger, studying the exquisiteness of his nature standing at attention for her.

Her freak flag flew above her head as the mood and sight of his polished, shiny penis enticed her to lower her inhibitions. The growing curiosity to please the beautiful specimen jumping side to side put her in the mood to say, "fuck the judgement." She licked the tip of his dick, then looked him in the eyes.

Walt's face said everything his mouth couldn't utter. His eyes turned glossy and his mouth pressed shut, holding back the request he desperately hoped she fulfilled without instruction.

She licked it a second time. This time slower, dragging her tongue across the eye of his pipe. Then, she gripped the width of his head with her mouth. Walt shivered and grunted through his teeth. The tightening of his thigh muscles, and the sound of him partially breathing and quietly muttering "fuck" with shattered breaths, made her mouth water.

Fully covered in desire, she yearned to hear him make those sounds again. She inhaled a long breath and slicked his dick from the tip down to the bottom of his shaft. Up and down she served him, holding her position steady with her hands pressed against his thighs.

Walt shuddered. "My God, baby don't stop."

Landon respected his request, living for the oral challenge with tight pulls to his strong bone—Holding her breath, then releasing with pride to the vibration of him whimpering, begging her not to stop until he felt a rush rising too fast, too soon.

He jerked back and sat up with the look of love in his eyes for her. Landon confused it to be the look of lust, hoping the risqué act she performed so soon in their courtship wouldn't make him see her in a negative light.

Still she yearned for more praise, and mounted him like a bull. Walt lied back in submission, gazing at her take control with a wild look in her eyes. She appeared entranced by the magic bridged between them, caging them together like animals stolen from the jungle.

Lust clouded the responsibility of using protection as the surreal connection they shared in the heat of passion, overpowered them both. His needy skin longed to be inside her pure exposed flesh...Her appetite pined to feel his gifted girth stretch her open.

"Aye," she gasped.

Walt cuffed her hips, studying her ascend and cascade on his wood. "I love this view."

Landon rested her finger on the corner of her mouth. Her flowing free hair covered the top lids of her eyes, captivating Walt as he gazed at her roll her pussy on his dick. His hands reached upward and cupped her face, brushing his fingers across her cheeks and mouth. She caught them with her teeth and smiled at him with slightly parted lips.

"Aw, baby," he whispered. "You look beautiful when you're in charge."

She smiled, gripping her muscles tight around his dick, then releasing her hold of it. "You gettin' what you came for?"

He placed his hands around her waist. "More than what I came for."

She cupped her breasts and pinched her nipples, rocking hard to finish him off. Easing her stride when the sound of euphoric peaks and pleasure echoed between the walls, she freely let her pussy throb, causing Walt to tremble below her. He howled with stunted breaths, locked thighs, and a grip so tight on her waist she couldn't break free from him if she wanted to.

"Don't move your pretty ass," he said, stroking the side of her face, dragging his thumb across her mouth.

She obeyed his command, posed like a Goddess worthy of being worshipped.

Walt did exactly that, strumming the tips of his fingers across her silky skin, leaving his prints on her like she was the scene of a beautiful crime, adulated in a trance.

With her legs wrapped around him, he kissed her lips and rose from the floor, exchanging a moment of understanding without speaking a word. Sealed together with a burgeoning bond growing between them.

Chapter 62

No Shame

Walt

The takeout served as refuel in between rounds of love making. While lying out of breath and flat on their backs, Walt reached over and held Landon's hand.

"I can't get enough of you, Landon."

"Same," she answered, reaching for a bottle of water on the nightstand.

"We were a bit irresponsible, but put the blame solely on me."

Landon choked from her sip of water. "I'm to blame, not you. I've never been careless like that before." She buried her head. "Forgive me."

"Baby, I am not complaining, and please don't ever apologize for doing what we did tonight."

"I got caught up in the moment."

"Shiiit. I'm glad you did." He pulled her over to his chest. "I trust you."

"But it was so unlike me."

He pecked her on the lips. "I liked that version of you. What shall we call her?"

Landon buried her head on his shoulder. "Stop."

"And I'm good in that department, in case you start to question what we've done."

"So am I. And that's good to know. I..." She maneuvered to the other side of the bed."

"What is it?"

"Since my divorce, I haven't been with…"

Walt cut her off. "Landon. I really enjoy spending time with you."

"Are you seeing anyone else?"

"So you *do* like labels." He laughed. "I'm seeing you."

"Why are you available?"

"Am I?"

Landon looked at him over her shoulder.

"I'd like to think I'm no longer available, or am I moving too fast?"

"Yes. Extremely fast. But I like it." She burst into laughter. "We've only known each other for two days."

"Two days? I'm counting back to the day I met you."

She rolled over to her side, propped up by a pillow and her elbow. "You can't do that."

"Why not?" He mimicked her position and flashed his white teeth her way.

"Because I was married, and you were here for—you know who."

"Technically, I never went out with her. The night of our date I ended up spending it with you. I left here thinking to myself, *'now that's an intriguing woman.'*"

"Now you're just being cute."

He huffed. "Since we're talking about former interests and our strange dilemma, may I ask you a serious question?"

"What is it?"

"Why in the hell would your ex-husband let you go?"

Landon shifted her eyes past him to the photograph of her on her wedding day glaring at her from the dresser. She rolled to her back as her eyes fell into a daze staring up at the ceiling.

She exhaled a deep sigh. "To put it short, he fathered a kid long before we met, and the child came between us." She pursed her lips while crossing her arms to cover her breasts.

"Is that why you asked me if I had children?"

She nodded.

"So, if I had said yes, this wouldn't have happened?"

"Probably not."

Walt muttered. "Thank God I don't have any kids then."

Landon held up her hands. "Don't get me wrong, I don't hate children or anything. I just know they come first, and I didn't get married to compete with the needs of another woman, or a child who should have his father in his life."

"All valid points, but do you want kids of your own?"

"One day. With my husband."

Walt closed in on her, then delivered a kiss to the back of her hand. His lips traveled up to her neck where his hands slowly crept upwards to her hair, massaging her scalp with sturdy finger strokes that made her back wilt her forward in his arms.

"I love the way you do that," she said, weak and raspy in tone.

"I can tell."

"If you keep going, you're going to put me to sleep."

"Then, I better stop."

"Why?" Landon asked, unable to open her eyes.

Walt passionately groaned. "I didn't come here to sleep."

CHAPTER 63

GROWNUPS

MILLICENT

With only a few hours of sleep under their belt, the alarm buzzed on Walt's phone, waking the new couple after a long, lustful night.

"Should we call in sick today?" he asked.

"I can't. I have meetings I can't miss."

"Then I'll get out of your hair and head in so I can daydream about you all day at work again." He kissed her exposed nipple above the covers.

Landon shied away from his advances. "I won't be any good today if I let you get under me this morning."

Walt kissed her lips, once, twice, then once more. "I'll call you tonight."

Landon strolled into work with the glow of the moon on her skin, and the eyes of a raccoon hidden behind tortoise frames.

"Margie, will you call Millicent St. James and see if she's free for lunch? Thank you."

Margie nodded with a curve on the side of her mouth.

"What's that look for?" Landon asked her.

"I feel I should be asking you that." She snickered.

Landon lowered her frames and shared a smile with her. It was the only answer Margie would get.

Moments later she buzzed her boss. "Ms. St. James is unavailable for lunch and would like to meet for dinner instead."

"Reply yes. My house. 7:00."

Mentally preparing for her overdue bout with her longtime friend, gave Landon the energy she desperately needed to make it through the work day. But by the time she arrived home with groceries for the airing out grievances dinner, her activities from the previous night crept up on her.

She felt sluggish, but still prepped the kitchen to sauté lamb, and roast baby reds. Thoughts of the man who kept her up the night before put a little pep in her step as she rubbed olive oil and salt on the potatoes, wrapped them in foil, and placed them in the oven.

'I'd love to see him again tonight. He could rub my feet and work me over into a good, deep sleep. But then again, I need to recharge. If he were to show up I'd let him have his way with me, and though he feels good, I need to rest at least one night. Maybe we could spend a night just holding one another.'

Landon laughed out loud at how challenging that would be.

Millicent arrived, looking around the home as if she had never been inside. She made subtle remarks about the change in décor, the color of the walls, and gave off a negative vibe, setting the tone of the evening. Eventually, Landon met her halfway and killed her plan for a nice evening to salvage their friendship.

"What are you doing?" Landon asked her.

"I don't know what you mean."

"Yeah, you do. For the past ten minutes, you and I have been carrying on as if we don't know what makes the other one tick. I wanted to meet with you to see if our friendship was worth repairing, but I gotta say, you are helping me see that us—not talking might be for the best."

Millicent gasped. "I can't believe after the history we have shared you would say that to me."

"It is what it is. Do I miss you? Yes. Do I want to be fighting with you? No. Can I move on? I can. But not if you're going to be acting like this."

"Landon, I'm not going to beg you to be in my life."

"Good. I have no plans to beg you to be in mine. I wanted to meet with you to tell you I'm not mad at you anymore."

Millicent clapped her hands. "And that's supposed to mean what? I can now come out from hiding? People make mistakes, Landon. You have this perception that everything and everyone is supposed to be perfect. Sorry if we can't all be as perfect as you."

"I know people make mistakes. But if you had been honest about you and old community peen, we might not be at odds with each other regarding trust. All you had to do was come clean."

"If I could, I'd go back and undo it. Living with the shame of it all was painful enough, and now this hole is between us. I swear I would handle myself differently if I could, but I can't."

"I'm ready to move on from this. I'm not saying we can be like we used to be, but we can try to mend our friendship. It's going to take some time."

"You don't sound like you've forgiven me."

"I have. I just question if you would have slept with Todd like you did Reynaldo, and now Jay."

"So you see me as the town slut." Millicent blew from her mouth. "I would never. That really hurts my feelings."

"I didn't want this evening to go this way."

"It's obvious there's still tension between us. You always could hold a grudge, and this is your way of carrying out one against me."

"I don't have a grudge against you. I invited you over here, didn't I? We're finally talking. And I'm not mad anymore. Shall I fix us a plate, and start this conversation over?"

"I guess it's safe to say you won't poison me."

"You won't know until you eat." Landon snickered below a smirk on the side of her face. "I'm kidding."

The joke minimized the tension in the room. Landon led Millicent to her newly decorated dining room, filled their glasses with wine, and served the smothered lamb chops and fully loaded baked potatoes on the good china she gave her and Todd as a wedding gift.

"I'm glad you didn't throw these away like you did me." Millicent sipped on her glass of Chardonnay.

"Ha ha."

"So, what have you been up to, besides giving your house an unnecessary face lift? It's beautiful, by the way."

"Thank you. And it was necessary for my mental health. The old furniture reminded me too much of what was taken from me, so..."

"Did you sell it?"

"I put it in storage for whenever Launa buys her first house."

Millicent glanced at Landon above the rim of her glass. "You seem different."

Landon avoided making eye contact with her. "How so?"

"I don't know. Just different. Is the single ready to mingle life fun these days?"

"I wouldn't know. I just recently started seeing someone."

"Really? Maybe that's what's different about you. What's this guy like?"

"Um, I don't care to share that right now."

"Why not? It can't be serious."

"It *could* be. It's still new, so, we'll see how it pans out. How is Todd doing?"

"He's doing pretty good as of late. It was tough for him in the beginning, as you know, but he's getting his feet wet, or at least that's what Jay tells me. Sometimes I think he only tells me this stuff so I can run and tell you. He pretends to forget we aren't on the best terms."

Landon sighed. "Well, I hope he's happy."

"Wow. Whoever this guy is must really be running a number on you."

"What do you mean by that?"

"*You* are wishing Todd happiness with someone else. This is Todd we're talking about."

"We're divorced, but I'll always care about him."

Millicent spoke in a bold tone. "You mean love him."

"Of course I'll always love him. But it wasn't going to work. Life goes on."

Millicent scoffed. "Shit really has changed."

"Yes, it has—Because for the first time ever I am asking...How are you and Jay doing?"

She stopped chewing. "I could cry right now."

"Why?"

"I'm so happy you and I are doing this." Millicent's voice wavered. "We're great. Thank you for asking."

"I would have never put you and him together, but it's good you two found happiness in each other."

Chapter 64

Wild Card

Jen

Conflicting schedules didn't align with Jules traveling with Jen to Detroit, but Jay made time to oversee her meeting with the construction team about the plans for her makeup bar.

She left Midtown and arrived at Landon's house out in University West, just as she was off to spend the weekend with Walt.

"Take care of our girl." Jen teased him.

"Yes ma'am." He grinned.

Landon widened her eyes at Jen. "Watch after this one." Her head turned towards Launa.

"I'll try."

Launa pinched her sister's ass. "Don't do anything I *would* do."

"Too late for that." Landon winked, then followed Walt out of the door.

"Somebody's smitten," said Jen.

"You see it, too?" Launa gawked with her mouth open. "They were looking at each other like two lost puppies. God, my sister is so sappy."

Jen tapped her arm. "So, what's been going on with you?"

"Your brother-in-law has been going in me." Launa snickered.

"Eww, Launa." Jen's face wrinkled. "And I heard. I was hoping that was a Vegas fling. A getaway jumpoff. A one and done." She shook her head. "Landon is under the impression you're seeing that Caleb guy."

"I am. I'm not exclusive with anyone. Caleb is my sweetheart. Always there for me when I need him. But Juan is unpredictable, and sexy, and spontaneous, and keeps me guessing. Something about his erratic behavior turns me on."

Jen scoffed. "You're attracted to toxicity. You can do better."

"What do you mean? They both give me whatever I want and spoil my boy."

"Your family spoils your boy."

Launa sharply exhaled. "Juan drives me crazy. I can't explain it."

"I can. You like drama. Men with issues and baggage. You know he has a daughter he hardly ever sees, and treats the girl's mother like shit, and...I don't trust him."

"What aren't you telling me?"

"I just told you. I don't trust him. When he comes to Miami, I catch him staring at me like he hates me or something. I mean their mother really hates me, but for a man to make you feel uneasy with a stare worries me. I hardly get any sleep when he's in town. One night I felt someone standing over me, and I was too afraid to open my eyes. I thought, 'This is my last breath,' clung on to Jules, and waited for the worst. I squeezed him so tight he woke up calling my name. When he made no mention of it, I realized the room was clear, and I searched for the presence of something, or someone lurking in the shadows. My gut told me Juan was in our room. My gut never lies to me. But nothing was there. The next morning, I asked him if he got lost in the middle of the night and he said no. But the way he answered me bothers me to this day."

"Fuck, Jen. You really think he was trying to spook you?"

"I do."

"Why?"

"You remember how he was against the wedding."

Launa grunted. "I'm supposed to hook up with him tonight."

"It better not be in here. Landon would have a fit."

"No. Some new hotel downtown."

Jen twisted her face. "Don't say I didn't warn you. Sleep with one eye open."

"Will do. Launa grabbed her phone from the counter. "Don't tell Landon," she whispered on her way out.

Jen muttered, "Trust me. I won't."

CHAPTER 65

THE WOODSMAN

WALT

Landon was tickled at how early Walt arrived to pick her up for the weekend.

"What's with the grin?" she asked.

His dark cheeks flushed. "I'm excited to show you my place. And to have you all to myself this weekend." Walt lifted her inside his Silverado. "I think you'll like it." Seducing her with his eyes as he buckled her seatbelt, he stole a quick kiss. "At least I hope you do."

Along the short drive, Landon pointed out she wanted to stop at the candy store exit on the drive back. Walt agreed, searching for a channel of upbeat tunes to fill the car. A satellite channel mixing old songs with the modern versions tested their wits about the history of classics. The blend set the perfect mood for the short drive until Walt veered off the highway on his exit.

Landon readjusted herself in the passenger seat. Noticing the shift in her facial expressions, he faced the awkward moment head on.

"Did you come visit your friend out here a lot?" Walt pointed to the left. "Her house was that way, right?"

"Not as much as she came into the city. But things can change–me driving out here to the boonies." Landon smirked.

"You won't have to drive if you never leave." Walt squeezed her thigh. "What happened to her that night was messed up, but then again, fate has a way of doing things."

The paint on Landon's lips stained her teeth as she sank the top row into her bottom lip.

"I keep a tight place. You won't find a spot of dust in the house. You had me cleaning like The Evans family on Good Times competing for the cleanest house in the projects." Walt chuckled to himself. "You ever watched that show?"

"I hated that show."

"Excuse me?" Walt toyed with the breaks.

"I was depressed after every episode. Who wants to almost reach a goal, only to have their piece of the pie snatched away every week?"

"Damn." Walt's face drew a blank. "I never looked at it like that."

"That's why I enjoy romance. The characters get their happy ever after."

"Then, I'm in a romance right now."

Landon blushed. "Are you?"

"Damn sure feels like it."

After a few twists and turns down a two lane country road, Landon grew anxious to see Walt's house, praying it was clean and cozy like he said. She created a scenario in her head of what she would do if it *was* how he described.

'I'll rip off his clothes and take charge of my needs. I can tell he's missed me these past few nights as much as I've missed him. Damn, am I ad-dick-ted?'

Upon pulling into the neighborhood, she realized their difference in salary, and her taste in real estate was more extravagant. She was modern, ritzy, and artsy. Walt, on the other hand, was earthy and rustic, judging from the log cabin style home he owned.

'Not what I was expecting from a police officer.' She braced herself. *'He said it was clean and cozy. Don't freak out. You really like this man. If it ain't clean, clean it for him. He's gone above and beyond for you. Stop being boujee like Launa said.'*

"We're here." Walt interrupted her in deep thought. "Everything alright?"

"Yeah. Everything's fine. Just a little nervous."

"Don't be. I made sure everything would go perfect this weekend."

He opened her door and helped her down from the high seats. Dogs barked behind a wooden fence secluding his backyard.

"Don't mind them. They sense the presence of a stranger on the premises."

Landon stopped in her tracks. "Please, tell me you don't have a dog in the house?"

"Potro and Patience have their own house out back."

'Thank God.'

Walt dropped his head. "You hate dogs, don't you?"

"No. I'm terrified of them. Well, big ones. The small ones I can handle, but big ones—that fear will be with me always. And if you dare say my dogs don't bite, you can take me home right now."

Walt held up his keys. "Okay. I won't say it. Do you still want to come inside?"

"If you'll still have me."

Apprehensive for a moment, he welcomed her inside, but the look of approval on her face helped him reclaim the excitement of inviting her into his home. Landon's eyes grew big at the beautiful, wooden craftsmanship he created as his signature. Their tastes were opposite–him being outdoorsy, crafty, and mid-century, but she vibed with his vision, and had to admit that her house was bigger, but his house was better.

"So you brought me all the way out here to show me up?"

Walt's eyes widened. "Does that mean you like my place?"

"I love it. So much love is in the details."

"Thank you, babe. I'm flattered."

"Why are you single again?"

"Because I hadn't met you. Let me give you the tour."

Landon was sure Walt put every room to use unlike her empty house.

She was also impressed he remodeled the interior with his own two hands. And in learning they shared an interest in interior design, home renovation shows, and art, she felt herself falling deeper for her new beau with every passing minute.

As she walked through his house, she searched for the trace of a woman's touch, but nothing suspicious called out to her. Once they made it past the bedrooms, he took a gamble.

"Can I take you to meet the married couple out back?"

Landon sighed.

"I'm not going to say those fateful words that'll put me in the dog house with them, but I'm going to ask that you let them smell you."

Landon took a step back.

"I'll hold them so you don't have to be afraid."

Landon masked her frustration by inhaling a deep breath. "Okay," she said, closing her eyes.

Walt eased Potro over towards her first, then Patience. Commanding them with hand signals, he ordered them to sit at his side.

"How many times do they need to sniff me?" Landon asked.

Walt snickered. "They stopped sniffing you a few seconds ago."

Landon squinted at the dogs obediently sitting upright a few feet away.

"They like you. As I knew they would. My babies are smart." He rubbed their heads. "Let me show you what I'm growing." He raised two fingers. The dogs trotted inside their house.

"I take it you built them that mansion."

"And they love it. Fans in the summertime, heat in the winter."

He escorted her over to his miniature garden, discussing his plans of one day having his own home grown vegetables, a weekend stand at the market where they met, with plans to expand in other ventures. Landon gazed at him while he yapped on, seeing a side to him she hadn't seen in any other man before—A nurturer in tune with the simple things in life. A man deserving of love.

Watching him talk about his garden and projects with so much passion made him sexier in her eyes. She stared at his lips as he said words like "plow" and "drill." Losing control to her lustful thoughts.

She shut him up with a kiss. "You learn a lot about a person when you're not lying on your back." She dragged her cheek against his, then gently bit his ear. "I'm gonna go inside. You wait out here for one minute, then come find me."

"I like you giving orders...In my house." He grinned. "Yes, ma'am. I'll do as I'm told."

One minute passed. He went inside and followed the trail of clothes leading him to the living room. Landon sat posed on her knees, bare in front of the fireplace.

"Please, Mr. Gardner. Plow and drill me."

"I should have brought you here sooner," said Walt, kicking off his shoes.

"They say you're a woodsman. I want you to put your personal touch on me."

"Baby, I can't get undressed fast enough."

"Come here. Let me help you."

Walt's jeans hit the rug, but not before Landon placed his dick in her mouth and sucked him fast with a wet mouth and slick jaws. His knees locked with his back straight. He choked as he gasped, then sighed from the sensation.

"Shit baby. Whatever I did, I swear I'll keep doing it," he whispered.

Landon embraced the inner exploratory side she discovered earlier in the week. She stroked his paintbrush like it was the canvas for a Picasso, sending him to euphoric heights with the intent to make him feel as good as he made her.

"Baby, please take it easy on me. I wanna feel your sweet ass, but the way you're handling me is gonna cause me to..." he pled in a low voice.

But she didn't stop. She enjoyed hearing how she drove him crazy. His verbal expression excited her, making her want to be more forth giving when it came to servicing him. More sensual when her lips were on him. More adventurous when it came to pleasure. And she got off wetting his whistle.

When she scaled back for air, Walt dropped to the floor to color Landon's pussy as his own masterpiece. She trembled when his fingers touched her, and as he slid in her saturated pink walls, the penetration of his dick caused her to feel as if she was losing her mind.

The closer they came to orgasmic relief, Walt succumbed to the intensity knotting in his chest. Looking down at her, he lifted her chin and transferred that intensity with a kiss.

"Landon, I know it's soon, but I'm in love with you," he said, stroking her deep.

She held onto his shoulders and whispered in his mouth, "I've fallen for you, too. I didn't want to be the first to say it." She smiled.

He bit her bottom lip, then sucked it as he dove in deeper. "Say it when you're ready."

"I'm ready," she said, looking him in the eyes.

"Then let me hear it." He applied pressure to her walls, swimming deep with a winding motion.

Landon moaned. "I'm in love with you, too."

Walt lost all of his composure. Hearing Landon say she shared the same sentiments as him, led to a premature eruption.

Their fingers intertwined as he clamped down and released his warm load in her sugar walls. Landon squeezed her pussy tighter around him, discharging a release of her own. And together they came in a beautiful moment of expression, confession, and profession. Enclosed as one. Fallen to the depths of love.

CHAPTER 66

LET IT GO

JAY

While Landon was enjoying her time away, Jen and Jay met up at the makeup bar to discuss changes to the layout. He brought Max along to leave him with his mother after their business was settled.

While Max ran wild in the open space, his parents battled wits, but not for long as Launa stopped by to see the place before her night out.

Jay appeared smitten at the likes of Launa walking in. He flashed his teeth in her face just as Todd strolled through the door.

"Bruh?" Todd frowned at him.

"One of my friends ain't enough?" Jen mugged Jay's forehead.

"Aw, come on now. I just like to hear Launa talk her shit."

"What's up, Bruh-law?" Launa hugged Todd.

"You ain't hug me?" Jay opened his arms.

Launa and Todd laughed.

"Bring it in, Loverboy." Launa teased Jay.

"Always a pleasure." Jay smelled her hair, smiling at Todd and Jen with a devilish grin.

Jen shook her head. "You can't help but not be shit."

Jay's smile fell to a grin as he winked at Jen. "Lil' Launa. Whatchu doing 'round these parts?"

"Meeting up with Caleb in a few. He loves him some me."

"So you listened to my advice earlier. Good. I'm proud of you," said Jen.

Launa rolled her shoulders. "What y'all got goin' on?"

"Making money as always." Jay tugged on his beard. "Where's L?"

The room fell silent.

"Not here." Launa peered at him as a warning to back off. "Where's your supervisor?"

"Shit, at the house. I guess."

"You guess?" Jen snickered. "He knows she's at the house waiting on him."

Launa chuckled. "She's got your old job." She and Jen leaned into each other snickering.

Jay sighed. "Well, I can tell I won't be over here too long."

Launa rubbed his shoulder. "You mean to tell me a big, scrappy gangsta named John Jay Lloyd can't take a joke?"

"Whoa. Whoa with the government name." He couldn't help but smile with Launa.

Jen parted her lips. "Millicent might be getting her walking papers. Ain't that right, Todd?"

Todd held up his hands. "I'm surprised you're just now noticing whatever this is these two do when they get around each other." He watched Jen study Jay. "How's my—How's Landon? Everything alright with my girl?"

"She seemed fine when she picked me up earlier." Jen leaned over and tapped the back of his hand. "You hangin' in there?"

"You know. Maintaining." His voice rose when he lied. "Tell my...tell *her* I asked about her."

"You thought she was going to be here tonight, didn't you?"

Todd shrugged his shoulders.

Jay interrupted. "Jen, let me holla at you for a minute."

Todd and Launa played catch up at one of the stations while Jay and Jen excused themselves to the back office.

"Who is Landon seeing?" Jay interrogated her.

"Why are you asking me?"

"'Cause I know you know."

"Why are you getting involved?"

"You see him out there. He wants his wife back."

"Look at you. Caring about someone other than yourself. I'm proud of you, Jay. I really am. But you should encourage Todd to move on. That's all I know."

"You say that like you're positive he has no shot of winning her back."

Jen raised her brows and changed the subject. "I have news. Jules didn't get the offer to transfer. But word got out, and he may have worked something out with the football team instead. Hopefully he gets it, and we'll be one big happy family back in the D."

"You need me to pull some strings?"

Jen shook her head side to side. "Let him handle that on his own."

"No foul, no funny." Jay put his hands up. "I'm just trying to help. *Why you making that face?*"

"I looked at the schedule. The football team has an exhibition game in Sweden, Week 10. If he gets the job, he is going to Stockholm."

"Leave it alone, Jen."

"If he goes, I'm going with him. It's the perfect cover for me to get into the country."

"Why are you hell bent on going after something you don't need?"

"I have to, Jay. And I want you to come out there, too."

"Nah."

"Come on. I'll go to the bank, transfer some of the money, and cash out the rest. Boom, it's done. I only trust you to watch my back."

"I don't know shit about that place. And neither do you."

"If it looks risky, or doesn't feel right, I won't go through with it. At least think about it."

Jay pursed his lips, biting on the inside of his bottom lip. "I've already thought about it. Neither of us are going to Sweden," he said, then walked back to the front. "Launa, bring Caleb over to the house tonight. Max is staying with his mother, so party at my house. Let's get out of here, T."

CHAPTER 67

PARTY UP

MILLICENT

Jay strolled in the house, quietly fuming his former love had walked out on him and their son, and was now attempting to bring danger to their doorsteps. Money was never a problem for them, so a few million attached to strange cities, killers, and loved ones already lost, wasn't enough to risk the good life they were already living in his opinion.

Millicent peered over at him pouring a shot of gin. Instead of pestering him, she kept silent and set up the games, drinks, and food for the house full of guests he sprung on her at the last minute.

"Y'all know the drill." She welcomed their friends inside. "Liquor's on the table, beers in the cooler, and the wine is on chill in the bucket. If you're gonna smoke, go out back. That's also where you'll find Jay and Todd, of course."

She kept a close eye on Jay mingling with the fellas smoking out back, barely paying attention to the conversation amongst the ladies.

"Mills, you alright?" Tammy asked.

She jolted. "Yeah. Why do you ask?"

"Because you've yet to add anything to the conversation."

"Sorry, my mind wandered. What are y'all talking about?"

Tammy and Kim glared at one another with a side eye.

"Is Landon coming tonight?" Kim asked.

"Jay set this thing up like two hours ago. I have no idea who he invited."

Kim glanced out to the balcony. "It's probably best she doesn't show tonight."

"Why?" Tammy and Millicent asked at the same time.

"Because Todd's date is glued to his side." Kim nudged her head for them to look at the smoke-filled balcony.

"She wouldn't care." Tammy snickered. "I hear she's boo'd up."

"With who?" Kim whispered.

Millicent shrugged her shoulders. "She wouldn't give up his name when we had lunch the other day."

Tammy bit her tongue and raised a brow. "How did that go?"

"Surprisingly...well. We decided to take it slow in trying to rebuild our friendship."

"Good." Tammy sighed. "I'm sick of this divided shit. It's time we bring harmony back into the group."

The doorbell rang.

"Maybe this is her now." Millicent went to the door, looked through the peep-hole, and made eyes with the girls. "Launa, I didn't know you were in town. Come in." She waved her and Caleb inside. "I remember you."

Launa sighed. "Caleb, you remember Millicent from the last time, don't you?"

"How are you?" He tipped his hat.

"Good. Good." Millicent smiled. "The fellas are out back."

"Looks like they're coming in and ready to lose their money." Launa rubbed her hands together. "Oh God, who is the bird with Todd?"

"Launa, be nice tonight." Millicent held her hands in prayer pose. "Please."

Launa tittered. "Bruh-law! We meet again!" She sashayed across the room.

"Help me out here," Millicent said to Caleb.

"I'll try."

The crew vetoed a game of Pictionary to play Taboo before engaging in the heated game of Spades.

"Let's make this quick." McCaine narrowed his eyes at Launa. "I got a taste of vengeance on my tongue."

"That ain't the taste that needs to be on your tongue." Launa pointed to Tammy. "He ain't servicing you, sis?" She turned back to McCaine. "You ain't learn nothing at Castillo Mas?"

"I learned not to go back," McCaine replied.

"I enjoyed it," Kim added.

Brian sighed. "Yes, you did."

"I wish Brian would co-sign on going back. I wouldn't mind getting it on in the voyeur room. Letting people see how love should be made."

Jay led the snickers around the room. "Go 'head Brian. Take ya ole lady back to that stank house and show everybody you have no clue what you doing."

Brian shook his head. "Ask the limo driver if I don't know what I'm doing."

"Oh shit." Launa's surprised eyes widened.

"That was a wild night." Jay chuckled.

"Damn sure was. I don't know about y'all, but my house got a whole lot freakier after that night," said McCaine.

Tammy silenced him. "But he still won't consent to my threesome request?"

"That shit is never going to happen."

"It might—Without you."

McCaine held his chest.

His wife patted him on the head. "I'm joking, baby, but I do want to know what those shock clamps felt like. The lady in that room looked half pleasured and half tortured. Inquiring minds wanna know."

"Now *that* I might can work with. But I'm not watching another man plow my wife."

Tammy called out to Millicent. "If my memory serves me correctly, you, Mills, said you were curious about sleeping with a white man. Did you do it? Do you still want to compare notes?"

"No, I'm good." She hugged on Jay's arm.

"Damn right she's good." Jay gnawed on her cheek.

Launa frowned. "That is still gonna take some getting used to."

Everyone snickered.

Todd's date spoke up. "I didn't know you all would be this open when Todd invited me to come tonight. But since you *are*, my friends and I are having a don't choke party in a few weeks. You ladies are welcome to come if you want."

"Sign my wife up right now!" McCaine shouted.

Tammy hit his arm. "I don't need a class."

The men's eyes shifted amongst the room.

"When is this party? I'll pay for it." Jay threw a wad of cash on the table.

Caleb laughed out loud. "Y'all are a wild bunch."

"*We tryna get wild*," said McCaine, adding one dollar bills to Jay's stack.

"Relax, big spender." Launa silenced McCaine. "I'm about to take your lil' money right now. Let's get the real party started."

[illegible]

[illegible] people [illegible]

[illegible] about the name [illegible]

[illegible]

[illegible]

"But we're nobody's [illegible]

[illegible]

[illegible] to bed, ghost [illegible]

[illegible] "Time [illegible]

[illegible] Goodnight.

[illegible]

[illegible] he whispered that [illegible] would stop [illegible]

[illegible]

[illegible]

[illegible]

[illegible]

[illegible]

[illegible]

[illegible]

[illegible]

[illegible]

[illegible]

[illegible]

[illegible]

[illegible]

CHAPTER 68

LUCK BE A LADY

LANDON

While Launa was off stealing books and taking her sister's place, Landon was busy finding a similar luck in Ohio at a casino. The thrill of winning set the tone for the weekend.

Walt rolled the dice.

"Seven!" the dealer shouted.

Walt pulled at Landon hips. "My good luck charm, Lucky Landon."

She rested her hands on his broad shoulders. "I am feeling pretty lucky at the moment."

"Then, with all the respect in the world I say this to you, baby. Blow." He held up the dice.

Their foreheads touched. They shared a private chuckle as Landon's cheeks bled a pink, reddish hue. She gazed into his eyes and blew on the dice. Walt tossed them onto the table without looking.

"Seven!" the dealer shouted.

"Shall we take our winnings, throw it across the bed, and wrinkle it with the sheets?" he asked.

Landon stammered. "That sounds sexy and unsanitary. What if we donate it and just wrinkle the sheets?"

Walt kissed the back of her hand. "You pick the charity. I'll get us home."

Back at his house, he kept his promise of jumping her bones. Neither expected to pass out soon after. When he woke to her laying naked next to him with the sheets covering the lower half of her body, he wished he could wake up to her laying in his bed all the time.

He slid her to the middle of the bed, widened her legs just enough to plant his face between her thighs, and replaced his cup of morning joe with her special blend.

"I always heard this is how a man prefers to wake up in the morning." Landon sighed, rolling her fingers around his crown.

"We do," he mumbled. "But I like waking you up like this instead."

But they didn't stay awake for long. A few tight, intense thrusts and moaning into each other's ears ended with an early withdrawal of explosive climaxing, and a nap cuddled in sweat.

Potro and Patience barked, alerting Walt he was off schedule for their breakfast. Landon tapped the line of his muscle holding her close.

"I hear them," he groaned. "I'm in too good of a position to take care of them right now."

"This does feel good, but I need a shower, and you deserve some food to refuel."

"Can I make a request?"

"Sure."

"You know how to make French toast?"

"Coming right up."

Walt threw on a ratty sweat suit and tended to his babies outside. He came back inside to the smell of vanilla and cinnamon drawing a smile on his face. He sat at the bar and watched Landon dip, flip, and fry coated bread in a pan, realizing he hadn't told her he loved her since the first night he brought her home.

"The boys said to tell you hello."

Landon peered over at him. "Don't ruin a perfectly good morning guilting me about your babies out back."

"You should say hi."

"I'll do them one better." She opened the back door and threw each pup a sausage link. "Was that good enough?"

"Not really. Now they're going to see you as the lady who feeds us table food, and I'm now the mean man who keeps them from it. Nice play."

Landon laughed at his jealous quip so loud she missed him saying I love you at the end.

"I love you," he said a second time.

Her laughing spell halted. She flipped the toast a final time, turned off the stove, and made her way to her side of the bar. Leaning halfway over, she stared into his eyes and recognized the same look in them around the iris when he said it the first time. She saw sincerity in his face, felt the honesty in his voice, and followed her first mind telling her she could trust him.

"I love you, too."

He leaned forward and kissed her. "Since you love me, too, there is something I want to ask you?"

Landon gulped hard. "Okay?"

"How do you feel about costumes?"

"I'm sorry?" Her brows raised.

"The precinct is having its annual costume party. We do it because we're always in uniform, so I was wondering if you'll go with me this year? I really want to introduce you to everyone."

"Is it an I-can-dress sexy type of costume party, or are you asking me to be the tail of a donkey—'cause if you are…"

"I would never ask you to do such a thing. And yes, you can dress sexy. You're sexy even when you're not trying. Whaddya say?"

"Can we be Batman and Catwoman?"

Walt snickered. "You got a thing for the Dark Knight?"

She tapped her fingers together. "All those gadgets."

Walt choked, trying not to laugh. "I haven't been this excited for Halloween since I was a kid. Pretty girls like you don't often like geeks into comics and stuff."

"Now look…you can get away with it for Halloween. But don't let me catch you running around in costumes all year long." She raised a brow.

"Only if you like it. I wish I had those gadgets right now."

"You can make up for it by staying the night when you drive me home."

"I was just waiting on you to ask."

Chapter 69

Opps

Launa

Scrolling through her messages, Launa sat in the kitchen indecisive if she should press the send button to call Juan, or erase him from her contacts. Startled by the garage door lifting, she locked her screen and waited for Landon to make it inside.

"I guess it went well!" she shouted from the kitchen.

Landon stood at the entrance with Walt on her heels.

"Well, well, well. Look who remembered where she lives." Launa chortled, looking down at Walt's hands carrying an overnight bag. "Hey Cowboy. What you got there?"

Landon shook her head. "You remember my sister, Launa."

"Nice seeing you again."

"Same here." Launa grinned at her sister. "Two days not enough?"

Landon looked over her shoulder at Walt and blushed. "I tried to catch Jen before her flight, but time got the best of us."

"Time. Right." Launa chortled, peering at Walt. "You're a cop, right?"

"Detective."

"What's the difference?"

"I don't patrol the streets like when I first joined the force."

"I see...You like policing people?"

"I like protecting and serving the people."

"Un huh. *What you* been serving my sister?"

"Launa!" Landon pinched her arm. "Ignore her. She's always had a sharp tongue."

Walt laughed. "It's fine. I have nothing to hide."

He whispered in Launa's ear. "I'm hoping to serve her for the rest of my days if she'll have me."

Launa's eyes broadened.

"I've never seen my sister speechless," said Landon.

Launa was happy her sister found someone that adored her, but was at a loss for words as her loyalty lied with Todd. The revelation stunned her, so much so, she drove back to Flint earlier than she planned with a racing mind and near catatonic tongue.

The glow on Landon's face made her question the men she took up with. Caleb was nice, giving, and verbal about testing coupledom with her, but she didn't see him as a candidate to bring home to Papa Davis.

Being honest with herself, she was more attracted to Juan—the questionable, unreliable mystery she met in secret—and she hated herself for it. Once again, Landon was showing her up with a man she could build a future with, while she was still making unwise choices with wise guys.

She pulled up his number in her phone, ran her finger across the call button, then went to the top of the screen, and erased him out of her contacts.

Her phone vibrated at that moment. 'What does Jay want?' She thought to herself.

"Sup?" She answered.

"Swing by before you head out. I'll be at the house."

"Everything cool?"

"Yeah. Just need to holla at you 'bout somethin'."

"What's so important you didn't want to speak on the phone?"

"Speaking of phones, leave yours in here. Follow me." Jay led her to his office in the back of the house.

"Tell me you have trust issues without telling me you have trust issues," Launa joked.

Millicent peeped in. "Hey, Launa. What are you gonna do with all that money you won last night?"

"Spoil my little man." She turned to Jay. "So what's up? I was getting ready to hit the road when you called."

"Mills, close the door." Jay twitched his finger. "Whatchu know about this Juan fella *you been* running around with?"

"I literally just erased his number from my phone. And how did you know?"

"I know 'cause I'm me. I got eyes and ears everywhere. Why'd you delete him?"

"Jen mentioned some things about him. He ain't the best man to bring around my son."

"Or mine." Jay expressed in a stern manner. "Now Caleb, I like. And he likes you. He's a good cat."

"Now Jay, I know we shoot the shit a lot, but I'm not about to let *you* tell me who to date."

"I'm not trying to. I'm just letting you know he's a good lad. But this Juan character—Anything stand out to you that I might need to know."

"Like what?" Launa scowled.

"Like maybe you've heard something you shouldn't have, or have you ever heard him talking about Miami?"

"Not that I recall. He's a guy with a million secrets. I always thought it was women, 'cause when is it not, but I don't know. He's just real shady, and unkind at times, and questionable. I don't plan on seeing him again."

Jay applauded. "Good for you."

"Now tell me what this is really about."

"This is about family. I know you go for a badass, but you got yourself mixed up with a guy who, as you said, is questionable. I can't say more than that right now, so just take heed, and keep this conversation between us."

"I can keep secrets, Jay." Launa pointed to Millicent. "No shade, Mills. I'm just simply pointing out..."

"And don't do that shit right there with him." Jay wiggled his finger between her and Millicent. "No flying off the handle, or running your mouth with this cat. He's got some heat on his name out of state."

Launa's voice raised. "What state?"

"Doesn't matter."

Her brows lifted. "You think he's dangerous?"

"I know so."

"Jen was telling the truth, I bet," Launa muttered.

"Jen?" Jay and Millicent replied together.

"Yeah. She told me she thought he was standing over her in their bedroom one night."

Jay's chest pounded through his shirt. "What the fuck did you just say?"

"Apparently too much."

"You two can go now. I need the room."

Millicent held his arm. "Babe, do you think Jen is in trouble?"

Jay stepped back and looked down at Millicent. "Why would you ask that?"

"We'll talk later." Millicent hushed, pressing on Launa's heels on her way out. "Launa, I know we've had our differences, but watch your back. Alright."

"Do you know something I don't?" Launa asked.

"Just do what Jay says and be careful. And my vote doesn't matter, but Caleb is the right choice. Not that you asked."

Launa scoffed. "Whatever. Don't worry about me. My pop taught me how to shoot."

Chapter 70

Take Charge
Todd

An assembled team met at the office at the bar. The second place Jay trusted to discuss business. Without disclosing Jen's history and true identity, he warned his members about Juan.

Todd sat rattled on the couch. "Jules's brother?"

Jay nodded.

Todd assessed the look in Jay's eyes. "Anything pertaining to security goes through me or Jay. No one else. That goes for detail assignments, too. If someone comes up missing, don't show up for a post–Anything. If you don't hear it from me, or Jay, you don't change shit we put in place."

Jay cut in. "And as of today, no newcomers are allowed at The Alley. Anybody new shows up talking about placing a bet, or asking for entry, tell 'em it's a private event and put a tail on 'em."

"Got a picture of this asshole?" Caleb asked.

Trap pulled out Juan's photograph from a yellow envelope. The team passed it around until it wound up in Jay's hands. He studied the image for a few seconds, tossed it in the can by his desk, reached in his pocket, and struck the wooden stick on the lighting strip.

As the photograph burned, the team dispersed to their posts.

Todd hung back. "Now is the time to get rid of any moles, or anyone we've ever doubted."

"You realize what that entails?"

"I do." Todd nodded.

"Have Hush do it."

"How long have you been sitting on this, man?"

Jay spewed between his teeth. "You have no idea what I'm really sitting on, but what we discussed tonight fell into my lap a few hours ago. It goes all the way to Flint."

Todd sat up. "Flint?"

"Launa."

"The fuck you talking about?" Todd rose from his chair.

"Launa's been seeing this fuckboy while keeping our boy Caleb hanging on by a string."

"Does Caleb know this part?"

"Nah. I'll tell him eventually, but I had a chat with Launa, and she said she cut Jules's brother off this morning."

"I want a rotating detail on her house. 24/7."

"Fa sho. Took care of that as soon as I learned what was what."

Todd exhaled through his nose. "I'll pay for extra lookout boys down in Flint. I want them on Landon's house, too."

"I'm way ahead of you on that. I need you to run shit solo for a short. I need to feel out what's going on down in Miami."

"Red flags flying all the way to the bottom?"

"Seems so." Jay poured water on the flailing fire dancing in the can.

"Handle your biz. I'm going to handle mine as soon as I leave here."

Jay grinned, and passed a wad of cash to Todd. "Don't do that to yourself. We 'gon get you back in there, man. I'm working on it."

Todd lifted his shirt and stuck the money in a hidden lining in his denim. "Well, hurry the fuck up and do it."

Chapter 71

The Mirror

Launa

Launa remembered nothing about the drive back to Flint. Her mind was so occupied with her conversation with Jay, and cancelling Juan from her life, that when she blinked, she was parking her car in her spot in front of the house.

She sat there in a daze thinking about the rough sex she was going to miss, the extravagant gifts he'd give her after he acted like an asshole, and the middle of the night meetups. The spontaneity and manhandling in the sack almost made risking her safety worthwhile, until she replayed him blowing her off Friday night without as much as a phone call.

"You're better off without him, Launa," she said to herself in the rearview mirror, hit the steering wheel, then hopped out of her car.

She gasped.

"What'd you do this weekend?" Juan cornered her against the door.

Launa held her chest. "You fuckin' scared me."

"That's not a fuckin' answer." Juan's deep tone raised the hairs on Launa's neck.

She stuttered. "Wha...What'd you do this weekend? Oh, I know. Not call me." She looked behind him. "Nice wheels."

"It's a rental. Now stop fucking dodging my question and tell me where you were."

"You know where I was. Why didn't you call me?"

"I could ask you the same."

"I'm not calling you to give you pussy. Do you take me as desperate?"

Juan stepped in her face. "I take you as mine. If you don't hear from me, you call to make sure everything with me is straight. You hear me?" His voice groused. "Every time you go around those sadity ass people you act like them."

"I don't like you talking about my friends like that."

Juan grinned. "They really gas you up, don't they? Stop fuckin' with me, Launa. Why you ain't call?"

"'Cause I'm done with you. I'm done waiting for you to say when we're gonna meet, and you stand me up. I'm done listening to your false promises about moving in together. I'm done waiting around for you to say you'll come meet my folks and then I don't hear from you for days. I'm just done." Launa took a step back.

Juan grabbed her arm. "You think you can snap your fingers and be rid of me like that?"

"Tell the bitch you were with this weekend I said congratulations. You are all hers. Now let go of me."

A light turned on in the house.

Juan eased back. "I think it's time I met ole Moms and Pops." He took her bag from her hands and headed towards the front door.

Launa ran past him and cut him off on the steps. "Juan, I am not fuckin' around. I want you to leave, and I never want to see you again."

The front door opened.

"I heard your car pull up. What's taking you so long to come in?" Mother Davis asked.

Juan smiled like a psycho. "We finally meet. You must be Mrs. Davis." He reached for her hand.

"I am."

"I'm Launa's boyfriend, Juan."

"Boyfriend?"

"Yeah, Ma. Boy...friend." Launa raised her brows.

Mother Davis extended her hand forward. "Well, I guess it's nice to meet you, too."

Juan shook her hand, then kissed the back of it. "Launa here has been giving me the run around on introducing me to her folks."

"Well, everyone else is settled in. You should come back one night for dinner to meet all of us. Launa, it's late and your baby has school tomorrow, so wrap this up, will ya."

"Yes ma'am."

Mother Davis left the door cracked. Launa listened for the sound of her bedroom door closing, with Juan so close in her face, he could have been a mole.

She whispered, "What the fuck is wrong with you?"

"I told you. You are mine." He stroked her cheek. "And I wanna hear from your fuckin' mouth what you did this weekend."

Launa glared into his crazy, glazed, brunette eyes and realized he already knew what she had done over the weekend.

'Why do I pick loser after loser?'

After the conversation she had with Jay, her legs twitched below her.

'Don't rile this one up.' She heard Jay's voice in her head.

She suppressed her rage and waited out his intimidation. Fear flowed through her bones as she studied his split personality rise to the surface.

"Go tell your mother you'll be back in the morning."

Scared to pieces, she pretended to be bold. "I'm not going anywhere with you."

"I didn't ask. I'm telling you."

Launa sighed. "What do you want from me?"

"To not play in my fuckin' face like I'm some gotdamn simp. I saw you, Launa. And if I see you with another mufucka, I'll kill you and him."

"I was with friends all weekend. I don't know what you think you saw."

"That chubby mufucka ain't no friend." He pointed two fingers in her face. "I told you not to play with me."

"When did we become exclusive?"

Juan stepped back and ran his hands across his head. "What?"

"We never said we were exclusive."

Juan paced back and forth.

"Look, it's late and I'm tired. Once I drop my kid off to school, I'll meet you wherever you're staying, and we can get this sorted out. Cool?"

Juan invaded her space again. "Im'ma give you this one time to prove yourself to me. If you don't show up..." He paused and smiled. "I'm at our usual spot. Room 301." He planted a swift, rough kiss on her lips. "And that pussy better be wet when you get there."

Launa went inside, opened her father's safe, and placed his revolver in her purse. She slept with one eye open, began her day like normal, dropped off her son, and found herself standing in front of Room 301.

Juan opened the door, wiping the cold from his eyes. "It's good to see you, baby." He pulled her inside. "You mad at me?"

Launa kept quiet.

Juan took her hand and forced it down his boxers. "I've been thinking about your sexy ass all night." He kissed her cheek. "You feel it. I'm sorry about last night. I ain't mean to scare you. You know I love you."

Launa remained silent.

"Say something, baby. You know I hate that silent treatment shit."

"We're good," she said, hiding her real emotions behind a smile.

"Come on and sit on this dick."

Launa succumbed to the passion of Juan sucking clots of blood on her neck, down the center trail of her stomach. He licked the burgundy marks he left on her until she could no longer pretend she didn't miss the rough manhandling. The carnivorous way he devoured her skin that put her in a sensual trance.

Before he revealed his crazy side, she craved to feel his tongue molesting her body, and in that moment, she temporarily caught amnesia for the sake of indulging him.

Lost in his commanding mannerisms of euphoric pleasure, she maneuvered his dick inside of her.

"I knew you would come for this dick," he groaned. "And you came with that pussy drenched just for me like I told you to. You better had been a good fuckin' girl." Juan stroked hard and fast with enough friction between them, it felt like flicks of static shock sparked on each lunge forward.

Launa shrieked, empty of words to express the pleasure he gave her.

"Mmm, I love this shit. This is my pussy. You hear me." He scraped her walls side to side and rolled his hips forward until she grunted a sigh of pleasurable pain. "You better not had let that fat mufucka feel my shit."

Launa stuck her fingers in his mouth to shut him up. In the middle of their battlefield of fuckery, Juan growled above her, mercilessly stroking her silly and sideways, bending her knees to her chest, and drilling his dick as far back as it could reach.

He spit her finger out from his mouth. "I wanna give you something to suck on, but this pussy is too good to pull out." He lowered her legs, hovered above her, and wrapped his hands around her neck.

Crick. Crick. The headboard banged against the wall.

"You give my pussy away?" He thrusted deep.

Launa's eyes bulged as she shook her head side to side.

"You give my pussy away?" he tested her, this time with a crazy look in his eyes.

Launa squeezed out a, "No," counting the minutes until the lashing would end.

She tolerated the switch for a minute more, winding her hips and squeezing her walls to make him pop.

He howled and sighed out of breath with his eyes closed. Launa glanced at her purse, afraid she was going to have to put a bullet in her crazed lover's head.

Juan fell forward, kissing her cheeks and moaning indistinctly until he drifted off with his cock still loaded inside of her. When his mouth fell open, she maneuvered from below him and slid to the edge of the bed.

Juan pulled her back and imprisoned her in his arms. She lied there, listening to him snort and grit his teeth for an hour.

Then, his phone rang. Launa pretended to be asleep when he answered. He peered over at her while he crept into the bathroom and closed the door.

She opened her eyes, eavesdropping on his conversation, making out every other word he uttered through the thin walls.

"I got that bitch under lock and key," he said. "Sweden." And "He don't suspect a thing. I'm handling it." He ended the call and returned to the bed.

Launa felt his eyes burning her in the back of the head. She continued to pretend she was fast asleep, faking a light wheeze knowing Juan hated to hear her snore.

He smacked her ass. "It's time to go."

She grunted and stretched, holding her eyes tight. "What?"

"Time to go."

"But I called out to hang with you today."

"I'll make it up to you." He kissed her shoulder.

"When?"

"Soon. Now get dressed. I got a flight to catch."

Launa jumped up and dressed faster than him. She draped her bag over her shoulder and clung to him, playing the role of dicmatized, desperate dummy, convincing Juan his talents between the sheets had Jedi mind-tricked her into believing his lies.

"I'll call you when I land." He palmed her ass.

Launa stood on her toes and kissed him. "You better," she said, then dashed through the door, nervous as she walked to her car.

Slowly, she trailed, never looking back, careful to keep her movements simple. Holding one hand over her chest, she cranked her car as a tear strolled down her cheek. "Ten, nine, eight," she counted aloud to herself, easing out of the lot before she dried her eyes with the sleeve of her shirt. "God help me," she said, trembling while she steered the wheel, confused if God was the right person to call on —Or Jay.

CHAPTER 72

OLD HABITS

TODD

Todd took a deep breath as he parked in his old driveway. He psyched himself into knocking on the door just as Landon lifted the garage to head out to work.

She hopped out and smiled at him. "What are you doing here?" she asked with her hand on her hip.

Todd jogged down the front steps. "I won't hold you long. I need to run something by you."

"This early?"

He bit his bottom lip. "I just came by to give you a heads up. It's some activity going on that I can't fully explain right now. I need you to be extra alert, and make sure you keep the doors locked. And don't freak out, but I'm putting eyes on your house."

"No."

"Whatchu mean, no?"

"No. I don't need all of that. I'm not a part of that world with you anymore. Whatever you and Jay have got going on, no longer involves me."

"This has nothing to do with Jay, or myself."

"Then what is it about?"

Todd lifted his chin, stuck his hands in his pocket and stood in the stance that Landon found arousing. "Can I talk to you like I did when we were together? In the vault?"

"Is it that serious?"

"As of yesterday, and this morning, yeah."

Landon closed her car door and followed Todd to his car.

He turned up the heat. "I can't tell you everything, but whatever is going on has to do with Jen, and possibly Launa."

"Launa?"

"Yes, but don't worry. I'm on top of it. I just wanted you to be aware. That's all."

Landon turned up her lip and breathed out. "What has Launa done?"

"Nothing. It's more-so the company she keeps. But I promise you, I'm on it." His eyes roamed over her.

Landon avoided eye contact with him. "Will you keep me posted?"

"I will. I came by last night as soon as I heard, but a car was..."

Landon's chest fluttered. "I'll be mindful of my surroundings and make sure the alarm is on."

"I'll bring you an extra piece tonight."

"I can swing by after work and pick it up. Will you be at the shop?"

"I will."

She finally looked at him. "Then I'll see you in a few. Thanks for still looking out for me. And my sister."

"Always."

Landon held her arms as she strutted back to her car. Todd gave himself the pleasure of savoring every second of her walking away, hung up on how she didn't want to acknowledge the car parked outside of the house the night before.

He raced to Flint, welcomed by the family with open arms.

"To what do we owe the pleasure," Papa Davis stood aside for him to come in.

"I had a few orders out here and thought I would pop in on my people. How is everyone?"

"Good, son. We're doing good."

Launa came downstairs. "Bruh-law! Come ride with me to the store."

Todd looked at his phone. "I got a little time to spare, but then I gotta get back to the shop."

"It's good to see you, son." Papa Davis hugged his shoulders. "Sure do miss you, boy."

"Todd, make sure Launa gets everything on my list, please." Laura Lee walked off into the kitchen singing a hymn.

"Sure thing, Ma." He turned to Launa. "I'll drive."

Launa loosened her scarf and spilled what she endured. The vein in Todd's neck bubbled when she repeated the threat Juan made about her and Caleb, but the maroon mark halfway hiding behind worn off concealer, and an opening between her scarf and sweater made him seethe.

"You are not to see him again." He opened the hole wider for a closer look at the bruise.

"Oh, that. That's not what you think it is."

"I promised your sister I was taking care of this problem."

"She knows?"

"Not everything. So don't say nothin'."

"How was it seeing her?"

"Brutal. I swung by the house last night, and a car was parked out front. It took everything in me not to kick that fuckin' door in. That's the first time I ever rode by and a car was there. Shit don't feel right."

"I'm sorry."

"Not as sorry as I am. But back to you. Don't take that fucker's calls. Don't let him in the house. And don't meet him anywhere."

"I promise. I'm keeping my distance." Launa exhaled and relaxed her back in the seat. "Where is Jay?"

"Headed to see Jen."

"Tell him to call me. And tell him it's important."

Todd narrowed his eyes. "Will do."

CHAPTER 73

TRIPPIN'

JAY

Walking through Miami-Dade, Jay looked over his shoulder every few seconds. Being on territory he didn't trust, and the constant vibration of his phone with coded texts from Todd unnerved him.

"My man, no stops. Take me straight to the shop at that address," he instructed the connect who picked him up.

With straight shoulders and a cocky grin on his lips, he walked in without acknowledging anyone, and let himself inside her office. Jen followed him a few seconds later and cleared her throat.

"Remember that walk we went on?" Jay looked around the barren room.

"Si. And hey to you, too."

He handed her his cell phone. "I could use one of those right now."

Jen took his phone, unlocked the bottom drawer on her desk, and tossed it inside. "Let's go," she said, pulling out a burner phone.

Jay followed Jen through the back entrance into the alleyway. A few twists and turns between buildings, led them to the end of a road where the sand from the beach blew past the dead end sign leaning sideways.

She connected the phone to the wifi in the nearest building. "Make the call, and make it quick."

Jay dialed Todd. "Sun's shining."

"Had a drizzle here." Todd coughed. "Might be raining soon."

"Was it in the forecast?"

"Nah. A downburst."

"Storms help ya sleep. As long as it don't flood." Jay ended the call on the burner and handed it to Jen.

She dropped it on the rocks and crushed it with her heel. "You wanna tell me why you rolled up on me with no warning?"

"Pretty boy's brother is a problem."

"Whatchu know?"

"He was spotted scoping my house. Either for me, or Launa it turns out."

"Ugh. So you know about them?"

"Mmm hmm."

"She says she cut him loose, but it sounds like he's been busy, so I won't keep you long. You trust your house?"

"100."

"Ahite. If you say so, just…"

Jen cut him off. "Always."

Jay sneered. "I trust you, but not on that."

The side of Jen's mouth curved. "You got me worried now." She popped her lips. "Let's head back so I can call Launa."

Jay checked out the goods he missed from time to time, rising and falling in her shorts.

"Stop looking at my ass," Jen said, leading him through the maze of alleys back to the shop.

Jen pulled out a second burner from the drawer and dialed Launa. Jay listened in on the call with clenched teeth as he heard firsthand what she endured with Juan. Jen shook her head at what she suffered, while Jay noticeably grew angry when Launa's voice began to crack.

"I heard him tell someone on the phone he has that little bitch in check. And I think he was talkin' 'bout me," she said to Jen.

Jay clicked his tongue.

"Then he mentioned something about Sweden," Launa added.

Jay and Jen's ears perked up.

Jen took a deep breath. "When L needed to get away, I offered my home to her. The same goes for you."

"I would take you up on that offer if I knew for sure he wasn't down there."

Jen mumbled to Jay, "If he knows what's good for him, he…"

Jay touched the back of her hand. When their eyes met, Jen read his gaze, recognizing he still loved her.

She pulled her hand away. "Launa, I love you like a sister. I don't want you to worry. Just be careful up there. I'll call you later tonight." Jen hung up the line and turned to Jay. "You think she's telling us everything?"

"I think she watered it down. I'll get the full story tonight." Jay stared her down. "I saw that look in your eye, Jen. You don't need to go after that money. We're straight."

"I hear you."

"Where is pretty boy?"

"At the house waiting to see if he got the job."

Jay's forehead crumpled as he sighed. "He'll get it." Jay looked away. "At least I hope he does. That would save me from making these trips checking on you."

"Either that, or get rid of the problem before it comes knocking on my door."

Jay couldn't hide his teeth. Hearing her talk with such fearlessness and cockiness turned him on, and the memory of her giving him hell the night they met crossed his mind. He watched her lips smack, filling with desire to kiss them for old time's sake, but restrained the urge in fear of rejection.

"We make a great team." He tested her.

"You mean made. And no sense in going down that road. Yo ass is gonna lie in that bed you made."

Jay grinned. "Listen to you."

"You fucked around and I found out. Too many times. Don't make me do what I should have done back then."

He fanned her off. "You all talk. I don't think you're the badass you claim to be. You ain't said shit about the guys I put on you."

"You mean the guys outside in the brown Chevy? Or the guys you had posted outside of Landon's house this past weekend?"

Jay smiled. "Say no more." He laughed off the thoughts of when they were a couple playing in his head, and hugged her. "My work here is done. I'll show myself out."

CHAPTER 74

UNDOUBTEDLY

JEN

Walking in the house with a million outcomes of murder and mayhem plaguing Jen's mind, Jules welcomed her home in the happiest of moods.

"I accepted their offer." A proud smile rose on his lips from ear to ear.

Jen's face lit up, pleased to hear the good news, but not as spirited as Jules expected.

"I thought you'd be a little more excited." He placed his hands around her waist to the small of her back. "Bad day?"

"Something like that. But don't let my reaction fool you. I'm thrilled you got the job."

"Not as much as I am. I get to make the woman of my dreams the happiest she's ever been by reuniting her with her son. I know it's been hell living without little man. It's been even more hell for me knowing our union separated you from him. Now I get to right that wrong. You can't tell me fate isn't on our side."

A lightness overwhelmed Jen, and her face beamed the way Jules imagined it would when he first announced the news.

"That's it right there. That's the look I was hoping to see on your face."

"I love you, too," she said, then rested her head on his shoulder.

"I'm glad you know how I feel about you without me having to say it." He leaned down and kissed her forehead.

"I saw a house over the weekend. Let's fly up and take a look at it in a few days."

"The sooner the better."

"I wouldn't mind hanging back through the weekend and taking my boy to the Halloween carnival at his school. It's all he talked about before I left yesterday."

"Think he'll mind if I come along?"

"He likes you, Jules. Don't worry about that." She ran her fingers across his face. "We'll have a good time."

CHAPTER 75

CRY FOUL

JAY

As soon as the plane landed, Jay headed to his bar. Todd sat in the office smoking a blunt when he strolled in. He took one look at him and passed him the fat, tightly rolled cigar. Jay took a toke, exhaled a thick cloud above him, then plopped down in his chair behind the desk.

"How bad is the Launa situation?" Jay kicked up his feet.

"Bruises on her neck from what I seen. She played it off like they were sex scars though, so..."

Jay narrowed one eye and enlarged the other. "Damn, Launa get down like that?"

Todd furrowed his brows at him. "She's still my little sister, man."

"I'm just saying." He leaned back and crossed his hands on his chest. "Whatchu think? Passion or force?"

Todd shrugged his shoulders. "Either way, I disapprove."

"Little ass Launa. I shoulda... So whatchu come up with?"

"I say add him to the Hush count."

"He ain't low on that roster they got down there in Texas, though. Gotta make this one look like a bitch did it."

"Nah. That puts a target on Launa's back. I ain't witchu on that idea."

"It'll be a huge disadvantage carrying out his hit without a proper plan. And my intel disclosed he's fuckin' wit' more than Launa. Any of the other ones could want him dead. Especially his kid's mother."

"So whatchu wanna do? Set her up and make her do time behind his punk ass? Un-uh. Gotta be a better way." Todd reached for the blunt. He inhaled, choked, and placed it back in the tray. "He lives a street life. He deserves a street death. Leave the females out of this."

"Let me think on it some more then. 'Cause if I had my way, I'd take him and his brother out."

"Jen having problems down bottom?"

"According to her, no. She doesn't suspect her husband at all. The good news is she's moving back soon. The stadium hired him so I can keep a closer watch on him, and my boy gets his mama back full time."

"It's gonna be good to have her back."

"Yeah." Jay glanced over at Todd staring off. "One down. One more to go."

CHAPTER 76

HALLOW'S EVE

LANDON

It took forever for the sun to rise once autumn arrived, but if you blinked, the sky would be dark before heading into five o'clock traffic.

The night Landon was leery about had arrived—Halloween surrounded by a bunch of strangers.

Uncomfortable in his tight suit and leather mask, Walt's mouth dropped open when Landon stepped out of his bedroom. The curves of her wide hips cascading from her waist line made him shudder. He stood there speechless with a watering mouth and bulging cock he couldn't hide.

"Well?" she asked, blotting her deep red lips and adjusting her face mask.

Walt looked down at his crotch. "I don't think we thought these costumes through."

Landon followed his eyes and chuckled. "I take it my Dark Knight likes what he sees?"

"I've changed my mind. I don't want to go tonight."

Landon approached him. "Why?"

"I can't walk around the office with a dick print."

Landon laughed. "I tell you what. We'll wrap the cape around your waist, do a quick walkthrough to show our faces, then leave."

"The minute I swell up, we're out of there."

Landon's sex appeal brought silence to the party. Walt was overwhelmed with pride to have her on his arm, but his co-workers deflated his ego with embarrassing stories to remind him he was an *Average Joe*.

He fought his arousal with everything in him when he and the men gawked at his date excusing herself to visit the ladies room.

"How did your corny ass pull her?" his former partner asked.

"If being corny pulled that amazing woman, I highly recommend you get like me," said Walt.

"She got a sister?"

"She does. And, no, I will not introduce you to her."

"What's wrong with me?"

"A lot. And I'm not doing anything to jeopardize my relationship with that woman. Fellas, y'all are looking at my wife right there. Put your eyes back in your heads."

Walt stepped away and waited for her by the door.

"I think we've made enough rounds," he said, taking her by the hand when she exited the ladies room.

Landon raised her brows.

"Yes. I'm about to burst these gotdamn tights. Let's get out of here."

They rushed back to the house where he carried her inside. He threw her on the bed, lowering his voice into a masterful cadence.

"You've been naughty tonight, Cat Woman." He smacked her leather covered ass.

Landon gasped. "Have I?"

"Bad girls have to be taught a lesson according to the laws." He spoke in character, seducing her with a low baritone rasp and commanding eyes behind his mask.

"I've been really bad lately." She purred.

"Yes, you have." Walt ripped the seam of her pants. "I thought you had on a thong."

"No panties. Just for tonight."

Walt flicked her pussy and groaned. "A bad girl you are indeed." He lifted her legs and licked her pussy. "And bad tastes good on your foxy ass."

She removed his mask to grip on his head. "Mmm, Mr. Dark Knight seems thirsty. Drink."

Landon wiggled in his mouth, unzipping the leather top stuck to her bosom. Walt sucked her southern lips between the leather, struggling to strip off her pants. She moaned from the friction and suction of his lips lathering hers, then handed him an assist with the pants glued to her ass.

She pulled until they lowered past her thighs. Walt squeezed her buttery cheeks and sucked the meat captured between his fingers.

Landon tugged on the leather sticking to her shoulders. Her entire body wet from the heat of arousal. She sighed as her top fell to the side—almost naked with her pants stuck at her knees and tucked in her boots.

Walt paced himself, slowing down the inevitable moment. He unfastened her bra, then stood over her with his hand on his belt. Landon reached up and grabbed the handcuffs.

Walt placed his hand on top of hers. "I would never arrest you, but you have the right to assume the position."

Landon rolled over to her stomach, resting her hands behind her back. Her ass jiggled from the pulses of her pussy starving for attention–squeezing tight then opening up as she yearned for his dick to remedy her wanton need.

Walt placed one cuff around her wrist. "How does that feel?"

"Like I'm ready to be taught a lesson for my bad ways."

He cuffed the other wrist, unzipped her four inch heeled boots, then yanked off the unruly leather keeping them apart.

Landon looked at him over her shoulder, biting her lips.

Walt studied the suspense dancing in her eyes and revealed his next gadget. He reached inside a hidden compartment of his cape, pulled out a flogger, and tapped her ass with the frills. Landon sighed with delight from the flailing.

He untied the cape from his waist and tapped her harder, putting a reddish print on her right cheek.

"Did I hurt you?" He rubbed the inflaming bruise.

"No, sir."

He struck her with the same force. "I think my naughty girl likes this."

"I love it," she whispered.

Walt unbuckled his gadget belt and tore out of his costume. "Then let's continue the lesson," he said, revealing the power that made him a man.

Gently he rubbed his dick across her lips. Landon stuck out her tongue and circled the tip, making him jolt.

He sighed. "Not yet, rulebreaker."

She ignored him, lifting her head and leaning forward until his head touched her tonsils.

Walt dropped the flog and called out her name. "Landon! Aah!" Then he muttered. "You fuckin' bad girl." He rolled his dick around her mouth, leaned forward, then slapped her ass with his hand. "That's it. Yes. Just like that. Look at me. Let me see those pretty brown eyes."

She held his gaze as she succumbed to his dominance. His appeal. His authority. Heavily turned on with her performance, she smiled at him as she spat him out, rolling her tongue around his tip lingering in her face, eager to return to the warmth of her mouth.

Arousing sighs of gratification spilled from Walt's lips. He grabbed her hair and fed his dick down her throat, wetting the bed as her saliva dripped from the side of her mouth.

Her confined hands jittered, unable to hold him back. Walt huffed, guiding her full lips back and forth as they caressed his yardage eloquently, and effortlessly, until he felt the burst of the moment building inside of him.

He retreated from her bordeaux colored lips. "Have you learned your lesson?"

"No." She sighed, catching her breath.

He cuffed her lips with his fingers and kissed them gently. "You handled that like a good girl," he said, then flipped her over to her back.

Landon gyrated from anticipation. Her lower back lifted up and down on the bed. Walt unhooked a second toy from his belt hiding in a black silk bag.

"Tell me if this hurts." He clamped nipple stimulants to her breasts.

Landon panted as they whirred, at first loose, then tight. "Mr. Batman, are your tools just for me?"

"Yes." His voice still raspy and deep in tone holding character.

With her pussy glued to his mouth, he elevated her ass off the bed, flicking his tongue inside her pulsing walls. As he slurped on her sweet waters pouring into his mouth, Landon shivered, shuddered, juddered, and quivered sensations of a novice.

She pleaded. "Stop. No, don't stop. Suck me. Stop. Please fuck me."

"Un-uh." Walt shook his head. "I'm in charge tonight. I give the orders."

Landon felt a full-fledged freak blossoming inside of her. She whined at the torturous pleasure of being serviced to the brink of an oral derived orgasm. Walt plunged inside her yearning yoni like a mad man, feeling his way around her body with an engorged tip ready to shoot upon entry. He slowed down his strokes, rubbed his tip against the back of her wall, then paused when she exhaled a deep breath.

"I told you to fuck me."

Walt pulled out, then lunged back inside, pressing his dick in the same spot.

Landon moaned. "Yes, Detective. Give me what I want."

Walt stroked her fast and hard, then paused again. "For a bad girl, you're very demanding. Now shut up and take this dick before I put it back in your mouth to make you see the error of your ways."

"Do it," Landon demanded.

"I would if I could," Walt grumbled through his teeth, locked his knees and emptied his clip inside Landon's warmth. "Ooahh!" He shrieked with stiff thighs holding him steady.

Landon's eyes held his as they culminated together. Something beyond a deep connection bridged them in that moment.

With his barrel hollow, he removed himself, uncuffed her hands, and unclipped the clamps from her breasts. His lips traced her body as he rolled her over to her stomach to knead his fists across her back, while kissing the print he marked on her ass. He massaged her head to toe with both his hands and his mouth until she fell asleep, loving that she was in his bed. Loving that she was in his life.

Landon woke up in the middle of the night covered in one of his white t-shirts, and cuddled in his arms. She admired him in the dim light and kissed the muscle locking her in place, smiling to herself, feeling like she was in a dream. Then, she pinched herself to make sure this was her new reality. And she settled in his embrace, thankful for a second chance to be loved—with no strings attached.

[illegible]

CHAPTER 77

STOCK & HOME

JEN

Escrow on a four bedroom house fifteen miles outside the downtown city limits made the transition a win, limiting the time they had to camp out at Landon's house. It wasn't the home Jen picked, but with Tammy excelling in real estate, her friend in high places locked them in on a short sale within no time.

Looking to earn bonus points with Landon, Walt joined her and Launa to help with the move. Hours after the heavy lifting had been completed, and only fragile packages stuffed in the middle of the living room remained to be cleared, he and Landon disappeared somewhere in the house.

"Landon must have that power ooh wee." Jen snickered. "She has that man by the balls."

Launa scoffed. "He asked for my parents' number."

"Already?" Jen scowled.

Launa nodded.

"You don't think he's about to..."

"For Todd's sake, I hope not."

"Poor Todd."

"Poor me. I haven't tackled one husband, and Little Miss Ambitious is about to score her second."

Jen held back a rising cackle in her throat when she saw Launa's face. "Any word from *him*?"

Launa pulled up the monument of texts from Juan.

"Keep him on read."

"How long 'til you think he shows up here since y'all have moved back?"

"Any day now. But I'm ready for him."

"So am I." Launa pointed to her hip. "Can I ask you something?"

"Anything."

"Why do I feel like there's some big secret around this you and Jules and Juan and Jay fiasco? And why am I in it for simply thinking with my twat and not with my head."

"You ain't the first, and definitely not the last to pick the wrong man to get into bed with. Women as a whole share that fault. My track record ain't that peachy. Shit. Look at Jay."

They laughed out loud.

"But there is something else going on, right? I mean one minute I'm enjoying a good lay, then the next minute he's standing over you in bed, talking to me reckless; and now I'm toting my daddy's pistol, thinking of the different ways I'm gonna have to lay him on his back."

Jen took a breath. "I trust Landon. She can keep a secret. And I feel like you're just as much my sister as hers. I hope I can trust you, too. Let's take this outside."

Away from everyone, the two of them sat on the deck where Jen revealed her dark past. As she shared her secrets, she enlisted Launa to play a part in her plan of collecting her money.

"Jules's new job is going to Stockholm over the holidays. While I'm gone, I need you to open bank accounts in your name, and Landon's name, and give me the account numbers when I get back."

"Any way I can talk you out of going through with this?"

Jen stared off to herself and continued. "I'm not gonna do anything on this trip. But one day, I will, and if a large sum of money appears in those accounts, it'll mean I'm okay, but also mean you'll never see me again. I want you and Landon to take care of my boy. I trust you two will make sure he gets what I set aside for him. I'll leave a breakdown with you before I go."

"Is there no talking you out of this?"

"My mind's made up. And you're the right person to share this with. Only you know what I'm planning. Only you will know I survived."

"Why me?"

"'Cause we're more alike than you think. You know what it's like to be a single mother. And fuckin' wit' Juan, you know what it's like to be in danger."

Launa sighed.

"To make my disappearance look real, I need you to convince Jay to have a funeral for me. He's quite fond of you, ya know. Think you can handle that?"

Launa nodded. "And if the accounts never get a deposit?"

Jen looked down at her feet. "Then you'll be having a real funeral for me."

Launa grabbed her hand. "Is this money worth going after?"

"My father lost his life giving it to me. I can't let that be in vain."

"Then you better make it back here to give it to Max."

"God willing." Jen looked at the door behind her. "One more thing. Landon doesn't need to know about this until after the fact."

Days before her departure, Jay raised hell at Jen. "How much money do you need to keep yo' ass here with us? With our son?" He fumed in her face, squeezing his hands out front, acting as if he was choking her. "I got ahead of myself thinking since you were back, you'd be trying to have some fancy meal on Thursday. Yet here you are, scheming on money you don't need. I got us." He beat his chest. "The businesses got us."

"You got Millicent. And this exhibition game is the perfect cover for me to scope out the city. Plus, the other wives are going, so there's no reason I'll be seen as suspicious."

"Jen, I can't help you if something goes wrong."

"I'm not going to do anything on this trip."

"If you do, that's all on you."

Jen kept those words in mind while freezing in the frigid temperatures of northern Europe. They reminded her that for her entire life it was "all on her." She was all she had until her friendship with the Davis girls blossomed into a sisterhood. And not even *they* knew the mindfuck that went on in her head at times when she felt low. So low that sometimes she welcomed death, as she was tired of looking over her shoulder. The night when Juan stood over her in her bedroom, she embraced it, feeling as though he would be doing her a favor.

Jules squeezed her tight. "I'm not a mind reader, but I'm guessing you're wondering why we came over here. It's cold as a bitch." He rubbed his hands up and down the back of her coat. "You alright?"

Jen's shuddering teeth tapped together. "Yeah. I'm praying they have the heat on hell inside this stadium."

"The wives are sitting in a skybox, so I'm sure it's nice and toasty."

"If it's not, I'll find my way back to the hotel where I know it's warm."

She watched the team practice until her fingers were fully thawed and her toes no longer shivered in her boots. As the wives ran in and out of the skybox, she disappeared with a group visiting the loo and circled the stadium, overlooking the skyline of the city below them. She pulled out the map she swiped at the airport, studying the streets they crossed on their way to the arena, then blended back in with the ladies before her absence was noticed.

Post practice, Jules vowed to keep her warm on a stroll down the street from the hotel to grab dinner.

"Stroll? It's colder now than it was earlier."

"It may be the only time we get to trek through the night temps together, and who knows? Could be one of those rare nights the northern lights show up here. Just for you and me."

Jen bundled up in scarves as they took to the icy streets, stopping at a quaint little restaurant. Soused on wine, they briefly dove back into the cold streets and found warmth inside a pub on the corner.

They danced and made out in the middle of the floor, celebrating their upcoming anniversary, surrounded by strangers treating them to free drinks at the bar.

"A year ago she said yes to me!" Jules shouted. A Duchenne smile lifting the corners of his mouth.

Jen buried her head on his shoulder with the look on his face planted in her thoughts. That moment convinced her what they shared was real. He was not the enemy. He was her true love.

Wrapped in his arms for the brave battle to stampede through the icy streets back to the hotel, they took a detour to the right instead of the left, crossing two branches of Forex Banc within three blocks. Jen peered at the signs, keeping her main focus on her husband, waiting for a change in his behavior.

Jules didn't flinch at the sight of the bank.

"Either the alcohol is wearing off, or the temperature just dropped to fuck you Celsius," Jen joked.

Jules pushed them inside the nearest hotel lobby. "Can you call us a cab?" he asked the bellman.

A night of endless sex carried them into the morning. Jen endured the pleasure of his willingness and determination to please her. He eased her mind of real world problems by pulling her into him, and in ways she enjoyed being drawn, mounted above her with her feet flung past her head.

The pain that coincided with the pleasure of his long-winded, alcohol induced endurance finally subsided.

"It's unfair." He sighed, stealing open-mouthed kisses.

"What is?"

"You get to lie around all day while I have to tend to a bunch of sweaty men on an hour of sleep."

"So, you wanna erase the last six hours?"

Jules dropped low and licked the slick from her folds. "Never *dat*. What are you and the ladies doing today?"

"Museums, exhibits, lunch, visit a palace, and shopping for antiques are on the itinerary."

But Jen did none of that with the ladies. Using her time wisely, she broke free from the group after the first museum visit, giving herself a tour of side streets near the two bank locations, and making mental notes of crowded cafes and bars, second hand shops, and antique stores.

She grabbed brochures and trinkets along her route, then waltzed inside a costume shop with questions about the early advertisement for St. Patrick's Day.

"Your place is excited for the parade, I see." Jen looked over her shoulder.

The store clerk smiled. "Oh, yes. Crowded streets, nonstop parties, and drunk people spending money is a fun time."

Jen eyed a bright green wig behind the counter. "I'll take that wig behind you."

"Good choice. It'll sell out before February."

"Well, I like the short black one, too. I better grab that one before it's too late. And the hat next to it, please."

The clerk rang up the items. "Be sure and come by when you wear them so I can add you to the wall." She pointed behind her.

Jen glanced at the wall then peered quickly at the entrance. "By chance, do you know when the next trolley arrives?"

"Every fifteen minutes. If you turn left on your way out, you should catch the next one right on time."

"Thanks. You can keep the bag. I'll be back to be featured on the wall," she said, stuffing the wigs and hat in her tote.

She followed the clerk's directions, and sat behind the driver of the bus pulling up to the stop, studying his rearview mirror while learning the main streets on the route.

"Do you know where you're headed?" the bus driver asked.

"Nowhere in particular. I hopped on to get warm and see your beautiful city."

"I know an American accent when I hear one."

Jen smiled.

"Also, your coat screams tourist. You need a goose down in these temperatures."

"Thanks for the tip. And here I thought if I bundled up in a wool scarf, I would fit right in. I've been freezing my butt off out there."

The driver chuckled. "Good thing you hopped on. You'll be warm in here."

"Will I see any famous landmarks on your route?"

"Only a few." He handed her a schedule. "My main stop is the train station. Just up a mile ahead, I'll pick up some transfers and spend about twenty minutes in the lot. From there, I'll point out some things you wouldn't want to miss on the way back into the city."

"I'd appreciate that."

"The name's Bennie. And you are?"

"Therecita," Jen lied.

Jen browsed back and forth from the rear view mirrors to the streets, confirming her suspicion she was being followed.

Two cars back, a vehicle followed the trolley's every turn. She kept her cool, probing the bus driver with questions all the while keeping an eye out. Contemplating her next move. Grateful, she bought a pocket knife from the gift shop at the museum.

Bennie picked up the transfers and drove to the train station. "We have a good twenty minutes before we pull out. Take a tour of the place. Grab a coffee. Then let's meet back here." He placed a reserved card on her seat.

Jen followed the travelers inside. In her peripheral she noticed the same figure as before keeping tabs on her every move.

From a yard away he watched her while pretending to read at different kiosks. Jen slipped into the bathroom, locked herself in one of the stalls, and removed her scarf. She turned her jacket inside out, tucked her hair below the short, black wig and hat stuffed in her tote, and cuffed the knife below the hem of her sleeve.

As a group of women exited the lounge, she blended in with them, walking past Juan eyeing the door. Her chest tightened as she gripped onto her knife. Madness played in her head. Her past trauma resurfaced.

Bennie stood near the coffee shop talking with one of his colleagues. Jen eased over to the service counter, swiping pamphlets of departure and arrival schedules, sightseeing brochures, and taxi cab companies.

She ordered a coffee and sat with her back to the wall in a corner near a man reading a newspaper, watching Juan search for her in the station.

When Bennie headed towards the bus, Jen moved closer to the windows. She sipped her coffee, studying the anguish written across Juan's eyebrows surveying the bathroom.

The next group of departures loaded the trolley as Juan barged into the ladies room causing a stir. Jen sat back and watched her stalker push his way through the horde and run towards the bus.

Bennie peaked out from the bottom step, searching for Jen before closing his doors and leaving the lot. Juan smacked the back of the bus with his hands and dashed for his car.

When he screeched out of the lot, Jen hopped into a taxi. "Stockholm Suites, please."

The taxi driver nodded.

Jen removed the hat and wig. "A little privacy, please," she said to the driver, eyeing her in the rearview mirror.

"Yes, ma'am," he said, still watching her remove the disguise.

She turned her jacket back to the other side and sharply exhaled. Her back sunk against the seat. Her heart racing so hard she could feel it thud in her chest.

Disturbed that Juan followed her and Jules to Sweden, she shook her head in disbelief, then recomposed herself as she now had confirmation that with, or without the money her father left for her to claim, a target would forever be on her back.

Quickly, the old Jen resurfaced. That night, she slept with one eye open, and staged the hotel suite with steak knives from room service behind the mirror, below the mattress, and under her pillow—Plagued with the only answer to her problem. Murder.

'It's time I disappear. For good.'

Chapter 78

It's Giving Thanks

The Davises

With Jen and Jules out on their own, and Walt back in Ohio for the start of a new week, an empty house suddenly felt like loneliness to Landon.

Work was slow with the holidays approaching, so she worked half days, but the deafening silence at home became too much. She'd grown accustomed to laughter, grown up conversations at all hours of the night, and a child running amuck. She missed the noise. She missed being around people. She missed Walter.

Midday Wednesday, Walt called her at work.

"You just caught me." Her face brightened at the sound of his voice. "I'm done here for the rest of the week."

"I'll be following your lead in a few hours. Gonna head home. All alone. Wishing a certain pretty face was there to keep me company."

"Hmmm. I wonder who you could be talking about?"

"Ya know, I've been waiting for you to say something about the holidays. I've seen firsthand you know how to cook, so what gives?"

"I think maybe a little holiday blues."

"I'm sorry to hear that. Anything I can do?"

"You do enough already. I'm sure it'll pass."

"Think it'll pass by the morning?"

Landon grinned. "My mother called this morning and asked what time she could expect *us*. What did you do?"

"I paid your sister for your parents' number."

Landon gritted her sister's name through her teeth. "Launa."

"A hundred bucks for the number. Another hundred to keep quiet."

"What else am I in the dark about?"

"I had to agree to go with you two to your friend's house for game night on Saturday."

Landon kissed her teeth. "We aren't going to that."

"I gave Launa my word I would get you to go."

"You let me deal with my sister."

"Why don't you wanna go?"

"You don't know how my friends are when they get together."

Walt stammered. "Are you hiding me from them?"

"No." Landon's voice cracked. "I haven't been to any of their events in like a year, and the last one was a total disaster. Trust me when I say, you don't want to go."

"You're right. I want *us* to go."

Landon sang while chuckling. "Do you not remember Jay? My asshole friend? He by himself will get under your skin, and you being an officer... It's not a good mix of company."

"I'm a man, Landon. I can handle myself. Let's go. I don't wanna be the reason you don't hang out with your friends."

Landon huffed. "Don't say I didn't warn you."

"So, that's a yes?"

"Yes. And just so you know, I play to win."

It felt strange to walk in her childhood home with someone other than Todd on her side. She paused on the top step with her fingers shivering on the knob.

Walt kissed her cheek. "You've had the jitters the entire trip. Did I mess up calling your folks?"

Landon shook her head side to side. "It's me, not you."

"Words no one ever wants to hear."

"I'll be fine. Why aren't you nervous?"

"Maybe I'm good at hiding it."

The front door opened.

"My baby's home." Papa Davis hugged Landon. "And this must be the detective Launa told us about. Odd not hearing anything about the man from *you*, Landon." He extended his hand. "Nice to meet you, son."

"You too, Sir."

"Come on in and tell your mother hey." Papa Davis pointed to the kitchen. "Now, son tell me, who are you rooting for today?"

"If I answer wrong, do I get to stay?"

"Uh oh. Just keep it a secret, son." Papa Davis chuckled.

"That's probably for the best."

While the women piled into the kitchen to help Laura Lee cook her feast, Landon snuck evil eyes towards Launa.

She whispered, "What kind of mess are you starting, inviting Walt to game night?"

"That explains the dirty looks you've been throwing my way."

"What do I look like bringing a cop around them?"

"You mean around Todd?"

"Walt thinks I'm hiding him, so now we have to go so I can show him I'm not ashamed of him."

"Good. Then, everything's settled."

"*What you* two over there whispering about?" Laura Lee inquired.

"Whatcha think about Landon's man, Mama?"

"Sure is nice on the eyes." Laura Lee pursed her lips. "And he was real nice over the telephone. But definitely nice on the eyes."

Launa cackled out loud. "You already said that, Mama."

"It was worth mentioning twice." Laura Lee smiled at Landon. "What do you think about him, dear?"

"I think I might love him. I mean, he's told me, and I've told him."

Laura Lee and Launa glanced at each other.

"What was that?" Landon asked them.

"Your sister told me you and this man were moving real fast. I see she wasn't lying." Laura Lee pinched Landon's cheeks. "We were just hoping you and–Never mind. You two start taking the dishes to the table."

Laura Lee basted the turkey one last time and set it in the center of the table. Landon squeezed Walt's shoulders, standing behind him on the couch, pleased to see how great he was getting along with her father.

"Turn that game off," said Laura Lee.

Papa Davis turned down the volume. "I bet you she's rolling her eyes at me."

Walt peered over his shoulder and laughed.

"Told ya." Papa Davis scoffed.

"Walter, don't be like this old man and waste away your days following sports." Laura Lee grumbled. "Can't even have dinner with his family without checking a score."

"Yes, ma'am." Walt jumped up from the old plaid sofa her father refused to replace.

Papa Davis rose from his sunken spot on the couch, slowly backing away from the television flashing highlights of the previous plays. Laura Lee huffed and tapped her heel on the hardwood.

"Daddy, just pause it," said Launa.

Her father pulled out his wife's chair, then sat next to her at the head of the table.

"Walter, we're so happy you could join us. Now, Tim, bless the food."

Launa placed her hand on his shoulder as he bowed his head. "Lord, bless this food we are about to receive. Amen."

"Short and sweet. I like it," said Walt.

"It does smell good in here, don't it?" Papa Davis added.

"Yes, it does. Mr. and Mrs. Davis. Thank you for having me today." Walt smiled at Landon.

The conversation went in many directions, from learning more about Walt's background and family, the latest stories in the news, the bad weather moving into the area, old stories of the girls growing up, and Tim's latest video game addiction.

As the hour wound down, the men complimented the chef.

Papa Davis stared at Walt and cleared his throat. "Yes, Laura Lee, you've been making me the best dinners for thirty-five years. Not just on holidays. Every day. And I thank ya, my love."

Laura Lee blushed with her head hanging to the side.

Walt followed the segue. "Thirty-five years is a long time."

"It flies by when you're happy, son."

"Well, there is definitely a lot of happiness in this house. And I would love to one day say thank you to my wife for allowing me to be graced by her presence." Walt looked at Landon.

"Did I miss something?" Landon asked.

"Actually, I'm the one that's been missing something. You." He held her hand. "I have been searching for that one special woman to complete me since I became a man, and I'm looking at her. Landon, you fill my empty life."

Landon sharply inhaled.

Walt reached in his pocket and placed the engagement ring box in front of her. "I asked your father for your hand, and he was concerned about how fast this is happening. But I told him how much I love you, and know we are meant for each other. He was a tough one to crack, but he gave me his blessing. And so I'm asking, will you do me the honor of becoming my wife?"

"Lord have mercy," said Laura Lee, holding her chest.

Walt slid the ring on her finger. "Say you'll marry me?"

Landon released the breath she was holding. "Yes. I'll marry you."

"Yeah?"

"Yeah." She nodded repeatedly.

Walt pulled her in and kissed her lips, holding them against his.

Launa cleared her throat. "There are children present."

Landon and Walt pulled away from each other giggling.

"Congratulations." Launa hugged her sister. "Let's see this ring."

CHAPTER 79

THE WINNING HAND

WALT

The excitement of the engagement kept the house warm as the fire burned low. It was hours after dinner when a chill traveled through the house.

"Is there wood outback?" Walt asked Papa Davis.

"Near the shed. I was supposed to bring some in hours ago." Launa threw her head back on the couch.

"Relax. I'll go get it."

"I'll come with. I need to lock up the shed anyway," she said.

Being the detective he was, Walt observed two men sitting in a car parked a few houses up. He kept an eye on them, as they kept an eye on Launa.

"Everything alright?" he asked.

"Yeah." She sighed. "If I seem a little jealous, I am. Don't get me wrong, I'm happy for you two. I'm just wondering when it's gonna be my turn. I don't want to be a career girlfriend all of my life."

"You won't be. And that isn't what I was referring to."

Their eyes met, and he gestured to the car on the stakeout.

"Oh, don't mind them. They're here for me. I'm having trouble getting rid of a guy I was seeing. Those guys are friends, making sure I'm okay."

"If you need my help, just say the word. Not to sound too cocky, but you are about to be my little sister, and I look after my family."

"Thanks, but I have it under control. My sister knows nothing about this and I'd like to keep it that way." Launa shook her head.

"Give me his name," Walt demanded.

"If he bothers me again, I will."

"What's he done so far?"

"Umm. Verbal threats like he better not see me with anyone else, and I belong to him. That sort of thing."

"Launa, you and I need to have a serious conversation about this after tonight."

"I've got your number if I need you."

Walt looked back at the car. "Don't make me call you first." He picked up three logs and waited for Launa to lock the deadbolt on the shed. "You still think Landon and I should go to that party on Saturday?"

Launa chuckled. "Now that we're almost family, I feel I should confess that I was being facetious in asking you to go to that."

"I sorta gathered that from your sister, who is against going, by the way."

"But you're not. Why is that?"

"Since we're confessing truths, I wasn't sure until tonight Landon wasn't ashamed of me."

"Why would she be?"

"Because of how we met."

"Well, she said yes."

"And I can't wait to call her my wife."

Launa tapped his shoulder, then opened the back door of the house. "And I'm sure she can't wait to show off that rock."

The engaged couple collided in coitus on the way back to Landon's house, a second time in the garage when they made it home, and a third time in the morning. The sales were worth missing, lying in each other's arms, studying the calendar for a wedding date.

Landon propped up on Walt's chest. "I don't want a long engagement, or a huge wedding. I've done that. But I also don't want to rob you of the experience."

"So what are you proposing?"

"Something small and intimate. Maybe on a beach somewhere."

"The majority of my family is back home in Hilton Head. The weather is normally nice around New Year's."

"I love that idea. But can we pull it off in a few weeks?"

Walt kissed her delicately. "I don't care who shows up. As long as you are standing in front of me, the day will be perfect."

In the middle of the night, Landon woke up with Todd on her mind. She laid on her back, mentally crossing off excuses why they couldn't make it to game night. She prayed for a blizzard to cover the city, for Walt to have a work emergency, or Mrs. Latham needing someone else to babysit Max at the last minute. Anything would be better than facing Todd and her friends bombarding her for moving on with her life.

By morning, it was clear her prayer for a blizzard wasn't heard. The sky was clear, the temperatures unseasonably warm, and she and Walt walked into the lion's den together.

The room fell silent when he walked in behind her. Landon swore she could hear Millicent swallow, Jay's throat itch, Todd's knuckles crack, and Tammy humming to herself.

McCaine stepped forward, obviously having been briefed by his wife. "Nice to meet you, man. They call me McCaine by my last name, and this here is my wife, Tammy."

Walt extended his hand. "Walter Reed."

"I feel like we've met before," McCaine probed.

"Yeah, we did. About a year ago."

"Landon!" Jay shouted across the room.

Every eye in the room shifted in Jay's direction.

"Come holla at me for a minute." Jay rose from his chair and walked into the kitchen.

Landon touched Walt's shoulder. "Be right back."

Walt's eyes followed her across the room, avoiding the heat blazing at him from the couch.

Jay squinted one eye as he scowled. "Sis, what the fuck you doin'?" he exclaimed in a whisper.

Landon eased backwards. "Do we need to leave?"

"Anybody but this clown."

Landon aimed for the door. "We'll leave."

Jay pulled her back. "What would possess you to show up here with *him* of all people? You know *my man* is still waiting for you to take him back."

"Didn't I see a woman sitting mighty close to him just now?"

"He don't give a fuck about that bird. You know this." Jay dropped his head.

"Talk to me, sis. What's going on witchu? Is it a date, y'all just hanging out? What?"

"We're exclusive. And it's obviously a problem, like I figured it would be." Landon sighed, then whispered. "Listening to Launa. What the hell was I thinking?"

"Launa told you to bring him." Jay burst into laughter. "Your sister is a trip. I swear I love that trouble making ass girl."

Millicent waltzed in. "The night we resolved our issues, you said you were seeing someone and it was serious. Were you talking about him?"

"Yes."

Millicent smiled and folded her arms. "So I guess we're even then."

Landon scoffed. "You would make this about you. Unbelievable."

"Landon, you rolled up with my ex on your arm."

"Your ex? You never went out with him. He drove you to *my* house, and you ghosted him." Landon pointed to Jay. "So you could let this one fuck you in my guest room, remember?"

Jay grinned, humored from Landon's choice of words. "You two calm down."

Landon ignored him. "You never even kissed him."

"So, he still liked me, and it feels weird seeing you with him."

"Trust, the last thing I would do is entertain your sloppy seconds. If you *had of kissed, or slept with him*, I wouldn't have given him a second glance—At least, I don't think I would have."

Millicent's eyes grew as big as Jay's grin when Walt entered the room. "Is everything okay in here?" His hands clutched onto Landon's waist.

She leaned into him. "Everything is just fine."

Walt reached for Jay's hand and glanced at Millicent. "Thanks for having us tonight. How have you been?"

Jay shook his hand. "I see you, man. I see you," he said, then led Millicent back to their guests.

Millicent whispered, "Normally it's Launa bringing the drama."

"Still is." Jay chuckled.

Brian and Kim distracted the elephant in the great room with a list of games to choose from. The energy was unsettling for Kim, who had been excited everyone, minus Jen, was going to be together for the first time in over a year.

She chastised them. "Do y'all need more liquor to liven up or what?"

"Yeah, what's the deal with everyone tonight?" Brian asked.

"Do you two not recognize Landon's date?" McCaine pointed to the kitchen.

Launa stood up. "Okay, my sister is not going to be the spectacle everyone whispers about tonight, so let's get it all out so I can whip his ass in Spades again." Launa pointed at McCaine.

McCaine's nostrils flared as he stared at his wife. "This little girl keeps coming for me."

"Little girl with big bank. Your bank to be exact. Let's get this party started."

Landon and Walt returned to the room.

Launa rolled her hands towards them. "Everyone, my sister has graced us with her presence and brought along a new face. Everyone, meet Walt, and Walt meet the crew." Launa pointed as she called out everyone's name in attendance. "Now, let's do this." She rubbed her hands together. "Who's gonna cry on their way home tonight?"

Pictionary didn't liven up the room. Taboo was removed as a choice, to omit adding fuel to the burning fire simmering in the room. The couples settled for a game of Clue, where the build-up of mystery finally eased over the tension with laughs. For the final game before hitting the Spades table, the couples selected Two Truths and A Lie.

McCaine brought the laughs as always. "We went back to Castillo Mas and didn't tell you guys. We had a threesome idea. And we are going to the Bahamas for our next anniversary."

Jay chimed in, "I'm calling bullshit on all three."

Brian laughed at the choices and passed on giving an answer.

Launa threw an empty cup at McCaine. "Follow up question. Who was the third party in the threesome?"

"That's not how the game works." McCaine threw the cup back at her.

Launa made her selection. "The threesome is the truth."

Tammy laughed. "She's right."

The room went into a roar.

"I know y'all lying," said Jay.

Tammy confirmed. "We made a deal. If I let him bring in a woman, he would have to let me bring in a man the next go 'round. We went out and flirted with some people. Caine here picked some young, hot thing way out of his league who was down with it. Yes, I was a little jealous, and shocked she said yes, but when I brought over this strapping replica of Jesus with a chest you could bounce a coin off of, this one here called it off."

"Damn straight I did." McCaine nodded.

"I knew he was bluffing the whole time." Tammy fanned her hands at her husband.

"No, I wasn't. If you would have brought over a Brian or something, I would have gone along with it."

Brian stood up. "So what are you saying?"

"I mean, you know. A little nerdy cat like you wasn't gonna out do me."

"Says who?" Brian's voice raised like a soprano. "You don't know how I handle my business."

Jay butt in. "Brian, sit yo ass down and go next."

"Suddenly, I don't want to give my two truths and a lie."

"Why am I not surprised?" Jay fanned him off. "Say, Mr. Officer, why don't you go next?"

Landon whispered to Walt, "You can pass."

"You want me to?"

Landon nodded.

"I'll do as the lady asks and pass this round."

Todd said below his breath, "Smart move."

"What was that?" Walt asked Todd.

"I said smart move—Listening to the lady." Todd chuckled and kissed his teeth.

"I changed my mind," said Walt. "I'd like to tell my truth."

The room returned to the awkward silence.

"Nah, you straight, man," said Jay. "T is just fuckin' witchu. I know you didn't think it was gon' be easy comin' 'round us." Jay put his hand on Todd's shoulder. "You here with this man's wife."

"Ex-wife," said Carla, Todd's date, tugging on his arm.

Launa snickered. "Who are you again?"

"Carla. We met earlier."

"Yeah, I don't remember that. Nice boots."

"Thank you." Carla smiled.

"They're made for walking out of this here situation."

Silent jeers and snickers rose around the room as Carla sat with her mouth open. Landon's eyes met with Todd's for the first time of the night. The emotion stirring inside of her sweltered to an uncomfortable heat.

"Let's call it a night," she said to Walt.

"So you're a runner now?" Todd's voice raised over the dying chuckles. "You bring this motherfucker around our friends, and you gonna run away? Don't do that." His glare shifted to Walt. "Inquiring minds wanna know how long you been sniffing around my house."

Carla chimed in, "Can someone explain what's going on here?"

"I'd be glad to." Landon stood. "We're leaving."

Todd stood. "What's going on is this sneaky motherfucker's been snooping around my house and shoplifted my woman."

"What!" Landon shrieked.

"How long!" The bass in Todd's voice shook the room. He stared at Landon. "Were you seeing him when we were trying to work things out?"

"No. I wouldn't do that to you, and you know it."

Walt stood next to Landon. "Hey man, watch the way you address my lady."

"Playboy, I'm doing my best not to get on yo ass right now. Don't address me."

Walt ignored the warning. "Look, I don't want a problem with you. And for your information, I ran into Landon two months ago. She and I started dating well after your divorce. No one was sneaking around."

Todd's shoulders began to swell. "Landon." His voice desperately searched for answers. "Him?" He pointed at Walt with furrowed brows nearly reaching the taped line on his forehead. "You bring him here to hurt me?"

Tears formed in Landon's eyes staring at the reddish hue forming in the corner of Todd's. She broke away from his gaze and made a move towards the door. Walt held her with his hand planted on her hips.

"I'm to blame here. Not Landon. I thought she missed being around her friends. She shouldn't have to be alienated from the people she loves because of me. Again, I don't want any problems with you, Todd. Landon didn't want to come tonight. She's a good woman."

"You don't have to tell me how good she is," Todd said with his chest.

"Okaaaay, Bruh-law," Launa muttered.

"Thank you," Todd and Walt responded in unison.

A collective gasp filled the room. Landon pulled away as Walt held onto her, while Brian choked on a cough that failed to get any sympathy from his guests.

"She was talking to me." Todd's shoulders straightened.

Walt lifted Landon's hand. "I think she was talking to me."

"Oh shit." Millicent held her chest.

Todd's caramel skin turned red. "Everybody clear the room. I need to have a word with my wife."

Walt glared down at Todd. "You mean my wife."

"You gotta make it down that aisle first." Todd cuffed his fists together and raised his head back.

Brian took a shot and hissed from the burning in his chest. "Everyone, come check out the movie room we had installed. That goes for you, too, Mr. New Addition." He pointed to Walt. "She'll be fine. Let's go. Everyone follow me."

In the middle of the room, the former couple stood feet apart with tension between them. Landon grew sick at the hurt written on Todd's face, and the madness growing in his eyes.

Todd's voice cracked. "Tell me that's a friendship ring. A purity ring. A promise ring. Anything but..."

"It's an engagement ring."

"I honestly thought we were taking a break. I thought one day you would wake up and realize that us not being together is a mistake. I thought in a few years when my son turned eighteen that I would get my wife back. My life back."

"Why have you never shared that with me?"

"Would it have mattered? Does it matter now that you know?"

"I don't know... It's too late... Maybe?"

"Was he telling the truth? Were you faithful to me and not tiptoeing with him behind my back?"

"What he said was true. We ran into each other at a charity race back in September."

"It's moving hella fast, don't you think?"

Landon looked away.

"You don't know this guy well enough to take his last name and get rid of mine."

"Let's not do that."

"Is he planning on moving in the house I'm paying for?"

"I told you we could sell it and split the money."

"I bought that house for you. Not for some gigolo cop to live in for free."

"He has his own house."

"You got an answer for everything regarding him. I don't like this shit at all."

"I'll tell Tammy to put the house on the market."

Todd took a step towards her. "Can you honestly say you don't love me at all?"

"I'll always love you, Todd, but now I am in love with him."

The madness in Todd's eyes turned to clay.

"We won't come around anymore. It's best if we just go." Landon stepped to the side.

"No. Don't leave."

"Why not?"

"Because—if you leave, I won't get to look at you."

Landon held back her response and accepted what she knew was his truth. She considered giving into his request as they stared at each other in silence until a smile formed between them.

Kim re-entered the room. "It got quiet in here. I thought I should make sure you two were okay, or at least not violating my new furniture with a moment of weakness. I know how you two used to get down."

"If only she'd let me." Todd chuckled.

"Everyone, come on back in!" Kim shouted, then whispered to Landon. "You alright?"

Landon sighed. "I don't think I'll ever be fully alright."

Kim squeezed her hand.

Walt approached Todd and held out his hand. "I mean it, man. No disrespect on my part."

Todd placed his hands in his pocket. "We're straight," he said, looking him up and down.

"And we're leaving so you all can enjoy the card game. See you soon." Landon led Walt outside.

On her heels he whispered, "That's not how I imagined this evening."

She tossed her wrap around her shoulders. "It went exactly how I expected. I did warn you."

CHAPTER 80

BLIZZARDS & BLISS

JEN

The rumbling of the wheels touching down on the runway eased Jen's mind for the first time in days. Her busy mind had little time to think clearly, let alone the grand opening of her makeup bar.

Jay met with her and the contractors putting the finishing touches on the place. He could sense she was different since her return, and patiently waited for the team to disperse before laying into her.

"Speak," he said.

"That has never worked on me. I know you technically own this place, but I'm not your employee."

"Whatchu holding back, Jen?"

"Some shit that's gonna make you spazz."

"You went for it, didn't you?"

Jen shook her head no. "I scoped the city like I told you I would, and had a tail on my ass." She paused. "Juan."

Jay kissed his teeth and flicked his tongue. "What kind of man terrorizes women? A bitch ass one, that's who. He's getting put down." Jay wiped his nose with his hand. "You alright?"

"Yeah. Just tired of looking over my shoulder and being Jen Mendez, Jen Carson, and now Jen Rosetti. Hunted by her own in-laws."

"Not for long."

The blizzard Landon prayed for arrived weeks later during Christmas. She and Walt brought in the holiday at his home in Ohio, while Jules and Jen celebrated the morning with Max in their new home.

"Maybe next year we can spend Christmas at my mother's house. She's been hounding me about us having a baby ya know?"

"Really? She would accept my demon spawn?"

"You still think she doesn't like you?"

"I'm still waiting for my congratulations and welcome to the family from her."

Jules's face crumpled.

"Yeah." Jen scoffed. "I won't hold my breath."

"My brother will be here tomorrow. Sure you can't postpone going down to Carolina?"

"Landon is a nervous wreck. And she's been more than kind, hospitable, and helpful to us. I can't say no."

"I know. I know. Forgive me for asking. I just kind of feel Juan isn't going to show up alone."

"What? I hope you aren't going to let him, and whoever he brings with him stay here."

"Um. I think it's my niece and her mother. Mama says they've been getting close again."

"Good for them. But I don't want a woman staying here and I'm not around. Make them get a hotel."

"Are you being serious right now?"

Jen raised her brows and tilted her head to the side. "I am."

"I don't like it, but if that's what you wish. I won't let them stay here."

"And let's not let it come between us. It's our anniversary, remember?"

Jen reeled in her husband for a smooch to smooth things over on the surface, while on the inside she knew Jules popping up like a pimple on picture day during their anniversary was no coincidence. He wanted to antagonize Jen, and also put eyes on Launa who stopped taking his calls.

"You're right. And as soon as he's gone I'll be on my flight to join you, and start working on that baby."

A quick slip of information occurred the following morning. Jen dropped Max off with Jay and stared deep into his eyes.

Millicent peeked around the corner. "Welcome home, baby. Come in before you catch a cold," she said to Max.

He hugged his mom. "See you in a few days." He ran inside.

Jen waved to Millicent. "And I'll see you down south, right?"

"Yup. Looking forward to spending time in warm weather." She and Max went further into the house.

Jay looked over his shoulder then back to Jen. "You got that look in your eye."

"There's a present for you arriving at my house tomorrow. Let me know how you like it after the wedding."

"Will do. And tell Landon congratulations for me. I'm sure she'll understand why I can't be there for her on this one."

Jen saluted him and ran back to the cab.

[illegible]
[illegible]
[illegible]
[illegible]
[illegible]
[illegible]
[illegible]
[illegible]
[illegible]
[illegible]
[illegible]
[illegible]
[illegible]

CHAPTER 81

UNBROTHERLY LOVE

JULES

"I was expecting you to arrive with company." Jules stepped out of the way for Juan to come inside. "Mama said you were making things right with…"

"Mama has false hopes. I did what needed to be done to make her happy Christmas morning with a child being in the house. Why haven't you contributed to her wish?"

"Who says I haven't?"

Juan squinted. "So Jen is?"

"I didn't say that. I said I've been contributing."

"She's probably on the pill and you don't even know it," Juan grunted below his breath.

"What was that?"

Juan kept quiet and threw his coat on the sofa.

Jules inhaled sharply, eyeing his brother as he bit his tongue. He paid close attention to how he looked around the house with the tattooed envious shade of green in his eyes.

"Another nice house you got yourself."

"Being a doctor pays well."

"This one's bigger than the one in Miami."

"Miami is more expensive. Less space equals more money down there. Up here, I could own three homes for the price of that one house on the beach."

"You sure Jen didn't contribute to this one, brother?"

Jules scoffed. "I thought we agreed the moment I married Jen, all bets were off!"

"We didn't agree on anything." Juan poked his brother in the chest. "You asked me to get the hit called off, and I did. But I still want our father's money."

"She doesn't have it."

"That's what I told Caesar. His fondness of you is the only reason that bitch is still living. But she isn't fooling me. She knows where that money is, and I want it." Juan tittered. "It's funny how you think your hands are clean in all of this. You can't just get out of the business. Caesar is still watching you. Just because you're pussy whipped and believe she's innocent doesn't mean she is. He's simply showing her grace because he trusts you."

"Speaking of trust, what were you doing in our room that night?"

"I have no idea what you're talking about." Juan grinned on the side of his mouth.

"For the last time, she doesn't have the money!"

"No. But she will. She's a smart one, that one. Making you think she was sightseeing in Stockholm." Juan laughed. "Must be some good pussy. Maybe you should let me hit it, so I can believe her lies like you do."

Jules punched his brother in the mouth.

"There he is. That's the man I know." Juan pressed his fingers to his lower lip. "You've been playing the good doctor too long."

"Hear me good, brother. Stay away from my wife. If any harm comes her way, you can forget we're brothers. I *will* kill you."

"Of course you would. You want the money for yourself. How about we forget we're brothers right now?"

"Get the fuck out of my house!"

"Gladly." Juan threw on his coat. "I gotta say, Julian, it's good to see you still have it in you. I'll let Caesar know you're still doing recon. I'll be in touch."

"Then you'll be telling him a lie."

Juan allowed the cold air to blow past him as he stood on the porch. "Julian, there is no such thing as out until you're dead. You know the rules."

With his brother gone, he brushed his fingers across the photograph of his wedding day, circling Jen's face. Concerned for her safety, he hopped on the next flight to South Carolina.

"We need to talk," he said, exasperated, standing in front of Jen's hotel room door.

"What are you doing here so early?" Jen asked, bright eyed with a scowl on her face. She looked past him down the hall. "Come inside. What's going on?"

Jules stared into her eyes. "I need you to promise you will listen to everything I have to say before you react."

"I promise." Jen backed away from the door and sat in the chair next to her purse.

"We're not safe."

"Safe?" Jen acted surprised and reached into her purse, feeling for her pistol. "What are you talking about?" she asked, pulling out her lip moisturizer.

"Is there a reason you won't tell me why your family disappeared into thin air when we were kids?"

"There is. Why are you bringing this up?"

"Because I know what happened back then."

Jen placed her hand back into her purse and clutched her gun.

Jules paced the room. "My pops told me the story. He and your dad were in cahoots together stealing money from a large company back home. Your pop was better at laundering and got greedy. He stole the whole pie from up under my dad's nose, and so, he blabbed to the man they stole from, Caesar. Caesar, in turn, put out a hit on your dad."

"And spared yours?"

Jules shook his head. "But only for a short while. He died in an "accident," but I know better."

"Why would your dad tell you this?"

"Because before his "accident", Juan and I were forced to work for Caesar. Not long after you disappeared."

"What does any of this have to do with you showing up here like this?"

"When I suspected Caesar was responsible for my father's murder, I turned my back on the organization, but Juan didn't. And when we got married, Juan claims he reported to Caesar you have been found. But I know when my brother's lying. He hasn't reported any sighting of you."

"How do you know?"

"Because Juan wants that missing money for himself."

"But I don't have it."

"I have told him that."

"Does this mean that night when I said it felt like someone was in our room..."

Jules lowered his head. "You were right."

Jen raised her voice. "Then why didn't you tell me I was justified to be creeped out by him? Why keep his motives from me!"

"Because he is my brother, and I thought I could keep him in line."

Jen stared at Jules with her hand on the trigger. His story had holes in it, and she wondered what other secrets he was hiding—finding him untrustworthy by glossing over his role in the matter.

Dreading the man she loved would be the death of her, she asked him, "Why are you here?"

"To protect you. I've always known my brother had a taste for blood, but I thought this one time he would look past his thirst for family. My family."

"So you don't have a role in any of this?"

"Jen, I love you."

"Are you even a real doctor, or is that a cover?"

Jules huffed and ran his hands to the back of his head. "I'm a real doctor. I came down here to tell you what's going on because my brother and I are at odds over you. And I will choose you over him every time. I lost you once. I won't lose you again. And I am here because I needed to tell you in person—I may have to kill my brother."

Jen removed her hand from the gun and went to Jules pacing back and forth in the middle of the room. "You would do that for me?"

Jules nodded. "He just sat in our home and told me he stalked you in Stockholm. How can I stand for that? Were you not aware you were being followed?"

Jen played along. "I was enjoying the scenery. I saw so much without you, I was going to suggest we go back one day so I could see it *with* you."

"And I owe you that. Especially since we didn't get to see the northern lights."

"Shall we call the travel agent when we get home?"

"Yes. And I promise to make it a trip to remember."

Jen slipped her weapon beneath her pillow when Jules turned on the shower to let the steam build. She questioned his honesty while preparing for a sleepless night.

'Is he a double agent? Are my whereabouts being tracked through him?'

Clutching her pistol all night, she watched the sun rise, and prepared to put on a happy face for the bride, while in the back of her mind she wondered if she had slept next to an enemy.

CHAPTER 82

GOLDEN HOUR

LANDON

God smiled down on the beach as Walt stood below an arch draped with white lilies and orchids during golden hour. As the sun began to set in the backdrop, Landon faced the photographer leading her bare feet down a white satin runner half covered in sand.

In the white chairs to her right, Walt's family, a few co-workers, and friends smiled at the beauty slowly walking the path to matrimony. On her left, her family and friends gasped and whispered how gorgeous she looked with the orange glow beaming down on her from the sun.

Her mother of pearl silk dress agreed with her light brown skin tone, radiating behind the spaghetti straps of her dress fitting her gently exposed curves silhouetting with every step she took in her gown. Her thick, flowing hair blew wild in the wind below a cream and pearl infused tiara. And her nude lips outlined in chestnut, pressed tightly together, concealed her trembling teeth.

Papa Davis released her hand to her betrothed, and the chaplain started the ceremony with a spiel about the rarity of true love, and the importance of respect for a husband and wife.

Walt never took his eyes off of Landon. He stared into her eyes as he vowed to be a loving husband, and leaned in to kiss her before completing the vows.

"Get back on your side," the chaplain joked.

A collective laugh roared louder than the waves rushing in.

Walt kissed Landon one more time and spoke from the heart. "You breathed life into me. From the moment you said you would go out with me, my world shifted for the better. It was then that I knew living without the kind of love you put in my heart, meant that I was living a half-life. But now it is full because I have the most amazing woman I have ever laid eyes on to live it with. I am now yours and you are my everything. My morning, noon, and night. My forever golden hour."

A tear fell from Landon's eyes.

Walt caught the black drip before it strolled down her cheek. "Chaplain, I'm ready to finish my vows."

The chaplain teased Walt with the telling of a funny story to prolong him from kissing the bride.

Walt pulled Landon in close and said to him, "No disrespect, but I'm kissing this woman."

The chaplain laughed along with the guests. "Ladies and gentlemen, the groom has caught on to me. I better stop telling this story before he throws me in the ocean." He winked at Walt. "I now pronounce you man and wife. You may kiss your bride."

Their kiss created chatter from both sides of the aisle. The newlyweds' lengthy lip lock lasted too long for Papa Davis's taste.

He cleared his throat and shouted at his new son-in-law. "I'm still here!"

CHAPTER 83

NOTICE

JEN

Standing over her sleeping son, Jen threw her coat on his desk chair. She stepped back and read the prescription dosage on Max's medicine.

"You looked nice at the wedding," said Jay. "You didn't have to end your getaway so soon."

Jen sat on the bed and brushed her hands through her son's hair. "What you got a fake Facebook account stalking folks?" Jen joked.

"Be fuckin' for real. Millicent was stalking y'all. I saw that look in your eyes, though. What was that about?"

"Before I tell you, let's get the first thing straight. Don't wait to call me when my son is sick."

"It wasn't that serious. If it was the flu or something, I would have called you. But once his fever came down, we had it under control," Jay explained.

"I would have been here sooner."

"To avoid you rolling your eyes at me, I'll make sure to call you no matter what...God forbid he gets sick again."

"Thank you. And thank Millicent for missing the wedding to watch over him for me."

"She loves him, ya know."

"I know she does."

"Now tell me what's going on?"

"I'm kind of in the dark. Jules told me some things about his brother. And I'm feeling a bit uneasy."

Jay grunted. "You said a hundred, remember?"

"I did." She sighed.

"So if you ain't still at a hundred on him, what are you?"

Jen looked away. "Maybe fifty-five."

Jay whistled. "That's drastic, Jen. Max definitely ain't coming over there anymore."

"I would argue with you, but I'm not because I was hoping you said that. Until I get back to a hundred with him."

"I'd like to see that."

"You don't understand, Jay. He said he would..." Jen swiped her hand below her chin. "...his own brother for me."

"Oh, he most definitely knows some shit saying something like that. I hate to have somebody's son looking up at me, but if he fucks around he will find out. I'll do more digging on him. Anything you learn, you tell me. Ya hear?" Jay's head leaned back.

Jen nodded.

"And you left me for that pretty motherfucker." Jay shook his head. "I ain't looking so bad now, am I?"

Jen rolled her eyes. "You can leave us now. I'd like to be alone with my son."

CHAPTER 84

HERE & NOW

WALT

Jetting across the states, the happy couple spent one night in San Francisco looking out at the fog veiling the Bay Bridge, then drove to wine country. Walt dropped their bags in the presidential suite, covered in white roses and champagne in a bucket on the bar.

"Aht, aht, aht." He kissed between his teeth. "I have to carry you in."

"We did that already."

"I'm gonna do it until you tire of it."

Landon snickered. "It's only meant for the house, so after that, you can stop."

He lifted her into his arms. "Maybe I will. Maybe I won't," he said, carrying her over the threshold. "What would you like to do first?"

"I know what you wanna do." She nudged her nose against his. "But I really would love a hot bath."

Walt placed her on the bed. "Wait here."

The steam between the newlyweds matched that of the water in the tub. Landon sat with her back against her husband's chest as he lathered her body, gliding his heavy hands across her tanned skin. Tender kisses trailed from shoulder to shoulder, while the silkening of her soft breasts received the attention she craved.

He fondled her mounds and nipples, causing them to pebble from his light touch. Landon sunk lower in the water, soaking the ends of her hair until her curls fell heavy on her arms. Walt clenched the cloth, dropping water from it to rinse away the lathery lube between them, sucking beads of water from his bride's neck. She moaned to the sensation of his mouth drying her dampened skin.

"Stand up, Mrs. Reed. I missed a few spots."

His tongue cleansed, suctioned and dried the trickles of water dripping on her skin, replacing the moisture with wet kisses from his mouth. His fingers imprinted on her ass cheeks, holding her steady as she leaned forward on the slippery tile moist with condensation.

Licks, kisses, suction, and tongue swabs withdrew slick from her hidden walls, oozing down her inner thigh from Walt's oral play.

He groaned sinisterly. "That's it. Come for me, baby. I haven't even started yet."

His fingers spread her cheeks wide and he dove below, cleaning the crème de la crème clotted on her folds, then dragged his tongue up to her back road.

Landon jolted. Her hands slipped on the tile. She reached upward and clung to the shower head, withstanding the swirls of her husband's tongue eating her exit like it was the dinner they were missing.

Kneeling below her hidden treasures, Walt gently teased her pussy with finger flicks as her ass rolled on his face. He mixed the flicks with soft rubs forcing her to cry out his name. He groaned, getting off on giving her pleasure, though his dick jerked against her calf ready for insertion.

He continued to fuck her mind before her body, dragging his tongue from the pink hole to the black one. Landon lost her posture. Her back weakened, pressing her breasts against the warm, wet tile, fully relaxed in Walt's strong hold.

Her pussy throbbed in his mouth, and she cried out in ecstasy. "Don't let me fall," she mumbled.

Walt rose higher on his knees and gripped her waist. "I got you. I just want to watch this pretty pussy pulse up close a little longer."

Each pulse was rewarded with a lick. Landon's arms fell from the spout searching for his shoulders.

Walt restricted them with one hand. "I should have brought my cuffs." He apprehended them above his head finishing his flesh meal tour with swift finger rolls, and flicks to her clit, while his mouth gently kissed the lining of her ass cheeks. "Mmm." He sighed. "I won't stop until I see that sweet cream coat your sweet ass pussy."

"I'm close," she whined. "Just don't stop."

He trailed his face down her track, then tongue flicked her folds from the back, using his knuckle to finish her off with a gentle swab of her clit from side to side. Landon's cuffed hands tightened against her back. She shrieked quietly, gyrating on his face, experiencing complete euphoria.

Walt carried his weary wife to the bedroom and laid her soaked body on top of a pillow folded in half below her stomach. He stretched her legs out wide and penetrated her throbbing walls, greeted with a squeeze to welcome, and hold him inside.

Landon panted. The patient torture of his teasing transitioned into jabs of sensual pleasure. His sturdy cock *grinded* her drenched, hidden heaven. Her thrusting hips rolled with his punches.

Walt held her legs out wide with his hands wrapped around her waist, pressing her lower back into the pillow, carving every corner of her pussy with his dick. He kissed her back sparingly, relishing her sounds of pleasure into his memory.

"Oh! Ah! Ugh! Walt!" she called out to him. "What are you doing to me?"

"I'm writing my name on your pussy, Mrs. Reed," he said, rolling his hips so the tip of his dick wrote the letters in cursive. "What's your name?"

"Landon!"

"Landon what?"

"Landon Reed!"

"Yes. I love hearing you say that. Say it again." He smacked her ass.

His strokes slowed down as his hands slid from around her waist down to her thighs. An intense orgasm expelled from the pressure of the gesture at the top of her warm walls. Walt's body locked. His legs turned stiff, his back as erect as his cock.

"Ah yes!" he bellowed, short of breath.

Landon whimpered and whined below him. "I want more of that when I wake up."

Morning passed them by as Walt fulfilled her request. Pillaging her when she woke. Working up an appetite.

With a few hours left in the day, they strolled to the chateau's café, tasting fresh farm to table cuisine, then over to the neighboring fields where the vineyards produced the grapes for their in house wine.

The buds of tulips and daffodils hung from intertwined stems in the garden, overshadowed by the beauty of the olive oil grove leading out to a lake past the vineyards.

Too late to tour the fields and smash grapes with their bare feet, they drove towards Napa, taking in the view of mile wide vineyards and shaded pavilions before their dinner reservation.

After tasting the flavors prepared by a world renowned chef at the chateau's five star Michelin restaurant, they cozied up in the courtyard, opposite other couples sitting in the moonlight.

"I wish I could make out with you right here," Walt whispered in her ear.

"And be caught on camera. No way."

"Don't mind me. I'm just tipsy from the pairings. And you in that dress is adding to my buzz."

"Maybe we can sneak one out in the field tomorrow on the tour. I saw a porno like that once."

"I have to be the luckiest man alive." His voice fell deeper. "Now, tell me about this flick."

Landon's phone vibrated in her purse. "Wonder who that is? I haven't checked in with anyone."

> Congratulations. I hope he makes you happy.
>
> Todd

Landon suddenly went cold. The vibrancy in her face lost its shine. The glee in her eyes turned dark.

"Everything alright?" Walt rubbed her back.

"Yeah," she lied. Her cheeks turned red as an apple.

"Don't lie to me, baby. What's wrong?"

She handed him the phone.

Walt flicked his tongue against the back of his teeth. "I'm sure he's aware we're on our honeymoon."

"At least he's congratulating us. We can't let this ruin the good time we're having."

"I won't. But I want to address it."

"Can we just ignore it and stay in our happy bubble? Please?"

Walt's forehead crumpled, hiding his anger. "So, you're happy?"

"I don't think I have to tell you that." She placed his hand on her thigh.

His brows raised from the corners of his mouth hooked into a sly grin. "Mrs. Reed, have I ever told you how much I love you?"

CHAPTER 85

BOW AND ARROW

LANDON

A decision had to be made where the newly married couple would call home. With Todd paying the mortgage on Landon's house, Walt wanted out. Ohio was too far out for Landon to commute to work, and the drive back and forth from Detroit to Toledo was soon going to wear thin.

"I get two more times to carry you over the threshold." Walt picked up his wife and juggled her in his arms.

Landon shrieked. "What do you mean two more times?"

"I did some things before the wedding." He put her down and opened the drawer to the dresser in the foyer. "I added your name to the deed on our house in Toledo. I thought it could be our vacation home when we wanna get out of the city."

"So you've decided where we're living full time without considering my input?"

He unfolded a picture hidden in his wallet. "I was hoping we could look at this place in Waterford. Start out there together."

"I knew this would eventually come up, but not this soon." Landon walked into the kitchen. "I like my route to work."

"I timed it. It's thirty minutes to Elizabeth downtown. And, I've been looking at transfers in the area."

She opened the fridge and passed him a bottle of water. "Is there something you don't like about this house?"

Walt spread his arms out wide. "Yeah. That another man is paying for it."

"I'll think about selling. Todd most likely won't fight me on it now that you're living here."

Walt cornered her against the inside door of the fridge. "I wanna buy a house for my wife. Are you going to let me provide for us?"

The chill from the fridge and his authoritative stance electrified Landon. She squirmed with hardened nipples pressed against his chest.

"I asked you a question."

"Yes," she muttered.

Walt stole a kiss from her blood moon colored lips. They merged in front of the cool air, immersed in a frenzy of passion.

Landon raised her skirt. "I want you right here, right now."

Walt unzipped his jeans. "I can't get enough of you, woman."

"Do me as you please, husband."

In front of the open doors, Walt turned Landon around and bent her over. He licked his fingers, then rubbed them on her slit. "Aah. You're always wet," he whispered, lunging inside her wanton walls begging for punishment instead of mercy.

He wrapped her natural curls flowing down her back around his fist. "I could do this to you all day."

Wilder than a madman, he fucked her like she begged. The savage strokes of his delivery unyielded as she shrieked and her head banged into the shelves.

"You take this dick like a good girl, Mrs. Reed."

"And you...love...giving it..." Landon susurrated between sighs.

In walked Launa. "Oh shit. My bad." She ran out of the kitchen.

"Was that?" Landon tried to rise.

Walt released with her in his arms as the front door slammed.

Short of breath in the middle of a moan, Landon asked, "Did my sister just walk in on us?"

"She did." Walt squeezed her so tight she couldn't escape. "She's gone now."

The couple laughed, entangled in afternoon delight.

"I guess I should probably call her." Landon laughed.

"I would say apologize for me, but I'm not sorry." Walt eased his fingers to her clit.

"Neither am I."

In the morning, Walt left for Ohio. Launa waited for his car to cut the corner before she cut up with the shits and giggles.

"Well. I must say. I'm impressed. Here I was wondering how a snooty little thing like you had men wrapped around your finger, when it turns out Little Miss Perfect is a freak."

"I am not." Landon's eyes twinkled like stars. "What are you still doing in town?"

"I was using your crib for my love nest while you were away."

"With who?"

"Caleb."

"He doesn't steal, does he?"

"No. I don't think so. Anyways, I never let him spend the night."

"Good. Now stop looking at me like that?"

"Like what?"

"With that snarky face. I don't like it. "

Launa dragged the stool at the bar.

"Watch the floors. I might be selling this place." Landon sighed.

"As if you need bigger or better."

Landon shrugged her shoulders. "So what's up? Why the resting bitch face?"

Launa chuckled. "You know I love you, right?"

"Mmm hmm."

"Even when we've had bad blood between us, the love is still there. With that being said, I guess I can come clean and admit that I am a little jealous of you."

Landon wrinkled her face.

"I've always wondered why everything went your way. Why your life has been so favored compared to mine."

"What's wrong with your life?"

"I'm not complaining. I'm just saying, look at you. You're stunning, got Mama's hourglass shape, this big house, a career, money, you made it out of Mama and Daddy's house, and..." Launa paused.

"And what?" Landon's voice deepened.

"And you have two men that love the fuck out of you. Literally." Launa nervously giggled. "I often find myself wondering how that feels."

Landon's chest pounded to the point she couldn't breathe. She placed her elbows onto the counter and stared at the bubbles popping in her champagne glass. The image of Todd holding her gaze while he fucked her on that very counter popped into her head.

She traced the back of her neck and trembled as if she could still feel him inside of her. Her eyes then shifted to the refrigerator. The image of Walt fucking her a day earlier, and the countless times Todd had his way with her in the very same spot sent chills down her spine. She trembled a second time like she could feel the cool breeze blowing on her as it did while she took both lashings, stirring a craving inside of her to feel both encounters—all at once.

"Overwhelming," she answered her sister.

"That's it?"

Landon shook her head side to side. "No. Sometimes I feel gifted and cursed. Burdened. I hurt Todd for my personal happiness. That wasn't easy knowing how much he loved me."

"You mean still loves you."

"He doesn't make loving Walt easy at all." Landon slid her phone across the counter. "He texted me on our honeymoon. I had to pretend it didn't affect me for my husband's sake. But it did." She sipped from her glass. "It's hell at times."

"So, I shouldn't be jealous?"

The sisters stared at each other as a knock appeared at the door.

"Nope." Landon swallowed the remaining bubbles whole. "Be careful with love. It ain't all peaches and cream. Sometimes it hurts like hell."

CHAPTER 86

KINFOLK

MILLICENT

"We bought you a wedding present." Millicent raised an ivory wrapped box with a gold ribbon triple tied in the center. "May I come in?"

Landon stepped aside. "We missed you in Carolina."

"I heard everything was beautiful. Max came down with a fever, so I stayed home with him. I assumed you preferred having Jen there over me, so I didn't worry her."

"Is he okay?"

"Yeah. It was strep. *You're* looking well. Got that glow about you, I see."

"Happiness will do that."

Millicent placed the box on the dresser in the foyer. "I hope you both like it."

"I'm sure we will. I'll wait for Walter to come home tonight, and we'll open it together."

Launa strolled in. "Oh. It was you."

"Hey Launa. I didn't know you were still in town."

"I was just getting ready to leave."

"I'm right behind you. I just came by to drop off Landon's wedding gift." Millicent pointed to the present.

An awkward silence fell between the three of them. Launa clicked her tongue, doing an about face. Millicent fiddled with the strap on her purse. Landon's eyes roamed around the room.

Breaking the lull, Millicent asked Landon, "So, how long are we going to be fake with one another, because I can't stand it?"

"What do you mean?"

"A lot has gone on, but I thought when you invited me to dinner that night we were going to make an effort."

"Isn't that what we're doing?" Landon frowned. "Wait. Is that the real reason you didn't come to the wedding?"

"Max really was sick. I'm talking about how things seem forced with us just talking. I miss us. Our random chats. Our friendship."

"What's going on, Mills? You can talk to me."

"Good. Because what I have to say has been weighing on me for weeks."

"Everything good with you and Jay?"

Millicent crossed her fingers. "So far. Playing house and stepmom has been...surprising."

Landon glared at her from the corner of her eye, quiet and analyzing her word choice. Her eyes shifted toward Millicent, staring aloof like a struck deer mesmerized by lights. Landon clapped her hands and the two old friends laughed.

"What the fuck kind of answer was that?" Landon asked.

"An honest one. Sometimes I wake up and wonder how the hell did I end up in this situation." Millicent sighed. "Don't get me wrong, I love them both, but it's hard as hell some days."

Landon snickered. "That felt good just now, didn't it?"

"It did. Landon, I mean it from the bottom of my heart when I say I am sorry about everything."

"It's old news now. What did you want to talk about?"

Frown lines formed on the side of Millicent's mouth as it stretched wide. "It's about Todd."

"How is he?"

"Still fine as hell, of course."

Landon side-eyed her.

"He's got the facial hair growing in kind of wild, but seems like he isn't a stranger to the bottle. If you know what I mean."

Landon hid her face and lowered her head.

"I think he moved back in with his mama," Millicent reported.

"That I refuse to believe. Why would you say that?"

"When Jen returned from your wedding, Jay and I dropped Max off with her. Afterwards, Jay said he needed to swing by Todd's house. Well, we ended up at his mama's house. And get this. PJ remembered me. He was talking my head off while Jay and Todd wandered off behind the house. So then, Todd's son came up to the car, and I couldn't stop staring at how much he looked like PJ."

Landon's nostrils flared.

"I take it you get where I'm going with this?"

Landon muttered. "I kept begging him to get another test and he kept cursing at me that the boy was his."

"If he isn't, your marriage ended for no reason."

"Millicent, I appreciate you telling me this, but I just got married."

"I know, but being that I withheld information from you before, I didn't want to make that mistake again."

"And I appreciate it, but I removed myself from that situation so I wouldn't have to feel the way I'm feeling right now."

"Do you think I should mention this to Todd, or…"

"You know what?" Landon tapped her feet. "It has nothing to do with me. I no longer have to argue about a child that isn't mine. No one knows how horrible that dilemma made me feel. Like I was a witch for choosing peace over drama. I can only wish Todd well at this point." Landon opened the door. "I need to get some air."

With her bags in tow, Launa joined Millicent standing at the door. Together they watched Landon mosey in front of the budding gardenia leaves Todd planted because she casually mentioned their smell made her love being outside.

Millicent turned to Launa. "Think she'll be okay?"

"She will. The real question is how's Todd gonna take it if that boy isn't his?"

CHAPTER 87

LIFE AIN'T FAIR

LAUNA

The sight of Landon losing her composure was a hidden act to the world. And for Launa to witness her in that state was a first. She took a chance facing black ice to stay behind with her sister.

"You wanna talk about it?"

"There's nothing to talk about." Landon kicked off her shoes.

"You know damn well there is. What are you gonna do if that boy isn't Todd's?"

"Ain't nothing for me *to do*. If he is, he is. If he isn't, then..." Landon shrugged her shoulders.

"Then you threw away a perfectly good marriage."

"And landed into another one." Landon snapped.

"How is that fair to Todd?"

"How was what happened in our marriage fair to me?"

"It wasn't, but can you actually say if this boy isn't Todd's you won't feel a certain way?"

The sound of the garage lifting lulled a brief silence.

"I'm sure I will, and I'll get over it."

A sarcastic laugh inflamed Launa. "Bullshit. You're totally shutting off your feelings."

"You know what. I hope the boy is his so we can get off of this, and I can get on with enjoying my new husband."

"I don't believe you, but I'll respect your wishes and leave it alone. When you're ready to talk, call me."

Walt interrupted them. "What's going on, ladies? It's getting dark out there, Launa. You should have left earlier to avoid ice on the roads."

"I was actually about to jet."

"Does this have to do with last night?" Walt caressed Landon from behind. "I apologize about that. If I had known you were here…"

"Say no more." Launa chuckled. "It was my bad. And on that note, I'll see you two next time around."

The dim light from Tim's bedroom was lit when Launa pulled in the driveway. *'He's waiting for me to kiss him good night.'* Her lips curved in the corners, but the light smile was uprooted when a car slowly creeping by a few houses down the street with the lights off caught her attention.

Launa sat still in her car as the creeper's brakes lit the street bright red. She placed her hand in her purse, retrieving her father's pistol.

"I'm sick of this shit."

The car pulled in behind her. Launa breathed in and out with her finger on the trigger.

Juan knocked on her window. "Bet you thought I couldn't see your little head in here. What's up, stranger?"

Launa raised her voice. "Leave, Juan."

"Girl, stop tripping." He plastered a smile too big for his face to carry well. "Come on and get out so we can go inside and have a talk."

"Why would I have anything to say to you? Leave." Launa frowned, noticing for the first time his smile was haunting.

Her rejection of him turned his face red. "It's cold out here. Quit fuckin' around."

Launa cranked the engine.

Jules hit the hood. "You better not drive off. Open this fuckin' door."

Launa's eyes looked past him at one of the men Jay sent as protection running between the neighboring houses, and the other approaching Juan from behind.

Grunting like a wolf in the wilderness, his voice lowered. "Quit acting like you some fuckin' tough girl and more like my bitch."

Launa lowered the window an inch. "And if I don't, what are you gonna do?" She pointed the barrel at him through the crack.

Juan laughed. "The rule hasn't changed, little girl. You don't pull one of those out if you ain't gon' use it."

Click. The safety came off.

"You wanna mansplain something else to me?" Launa licked her lips and grinned. "I bet yo ass wishes you had of listened and left when I asked you to now. Don't ya?"

Juan looked over his shoulders. "The fuck?"

Hush, covered in a face mask, hit Juan in the back of the head with a lojack. "Get in the house," he ordered Launa.

Juan reached for his waist when the other man pressed his gun to his jaw. "Un uh uh. I wouldn't do that if I were you."

Launa broke down the sidewalk.

"Empty his pockets," Hush ordered his assistant while he tied Juan's hands behind his back. "You drive his car and follow me," he added, throwing Juan's body in the trunk.

In the dead of night, the wind whistled around the house as Launa swirled her phone between her fingers on the nightstand. Caleb's name popped up on the screen.

She answered, "Hey."

"How you doin'?"

"Um. Not sure how to answer that."

"I would ask you if I could pull up tonight, but something's come up. Can I take you to breakfast instead?"

"I can meet you at nine after I drop off my son."

"I'll send you a drop when I hit the exit."

With raccoon eyes after a sleepless night, Launa sat at The Crepe Spot waiting for Caleb to show. Coatless and dusty in a sweatshirt, he arrived looking like he hadn't showered in days. His eyes were bloodshot in the corner, and he kept his hands inside the pockets of his hoodie, pushed out from his pudgy belly.

"Due to the reason I think you drove all the way out here, I'll forgive you for making me wait thirty minutes," Launa complained.

"Under normal circumstances I wouldn't have been late. But I was taking care of something for you." His dark eyes shot straight into hers.

"Can I stop worrying about my family's safety?"

He nodded.

"And yours?"

"Why mine?"

"Ummm. A verbal threat was made if I was seen with you again..."

A crooked smile curved on the side of his mouth. "You don't have to worry about that."

Launa took a deep breath. "You've been hanging around Jay too long."

"Whatchu mean?"

"You reminded me of him just now. The look on your face. The mannerism. You even sounded like him. There is this sudden cockiness about you."

"Nah. That ain't like me."

"There it is again."

"I don't hear it."

Launa sat back and called over the waitress. Her eyes studied the pride in Caleb when Jay's name was mentioned. It made her realize she didn't want to be in a committed relationship with a Jay Jr. rising in the ranks of street life, whores, and double lives. She'd suffered enough foolishness with that kind of man, and it was time she raised her standards and selections.

"A pecan apple crepe for me. And an egg and sausage crepe for the big fella, with a side of house fried potatoes for the table please." She grinned at Caleb. "Trust me on this."

"It's your set."

The waitress removed the menus from the edge of the table. "Coming right up."

Launa glared at Caleb. "See how I ordered for you just now?"

"I like that you know the shit I like."

"That's because this friends with benefits arrangement has been working for us. I'd like to keep it that way, while I work some things out."

"I'm cool with that. Told ya I ain't rushing into nothing, or putting pressure on you 'bout being exclusive. We good like this until time says otherwise."

Launa's shoulders relaxed. "And thank you."

"For what?"

"Giving me my old life back."

Chapter 88

Behind Caleb's Eyes
Caleb

Sparks scraped across the plate of crepes Launa introduced to Caleb. Her parted lips chortled watching him swallow the sausage parts like gulps of water.

"Good shit, right?"

He smacked his lips. "Scrumptious. We need to make this our spot."

"We can do that." She twisted her fork to slice the dough. "So, can you tell me what happened, or does that go against protocol?"

"I don't know what you talkin' 'bout?" Caleb yawned and stretched his arms out wide. "Tell me 'bout your plans."

"I'm sorry?"

"A minute ago, you said you needed to work some things out. What you got goin' on?"

Launa swallowed the apples sticking to the roof of her mouth and wiped the goo from the corners. As she confessed her desire to leave the Midwest, and move down south after visiting the Carolinas for Landon's wedding, Caleb got lost in her story, and in her eyes, replaying the night's events in his head.

Two strong arms on Jay's payroll were positioned outside the three star lodge as lookouts. Jay rarely got his hands dirty, but since Juan stalked Jen and threatened Launa, he made an appearance at the club to Caleb's surprise.

"Tonight's the night you prove yourself. Show me you got what it takes to get the deed done." Jay tugged on his beard. "A woman sat on the other side of Caleb and passed him a gun, then disappeared in the shadows of the dark club. "Lesson number one. Always keep a bird that's gonna ride for you no matter what in yo' pocket. Don't keep no singin' ass bitch around you."

Caleb nodded.

One of the lookouts stepped inside and wiped sweat from his forehead.

"It's time." Jay rose from the stool and led Caleb to a back entrance out of the club.

Down the back alley they trekked to a metal door locked with chains. Clanging from the other side rung against the bricks in the small path, lifting the hidden entrance. Together they stepped, following a team member dressed in all black, and a ski mask revealing only his eyes. He pressed a code on a door. Beep. It opened to a red lit elevator. The guide input another code and the doors closed, stopping two floors down to a garage of SUVs.

Caleb hopped in the back of Jay's designated ride, listening to Jay give the order to be driven to the warehouse.

"I noticed you didn't check your gun." Jay grinned.

Caleb looked dumbfounded. "I didn't think I needed to, coming from one of the team." He opened the chamber to find an empty clip.

"Rule number two." Jay paused. "Always check your piece. Rule number three. Trust no one. Why would I ride in a car with someone packing heat who's never rocked with me before?"

"I thought we already had that understanding."

"Not yet."

The SUV turned down a white covered dirt road in the outskirts as flurries grew wider against the front shield. Miles down the road stood a gray warehouse next to a rundown barn with hanging steel shining from the headlights.

Inside they went. Guns pointed to Caleb as he was stripped of the empty gun.

His eyes stretched wide. "What's this about?"

Jay pointed to Hush. "Check him."

Hush patted Caleb down like a lineup in a prison. "Clean."

"You get one shot," said Jay, signaling for Hush to open the trunk.

Hush called him over. "You lookin' at a bitch in there," he said.

Juan wiggled and moaned below the silver tape glued to his mouth.

Jay eased over to the trunk. "This one's got a thing for abusing women. Especially *the one you like. Like my pops told me, bitches are made for fuckin', and this ain't no bitch I wanna stick my dick in."*

Hush laughed below his breath.

"That everything?" Jay asked Hush, dropping a bag of Juan's things. "Im'ma let you keep some." Jay tapped his chest with his fist. "How much he had on 'em?

Hush turned to his partner and pulled out wads of cash from below their hoodies. His helper dropped a duffle bag of cash they removed from the trunk, hidden in a bag with pear lotion.

"He's working with them diamond fat cats down south." Jay grinned at them. "Keep the wads. Im'ma need those bags." Hush placed them in his hand. "I need two eyes tailing me when I make this drop. We bout to get in on a new score." He walked back to the entrance. "These two decide if you're worthy or not. Make'm proud," he said, exiting the warehouse.

The rocks crackled as the SUV that drove them there skid down the snow covered road. The two gunmen pointing their guns at Caleb lowered the clasp.

Hush loaded the gun Caleb was given with one bullet. "One shot. If you miss, they won't." He pointed to the 2 shooters serving as witness, loaded the bullets, and handed him his weapon.

Caleb aimed the gun at Juan's head without hesitation.

Pop.

"We gon' like having you 'round." Hushed nodded to the shooter behind him picking up the shell.

Blood spooled from Juan's chest seeping deep into the carpet in the trunk. The shooters lifted his body with a sheet and placed it on a metal cart.

Hush ordered Caleb. "Push that motherfucka ova there." He pointed to an opening in the center of the wall with a fire burning.

The two shooters stepped alongside him wheeling the cart towards the fire. Together they lifted the edge of the cart and guided the sheet inside an incinerator.

Hush whistled and Caleb went to him. "Pull that end."

Caleb tore the right side of the carpet out of the trunk. Heat warmed the hairs on his neck as one of the shooters started a controlled fire in a ring of hay, while the other stood guard at the incinerator with a shovel in his hand.

Hush opened the roof as the fire's height began to tower them. While the cold air pulled the smoke through the top, he dragged Caleb back over to the car. He opened a locked cabinet with tools inside, then handed Caleb a crowbar.

Caleb stood with the bar in his hand unsure what to do.

"Chop it." Hush pointed to the car, cranking a power tool.

"Did anybody check to make sure it didn't have a GPS built in?"

Hush paused the loud buzzing of his tool. "You think you dealin' with amateurs?"

"Not at all." Caleb pushed through the challenge of disassembling the car and scrapping the serial numbers off the stripped parts.

Covered in oil, tar, grease, sweat, and specks of blood, he stood strong as the shooter scraped the smoldering ashes from the chamber, and watched him throw them into the fire where the carpet burned to small fibers. The second shooter poured water and ammonia into a bucket, dropping the bones and the guns in the liquid, then took off his clothes. Hush and the first shooter followed his lead.

"What you waiting on?" Hush asked Caleb.

Caleb shivered from the chill flowing down from the roof. "I haven't complained once, but I ain't down wit' no funny, ritual shit."

Hush and the shooter's eyes shifted amongst each other. Hush belted out a laugh Caleb was shocked he knew how to do. The shooters cackled along with him covering their dicks with their hands.

"Look in the cabinet, youngblood." Hush rolled his shoulders trying to keep warm.

Caleb turned his bare ass to the hitters and walked to the cabinets.

"Bottom drawer."

He opened the drawer and retrieved four sets of black and navy blue sweatsuits. Then, passed them around to his new brethren freezing near the fire.

Hush patted him on the back. "Jay'll be pleased with you, youngblood. Welcome to the fam."

"Caleb?" Launa waved her hands in his face. "Caleb? Where did you go just now?"

Ignorant to her full story, he clung to the last words he heard her spew and answered, "I was wondering if you'd let me go with you."

Chapter 89

Linestepper

Todd

It never dawned on Todd that PJ could be Ephram's father. He seethed at the notion of his brother sitting idly by, watching him lose everything, and not say a word.

He sat in his car outside of his mother's house replaying the argument he and Landon had the night she left for Flint. He could still hear her voice saying, "Take another test," and it saddened him to think how he cursed and yelled at her for begging him to take one extra step to save their marriage.

'Is it worth finding out the truth?' he wondered. *'I've lost my wife and my house, and now I could lose my brother and son.'*

Flashes of Landon laughing in his arms, the two of them winning on game night, and the final time her breasts rubbed against his chest while he stared into her eyes, and wiped the wisps of hair from her face, led him to open the car door and face his brother.

"Sup, man?" He sat the twelve pack of beer between them on the coffee table.

PJ plucked one from the slot. "My brother. You read my mind. I only got one left in the cooler. I was gonna make a run in a few."

"No need. What you do today?"

"Same ole, same ole."

"No luck on the job search?"

"Nothing worth getting up early for. But I wouldn't have to keep searching if my little brother would hire me."

Todd kissed his teeth and grinned. "It ain't never good to mix family with business. I'll make some calls, and see if someone's got an opening. But if you ain't gonna be serious about it, don't let me waste my time."

PJ's gaze with the TV screen didn't break.

"Did you ever sleep with Dee Dee back in college?" Todd asked him.

"Who didn't?" PJ laughed. "I don't know, man. Those days are a bit hazy. Why you askin'? You thinking about making another trip down the aisle to have your one big happy family since Landon married again?"

Todd clenched his fist. "How much of that shit you sniff today? Fuck outta here talking 'bout makin' that hoe my housewife."

"May as well. Y'all share a seed."

"Would you want to marry a woman who has fucked me?"

"Naw."

"Didn't think so. Just sip yo' beer and shut the fuck up then." Todd sipped from his bottle glaring at his brother. "If you do go out, holla at me. I'll give you some cash to bring me back some gars."

"Just give me the money now. I'll bring'em back when I tip out."

Todd slapped a twenty on the table. "Im'ma hit the shower. Leave'm in my coat when you get back."

PJ tipped out less than an hour later after clearing four bottles. Todd scooped them from the table with a plastic Ziploc, then hid two of them in his lunch bag in the fridge, and the other two in his room.

Like bags of sifting sand, Todd's fingers numbed with a tingling sensation when he dropped off the bottles to the lab.

"Two are cold. Two are room temperature. I didn't know what you needed to check DNA markers, so check them all if need be. I'll pay," he said to the clerk.

The anticipation of the results left Todd aloof at work, thinking how he and Landon would have been celebrating their fifth anniversary. But another man was filling his shoes and other places.

An angry chill covered him as he seethed to himself.

Jay and Caleb walked in without any notice. "Fuck got you going crazy, man?"

"I'm ahite."

"I beg to differ."

"What y'all doing here?"

"Comin' to holla at you. We brought lunch." Jay lifted the fast food bags. "Your office cool?"

"Sounds like it needs to be." Todd lifted the bridge and escorted them to the back. "Watch the front," he ordered the staff standing by, then locked the office door behind him. "What's this about?"

In the privacy of Todd's office, Jay spoke in code regarding the put downs and changes in their organization.

"This lad is one of us now." He pointed to Caleb. "Anything you need, we can go to him."

"Fa sho." Todd shook Caleb's hands and crumpled the bag of fries.

"Game birds coming in tonight. We gotta see which one the house is betting on," said Jay, flaring his nostrils at Todd's phone ringing.

Todd answered and Jay's eyes stretched wide. "This is Todd Jeffries."

Jay read his lips with the look of audacity furrowing his brows.

"Okay. Yes. I understand. I appreciate it. Thank you for your time." Todd hung up the line.

"So it's fuck the rules now?" Jay fumed.

"That was a top priority call. I wouldn't have picked up if it wasn't important."

"It must have been to answer during one of our meetings."

"What were you sayin'?"

"I'd much rather know what that was about."

"That was personal."

"You dying or something? Do you need us to go? 'Cause you do look a little sick?"

"I'll be alright. Just finish up."

"I'm finished." Jay rose to his feet. "I know you've been going through hell lately. I get it. Take some time for yourself and get at me later. It's success where I stand." He raised his brows. "You feel me. We can finish this another day."

Todd's t-shirt trembled as his chest pounded hard. He had never been dismissed by his long-time partner. "I hear you. Be easy."

The sun had set, and the moon rose high as he sat in the same spot of his office, sulking with the results as a million scenarios and his old life flashed before him. The thoughts of the past put him in a daze while the hours of the night flew by.

He slumbered peacefully in his office, waking to the tune of a special ringtone. "Good morning, gorgeous."

"Hi. Sorry to call so early. Are you free to talk?" Landon asked.

"Always. How are you?"

"I'm good and you?"

"Shiiid. I'm great, now. To what do I deserve the pleasure?"

"I need to run something by you. It's about the house."

"What about it?"

"I want to sell the house."

"No, you don't. You love that house."

"Walt isn't particularly comfortable living in a house that another man is paying for, and I don't think this situation is fair for either of you. I'm in a bad spot stuck between you two." She held back tears as her voice wavered.

"No need to cry. I hear it in your voice."

"So what do you think? Sell and split the profits?"

"I only want you to be happy, and if the house isn't making you happy, then I agree to sell it. I'll save a pretty penny not having to pay for it anymore, so tell you what—Keep my half for a rainy day. You never know if you'll need it."

Landon smiled on the other end, bringing a smile to Todd's face.

"Did I fix your problem?"

"You did. And, Todd... I want you to be happy, too."

"You know what would make me happy, but I'm not gonna go there with you."

Landon snickered. "Thank you, I guess."

"Landon, one more thing."

"Yeah?"

" Trade up, not down."

CHAPTER 90

MOVES OF A MENDES

JEN

Incessant phone calls day and night drove Jen nearly insane. As a mother, she understood her mother-in-law's pain to have a child go missing. But as a victim, she celebrated internally he was no longer a problem.

"It's been months since he's gone silent," Jules complained. "My mother won't give it a rest until we have answers."

"What does she expect us to do?"

Jules sensed the worst had happened. "All I *can* do is keep her hope alive. At least until we get proof."

To escape the rising tension of the unsolved mystery, Jen proposed she spend a few days in Miami.

"While you search for answers, I'm going to fly down to Miami and tell the staff in person that I'm closing the bar."

"I think you should handle it remotely. At least until we know more about my brother. He could be hiding out down there for all we know."

Jules turned up the television when the video of Juan at the car rental office popped up on the screen. He listened to the report, confusing Jen with the mixed emotions crossing his face as the journalist interviewed the clerk who rented Juan a car.

"MR. DIGGS IS A REPEAT CLIENT WHO ALWAYS RETURNED OUR

CARS ON TIME. BUT HE AND THE CAR APPEAR TO HAVE
VANISHED INTO THIN AIR. OUR OTHER OFFICES HAVE
REPORTED THE VEHICLE WAS NOT TURNED IN AT ANY OF THEIR
LOCATIONS, AND THE GPS TRACKER ISN'T PICKING UP A
SIGNAL."

THE REPORTER CLOSED: "MR. DIGGS AND THE LOANER CAR
HAVE BEEN MISSING FOR TWO MONTHS THIS PAST WEEKEND."

"They're still reporting my brother by his alias." Jules muted the television.

"What do you think he's up to?" Jen asked him.

"I wish I knew. But he's got my attention. It's what he's always wanted anyway."

"Should I be afraid?"

"Afraid. No. Alert. Yes. But without a body, I can't say."

"You don't think he's set all this up to hurt me—Do you?"

Jules sighed. "The thought has crossed my mind. If that's his play, he's doing a damn good job covering his tracks. But not reaching out to Ma makes me question if something foul is at play here."

"This is all too much...Which is why I want to get out of here for a few days. Between you being on edge, the news and your mother calling nonstop as a constant reminder—I feel like I'm losing my mind."

"You know what?" Jules swung her hands between them. "A getaway could do us some good. Let's say we leave early for that St. Patrick's Day festival?"

"How about you come with me to Miami, I break the bad news to my staff, then we leave from there?"

Smiling through laughter he said, "Always business first witchu." He kissed her forehead. "It'll be good to feel some heat before we freeze our asses off."

"I'll keep you warm."

The hardest moments of Jen's life were spent with Max the days before she revealed to Jay about her return to Sweden.

"The fuck you say!" The pictures vibrated on the wall as he shut the door on her trying to exit.

"I kept my word last time. I'll do the same this time. Trust me."

"I do trust you. I hate you won't let this go. You see shit is working out in your favor without it. Right?"

Jen pulled out her gloss and wrote on her arm. "J body?"

Jay smudged the clear liquid on her skin. He took the gloss from her hand and wrote. "*Ash.*" Then, began singing a verse from a southern rap song. "Blow in the wind," with a childish smile turned on his lips.

"So nothing to worry about then."

"That percent ain't never gonna be a hundred with me. Not because you chose him either. I ain't never liked him. And I don't trust him."

"What matters is you trust me." She hugged him on her way out.

Jay pulled her arm and whispered in her ear. "If shit goes sideways, send me a photo of you and Jules. I don't know that place, but I'll be on the first thing smokin'. You hear me?"

Jen squeezed both his hands, and slowly let it go before Millicent walked in. "I'll be seeing y'all."

It was clear to Jules the moment they stepped off the plane, Jen appeared lighter. The cloud of his brother's disappearance had been lifted, and not even the blistering cold could somber her spirit.

"It's nice to see you smile."

Jen nuzzled up to him. "We needed this."

His hands tightened around her waist. "Think we'll get lucky this time?" His head lifted towards the sky.

"I'm going to say yes. This time those lights will show up just for us."

As they settled in the suite, Jen held Max's baby shirt she packed to her nose. While Jules flicked the lights above the bar, she slipped it in her purse.

"It's only going to get colder outside. And I'm feeling a little jet lagged. Do you mind if we stay in, and you make good on that promise to keep me warm?" Jules crept behind her.

"What about the lights?"

"Fuck those lights if it means serving you." He buried his head in her bosom. "I've been neglecting you lately," he said in between his kisses.

"You can make up for that right now." Jen drove his hands inside her fleece leggings.

Jules watched her eyes shut tight as his fingers played inside of her like a violinist at the concerto desperado. Jen leaned her head back, expelling out the first moan of sexual pleasure she experienced in a month.

"I missed hearing you make that sound." Jules laid her on the bed and placed her cup in his mouth.

The level of excitement he withdrew from Jen when he took full control of her body had no limits. She swayed back and forth on his lips as he kissed, tongued, and maneuvered her up, down, left, and right, tasting every line and corner of her quivering body, nearly drowning from her waters.

As he emerged from below, he shoved her further towards the pillows at the top of the bed. Still entangled in her clothes with her pants mangled around her calves, and her boots tied to the knee, he raised them against the headboard and inserted his prized weapon, ramming her slicked lips with pressure.

His palms held her shoulders, controlling the bounce of her reflexes fighting against the full force of his strokes digging for her gold.

Jen came from the overdue friction, shrieking low *oh's* as his pipe remained stagnant, tending to her tender spot against the peak of her cavern.

He leaned down and tongued her open mouth, slowly lowering her legs as he slipped between the opening between the waist of her pants and her pussy.

"I'm locked in here now." He grinned, switching from the slow, sensual grind to a rough pace with a fist full of her hair wrapped in his grasp.

"Give me what you owe me."

Jules obliged with rhythmic grinds in the tightness of her walls. Their eyes locked, holding each other's gaze between oral expressions of fulfilled desire. He milked his wife to sexual abandonment, soaking the bed they had yet to sleep in.

"I'm going to lie in this," said Jules.

"Room service?"

"I was hoping you said that."

Jen caressed his face. "You needed this vacation just as much as me. We don't have to abide by any schedule. Deal?"

"Deal."

The lovers enjoyed their dinner at the table by the arched window, overlooking the green water outside the City Centre to honor the holiday festivities.

In the midst of a laugh, Jules pointed up. "I take back what I said earlier."

Jen's eyes opened wide. "You should. They are absolutely beautiful," she said, marveling at the blue and green streaks lighting up the black sky above them.

Jules popped the bottle of champagne he ordered. He poured Jen and himself a glass, then raised his for a toast.

"To us. And the trip of a lifetime."

Jen lifted her flute. "To us. And the northern lights gracing us with good luck."

The next morning, road crews blocked streets near and around the hotel, filling with people crowding the area while dancing to loud music, and throwing back spirits before the planned events began.

"The water is more vibrant now that the sun is out." Jen pointed out. "Kelly green I think."

Jules laughed. "The whole damn place is one color. You were right. This truly is a sight."

"Ready to go get lit?"

"This early?"

"Why not?"

"I was hoping we could nap, then hit the streets once everything gets underway." Jules fell back on the bed.

"Are you still feeling jet-lagged?"

"A little."

Jen sighed. "You hang back. Get some rest. I can take a stroll and see what's what. I don't mind." She threw her purse in a backpack and snuck in her passport and make-up kit.

"Be careful. And if you taste something good, bring me some back."

"You didn't have to ask."

The crowded streets were exactly how Jen wished they would be. She blended in with the crowd wearing a green Celtics toboggan, while the layers of sweaters beneath her reversible coat heated her as much as the adrenaline flowing inside her veins.

Sticking to her plan, she stopped by the costume store first.

"I kept my promise," she said to the clerk. "But I left my wig at home. I hope you have one you can sell me."

"Anything for a repeat customer."

Paranoid from her previous visit, she peeped over her shoulder. "Throw in that green scarf, and that brunette wig in the window, too."

Jen stuffed her bag and snaked her way through the crowd, swiping a purse from a drunk woman as she bypassed the bank closest to the hotel.

She walked around the block to the bus stop where she met Bennie. "Fuck," she mumbled, finding that the road was blocked.

One foot led the other along the route Bennie drove, peddling her to the other branch she spotted from the road.

Her lips quivered as she made her way inside. "Hello," she greeted the security guard at the entrance.

"How may I assist you?"

"I'd like to meet with an account manager."

The guard pointed at the end of the hall. "The concierge can find out who's available."

"Thank you."

The concierge took her name, and escorted her into an empty closed room with black, tinted windows. She sat in front of a desk with an old fashioned ink pen standing in a base, surrounded by plaques of achievement on the walls for an Officer Hyla Berg.

Jen fought off the shakes when she entered the office.

"Ms. Carson, I apologize for the brief wait. I understand you would like to make a withdrawal?"

"Yes. I'd like to transfer some funds to American accounts, as well as invest in some lucrative opportunities you may have to offer."

A man in a three piece suit entered the room.

"Upon looking at your account, to do such requests, the branch manager needs to be present when dealing with an amount of this magnitude. Ms. Carson, meet Noles Lindberg. He'll be present to witness your transactions today." Hyla handed Jen her identification cards and passport back to her.

"Nice to meet you, Mr. Lindberg."

He shook Jen's hand, then nodded for Hyla to proceed.

Hyla passed a green and gold folder with documents for Jen to view of the accumulated interest applied to the total of fifteen million.

"Do you know the account routing numbers you would like to make the transfer?"

Jen reached in her bag and unfolded a list of accounts. "I'd like to make more than one transfer. But while we do that, I'd like to withdraw 500,000, please. 25,000 in kronas, 400,000 in traveler's cheques, and 75,000 on a prepaid card, if possible."

"Very well, Ms. Carson." Hyla printed a withdrawal form for Noles to sign, then buzzed in the concierge. "Get this prepared for Ms. Carson."

"One million should be transferred to the business account of Made Up with Make Up. That's the account listed on the top. I'd like to add the interest on top of the 8 million into a trust fund to one Max Lloyd at the address listed. The age withdrawal stipulations have been notarized. The two accounts receiving the 3 million should be transferred to one Landon Reed, and Launa Davis with Max Lloyd as the co-owner of both accounts.

"And the remaining 2.5?"

"Invest 1.5 aggressively in the 5 different stocks specified, and transfer the remaining one million into a savings account in my name. Title it "Retirement Home," and name Max Lloyd, and Timothy Davis as the beneficiaries."

Hyla asked Jen to verify the correct spelling of the names listed, the address to mail statements, and a telephone number. The manager signed off on each transfer while Jen watched the amounts split into the specified accounts. When the computer transactions were complete, the concierge returned with a box containing the cash and cheques Jen requested, and a keypad for her to select her pin number for her card.

"Lovely doing business with you, Ms. Carson." Hyla extended her hand. "We'll be in touch with the information regarding your investment portfolio."

Jen stretched across the desk and shook her hand. "Thank you for your help today." She placed the wads of cash, cheques, and card in her backpack, then sat the box on Hyla's desk. Securely strapped with the bag draped across the front of her chest, she strolled towards the exit, listening to her heart beating a million miles a minute.

In disbelief, her father's plan for her had come true. Tears formed in her eyes as she stepped out of the bank, and took one final look over her shoulder. When the coast was clear, she exhaled a deep sigh with her shoulders relaxed as she tugged on the straps of the bag.

Her fluttering heart began to settle as she made her way back towards the blocked roads, and noise in the street. One block away from the hotel, a hand pulled on her in the crowd.

"Where have you been?"

Jen's breath hitched. "You scared the shit out of me." She punched Jules in the chest. "I thought you were tired."

"I was. But then I felt guilty letting you wander out here all alone, so I got dressed and tried to catch up with you."

'Odd you'd find my exact location with all of these people out here.'

Jules took Jen by the hand. "Have you eaten?"

A familiar feeling stirred in the pit of Jen's stomach. "I could eat."

They walked the streets, tasting fried dough and beers. Jen pretended to swallow the alcohol, spitting whatever she gulped back into the can.

Then, they maneuvered their way towards the pub where they dined during their last visit.

As the alcohol began to weigh on Jules, he interrogated Jen. "So, what all did you do when you left this morning?"

"Do I need to give you a step by step?"

"As your husband, I can tell when you're lying. What's the big secret?"

"Why do you think I have one?"

"You know you answer a question with a question when you're guilty," he slurred.

As his words danced, Jen's heart began to race. "I'm not a fan of the third degree, Jules."

"You're still dodging my question."

"I answered your question the first time you asked me, and I won't answer it again."

"Jen, what have you done?"

"I don't follow."

"But I did...I followed you this morning. Why were you at the bank?"

Jen slipped three kronas from her bag. "Transferring money. Thanks for ruining our vacation. I think I'm going to be sick." Jen held her stomach. "Excuse me."

Jules caught her hand. "Where are you going?"

"To the restroom, sir. Was I supposed to ask your permission?"

"Just hurry back. We need to get back to the room and have a real conversation."

Jen stole a steak knife from a table waiting to be bussed. She stood behind the door of the lounge, watching Jules from the crack when it opened. She took out her phone and texted a photo of them when they landed, and sent it to Jay.

She stuffed her green wig between her skin and the elastic on her pants, and escaped behind a woman exiting the lounge.

Ducking below the crowd, she dropped her coat to the ground, and placed the wig on her head.

Gusts of wind formed as a deterrent, but she blew hard against the wind, and hopped a taxi in the nearby stands waiting for drunks to leave the bars. "Train Station, please."

Jules's name lit her phone screen. She stared at his face smiling at her in the photograph and answered without greeting.

"Where are you?"

Jen sat quietly on the line.

"Just tell me what you've done and we can fix it. Together."

Jen's voice wavered. "Jules, I honestly loved you. I thought you loved me, too."

"I do love you. Baby, please tell me where you are. It's you and me against everybody else. Including my family. You're my family, Jennifer Rosetti. I love you! Where are you!"

"Goodbye, Jules."

In the blink of an eye, Jen found herself all alone once again. She tossed her phone on the tracks and rode the train to its final stop. Inside a bathroom stall, she held herself up, applying makeup to her face to resemble the identification of the woman's purse she swiped, and presented herself as Alexandria Stanton, for the next 24 hours on the train from Sweden to the United Kingdom.

The train ride was gruesome. Jen stayed awake the entire time, stealing ID cards from sleeping passengers who resembled her. Once she set foot in London, she borrowed the phone of a gentleman making a pass at her.

"Tell my boy I love him," she said to Jay when he answered.

"Talk to me, Jen."

"You were right. He can't be trusted. I don't know what his next move is going to be."

"Mine is to protect my son."

"Do me a favor."

"Anything."

"Show him my picture every day and tell him..."

"You're coming home." Jay insisted.

"No, I'm not. I'm done. I'm tired of looking over my shoulder, and worrying someone will hurt my baby because of me. The further away I am from him, the better."

"That's not true. He needs his mother."

"Make me gone, Jay."

"No, I won't do it."

"You have to." She paused as she stuttered. "I...I left you something at the bar. You know where to look. Just make everything better for my boy. Our boy. You're the greatest father he could ever have. I love you both."

Jen tossed the phone at the gentlemen and caught a cab to a five star hotel, testing her new identity. Once inside, she held Max's shirt against her chest, smelling what was left of his sweetness in the fabric, longing for the day she could one day hold him in her arms again.

For the next few days, she bought clothes and luggage before hiding out in France—discarding the clothes she'd been wearing in Sweden, and the identity of one Alexandria Stanton. There, in the French countryside, she sorted through the stacks of wallets she stole, plotting her next move, and who to pose as next until the dust settled.

CHAPTER 91

IN DEATH, THERE IS LIFE
JAY

The urgency to be free in Jen's voice rattled Jay into a frenzy. Torn between honoring her wish, and rounding up his troops, he froze before acting.

"Mills. I need to step out. You and Max stay put until I get back." He raised his brows.

"Everything okay?"

"We'll talk when I get back."

Jay's guards surveyed the outside of Jen's bar before he arrived. He slipped inside the dark open area where the hostess desk was newly installed. Using the light from the poles shining through the glass window above the sign on the door, he made his way into her office, and locked himself inside.

"What am I looking for, babe?" he muttered to himself, searching through the mounds of loose paper spread across her desk.

The contents inside the drawers had zero significance to him, and nothing in the accordion folders stuck out as relevant. He sat in her chair, looking around the room for a sign, waiting for Jen's clue to call out to him.

'What did you mean, I would know where to look?'

The mini fridge whirred behind him. Jay's eyes popped wide as he spun around in the chair then grinned.

He pulled the door open. "Bingo," he whispered, holding a white bag with a note attached.

Inside was a small plastic bottle filled with Jen's blood to tie her to the scene of whatever crime Jay cooked up. He chuckled to himself, impressed by the mastermind his former love was proving herself to be.

Tugging at his beard, he read her note.

Launa knows almost everything.
Name her Max's godmother.
The code is the day you gave Max your last name.
P.S. I don't have to tell you to burn this. Do I?
Love you all.

Jay, choked up by her words, shook his head as he realized Jen was ten steps ahead of him, and truly wanted him to "make her gone," as she said. He held the bag with a tight grip, wondering if they would still be together, had he known this side of her.

He locked up the office with the sample secured in his coat. "Miss you already, girl."

Jay hoped Jen would call before he set her plan in motion. For days Max questioned why he hadn't heard from, or seen his mother. It was *his* constant inquiries of Jen's whereabouts that led him to pass the sample on to Hush, and grant Jen's final wish.

He and Caleb set a camera inside the Rosetti house before Jules returned from Europe. They watched him pace back and forth while listening to the panic in his voice as he left message after message on Jen's voicemail—begging her to call him back.

The stammer in his voice raised the hairs on Caleb's arms. "He knows something. Think we need to report..."

"Shhhhhh." Hush cut him off. "Bossman knows what he's doing." He pointed to the screen. "And it's about that time."

Steam from the shower misted the background of the red coated image. Hush put in his ear piece, eased out of the vehicle, and entered through the front door using the code from the note.

Caleb whispered in Hush's earpiece, "He's still in there."

Hush crept inside the bathroom as his silhouette was concealed in the fog. The glass door creaked when he opened it halfway. Jules turned around, too slick to defend himself. Too stunned to react in time.

Hush banged his head against the soap dish, staging Jules's death as an accident. He hovered over his body while blood from the back of his head flowed down the drain with the water.

Placing two fingers on his wrist, he checked for a pulse. Once he confirmed the death, he dropped his wet shoes in a plastic bag, and left Jules to bleed out as he moved on to phase two.

He pulled one of Jen's sweaters from her closet, and a bra from the drawer, then stained them with the blood sample. He placed the soaked garments inside Jules's luggage, and yanked their surveillance cameras.

"It's a clear night," he said to Caleb.

"It's a clear sky." Caleb cranked the car and drove one block in the opposite direction.

Hush left the scene of the crime through the back door, trudging through the bushes to the next block. Caleb drove past Jen's bar and flashed his lights twice.

"Home," Jay ordered his driver, counting the days before Jules's name became the next headline.

⚬

The next evening, Jay called Landon.

"Have you heard from Jen?"

Landon took the bait. "I haven't, and I'm concerned myself. She hasn't replied to any of my texts."

"Never thought I'd ever ask your— the man you—you think Walt can do whatever it is he does to check on her for me? Max has been asking for his mother like crazy, and I'm running out of excuses."

"Of course."

"But don't tell him it's for me."

Landon snickered. "I'll tell him I want to know."

"Thanks, L. You still my G."

Chapter 92

Missed

Landon

As Jay premeditated, Walt's inquiry led to the police finding Jules's blue body in the shower, and sparked an investigation of Jen's whereabouts. The blood stained clothes in his bag, and the footage of their arrival at the airport in Sweden, formed questions around his solo return.

Jules was named the prime suspect of her disappearance, but with his death being ruled as an accident, the police filed the mystery as an international cold case.

Jen was finally free.

The media played out the events to Jay's liking. Reporters connected Jules as the brother of the car rental missing man, and dug up the Rosetti family history.

The outlets had a field day exploiting them as a family of crime with nonstop headlines.

'Missing Woman Married Into a Family of Crime.'
'A Murder Abroad.'
'Missing Wife, Missing Brother:
Who Was Julian Rosetti?'
'Bloody Business: What Happened to Jen Rosetti?'
'Wife Caught in Crime Crossfire.'

After weeks of receiving the same intel, Jay and Landon arranged a memorial to give Max closure. While preparing for the service, Landon attempted to comfort him with assurance his mother's love would be with him every day. The solemn look on his innocent face tore her to pieces.

Walt pulled her aside. "Give him some space. I don't think any words can comfort him right now."

"I can't believe this is happening." Landon leaned into him, thinking of the story Jen shared about her past.

"I know it's hard to accept."

"I just can't see Jules hurting her."

"It's hard to fathom, but what was he planning to do with that bloodied sweater and bra? And he returned home without her. He isn't looking innocent, my love."

She sobbed in her palms.

Walt held her close. "I'm sorry. I didn't mean to upset you. It's my job to figure out the parts that don't make sense. I shouldn't have said what I said."

The theme of the service was hope. Jay wanted the message to keep Max's spirits high, and only approved Landon to speak words of encouragement at the memorial.

"Jen will always be with us," she said, sniffling into the microphone.

Max wistfully smiled through her speech, confused about his sudden loss. Jay sat next to him, hiding his emotion during the short reflection of fond memories Landon shared. But as Max began to cry, Jay couldn't hold back his tears. Not because he feared for the worst. But because he could never tell the truth to his son, and had to watch him suffer in vain.

As the memorial came to a close, Max kissed his mother's picture gracing their presence at the front of the church. He stepped out in the middle of the runway, and exited the chapel with his head hung low, and his sadness bringing everyone to tears.

Jay welcomed their circle over to his house after the repast. They sat around drinking and sharing stories about Jen, the fun times of their friendship, and brainstormed a plan to set up a foundation in her honor.

"To Jen." Millicent toasted.

"To Jen!" The group raised their flutes.

"Has anyone been over to the house?" Tammy asked.

"Why? Are you grabbing for a listing?" Launa sassed her.

Tammy glanced over at Landon. "You know that's not why I'm asking. I was wondering if you all have come up with a day to retrieve her belongings, so Max and Jay can decide what to do with them. You know she had all of those jewels. I'd hate for someone to break in and steal her nice things."

"Jen left quite a few boxes here," said Jay. "They're stacked in the back room."

"I'd like to go through them, if you don't mind," Landon asked.

Walt tugged on Landon's hips. "Do you mind if I leave while you do that?" he whispered in her ear.

"I'm sorry. I didn't know you were ready to leave. I can come back and do this another day."

"No, please stay. I was thinking Launa could bring you home when you're done here."

"You sure everything's okay?"

He kissed Landon on the lips. "I need to return some calls, and check on the dogs. It's important for you to be around your friends right now. I'll see you when you get home."

Landon saw him out and made her way to the storage room in the back of the house. She kicked off her heels and peeled back the tape on the unmarked box stacked above the cambro.

"Achoo." She sneezed from the dust flaring up off the box.

She searched through the designer blouses folded neatly with the corners tucked, setting aside small truncates and photographs of her fallen friend. She wrapped scarves around her neck and placed rings on her fingers, reminiscing about their conversations.

'You sure had style, girl.'

Landon laughed to herself, remembering how Jen flung her hands about when she was passionate about a subject.

"You're finally free, friend," Landon mumbled.

Millicent joined Landon in her rummaging. "What are we going to do?"

"I have been thinking about that myself."

"Max is going to need all of us."

"I agree. And we're all happy to step in because we love him *and* Jen."

"That's good to know, because I can't do this on my own. I love him, and he's a great kid, but I have to admit that when Jen moved back up here, I felt a huge relief to get a break. I feel horrible for saying that."

"Don't. I'm sure mothers everywhere want to say that, but can't. I'm here to help."

"Please don't tell Jay."

"I won't."

The door screeched behind them. "Can I have a word with Landon?" Todd asked.

Millicent snickered below her breath and tapped Landon's shoulder. "See you up front."

"How have you been holding up?" Todd eased the door shut.

Landon pointed to her swollen eyes.

"Jen would want you to go on living, and be happy." He dug in the box. "What's all this stuff?"

"Things Jen left behind when she first left Jay." Landon chuckled.

"Oh damn. Jay kept this shit? Maybe I don't know him like I think I do."

"You know, I've finally come around to liking him with Millicent, but a part of me always felt he secretly wanted Jen back."

"I can't blame him. It's hard to get over a good woman." Todd stared at Landon. "I would know."

"Don't start." Landon glared at him with a side eye. "You seem different. Lighter than usual. What's going on with you?"

"Something I haven't told anyone."

Landon stood to one side and studied his face. "You've met someone?"

"No. No. God no. It turns out Ephram isn't my son."

"Say again?" Landon unwrapped Jen's scarf from around her neck.

"I had a DNA marker test done."

"I can't believe my ears."

"I know. We went through all of that for nothing. My life was turned upside down, and the boy wasn't even mine."

Landon held her chest and leaned against the boxes. She stared at Todd for a long time in silence replaying the conversations they had that ended in screaming matches.

'I pleaded with him to take another test– to pick me over that boy.'

"Landon, I apologize for everything I put you through. For making you feel second when you've always been first."

"I'm sorry, too. I know how badly you want to be a father. Are you okay?"

'Because I'm not. What the fuck am I supposed to do with this information?'

"I'm maintaining." Playfully, he swung his hands. "I put down the alcohol."

"That's what it is! You're sober."

"And clear headed." Todd gazed into her eyes, slowly moving in closer. "And I was thinking if only I could have the missing piece to my puzzle, my life would be perfect again." He pulled her into him by her waist.

"Todd," Landon whispered, breaking from his gaze.

'Don't look into his eyes.'

She shuddered from his touch.

Todd looked down at her fighting the impulse to look at him. He kissed her forehead. Then, on the lips. "Every time I see you I want to do that. And I think you want me to do it, too." He raised her chin and locked her in his gaze, admiring the reflection of himself in her eyes.

"You know this isn't right." Landon tapped her fingers on his chest.

"You and me will always be right." His deep voice sung to her soul. "Tell me I can have you." Todd pressed his swollen, throbbing bulge against her. "I miss you, baby."

"I never cheated on you, and I won't cheat on him either."

Todd stole another kiss. "You said 'him.'" He gently caressed her face with the brush of his fingers.

"What?"

"You normally say his name. And when you do, it burns me inside."

"Todd, I..."

His fingers pressed into her waist. "It's not cheating if it's with me."

Landon whispered, "I can't. This is wrong."

"Feels right to me. It has *always* felt right to me. You don't have to be afraid to tell me the truth." His lips nibbled on her neck. "I know you miss me, too baby. Tell me to stop and I will."

"Todd...st..." She exhaled, distracted by his hungry breath weakening her knees.

"Todd, what?" he respired against her skin. "You and me, we'll never be over. I know you still love me."

He caressed the nape of Landon's neck. He read the desire in her eyes and gave himself permission to touch her hidden abyss. "Oahh." He sighed from the slickness of her pussy throbbing in his hands.

He fell to his knees and tasted the lips he missed moisturizing his beard, digging his fingers into her round ass—tonguing her folds with the need to hear her sigh above him. The moment her voice cracked calling his name, he rose without sparing a second more to feel her warm walls welcome his dick. "Mmm. I miss you." He moaned, lifting her dress to her quivering thighs.

There, in the close quarters of his friend's spare room, Todd's dream materialized into reality, graced to feel Landon's love once again.

She covered his mouth upon entry, masking the wailing oh's he uttered when her wetness slicked around him. He stroked her vigorously against the wall, shaking the paintings like a light tremble of the earth passing below them.

Landon peered at the rattling frames tapping against the sheetrock. "Unh, Todd." She moaned.

"Fuck, I miss hearing you call my name like that, baby. You feel so fuckin' good," he said, fearing she'd try to stop him when he couldn't honor her request.

He lifted her thighs above his wrist, and carried her to the bed, silencing her with his lips pressed against hers. His thumb held her panties to the side through a hole he pierced in her stockings. The wide tip of his dick scraped her sides with wild, intense strides, exploring her palace he thought of as home.

Landon expelled a high pitched gasp. "Todd."

"Daddy's home, baby," he said, watching her react to the best strokes of his life. "I still love you." He buried his head in her chest.

'I wanna say it. He needs to hear me say it. God, I swear his dick was made just for me.'

Landon groaned silently, shrieking below her breath, encompassed on a mental high of pleasure she remembered, but amplified. She held Todd tight around his neck, secured in her arms, peeking at the bottom half of his abs wave while he lunged his dick into her like it was the first time.

Lust and indulgent yearning of what was familiar consumed her. The coital infliction, entangled with the emotions of her heart being pulled into two directions as Todd stroked and poked, rocked, grinded, and rekindled their flesh, took her to new heights.

Every thrust elevated her senses. Every broad stroke reminded her how good it used to be. How good it could be once again.

Todd rolled around her wet world with the intent to send her home with his face, and his penis imprinted on her brain. *And* her body. But he too was conquered by her mind, body, and spirit, grunting as he reprieved himself, latching on to her outer thighs.

"I will always love you, Landon." He squeezed her thighs, unloading inside her walls.

"Todd?" she whimpered.

He softly brushed her cheek. "Don't say this was a mistake. Just let me hold you for another minute."

"Okay," she agreed, breathless from his unyielding embrace.

"Come back to me, baby," he whispered in her ear.

"I can't, Todd. Consider this closure. It cannot happen again." She budged for him to release her.

Todd sucked on her cheek, savoring the taste of her skin. He slid out of her slickness, shifted her panties back in place, then playfully tapped her pussy.

"We have history." He helped her up from the bed. "And you know I will never get enough of you."

Landon placed her finger over his lips. "I'm going home, and I will tell him what I've done." She adjusted her dress at the waist.

"You said *him* again." Todd held her hands.

"Do you want me to say his name?" Landon pulled her hands from Todd's grasp and poked a finger in his chest. "Especially after what we've done?"

"Nah. And don't tell him."

"Why not?"

"'Cause I would worry about you."

"Worry?"

"Yeah. He's a cop. They know how to get away with shit, and if he hurt you, I'd take the risk of going toe to toe with the pol..." Todd's voice deepened. "You know I'd..." He exhaled. "Just keep it between us."

Landon curled her lips. "I don't think I should see you anymore."

"You don't mean that."

Launa burst into the room. "Are you done back here? Caleb and Jay are starting to annoy me, and it's trickling snow already."

"So, I'll see you around?" Todd grinned looking down at Landon.

"You take care of yourself," she said.

"I do whatever you tell me to, Gorgeous. Always a pleasure seeing you, sis-in-law." Todd winked at Launa, then blew Landon a kiss.

CHAPTER 93

ICY

TODD

Todd hung back with Jay, trading circles of smoke between them on the patio as the house cleared. Millicent fanned the earth's fumes stinging her nose as she sat two beers on the table.

She stood over Jay. "These are the last two." She shivered with folded arms. "I'm going to get Max ready for bed. It'd be good if you could sit with him after I read to him."

"Snow's coming down pretty good now. I'm getting ready to head out." Todd narrowed his eyes at Jay.

Jay looked up at Millicent. "Are you kicking my company out?"

"Never." Millicent massaged Jay's shoulder. "It's been a rough day for Max. I'm not sure I'm the one he wants to spend time with right now."

"Did he say something?"

"He didn't have to." She stepped towards the patio door. "Enjoy your beers. Good night, Todd."

Todd popped the cap on the edge of the table and raised the bottle. "Ahite, Mills." He waited for the door to close. "Either somebody is whipped, or some-body's gone soft."

Jay laughed. "I know you ain't talkin'. You got your dick wet in my house and acting like this ain't the most mellow you've been in 'bout a year."

Todd smiled and looked away. "I don't know whatchu talkin' 'bout."

"Man, please. You jumped on her like she was the first woman to give you some pussy. You really think I don't have cameras all around this house?"

"Yo creepy ass watched us?"

"Damn straight. It's my house. I mean, I didn't watch the whole thing, but I saw enough to make me happy for you, man." Jay cackled. "And shit, it wouldn't be the first time. Remember the side of the road?"

"Aw man." Todd's face burned with embarrassment.

"So, did you finally get it all out of your system?"

"I'll never get that woman out of my system."

"T, she ain't gonna leave that dude."

"She might." Todd blew smoke from the side of his mouth, jolting his legs nervously. "Are you gonna tell anyone what you saw?"

"Since when have I been a snitch?"

"You wouldn't tell Millicent?"

"Nah. I ain't *tryna* get in the middle of her and L again. Women shit is exhausting."

"Well, we'll see how this plays out. Landon said she's gonna tell ole boy."

Jay scoffed. "She's bluffing."

"Why you say?"

"You ain't gonna like this, but I think she fucked you to get you out of her system."

Todd tapped the short of the cigar in the tray. "You're right. I didn't like that shit."

"I'm just being real with you, T. She's torn. I see it in her eyes every time she's in the room with both of you."

"And if she does tell him?"

Jay scoffed. "If I'm wrong, I'll pay for y'alls wedding."

They tapped bottles.

"Bet. Im'ma get out of here. Take care of lil' man."

As the snow accumulated heavier than reported, Todd took the main roads towards his mother's house. He smiled to himself, inhaling the mixture of beer and Landon's scent on his top lip. The storm didn't faze him as he felt luckier than he had in months, driving with caution and glee along his route.

On the side of the road, he passed hazard lights flashing on a broken down vehicle with a small boy struggling to twist the bolts off a flat tire. His mother shivered, wrapped in a trench coat hovering above him, and hopping on both feet.

Feeling good about his day, he turned around at the next light and made his way back to help them.

"Your boy looks like he could use some help with that flat."

"I don't have any money to pay you, Sir."

"Money isn't a problem. Let's get you two out of this mess." Todd kneeled next to the boy. "You almost had it," he said to him, twisting the wrench. "How long have you been out here?" Todd yelled to the mother.

"Maybe an hour. We waited for someone to pull over and help, but people don't do that these days."

"You two look like you're freezing. Pop the trunk so I can put your spare on. I won't mind if you wait in the car."

The boy and the mother looked at each other.

"We ran out of gas, waiting for someone to stop. It's just as cold in there as it is out here."

"Damn." Todd muttered. "Then let me hurry up and get you two on the move."

He changed the tire and invited them to ride with him to the nearest gas station. The boy and his mother defrosted their hands in front of the vents. Their legs shivered, searching for warmth.

Todd noticed the boy's eyes widened when the fast food sign lit up across the street. He remembered when he was little, his mother taught them not to beg, or ask anyone for anything, and assumed this mother had trained her son to do the same.

His signal blinked on the dashboard and he whipped into the drive thru. "Let me get a one through six."

"You want six combo meals?" The worker's sassy tone made her question sound like a statement.

"Yeah."

"And what to drink?"

Todd looked at the boy.

"Pop," he answered.

"You heard him. Mix 'em up however you like."

The cashier raised a brow as she passed him his order. "Y'all real hungry tonight?"

Todd's bright smile put one on the cashier's face.

"Dig in," he said, placing the bags in the boy's lap.

While the boy and his mother chowed in the warmth of his truck, he filled two gas cans of petroleum, then drove them back to their car.

Shuddering, cold, and damp, Todd filtered the gasoline in the tank, started the car, turned the heat to mid, and concerned for their well-being placed three hundred dollars in the cup holder.

"Thank you," said the mother. "I never had a knight in shining armor before. Be blessed."

"It was no problem." Todd waved them off, heading back to his truck.

"Hey!" she shouted, holding up the cash. "Angel! I didn't get your name."

Screech! A car slid on a trail of black ice into the median. Todd's body plunged into the snow filled ditch. The driver of the swerving vehicle hopped out of his car and ran to the edge of the scene. The boy and his mother stood at his side.

"I lost control!" The man shouted, climbing down towards Todd's body. "Dial 911!"

The boy jumped into the ditch. "Mr. Angel, are you alright?"

Todd's eyes twitched. "Phone," he mumbled.

The boy crawled up the slick patch and snatched his phone from the seat. "I got it." He held it in front of Todd's face.

"My love," Todd muttered.

"I don't understand." The boy shivered, scratching his head.

"My..." Todd's lips shuddered, staring into a dandruff covered sky, blanketed in flakes of snow with ice freezing his back.

The blasting heat in the hospital lobby felt like a Godsend to the woman and her son.

"You stay put. I'm going to get a cup of coffee. Hospitals always have a pot brewing," said the boy's mother.

The boy didn't listen. He snuck back to the triage where Todd rested, held his phone up to his face, then rushed back to the waiting room.

As he scrolled through his contacts, he stopped at the name in bold caps that read **MY LOVE**, and hit the send button.

CHAPTER 94

OUT OF CHARACTER

LANDON

"What did I walk in on?" Launa questioned her big sister.

"Nothing."

"You mind if I smoke?"

"I do."

"It's only a lil' weed." Launa pulled out a pre-rolled joint from her pocket.

"Have you forgotten I'm married to the law?"

"So. He ain't gon' do shit to me."

"Fine. But wait to light it at my house. I only have jurisdiction over one cop."

Launa grinned. "Listen to you, all cocky and shit."

The sisters went outside to the screened patio and turned on the fire pit. The ignition of the heat nearly camouflaged the smell of ganja blowing in the air.

"Let me get a hit?" Landon asked.

"Say what?" Launa pulled the joint backwards, beating her chest and coughing through a crooked smile. She cleared her throat. "I need to know what is going on with you right this minute."

Landon swiped the joint from her hands and inhaled her first puff, bouncing back and forth on the cushioned lawn furniture. Cool and calm, she blew a thin cloud from her lips and smiled at her sister.

Launa giggled, waiting for the high to settle in. "I've never seen you smoke."

"I smoked my first joint with Todd on our wedding night."

"You never told me that."

Landon took a second toke. "I didn't know I was supposed to." Her voice rasped.

"What's going on between you two?"

Landon exhaled, then passed the joint back to Launa. "One of these days, I'm going to call you, and you are going to be my priest." She cleared her throat. "And I'm going to confess my secrets to you."

"Why wait? We just came from our friend's funeral. Tomorrow isn't promised to any of us."

"You got something you need to get off your mind?"

"In fact, I do." Launa puffed on the spliff. "I've been holding on to this for quite some time." She reached inside her bag. "A while ago, Jen asked me to open up bank accounts in both our names." She pulled out a sealed envelope and handed it to Landon. "This one's yours. We need to find some time to remove my name, or close it and transfer the funds wherever you like."

"Did she say why?"

"Just that if things didn't go well in Sweden, I need to check on these accounts. So, I did. And you won't believe what I found."

Landon opened the envelope and her eyes bugged.

"She said it's ours, but she wants us to look after Max until he can collect his trust."

Tears fell down Landon's cheeks. "She's really gone." She clutched the documents next to her heart.

"I assume you know her back story?"

"Shit blew my mind when she told me."

"Landon, we lost our sister."

"I miss her terribly."

Launa sniffled and put out the joint. "She saved me, you know. She warned me about Juan. Told me straight up I need to leave him alone, and I did." Launa's voice wavered. "You have no idea what that man did to me."

Landon sat still staring at her sister as Walt joined them on the patio. He looked at them both with interrogative eyes.

"It was me," they said in unison.

"I'm not an officer tonight. You two alright?"

Landon avoided looking him in the eyes. "I told her it was okay. And I had some myself."

"You've been through a lot recently." He sat next to her and squeezed her thigh.

Landon squirmed. "Don't be mad at me."

Walt laughed at her glossy eyes. "This is definitely a side of you I've never seen."

"Well, that's my cue. I'm gonna turn in and leave you two to it." Launa patted Walt's shoulder. "I'll take my evidence with me in the morning."

Landon and Walt cuddled in front of the pit of fire. The smell of marijuana and fabric softener from her blanket masked the smell of Todd on her dress, and her neck.

Walt let out a few jests every time he got a glimpse of Landon's bloodshot red eyes. "I didn't know you partake."

"I don't." She turned her head, deciding if the moment was right to tell him about the indiscretion.

Listening to his heartbeat, she waited for the next second, and then the next to come out with it. But every time he pulled her in close, she swallowed the hurtful words, convincing herself to wait until Launa was out of the house.

The fire pit lit their reflection in the glass of the windows. Landon's eyes were shaded red looking back at her. Guilt flooded her thoughts and drove her to relieve the pain pounding in her chest.

"Honey, I have something to tell you."

Walt squeezed her tighter. "I have something to tell you, too."

"You first." She exhaled.

"They offered me the job."

"So, we're moving?"

"I haven't accepted it yet. I told them I had to think it over. I wanted to discuss it with you first. They want my answer in the morning."

"You know what you want to do. Why would you need to discuss it with me?"

"You have no idea how much I love you, do you?"

Landon returned his gaze.

Walt kissed her smoky lips. "Taking the job means moving–Selling this house. I wanted to make sure you were really okay with that."

"Are you still going to keep the house in Toledo?"

"Yes. *We* are going to keep the house in Toledo. It'll be our getaway home whenever we want to escape the city, or just need a change of scenery."

"I think I should tell you what I have to say now."

"I don't think I want to know." Walt sighed.

"Huh?"

"You are inebriated, and I can't say that I'm fond of seeing you like this. Plus, you sound like you're gonna tell me something bad, and I think I would rather not know."

"But you *should* know."

"All I want to know is are we moving to Waterford or not?"

"Walter, Todd came over to Jay's house after you left, and…"

Walt raised his voice. "Didn't I say I don't wanna know!"

Landon shuddered. He never talked to her in that tone. The hurt in his eyes as if he already knew she had been unfaithful to him put her on pause. Her heart shredded seeing him like that. The vein in his neck, and the sweat forming on his forehead, alarmed her of the rage he'd been holding back whenever Todd was inserted into their equation. And after witnessing the pain on his face, she carried the hurt of her actions for the both of them.

"I'm sorry." Walt huffed.

"No, I'm sorry. I should have…"

He raised his hands. "I shouldn't have raised my voice. Not to you. If you have something to tell me, I should listen. What is it?"

Landon sat back in the chair and looked away. "He said Ephram is not his son!"

Walt scoffed. "And just what does he want you to do with that information?"

"I think he just wanted me to know, honestly."

"I could have sworn you were about to tell me something else."

"I was." Landon sighed looking at the envelope. "Jen left me some money and wants the girls to share as Max's caretaker."

"How much money?"

"Millions."

A glimmer glossed Walt's eyes. "Come again?"

Landon nodded and showed him the bank statement.

"Baby, for a second there, I thought I was about to lose you."

"I'm not going anywhere."

"I'm so glad to hear you say that." He leaned forward to kiss her lips again.

Landon pulled back. "We can do that after I get the smoke off my breath."

CHAPTER 95

SOULS TIED

TODD

Lathered from neck to toe, Walt stood outside the glass watching Landon shower.

"Need help in there?" He kicked off his shoes.

Her phone vibrated on the counter.

Walt eased over to the sink. "It's him. I swear he knows when to interrupt." He answered the call. "How can I help you, man?"

"I think the angel man wanted me to call you."

Walt tapped on the counter and placed the call on the speaker feature. "Say that again."

Landon stepped out of the shower. "What's going on?"

"The angel man is in the hospital," said the boy.

"Angel man?" Walt questioned him, holding up the phone for Landon to see Todd's name on the screen.

"Yes. The man who helped me and my mom."

Landon's fingers covered her mouth. "What hospital?"

"Memorial."

"We're on our way."

'We shouldn't have done what we did,' plagued Landon's mind on the way to the hospital, wondering if prayer was appropriate after the carnal sin she and Todd committed earlier. Her nails tapped on her phone, alerting everyone in a group text where to meet. Then, she dialed Todd's mother, hesitant to press send.

"Should I wait to have more news before I tell her?" she asked, breaking the silence in the car.

Walt pulled the car up to the emergency entrance. "You go in. I'll tell her and come find you." He kissed her, took her phone, then watched her skip over patches of ice on the sidewalk.

Inside, her eyes roamed around the waiting room. A frail boy hugged up with his mother sat next to the television holding Todd's phone. The woman stared at Landon when she approached them.

"Can I help you?"

"I believe your son called me." She pointed to the phone in his hand.

"Did you call someone?" She frowned at her son.

He nodded.

"May I ask why you called Todd the angel man?"

The boy froze, fearful he had done something wrong from the disappointment in his mother's eyes.

"Well." The mother stopped short when Walt wrapped his hand around Landon's.

"His family is on the way," Walt interrupted.

"Good. This is the boy who called us earlier." Landon pointed. "And his mother."

"Nice to meet you." Walt nodded. "If you don't mind, you were saying?"

"Well, he saved us tonight." She held up her hands as testimony. "So many cars passed us by. But not him. He turned around and came back to help us." Her prayer hands touched her lips.

Landon felt Walt's hands turn clammy.

"He'll pull through," he assured the woman.

Landon studied her appearance. She recognized the woman filled up on coffee, and the boy never stopped digging in the bags of fast food. When the lobby began to fill with friends and family, Landon slipped the mother some cash.

"It's getting late. If you need to get your son home, I understand. But if you don't mind, may I have a number to reach you, and give you an update."

The mother's eyes lit up. "I would love it if you did that."

Landon walked them to the entrance.

"What was that about?" Launa asked when she returned.

"All I could see was Jen when I looked at her. Single, struggling mother of a young boy in need of help. And Todd helped them because they needed it. I plan on continuing what he started. That windfall was meant to do something good."

The doctor walked into the room. "Jeffries family?"

Launa raised her hand. "That's us."

"I can only share medical information with the persons Mr. Jeffries has listed on the form from his previous visit."

"His mother is on her way." Landon advised.

"And you are?"

"The ex-wife."

"Landon Jeffries?" the doctor asked.

"Yes." She shook her head. "Reed, now."

"You were listed as his emergency contact a few months ago. May I speak with you?"

Landon followed the doctor behind the double doors. Through the square glass, Walt watched her fold her arms, shift her hands to her mouth, and shake her head pitifully.

The doctor placed his hands on her shoulder, then walked off in the opposite direction.

Launa and Walt met her at the door. "What did he say?"

Landon's eyes landed on Jay bursting through the door. "He's going to live, but he says he can't feel his legs. They don't know if the injuries are permanent or temporary. They have to run more tests."

Jay intercepted. "What's the word?"

"Launa, you relay what's going on to everyone." Landon turned to Walt. "I'm the only person they will allow back there until his mother arrives."

"You go ahead. I'll be here when you come back."

Landon hugged him. "I'm just going to tell him everyone is here, and he isn't alone."

Todd smiled the best he could when she walked into his room. His fingers tapped with the rhythm of the beeps of the machines flashing numbers and lines on computer screens.

"Get up here, baby." He croaked in a raspy tone.

Landon pulled a chair next to the bed. "You know I can't do that." She smiled at him. "How are you feeling?" She clutched his hand.

A tear dropped from Todd's eye. "I can't feel my legs."

Landon wiped the tear trailing down his cheek. "We're not going to claim that. Let them finish running the tests. Okay?"

"What am I gonna do?"

"What you always do. Live. Survive. And bless people like you did that boy and his mother out there. You're not alone, Todd."

"If I still had you I wouldn't feel this way."

"Todd. Don't turn to negativity. Not right now."

"Is he here with you?"

Landon nodded.

Todd looked away. "Did you tell him?"

"No."

"So you listened to me." He grinned.

"I did."

"This is what I get for..."

"Shhh."

"Is he mad I never changed you as my contact?"

Landon's shoulders shrugged. "If he is, he was wise enough not to mention it right now."

"I kept you on everything. You are my sole beneficiary, healthcare power of attorney, personal representative, owner of my business...Everything. I put my life in your hands. The smartest and prettiest girl in the room."

Landon teared up.

Todd's fingers tapped the bed. "Come sit up here with me, girl."

Landon squeezed his hand. "Behave yourself."

"Baby, don't let them stick me anywhere. Ya hear me?"

"You are going to be just fine." She looked at the fluid bags dripping from the stand. "I wonder what pain meds you're on that have you acting so mannish?" Landon joked.

"That ain't got nothin' to do with no meds. That's all you."

Landon forced a smile. "Your mother is on her way. Everyone else is out front. They want to see you."

Todd moved her hand to his chest. "I'm with the person I want here."

CHAPTER 96

MEASURES

LANDON

The morning didn't bring sunshine. Todd's mother sat at his bedside, holding his hand as the doctor briefed them on his ability to walk again.

"Myself and one of our best neurosurgeons reviewed your results, and we feel good about performing a surgical procedure that will put you in the seventy-five percent range of recovery."

"That's pretty high." Mother Jeffries tapped the back of Todd's hand.

"It won't be a quick turnaround, but with extensive physical therapy, you have a good chance to walk again."

"How soon can you do this procedure?" Todd asked.

"We can have you prepped and in the operating room tomorrow morning."

"Sign me up."

"Don't you want to know the risks?" his mother asked him.

"No! I can't live like this! I won't live like this! This was not a part of my plan."

Todd's mother sighed. "Does he need to sign anything beforehand?"

"The hospital clerical staff will be in shortly." The doctor excused himself.

"Tell Landon to come see me."

"Why do you want her back here?"

"Just do it, Mama."

Life returned to Todd's face when Landon walked through the door. The joy left him when Walt entered behind her seconds later.

"How you holding up?" Walt asked him.

Todd's lips pressed together tightly.

Landon shook her head. "Your mother said you're having surgery in the morning. See, I told you. Stay positive. You can beat this."

"You know I'm gonna try." Todd's eyes shifted to Walt. "I'm glad you came, man. I need to have a word with you."

Landon's chest pumped harder than an oil rig digging in dirt.

"You mind?" Todd raised his brows at Landon.

She looked at Walt.

"It's cool." Walt nodded. "What's up?"

Landon bit her nails as she stepped into the hallway. Mixing between the nurses and doctors hustling past the room, she fixated on a painting hanging on the wall near the vending machine. The swirling lines formed the backdrop of a beach below a setting sun with waves crashing ashore. It reminded her of her last wedding, flooding the guilt of her infidelity to the forefront.

She wiped the tears falling from her eyes, unsure of what was being said in the room between the two loves of her life, while the imagery in the artwork compelled her into a daze.

She hadn't realized Walt was standing behind her calling her name for over a minute. She gasped and jumped from the touch of his hand on her shoulder.

"Landon. He wants to see you."

She turned around. "Just like that? He wants to see me?" She rested her head on his chest. "What did he want with you?"

"To clear the air."

Landon exhaled as Walt embraced her. "So, you two are cool now?"

"I think so."

Landon leaned back. "How do you feel about that?"

"Like we might be able to finally coexist."

Landon pressed her hands into his chest, then returned to the room. She narrowed her eyes at Todd as she closed the door behind her.

"You know you don't fight fair."

Todd grinned on the side of his mouth. "He's actually alright."

Landon fumbled with the fluids on the stand. "Mmm hmm. They are pumping you up with some good stuff in here. What did you want with him?"

"Just discussing business amongst men."

"Is that all?" Landon glared at Todd over her shoulder.

"That's all."

"And what do you want with me?"

Todd's voice softened. "Come here."

Landon stood at his bedside.

He squeezed her hand. "To tell you I love you just in case."

"Stop."

"Wish me luck, babe."

"I wish, pray, and believe you'll be alright."

Staring up at her with the gaze that always weakened her he said, "Hope to see you when I wake up."

But he didn't see her. The sudden peace treaty between Walt and Todd overwhelmed her with shame and anguish. She couldn't handle being his friend and Walt's wife after the betrayal the two of them committed. To her, Walt didn't deserve the disrespect, and the secret of her disloyalty was painful enough. And so, when the doctors reported Todd's surgery was a success, she shied away from the hospital and never returned.

For months Todd begged to see Landon. Unanswered texts and calls sent his phone flying across the room. The closest he came to hearing her voice was when Launa paid him a visit and called her from her line. Even then, Landon refused to talk to him, forcing Launa to drive to Waterford unannounced, and scold her sister like a child.

"Do you want the man to heal?" Launa argued.

"I can't see him like that."

"Neither can he."

"Launa, I'm in a bad spot. I just can't get involved."

"This better not be about your husband's insecurities."

"It's not."

"It's been two months. How can you be so selfish when all that man has ever done is love you?"

"I know."

"Get Landon to come see me." Launa mimicked his deep voice. "He says it to me, Jay, Caleb, Mama, Daddy. Get Landon to come see me. Get Landon to come see me. Go see that fucking man!"

"I can't!" Landon's voice trembled.

"Why not?"

Tears dropped from Landon's eyes. "Remember when I told you one day I would tell you my secrets?"

Launa sighed. "Today better be that day."

Landon reached in her purse and handed Launa a sonogram.

Launa's mouth dropped. "Get the fuck outta here."

"I can't get involved. We divorced under false pretenses, I've had a fragment of time to enjoy my new husband, I've lost my best friend, then Todd nearly dies, and now I'm pregnant, and I don't know who the father is."

Launa pulled out a chair for her sister. "Say that last part again?"

Landon bowed her head. "Turns out I'm not as perfect as you thought I was." Together they snickered at their sibling rivalry.

"Does Walt know?"

"Yes. He's the happiest I've ever seen him." Bound in her sister's arms, Landon confessed, "But I'm so stressed out with this secret, I'm scared I'm gonna lose this baby."

"How far along are you?"

"Nine weeks."

"Landon, if this baby is Todd's, it could be what he needs to make him fight to get well."

"How is he?"

"Go see for yourself."

CHAPTER 97

FAMILY

LAUNA

The fight to walk again started out strong with Todd. But being in the dark about why Landon refused to pay him a visit, the overwhelming physical pain, the mental anguish he endured from the trauma, and the frustration of not achieving immediate results, caused him to lose the slight glimmer of hope he had.

Living with Mother Jeffries and PJ sent him spiraling down the deep end of darkness. Bottles covered the living room, despair floated from one room to the next, and while misery kept Todd company, the strain of tolerating one drunken son living at home increasing to two, infuriated Mother Jeffries.

She looked forward to Launa making her weekly rounds. To have a listening ear sympathize with her concerns regarding Todd's progress, as he and PJ took shots at each other in the den comforted her troubles.

"I don't know how we got here. Todd acts like he hates his brother, and he won't say why." She threw up her hands. "I know firsthand a sick man is meaner than a dog protecting his home. And my boy is meaner than that. I think it's got to do with your sister."

Launa's head bowed. "I thought she would have come to see him by now."

"Praise God when she does. 'Cause I don't know how much more of this bickering I can take."

Launa excused herself and intruded between the brothers feuding. Todd and

PJ shouted insults at each other, trading profane insults as if their mother wasn't in the other room.

"Enough!" Laura screamed. "You two are killing your mother!"

PJ tittered, smirking at Launa. "She's been here more than her sister."

"Thanks to you." Todd threw the bottle of beer in his hands at his brother.

PJ ducked. "The fuck does that mean!"

"You cost me everything!"

Mother Jeffries stormed in. "Why are you blaming your brother for your marriage falling apart!"

"Because he is Ephram's daddy! And the motherfucker never spoke up!"

"Millicent was right," Launa whispered through a gasp.

"Is this true?" Mother Jeffries asked PJ.

Todd rolled towards the door. "Get me out of here, Launa!"

*

"What are we doing here?" Launa asked Todd, sitting outside his old house.

"Your sister doesn't know this, but I drove by here every night."

"Before she remarried?"

Todd's silence conveyed his guilt.

He sighed. "I thought it would have sold by now."

"Maybe it hasn't for a reason." Launa turned off the engine. "You should buy her out. Move back in there. Become more independent."

"I would, but those walls are tainted with another man. Besides, I told her to keep all the profits. I ain't broke. I can find somewhere else to stay."

"If you do, I'll help you with your therapy."

"You'd do that for me?"

"We're family. But if you talk to me the way you talk to your mother and brother, I'll abandon ship quick, fast, and in a hurry."

"I can be in a place in two weeks."

"But we begin tonight. First things first. Clean yourself up."

"Is that why L won't come to see me?"

Launa scoffed. "If you were in her husband's shoes, how would you feel about her going to see him? And that the reason they broke up in the first place turned out to be a lie."

Todd sucked his teeth. "I get it. I mean, we made peace a while back. He may have my woman, but I still want my friend."

"Give her some time. A lot's gone on. Ya know." Launa cranked the car. "She still may surprise you yet."

"I'm waiting for that day."

Launa took the scenic route as she drove Todd home. The hostility died after they left, and the house was serene when they returned.

She got him settled inside. "Let tonight be the last time you lift that bottle."

Hypocritical of her own advice, she opened the side compartment and pulled out a half-smoked joint before whipping out into the street with her music turned up high. The first few puffs settled her nerves as she swerved onto the highway, releasing the tension transferred onto her from the events of the night.

Her phone buzzed against the middle dash, followed by consecutive messages drowning out the music. Launa veered off at the next exit to read what the commotion was about and lost her breath at the words on her screen.

The news just reported Walt was murdered while on duty.

CHAPTER 98

GRAY SHOWERS

LANDON

Racing to her sister's side, the hair on Launa's arms and neck rose from the screams and gibberish coming from inside Landon's house. She panicked from Landon's incoherent rant, fearing she would lose the baby if she failed to get her settled.

Outside a car door shut. The chime of the doorbell bounced against the bare walls. Launa opened the door to a silver haired captain standing at the door in his dress blues. He lowered his hat and pressed it near his stomach. The unit behind him followed his lead.

"Ma'am, it is with deep regret…" he said, drowned out by the wails of the weeping widow.

"We didn't want to believe it. But you being here makes it true." Launa held her sister.

"On behalf of the entire department, we are saddened to deliver this news," he added. "Please accept our condolences on the loss of a great man."

"He was a great man," Landon mumbled.

"When will we know the details of what happened?" Launa asked.

"I'll come by personally in the morning with a report. Our team is still investigating and verifying witness statements. Your family is in our prayers." The captain held Landon's hand, then gave her a salute.

The unit followed his lead as Landon and Launa watched their squad cars leave her driveway.

Short of an hour, The Davises arrived. Their presence helped remove the chill dancing down Launa's back with the memory of her sister's cries. Before they arrived, the house was so still you could hear an echo of Landon's pain bouncing off the walls.

"She's in here." Launa led her mother into the kitchen.

Landon was nowhere in sight.

"Maybe she's in the living room." Launa scratched her head. "I didn't hear her move around at all."

"She wasn't in there a second ago. Maybe she decided to lie down." Laura Lee suggested. "Let's look in the bedroom."

Still no sight of Landon.

"Where on earth could she have disappeared to?"

"Shhh." Launa silenced her mother, pointing to the closet.

They followed the sound of sniffles. Landon was crouched on the floor smelling one of Walt's shirts with a bottle of wine between her legs.

"I don't wanna hear it," she slurred.

"Mama's here."

"Baby."

Landon held up her hand. "There aren't any words anyone can say to comfort me right now."

Laura Lee sighed.

"You know I had this coming." Landon gulped another sip.

Launa took the bottle from her hand.

"I never deserved his love. That man loved me more than anything, and what did I do? I fucked my ex-husband, and now I don't have either one of them in my life. My Walt is gone. No more, baby I'm home. No more kisses in the middle of the night." Landon sniffled. "He did that, you know. My eyes would be closed, but I wouldn't be asleep. I just laid there and let him kiss on me."

"Let's get you cleaned up. That hard floor can't be good for the baby, and what are you doing drinking wine?" Laura Lee hugged her daughter. "And you did what with Todd?"

"I'll probably lose this baby, too. I've lost everything else."

"Stop it!" Laura Lee fussed. "You are not losing this baby. You're gonna get yourself together and use your baby to find your strength."

In the morning, Landon expressed she didn't want to host people coming to the house.

"We didn't get to have a housewarming. I'll be damned if I feed people because my husband is dead."

Laura Lee and Launa made eyes at each other.

"You let us worry about that."

"What time is that captain coming back? I should know why my husband was murdered."

"Calm down." Laura Lee sighed.

"How am I supposed to do that, Mama?"

"What's all the fuss in here?" Papa Davis strolled in the room.

"You calm your daughter down. She barks at every word I say. I need to make breakfast anyway."

While Laura Lee cooked, Launa handled the phone calls. As the bacon, eggs, and coffee brought a smell of country home cooking to Landon's freshly painted walls, the captain returned with the details the investigation provided from collected testimonies.

"Detective Reed died a hero. He and his partner responded to a robbery in the area, and he shielded his partner in the line of fire. Again, I'm sorry to be the bearer of bad news."

"He was a good boy." Papa Davis shook his head.

"He gave up his life with me so his partner could live?"

Laura Lee gasped. "Sir, she didn't mean that. She's not handling this well. Lan, apologize."

"Ma, leave her alone." Launa scowled. "She's not herself."

Landon inhaled and exhaled with tears running down her cheeks. "I'm sorry. My husband always looked out for others. And all that did was cut his life short. He should still be here."

"Here's my card." The captain passed his information to Papa Davis. "You all call me if you have any questions, or need anything. Anything at all."

Launa escorted Landon back to her bedroom while their father walked the captain out.

"Mama's been asking me about what you said last night." Launa paused. "What if the baby is...I mean, are you gonna tell Todd at all?"

Landon's shoulders dropped. "You didn't see how happy Walt was when I told him I was pregnant. Haven't I hurt him enough?"

"But, Landon?"

"And you better keep my secret." She bawled with a dripping red nose.

"I haven't said a word. And I won't. You better tell Mama not to say anything."

Laura Lee brought in a plate of food. "Here. Eat something for my grandchild in there."

"I'm not hungry."

"Try." She scooped up some eggs on the fork. "Since you don't want people coming here, I think it's best we take you home and host everybody there. That way, if you don't feel like being bothered with people, me, Davis, and your sister will host them. The man is going to have people who want to pay their respects."

"Fine with me."

"Your sister and I will handle all of the arrangements."

Walt's sister Gwen arrived in town with her family days before the memorial. Launa turned jealous at how much care and love Landon appeared to have with her.

"What's up with that?" Launa asked Laura Lee.

"I wish I knew. She's been snappy with us. And letting that sister's bunch run wild in her new house."

"She's already talking about selling it. Told me she can't stay in there with Walt gone."

"Can't say I don't blame her, but I am worried about these mood swings. One minute she's present. The next she's off into another world. That ain't good for that baby."

The sky was dim and gray with showers falling from the Heavens the morning of the funeral, and the mood swings Laura Lee was worried about turned for the worst.

Landon sat in bed nonresponsive to conversation. She had to be bathed, groomed, and dressed like an infant. She refused to speak. Barely blinked. And a rolling moan vibrating from her throat brought chills to whoever was in the room.

Along the drive to the service, the rolling moans made the hairs on Launa's body erect. Papa Davis stared out of the window silently weeping as he listened to his daughter mourn.

"I could never listen to either of you girls cry," he said to Launa.

She slipped him a Kleenex.

"That sound is unnatural to me. I always told your mother she had to be the tough one when it came to you two."

"Good thing I'm tough then, huh?" Launa leaned on her father's shoulder.

Drops of rain hit the car.

Laura Lee whispered in Landon's ear. "God has shown up to cleanse our pain with the rain."

The heaving moan continued from Landon's mouth as if she hadn't heard a word her mother said.

At the church, members from Walt's old job and new, as well as officers from surrounding precincts crowded the entrance. The widow paced past her supporters paying her respects, veiled in black lace with opaque dots covering her eyes locked straight to the casket ahead. She moved like a zombie, barely making complete steps–it was as if she was walking the plank of death towards her reserved seat in the front of the church.

As she passed the halfway mark, she laid eyes on her husband's body lying at the end of the aisle. Her escorts flinched as her feet paused. They held her upright by her arms so she wouldn't fall to the floor.

An usher approached, sifting through the family walking in behind her.

"Come on, dear. Let's get you seated." She flapped a mulberry fan on the path to the pew.

Distant whimpers and sniffles echoed in the house when the escorts sat her at the edge of the row between Papa Davis and Launa. She was in a daze. Catatonic with a heavy tongue. Her mind, trapped in her reality.

The captain from the office in Flint touched his hand and placed his old badge inside the casket. He was the last to view the body up close as the funeral home director crept behind him, waited for him to take his seat, then lowered the casket lid. *Click*. The lock clasped, trapping Walter inside.

Landon inhaled a sharp breath, waking from her dream state, and shattered into a low spell. "I won't see his face anymore," she mumbled, then moaned a crackling sound through gritted teeth withholding her tears from behind her veil.

The sound of her wail sent sharp bites through the ears of everyone sitting near her. Laura Lee reached over and lifted her veil, worried her daughter was in need of a sedative to cope with her pain.

Landon didn't blink. Her blood moon colored eyes sat lifeless staring at the sprays the ushers covered across the crown of the casket. Her ears, closed off to the words being spoken from the pulpit.

Launa whispered in her ear, "Landon, breathe. You've got to pull it together or the doctor will give you medicine that could harm the baby."

Landon's hands moved to her stomach. She didn't hear what had been said about her husband, but the mention of her baby pulled her from the depths of her hell.

A baritone humming sound moaned from her throat throughout the church. The sound pierced Todd's ears positioned in the aisle ten rows behind her.

He wheeled himself to the front row. "Help me," he whispered to Launa.

She lifted his feet from the plate as stares throughout the chapel held back whispers. Todd pushed himself upright into Launa's arms, then navigated himself into her seat.

Landon, sitting still as a broken clock, continued to moan the saddest sound he ever heard.

Launa pushed Todd's chair to the back of the church, dropping tears over a masked smile, pained by her sister's state, but overwhelmed by her former brother-in-law's warm heart. From the back of the church, she watched Todd hold his ex-wife's cold, lifeless hand.

He hoped to feel a twitch of her finger, but it remained numb below his. His brows raised at Papa Davis, clueless on what to say to the grief stricken widow resembling an inch of the woman he'd known. Papa Davis shook his head before his eyes shifted to Landon's profile. Todd followed his lead, requiring one look from her to know she was going to be alright.

"Landon," he whispered.

Her daze didn't break.

"Landon. It hurts me seeing you like this. Say something. Please."

Her face remained solemn. Her humming monotonous, growing louder and cracking in spurts.

Witnessing her in that state broke Todd. He could no longer suffer the pain transcending from her voice into his soul.

He placed both of his hands around hers. "That man in there loved you. And I know you loved him, too. Can you believe I'm saying these words to you?" He paused, waiting for her to move and the moans to stop. "You didn't think about me after you met him." Todd snickered. "You know that one was funny. Look at me showing up for you when you ghosted me." Todd paused. "So you not gonna respond to that one either?"

Todd hoped she would crack a smile at that line as her hum lowered to a droning croak resembling a broken vocal chord of a frog. She gave him zero inter-action. Lost in time. Never blinking or batting an eye.

"He knew you chose him. Go 'head and cry. Stop holding it in. Cry, Landon. Cry." He squeezed her hand. "I know you're in there somewhere, dammit. Cry, sweetheart. Cry for him. Cry for me. I hate seeing you like this."

A startling gasp for air expelled from Landon's mouth. The low wail deaf-ening the congregation ceased as a mute whimper bounced from her chest.

"Why!" she shouted, burying her face in her father's arms.

Todd rubbed the back of her hand, encouraging the sea of tears she'd been holding hostage to release. Gwen grew emotional listening to her sister-in-law cry over her brother. She bawled almost as loud, creating a chain reaction of tears and droning chatter around the church.

Laura Lee wiped the tears from her own eyes and looked over at Todd. She mouthed the words, "Thank you."

He pressed his lips together, acknowledging his former mother-in-law with a nod, and held Landon's hand until her cry tapered off. Once her hand slid from within his, he signaled for Launa to bring him his chair, and wheeled himself out of the church before the service was complete.

Jay followed him outside. "You alright, man?"

"Un-uh. I can't take seeing her like that."

"What'd you say up there?"

"What she needed to hear. That her husband loved her and she loved him."

"You actually said that?"

"Yeah. Why do you seem shocked?"

"'Cause you still love her yo' damn self. Everybody knows that." Jay dropped his shoulders. "I wonder which one of you loves her the most."

"I know the answer to that."

"So tell me."

"I wish I could say me, but I let her slip away, so Im'ma say he did. He would have never let her go."

"You say that, but that's impossible to know when they've never experienced a bump in the road."

"Actually, they did, and he still wouldn't let me have her. He made sure I never got a second chance."

"Well, Im'ma disagree witchu on this one. I think you love her just as much as he did."

"Why do you say?"

"Because you just sat next to her while she grieved for him. If that isn't the ultimate act of loving someone, then I don't know what is."

Todd scoffed with a curve on the corner of his lips. "She's the love of my life. I would do anything for her."

CHAPTER 99

HOME AWAY FROM HOME

LANDON

A change of scenery called to the widow. Hidden away in the closet of her childhood room, her family hosted the visitors in her honor. As the day wound down, the women of both families plotted together on what to do with the sorrowed mother to be.

Following the silent cry from the back of the bedroom, they found Landon squatting on the floor.

"Baby, we're going to move you home with us for a little while," said Laura Lee.

"No," Landon croaked between sniffles.

"Launa, pack her a bag." Her mother insisted.

"Gwen!" Landon called. "I was wondering if I could stay with you for a while."

"Down in South Carolina?" Laura Lee asked. "But what about the baby? Your doctor is here."

"We'll be fine, Ma. I can find a doctor there. Launa, I want you to work with Tammy on the sale of this house. And ask Daddy to take the dogs home with him while I'm gone."

Laura Lee shook her head. "Now, Landon, I…"

"Mrs. Davis, I'll see to it that she is well taken care of," Gwen confirmed.

"Ma, I have to get out of here."

Launa held her mother's shoulders. "I think she's right, Ma."

"I think you need to be with me, but I'll go along if you agree to check in daily."

Landon nodded. "Then that's settled."

"What do you want me to do about the house in Ohio?" Launa added.

"Walter's everywhere in that house. I'm keeping it."

The next morning, Gwen and her family flew home to make preparations for Landon's arrival. With a few days left before her departure, Landon draped herself in Walt's clothing, crying as she walked the halls of their home, and talked to him as if he could hear her.

In the middle of the night, she found herself driving to their house in Ohio. She had no memory of the roads she traveled, but there she was in front of their love nest. Their home away from home.

She ran her fingers across the wood crafted treasures her husband left behind. An electric sentiment encompassed her soul as she roamed from room to room, collecting items of sentimental value to take with her. But as the night came close to an end, she had a hard time leaving.

She sat in the quiet of the home. From chair to chair she sat, listening to the house settle and the birds fight in the bush near the kitchen. She laid in their bed, laughing out loud at the memories they made in that room, spellbound by the comfort it brought to her exhausted pregnant body.

Snuggled next to her husband's shirt, she caressed her belly as the baby swam around inside of her, closed her eyes, and breathed in the scent of him calming her nerves, inducing her first full night of sleep since his demise.

The sound of Walt's voice awakened her. There he was, lying in his spot on the bed with the prettiest smile she ever saw on a man.

Her hand slid across the cotton sheets towards him. "Say it's really you." Her face lit up brighter than the lights hanging above the courtyard on their honeymoon.

"I wish I could," he said.

"So, I'm dreaming?"

"Something like that."

Her lips curved outward. "Whatever it is, I don't want to wake up."

"Yes, you do and you will."

"I miss you so much."

"I miss you, too, my love. And I can tell."

"How?"

"You have my shirt wrapped around you."

"This is hard for me."

"I know it is."

"Why did you have to save that guy's life?"

"I was trained to."

"Do you think he would have done the same for you?"

Walt sighed and shrugged his shoulders. "I would like to think so."

"You always see the good in people."

"You have to, or you'll live in the world and only see misery. It loves company, you know."

"Why didn't you let me tell you what I did?"

"Because it didn't matter."

"I betrayed you, and you didn't deserve that. And I didn't deserve you. Now I've lost you. This is all my fault."

"You had nothing to do with my death."

"It's my karma. I did wrong by you, and losing you is my payback."

Walt placed his hand on top of hers. "Stop saying that. It was just my time. You had no control over that."

"I need you."

"You'll always have me."

A single tear rolled from her cheek onto the bed. "I love you. I'm so sorry. Do you forgive me?"

"I forgave you the night you tried to tell me."

Landon squeezed the pillow. "I don't want to live my life without you."

Walt turned to his side and inched closer to her, cupping her hand between them. "Promise me you'll keep on living."

"I'll try."

"Good. Now wake up." His voice faded into a whisper.

"Hiuuughh." Landon sprang forward with pain in her chest. She turned to Walt's side of the bed. The scent of vanilla musk and jasmine lingered around her as she rolled over, clutching the empty side that was once his.

His presence hovered above her. She reached up as her hands danced in the air feeling for him, then stretched her eyes as the baby turned in her stomach.

"Did you see that?" A smile lifted the corners of her eyes.

She imagined he said yes, and smiled back at her floating above the bed.

Two minutes shy of the alarm sounding off, Landon's hand brushed the cold spot where he used to lay. She eased to the edge of the bed, observing the fixtures on the wall and the pieces of her Walt sprinkled into the room. Questioning reality, she pondered if her conversation with Walt was real. Had she traveled to a spiritual plane to see him one last time?

Clack. A noise startled her from the front room. She rose from the bed, slowly creeping down the hall to investigate the sound. The hairs on her neck prickled so hard they itched. The racing beats of her heart pounded in her ear. "Aaah!" She exclaimed, her hands shivering against her chest.

The wedding photo of Walt lifting her above the water had fallen from the mantle above the fireplace.

She ran her fingers in a circle on the glass above his face. "I knew you were here last night. I'm taking you with me," she said to his ghost.

CHAPTER 100

THE THING ABOUT TIME
LAUNA

Sun bathing brought serenity to a troubled Landon. Gwen suggested she stay with her family until the baby arrived, but Landon used the windfall Jen gifted her to lease a house on the beach.

The hot weather agreed with her as the sun toned her a few shades darker. Giving her the tan of an amaretto shade that blended well with the glow of gestation.

The majority of her days were spent on the beach, and when that became monotonous, she enrolled in sewing and arts and crafts classes to keep busy. Her creative side flourished as she made decorative pillows and curtains for her new home, pivoting from an advertising career, and into home décor and interior design.

When Launa learned Landon had no plans of returning home with the baby, she reminded her of the reality she left back home, two unsold homes, a slew of condolence cards she hadn't replied to, junk mail from Spain, Walt's estate papers, the deed to the house in Toledo, and the insurance policy check requiring her signature.

Settled in the groove of finding herself and starting over, Landon mailed the documents back with her signature and a note.

I'm doing just fine down here. Trust me.

Her response by mail ticked off Launa. She bitched and moaned to Todd during his therapy sessions.

"Has my sister always been this pig-headed?"

"Not with me." Todd held himself up on the bars and took a step on his right leg.

"I thought for sure she would come home once she opened the package I sent her."

Todd's left leg skipped forward. "People grieve differently. In a way, I don't blame her. If I wasn't in my predicament, I'd leave, too." He exhaled.

"You're just saying that to take her side."

"I'm serious. Since my accident, I've been thinking about getting out of here. Your sister might have the right idea."

"I'm going down there."

"I'd be in the seat next to you if I could."

"We're getting there. And don't get too happy. I'll be back in time for our next appointment. Can't slow down your progress when we've come this far."

When Launa arrived on Landon's doorstep, tears welled in her eyes. She stood in the doorway half naked in a tube top and cotton shorts. Her shiny stomach poking out before her.

"Took you long enough." She held out her arms.

"Of course pregnancy would agree with you. You're keeping yourself up like it's easy." Launa hugged her and rubbed her belly. "And that tan. I'm jealous."

"And I'm mad at you."

"I just got here. What'd I do?"

"You could have warned me about pregnancy brain."

"Forgetful, are we?"

"Yes. And you know that's not like me." Landon opened the door wide. "Come on in. You look good. I'm gonna be jealous if I don't bounce back like you did."

Launa rolled in her suitcase. "I gotta say, it's a difference working because you have to, versus working to keep busy. I can thank Jen for this stress free look." She shook her hips. "I'm even thinking about taking a vacation. I got the same brochure from some place in Spain that I put in your package. Did you look at it?"

"Barely." Landon traced her belly. "I don't think I'll be going on a fancy vacation for a long time."

"If we go as a group you can. Think about it."

"How is everyone?"

"Great, last I checked in. The gang is always asking when are you coming home."

"I think I am home." Landon's eyes roamed around the front room. "How is Todd doing?"

"He'd be so happy to know you asked about him. He's doing really well." Launa felt Landon's loneliness reach for her through their sisterly bond. "You should call him."

"I want to...but I don't know what to say."

"Start with hello. It wouldn't matter what you said, honestly. He just wants to hear your voice."

Landon's lips curled and pressed tight. "Did you come down here to get me to call him?"

"Yeah. And to give you something."

"What is it?"

Launa unzipped her purse. She slipped a Genesee County envelope into her sister's hand.

Landon's breath hitched. "This is Walt's handwriting. Where did you get this?"

"The captain brought it over. He said it was in Walt's desk."

"I'm afraid to open it." Her hands trembled.

"I can't tell you what to do. But I was hoping he put something in there that would make you come home."

Landon broke the seal. "It's dated around the time of the accident."

Landon Honey,

I should make a candy bar and name it Landon Honey. It would be sold in all of those overpriced stores you love to shop in. Can't you see that? I can. Ignore my rambling, I couldn't sleep tonight. So while I watch your sweet face dream the night away, I thought I would clear my head and tell you what's on my mind. Though I hope you never have to read this.

If you do, then something has happened to me. And if that's the case, I am sorry I am not there with you now. Don't be upset with me. I'd never leave you by choice. Never.

So here is what's keeping me up tonight. I yelled at you when I didn't want to hear whatever it was you wanted to tell me. Something in my gut told me it would be best if I didn't know. Fear overwhelms me sometimes. I thought you were going to tell me you were leaving me to go back to Todd, or that something happened between you two. I think I get more angry knowing he refuses to let you move on. Whatever it was you wanted to tell me, I want you to know that I love you so much, there isn't anything you could do that I wouldn't forgive. I know your heart.

Then we got that terrible phone call and had to go to the hospital to see about Todd. I must confess that I said a horrible, selfish thing that night to myself and to God. If I could take it back I would. It was unlike me to think such a thing, and I am ashamed for the wicked thoughts that plagued me that night.

And when I heard the doctor say you were still listed as his emergency person, I knew then that I would be forced to share your love with him. And you know what. I'm glad to have the smallest piece of you if that is all I'm ever granted. I know you love me. But I know you love him, too. And that's okay. I can't be angry about that. You two share a past. We all have one.

With that being said, I want you to know that if something happens to me, and this letter finds you, I want you to forgive Todd. Do it for me. I forgave him that day we talked in the hospital. I know he would take care of you the way you should be taken care of, and I know he loves you just as much as I do. It would comfort me to know that you are in a good place and with a good person who isn't going to mistreat you, and that can give you a good life. The kind of life I wish to give you, and hope to spend with you forever.

I have loved you from the moment you were brought into my life, and it's an honor to have you carry my last name.

I Will Love You Always,
Your Walter

Landon's heart hurt all over again. Walt's love for her transcended from the page, overpowering her from the grave.

Teary-eyed, she folded the letter. "Make yourself at home. I'm going to lie down," she said to Launa.

"Did I do good bringing that to you?"

"You got it to me right on time."

Chapter 101

Oceans

An invitation announcing the engagement of Jay and Millicent couldn't draw Landon from the comfort she found in the south. 'Respectfully decline' she returned the invite, causing a stir amongst the friends.

Millicent asked Launa to come over the next time she was in town helping Todd.

Launa swung by. "If this is about helping with your wedding, you're asking the wrong sister."

"We need to talk about your sister. Is everything okay with her? She won't even come home for my engagement party. I thought we were cool."

"She's near her due date. I'm sure she won't miss the wedding, though."

"It's also Christmas. Are we going to let her spend it alone after everything that's happened?"

"Actually, my family is going down there to be with her."

Millicent sighed. "Our traditional holiday parties are getting smaller and smaller."

The timer in the kitchen chimed.

"Oh good. You can give me your opinion on these cookies I'm baking for Max. You want a water or something?"

"I could use a beer, but I'll take a water."

Millicent handed her a bottle from the fridge.

"Thanks." Launa took a sip. "Today was a trying one with Todd. He wants his recovery to happen with the snap of a finger, not realizing the strides he's already made are better than most people."

"I can't imagine what he's going through." Millicent pulled a batch of cookies from the oven.

Launa frowned. "I never pegged you for the domestic type."

"It's for Max's school."

Launa laughed. "Next time, grab a batch from the grocery store and put them in a container. They'll never know the difference."

"I did that one time before. One of the kids called me out, and said they tasted like the cookies from Rivertown. I was so embarrassed."

Launa burst out laughing. "Girl, fuck them kids."

Millicent joined her with a snicker. "Right. Like how rude was that? But in all honesty, I kind of like when Max is proud of me. That's why I actually baked them this time. Tell me what you think."

"Did you invite me over to be your guinea pig?"

"No, but since you're here..."

Launa bit a small corner. "They aren't my mother's, but they're good."

She gave her a thumbs up and finished off her water. Her foot pressed the lever of the garbage can to raise the lid. Launa tossed in her bottle and her eyes popped wide. The same brochure from Spain caught her eye in the trash.

"By chance, who in our circle would have signed us up for vacation solicitations?"

"Tammy or Kim would be my guess."

"I was thinking all of us should take a group trip somewhere after Landon has the baby."

"That actually sounds like fun. I'll mention it to Kim. She loves planning stuff like that."

"Cool." Launa swiped the brochure and hid it in her pocket. "I'll take another cookie for the road. And don't worry about my sister. I'm sure she'll come around after she has the baby."

A tingle tickled inside Launa as she drove home making the connection Jen was reaching out to them.

"She's okay," she said to herself.

Lila Leigh Davis graced the world with her presence on Christmas Eve. Coming into the world with both eyes open. Welcomed by The Davis family in town for the holidays, she sparked the conversation of Landon returning back to Detroit.

"Let us help you with the baby," Laura Lee begged.

"I like it down here, Mama."

"You're just squandering money away with three houses." Her mother picked up Lila from her crib.

Landon and Launa glanced at each other.

"Two houses. My first one finally sold."

"Well, you bought that house in Waterford to be close to us when you had children, and now you do."

"I can't return to that house. Stop worrying so much. I'll be fine here, and if things get too rough I know my way home. You'll be the first one I call."

Laura Lee kissed her teeth. "You talk some sense into her, Davis."

"You know your mother is going to worry me silly about you being down here by yourself with that baby."

"And you're not?" Landon sassed her father.

"Girl, just come home already." He fussed.

"Launa, tell them."

"Tell us what?" Laura Lee stopped bouncing Lila in her arms.

Launa traced her neck with her fingers.

Landon sat up in bed. "I don't know who Lila's father is."

Laura Lee tucked Lila next to her bosom like a football. "I was pretending that was your grief talking the first time I heard you say it."

"Come again?" Papa Davis turned down the sports news.

"She could be Walt's or Todd's."

Papa Davis held his chest. "So both of my grandbabies are bastards?"

"Daddy!" Landon and Launa shouted in unison.

Lila fussed from the commotion.

"Y'all keep it down. Babies can sense when their mother is upset. She'll holler all night if y'all don't hush this fuss." Laura Lee consoled Lila with light brushes of her hand on her back. "Grandma don't care who you belong to. That's why you need to come home with me. Let me look at you." She sat down and lowered Lila to her lap. "Right now, she looks too much like you when you were a baby to tell."

"Humph humph humph. Where did I go wrong with you girls?" Papa Davis shook his head.

"Davis, please." Laura Lee shushed her husband.

"Does Todd know any of this?" Papa Davis stood and leaned forward. "Sure he doesn't. 'Cause I know he would be here right now."

"Are you gonna tell him?" Laura Lee asked Landon.

"No. I don't want to know who she belongs to."

"I declare." Papa Davis left the room.

"Have mercy," Laura Lee muttered.

For months, Papa Davis badgered Launa to convince Landon keeping Lila a secret from Todd was wrong. Then, when Landon called in the middle of the night, stressed out of her mind from midnight feedings, little sleep, and colic cries, she gave him the clearance to spill the beans.

Launa hopped on the next flight. Landon cried when she saw her sister standing at the door with the glow of the morning sky behind her. She looked like an angel God sent to save her from herself.

"I thought I could do this alone. I thought I would reach out to Gwen if I needed help, but it doesn't feel right when she might not be Lila's aunt." She handed the baby to Launa. "I'm so tired. I can't think straight. I'd give anything to take a long, hot shower in peace."

Launa kissed her niece's round cheeks. "Go do that. Take a shower. Relax. We'll talk after you've had some sleep."

When Landon woke up, she slipped out of the house for some fresh air. She strolled along the beach, embracing the wind beating her face until it turned cold and red.

An empty wooden bench near a row of seaweeds leaning from a rough breeze invited her to sit. She rested there for a few moments, collecting herself as she listened to the waves wash ashore, took out a pen and unfolded a blank sheet of paper, then used the final moments of daylight to write below the sun setting in the horizon.

I miss you, Walter.

Life has changed drastically with you gone, and I must admit I have not handled it well. My sister delivered the note you wrote at work, and I need to say I'm sorry. I should have done better by you, but because you have been so understanding, and forgave me without knowing the truth, you've helped me realize how forgiveness works.

I can now forgive myself thanks to you.

I loved you, but I didn't deserve you. You are gone and still filling me with love as if it was your superpower. How you do it will forever be a mystery. But I thank you.

Motherhood is harder than I thought it would be, but even in my toughest moments, I feel joy just having her. Her name is Lila in case you want to know. And if you're looking down on us, you see where we are.

I thought coming down here would make me feel closer to you, and it did for a while. But now that I have this little life to look after, and time is pressing on, I'm finally ready to make peace with the fact you are gone.

It pains me to admit this to you, but I'm lonely, and ready to move on with my life. But I wanted you to know that I'll always love you.

Love Landon

She sealed her letter with a kiss, and secured it inside a plastic bag. She rolled it to fit inside a glass bottle, twisted the cap tight, then threw the bottle in the waves. Suddenly, the breeze paused like in the eye of a storm, and the final red rays of the sun reached the surface of the water from behind a cloud.

Landon closed her eyes smiling back at the sunless sky with tears running down her face. The cloud passed on, and a gust of wind circled her for a brief moment.

She exhaled, ready to begin again, opened her eyes, and watched the bottle dance in the waves as it carried it out to sea.

She trekked in the sand towards the house, then stopped to stare at the silhouette walking towards her. She smiled as the face came into form, and picked up her pace to see him up close.

"I just met my daughter." Todd reached for her hands.

"Your daughter?" Landon winced.

"She's mine. And I'm here to take you both home."

"I am home."

"Then I guess I'm home, too."

"Todd."

"Landon." He held her gaze. "I'm not going anywhere."

Butterflies fluttered in her chest as she stared into his brown eyes. "Look at you, back on your feet."

"I have you to thank for that."

"Me?" Her brows wrinkled. "I didn't do anything but run away."

"And you had enough reasons to. But I knew you needed me just as I have always needed you. I had to find my way back to you."

"From what I heard, my sister deserves all the credit."

"She does, but she knew why I was working so hard. She pushed me like hell to get to this moment. To get what I want. And what I want is you. And my pretty little girl inside that house. Say you'll have me."

Landon sniffled. "I'll have you."

Todd raised his long lost beloved in his arms. "Do you know how long I have dreamed of this moment?" His smile was wider than outside. "I've never known a love like this. I promise I will never let you slip through my fingers again." He tasted her sweet lips.

Landon caressed the sides of his face. "You better not."

"Now can we go inside so I can hold my daughter?"

Todd stole kisses from Lila's cheeks then studied her for a long time. Landon watched him observing her features from afar, puzzled by the way Lila reacted to him.

"She looks like her mama, but I know she's mine." Todd recognized a flaw he and the baby shared that Landon overlooked.

"And how is that?" Launa asked.

He kept the similarity they shared to himself. "You see her. She's been waiting on me."

Lila's tiny fingers reached up and touched Todd's face.

"See what I mean."

Landon and Launa chuckled.

"I love her. Just like I love her mama." He winked at Landon.

"So my work here is done." Launa clapped her hands.

"I got my woman back, and the family I wanted."

Lila cooed, having a conversation with Todd, then smiled at him while she giggled and kicked. Finding the tiny hole on the side of her ear like his, and her endearing, welcoming smile, filled him with a wave of emotions. Those emotions overflowed as he held her in his arms, feeling the bond between them serve as the only confirmation he needed that she did indeed belong to him. He didn't need a test to prove it.

"Your mama said we're staying down here," Todd inhaled the baby scent from her neck. "Daddy's gotta sell his business and find some work, baby girl."

Launa nodded at Landon.

"Since the house finally sold, we should be okay for a while." Landon took a deep breath. "There's a lot you and I need to catch up on."

Launa bit her tongue about her theory regarding Jen. She watched on as true love rekindled the flame between two people, destined to be together after many trials, separation, and distance.

Todd and Landon were finally reunited. Their love, back on track. Their story, tainted with character, but stronger in the end.

They settled into a new life on the waters off the Atlantic. Looking out across that same ocean was Jen, settled into the quiet northwestern corner of Spain.

Her tears melded in the waters on the beach, as she spent her days writing about her journey under an umbrella, with hope she and her son would one day be reunited. Confident, resilient, rich with the legacy her father left behind, and patient that one day she'd return to the people who became her family.

Thank you for following the story of this ensemble cast in The On Track But Off Course Series. Prepare for the crossover of this series with my Hummus series this Christmas, 'Levi & Launa Find Love'.

For more information about T.K. Richards, personalized orders, access to special deals, audio, character merchandise, and events, visit www.tkrichards.com and subscribe to my newsletter:

https://tkrichardsnewsletter.ck.page

REVIEWS
ENCOURAGE
VORACIOUS
INTEREST
EVERY
WHERE TO
SUPPORT

ME, THE AUTHOR

I GREATLY APPRECIATE IT

XOXO

Own The Series

Floral Discreet Cover Options

About the Author

T.K. RICHARDS is a multi-genre author of women's fiction and romance, featuring popular novels and novellas in Black Romance, Interracial/Multicultural Romance, Paranormal Romance, and YA Fiction. You can find her serialized fiction work on the Kindle Vella app. A graduate of Limestone University, T.K. has honors in Expository Writing, and was also the Poet Laureate of her graduating class. When she is not writing, she is immersed in the world of tennis, and binge watching movies—mostly comedy as she loves to laugh.

You can follow T.K. RICHARDS on the platforms listed below to interact with her personally:

facebook.com/Tkrichards

twitter.com/tkrichards1

instagram.com/t.k.richards

tiktok.com/@tkrwrites

youtube.com/tkrichards

goodreads.com/T.k.richards

bookbub.com/authors/t-k-richards

amazon.com/author/Tkrichards

Top Selling Romance Books by T.K. Richards

An Affair Abroad

The Vampiress

Juke: A Love Story